Concordia International School Shanghai

Stories Cast from a Restless Eighth Grade Class

iUniverse, Inc.
Bloomington

Stories Cast from a Restless Eighth Grade Class

iUniverse books may be ordered through booksellers or by contacting:

iUniverse
1663 Liberty Drive
Bloomington, IN 47403
www.iuniverse.com
1-800-Authors (1-800-288-4677)

ISBN: 978-1-4697-3716-4 (sc)
ISBN: 978-1-4697-3717-1 (e)

Printed in the United States of America

iUniverse rev. date: 1/9/2012

Foreword

By Terry Umphenour

Stories Cast from a Restless Eighth Grade Class is a book filled with delightful tales, through which imagination takes both the reader and the writer on an adventurous tour of the writing experience. For a third year, this project exposed the minds of eighth grade student writers from Concordia International School Shanghai to the demanding challenge of writing and refining a 5000-word story for publication. Collectively, the stories printed on the following pages take the reader on amazing adventure.

Brainstorming to determine the genre and story parameters started the process. Students expressed excitement at the freedom to write about a topic of their choosing. Some students expressed concerns about writing such a long story and the time it would take. The second phase of the assignment found students struggling to introduce their characters, develop the setting, and make their characters come alive with individual characteristics. After considerable thought, a first tentative outline, and a brief introduction, each student read and revised the plot and the storyline that provided the conflicts needed to bring the story to its climax and conclusion.

Usually the eighth grade writing process includes an outline, a rough draft, a final draft, and proofreading. *Stories Cast from a Restless Eighth Grade Class* required students to write an outline, an initial introduction, a first draft, and three additional drafts. After finishing the story's first draft, each student revised the story, ensuring that the facts remained consistent, that the story used the same tense throughout the manuscript, and that correct paragraph and sentence structure kept the story moving forward. Then each young writer edited his or her own story to make sure that the story used active voice and that pronouns, adjectives, and verbs used the correct tense. The final draft provided an opportunity for each writer to proofread. Proofreading such a long story, one that needed every mistake corrected, provided many opportunities to teach the conventions necessary to bring a story to publication.

Becoming insightful learners and effective communicators remains one of the expected student learning results at Concordia. *Stories Cast from a Restless Eighth Grade Class* tests Concordia's curriculum to see if it provides students the skills necessary to reach this expected student-learning result. As in Concordia's previous books, *Stories from Room 113: International Adventures* and *More Stories from Room 113: International Adventures*, only you—the reader—can determine the degree of success that each of these young writers has reached toward achieving that goal. The final stories are printed exactly as the students submitted them and may include errors or even missed comments that should have been deleted. In order to make this work a continuing education resource, the final submitted stories received no teacher or professional editing.

Concordia hopes that you enjoy reading these imaginative, adventurous stories as much the students enjoyed writing and editing them. To learn more about this writing process and its authors or to comment on this work, contact Terry Umphenour at the following email address: terry.umphenour@concordiashanghai. org.

Table of Contents

The Adventures of Denver

By Adam Brewer

"Please don't leave; I love you," Denver said to the child.

To the child it just seemed like Denver had been whining.

"Don't worry puppy. I will miss you very much," said the child as they left the house. The child had short blonde hair and blue eyes. He was short and thin and always knew how to cheer up Denver.

Denver watched his beloved family leave in the car, and he knew they weren't coming back. It had been decided that the kid's aunt would come to take care of Denver, but she was not the same as his real family. He had been sad all day and couldn't get them out of his head.

One day he lifted his head off his pillow. That day he walked around the house, and he found a letter on the floor. It was addressed to the aunt. The address read Shanghai, China.

"I need to go there, because my life is not the same

1

without them," Denver thought to himself. "I need them more than ever now."

So off he went on his trip to Shanghai in search for his family. Before he could leave his home, he had to get the right supplies to get on the plane. He got a pair of the father's blue jeans, one of the kid's shirts, a pair of the kid's old worn out sneakers, and a human mask that the kid wore for Halloween one year. He had a plan to go to O'Hare airport and take a plane to Shanghai.

He was going to disguise himself as his owner, and get a ticket with his family's credit card. He didn't know why his family left the credit card at home; they must have thought that it wouldn't work, out of the country. He took as much food as he could in his owner's bag, and he started his adventure. The bag that Denver had brought had been a rugged old one that the owner had thought about throwing out. However, it worked well for Denver because it was light and held a lot of food for him. He didn't know whether to bring human food or dog food; he loved human food. It was a treat to eat, but he didn't know if the food would be out of date by the time he got to Shanghai. So he chose to bring dog food, because he liked that too.

As he left the house, he wondered how he was going to get to the airport. He didn't even know where to start with his plan. So he decided to put his disguise into action, and try to get a ride by hitch hiking. He held up a sign saying that he wanted to go to the airport and needed a lift. Denver's handwriting didn't appear that good, considering he didn't have any thumbs. But fortunately for him, he got a ride from a trucker that could actually read his writing. The trucker said that the airport had been on the way to his destination, and he didn't mind dropping Denver off. The drive took only about forty-five minutes. He arrived at the airport and said good-bye to the helpful trucker and walked into the airport.

As he arrived at the airport he looked on the monitor to find the next flight out to Shanghai. He found one that was scheduled to leave in one hour.

"Great," Denver thought to himself.

He went up to the concierge and gave her the letter and pointed at the address with "Shanghai" on it.

"Are you trying to get a ticket to go to Shanghai, China, sir?" asked the lady.

Denver shook his head in agreement.

"Alright, there is a flight out of here in one hour. Is that fine, sir?" she said, "You want to check your bag for that flight?"

He just nodded and she checked him in.

He got through security in no time and boarded the plane. He was so excited as the plane took off, because he couldn't wait to see the expressions on his family's face when he showed up on their doorstep. He didn't know how he was going to find them. He thought that there would be signs there, and he would just follow them to the address on the letter. He had been on the plane and about to fall asleep, when the pilot came on the intercom saying that a bird got caught in one of the engines, and instructed everyone to prepare for a crash landing.

Denver got up from his seat and was really worried, because if he died he wouldn't be able to see his family. They would be heart-broken to know that he had died and they weren't there to help him. After the crash, he got help off the plane and went to the nearest ambulance that had been waiting right next to the crashed plane. The ambulance driver refused let him on considering he was a dog. He then observed the area.

"Snow, that's lucky for me I love the snow," Denver said to himself.

He ran out into the middle of the snow and dove in. The snow reminded him of the good times he had with his family. He became sad and focused on the important task at hand, reaching his family in China. As a husky,

Denver enjoyed being in the snow. So he decided not to take a chance on another plane ride, because next time he could really get hurt.

He set off through the Canadian snow in search of a way to reach his family. As a result of the plane crash, he had lost his food supply. So, he used his animal instincts to hunt for food. He was very good at finding food, but he also enjoyed his "comfy spot" in the house and his food being provided for him. Denver first started searching for bark or twigs to eat, but those just didn't taste right. Then he tried to catch his prey. So he found a group of birds on the snow and crouched down and crawled close enough to grab one of them. He finally caught one of them; his first catch of the day. He ate the bird and began to slowly stand up from his laying position. He then continued his search again.

It had been getting dark out, so Denver decided to find shelter for the night. "No need to try my chances in the dark," he thought to himself. "Better find shelter for the night."

He found a nice cozy cave to sleep in for the night. He found a comfy spot in the cave and lay down. He shut his eyes and went to sleep.

In the middle of the night he woke up to see a couple of huskies standing and looking at him strangely.

"Who are you?" he asked.

"I'm Shorty and that's Caramel," one of the huskies said.

"This is our cave, but you can stay the night if you want," Caramel said.

"Do you guys live here or what?" Denver said.

"No, we are on a journey to try to find a nice place where we can settle down and start a family together," Shorty said.

"Oh well, congratulations to you two, but if I may ask, can you guys help me? I am trying to get to China," Denver said.

"Oh sure we can. We know this area very well," Caramel said.

"But you also have to help us find a place in return," Shorty said.

"That works for me, but if we are going to go tomorrow, we will have to get some rest, so good night." Denver said.

"Good night," they said back.

Denver went to bed that night, feeling confident that he had made two new friends that knew the area. His destination was to see his family.

The next morning he woke up feeling confident and ready to go. He woke up Shorty and Caramel, determined to find his family. He easily got through the snow, but after awhile he started to get cold. Although he was a husky, being outside for long periods of time was new to him. His paws started to get cold and he began to shiver.

"What's wrong?" Shorty asked.

"Don't tell me you haven't been out in snow before?" Caramel said.

"No, I love snow; it is just that I haven't been out in it this long before." Denver explained.

"Don't worry you'll get used to it in about a day or so." Caramel said.

"Alright, that is reassuring." Denver said.

They kept going, barely talking to save their strength. The only time they said anything, happened when they had a controversy on whether or not they knew where to go. Just before noon, Denver began to get tired.

"Hey guys, can we stop for a second? I need to take a breather," Denver said to the others.

"Yes, I am also getting tired. Let's all stop for a second." Shorty told Caramel.

"Very well we can stop, but we can't stay for long," Caramel said. "We will soon lose daylight and need to find shelter."

So they tried to find the nearest cave to rest in. They found a nice cozy cave that gave them a dry and comfortable place to sleep. They went in and it didn't take long for Denver to doze off. He went right to sleep, and although it felt like forever, he slept only for about an hour. He woke up to the sound of Shorty humming to herself.

"That sounds so sweet." Denver said to Shorty, "Do you practice?"

"Sometimes when I'm alone," Shorty said back, "Caramel doesn't like it when I hum."

"Why?" asked Denver, "He should be proud that you have a talent that good."

"He thinks it is irritating, and told me never to do it around him," she said, "He told me if I wanted to hum, I had to do it when he wasn't around or when he was asleep."

"Oh, that's too bad because I would be glad to have someone that talented around, because if you can hum that good, imagine how you would be actually singing," Denver said to Shorty.

"Thanks Denver, but I don't think I'm that talented." Shorty said.

"What are we talking about?" Caramel interrupted.

"Nothing that important," Shorty said. "Are you up for good?"

"Well, I doubt I can go back to sleep with you both talking." Caramel said back, "So, let's return to our journey."

So, they gathered up their things and started walking. As time went on Denver's paws began to feel better and didn't become cold as quickly. He became used to the snow always being on his body. They ran into another Siberian Husky named "Buck". As a pure wolf, Buck disguised himself as a husky to trick the other dogs. He had rougher hair and had a different posture than an ordinary husky. But, to Denver, Shorty, and Caramel they thought Buck had just been rugged and very dirty.

"Hey, where are you heading?" asked Buck

"I'm heading to China, but these two are trying to find a house" Denver said, "I'm Denver, and that is Shorty and Caramel, and who are you?"

"My name is Buck," Buck said, "and if it isn't a burden, can I travel with you guys? I am on my way to Russia and I don't want to go alone."

"Well, if it is alright with Shorty and Caramel, you can, because it is their house that they are looking for," Denver said. "I mean, Russia is on the way to China, but it depends on where they want to search for their house."

"It's fine with me if it is alright with Caramel," said Shorty.

"It's fine with me," Caramel said.

"So lets start to make our way to Russia and start searching for places." said Buck, " I heard that Russia is such a great place for huskies to live."

"Well, I guess that we are off to Russia to find a home," Shorty said, with a smile as she looked at Caramel.

"I did hear the same thing from a friend of mine. So it's fine with me, if we go house hunting in Russia." Caramel said smiling back at Shorty.

"So let's get a move on people," Denver said.

"Fair enough, let's go," said Buck.

"If they only knew that I wasn't a husky and I was really a wolf, leading them into a trap so my friends and I could eat them as our dinner." Buck said softly.

"What was that?" asked Denver "something about you being a wolf?"

"Oh, no, I was just saying that there might be wolves around here and I'm very terrified of them," said Buck, trying to cover what he said before. "I just don't like them, they look like us and talk like us, but they are more ruthless and more dangerous then us."

"I hate them, too," said Caramel, "They could hurt us even though we are like family to them, and even though we appear alike, they don't care. They just hurt us without even thinking about it."

"Hey, let's just forget about wolf talk," Denver interrupted "If we run into wolves, we will deal with it and if we don't, that's good too. Let's just not worry about what will happen if we run into them."

"Yes, let's do what Denver said and move on and forget about wolves." Shorty said.

"Fine, let's start walking towards Russia." Said Buck.

So, they started walking and everything had been going well until they found water and a boat.

"What's with this? I thought there wasn't going to be any water on this journey." Denver said, with a weird expression on his face.

"Well, I guess we have to take that boat," Shorty said "I mean, the sign says that that boat is going to Russia"

"Yes, but look at the sign next to it," Caramel explained. "It says no pets are allowed."

"Well, I guess that we will have to sneak our way on," Buck said. "It won't be that hard. I mean all we will have to do is create a distraction. One of us has to run up as fast as they can and spray snow into the guards' faces, and then, the guards will run after the dog. With the guards gone, the others will run onto the storage boat. Since the distracting dog is much faster than the guards he can run out of sight of the guards, and quickly return to the boat with the others."

"I'll do it. I'm really fast," Denver said. "I used to run so much with my owner and I'm in really good shape so this will be easy."

So Denver got ready and left in a sprint. He went right past the guards and sprayed just enough snow in their faces for them to get angry. The guards chased after him in anger. They couldn't catch him. He outlasted them with his speed.

"We should go, I think the coast is clear," Buck told Shorty and Caramel.

After Denver distracted the guards, the other three dogs rushed onto the boat and into one of the containers. Denver quickly lost the guards, and got onto the boat.

"Where are you guys?" Denver whispered.

"We are over here," Shorty said.

"I don't see you. Are you in one of the containers?" Denver asked.

"Yes we are. We are in container twenty-nine," said Caramel.

The container Denver had been searching for stood at arms length away from him. He opened the container with his teeth and quickly glanced inside. He saw Buck, Shorty, and Caramel lying down in a circle.

"We should be fine here for the ride," Buck said. "The guards already made their rounds before we got on so we are safe for now."

They heard the boat's engine start up and Denver said, "Next stop, Russia!"

The next morning, Denver woke up and saw the beautiful face of Shorty standing up.

"Hey, I'm glad you are up," Shorty said, "I'm going to try to find some food, do you want to come with me?"

Denver nodded his head in agreement.

Early in the morning, neither Buck nor Caramel were up, as Denver and Shorty snuck by them and went outside of the crate. They started in the direction of the head of the boat, being cautious not to be found by any guards. They got to the front of the boat and peered through one of the windows. They then spotted a whole buffet of different food and drinks. Like heaven, the food looked unbelievable.

"That is a lot of food that we can eat," Denver said to Shorty.

"Yes, I know it is, but how are we going to get it all back to Buck and Caramel?" Shorty said, "I mean, they have to eat too."

"That's right," Denver said back. "I have a plan."

"We have to wait for there to be no one around that table, and when there isn't anyone, we have to grab what we can with our mouth, and run back as fast as we can," Denver said.

"That is a good plan, Denver but it isn't like we can grab that much food with just our mouths." Shorty answered.

Denver studied Shorty for a couple minutes. Golden and medium sized, Shorty stood there waiting for him. He then noticed that she had something around her neck.

"What is that?" asked Denver pointing at the thing.

"This? This is just a thing that my owner gave me before she had to release me into the wild," Shorty explained. "It's the only thing that reminds me of her."

"Oh, not to make this hard on you, but can we use that for our food attempt? I think you can carry more if you use that and I will just use my teeth to carry the rest back." Denver tried to explain to Shorty.

"That is a good idea, Denver. I would have never thought of that," Shorty said back,

They stayed there waiting until an opportunity appeared for them to raid the food table. When every one had left, they started to make their move. They looked at the door and were surprised to see that it had been left open. They crept inside trying not to make a sound. They got to the table and got on their hind legs to get up. Shorty scooped three pieces of bread, two carrots, and a hamburger. Denver took three hotdogs, still in the wrapper, and one chicken. They rushed out in case someone came back and saw them. They rushed back to the container that Buck and Caramel were in. As they got back they saw Caramel and Buck, up and talking to each other.

"Hi guys, how did you sleep?" asked Shorty.

"We slept well, but where were you guys?" responded Caramel.

"We were just getting some food to eat for the trip." Denver said back as he put the food on the table. "Enjoy!"

"Thank you, I was starving." Buck said, as he bit into one of the carrots. "I haven't eaten in four days."

"You haven't eaten in that long?" Denver asked, "Then you should eat up."

"Sounds good, thank you, Denver." Buck said

"Are you guys just going to talk or are you going to eat anything?" Caramel said.

"I think we should start eating, before they eat it all," Denver said to Buck.

"That's true, Caramel seems like he can eat the whole meal you brought back." Buck said back.

Denver looked at Caramel and studied him. As a bigger dog than most huskies Denver noticed Caramel appeared strong. Not a single piece of fat hung on his body. For that second, Denver thought Caramel was a nice dog but if you didn't know that you would be terrified of him. "Hey, Caramel, how did you get so big?" Denver said "Did you have a family that ran you and kept you in shape?"

"Yeah, I did have a family, but they moved to a smaller house and they couldn't afford to have me any more. I was in a house where the parents would take me to the gym every day to keep me in shape, and they ran with me all the time around the house," Caramel said "But I can not forgive them for putting me in the wild. I mean, when I was with them I was the happiest dog I could be, and when they left I just felt like there was something missing in my heart. But now I met Shorty and that hole is now full again."

"Awe, that is so sweet that you care that much about Shorty," Denver said to Caramel.

"Yes, I think I have a soft spot for beautiful ladies like this girl," Caramel said, as he kissed Shorty.

"Oh, thanks Caramel, I haven't seen this from you since we met," Shorty said.

"You guys, did you hear that?" Intruded Buck "I think that the boat hit land and we are in Russia."

Sure enough the boat docked in Russia. But the three dogs didn't know how to get off without the guards seeing them. They got out of their hiding place and they were about forty feet from the gate and freedom, when they noticed that the guards were checking the crates, as they were unloaded.

"Alright, I have a plan. We are going to wait until the guard goes with one of the boxes to put it away and that is when we are going to make our move," Buck said.

"That sounds like a plan to me," Denver said.

So they waited for the guards to leave to check a certain box, and then the four dogs made their move. The guards were so focused on the box, that they didn't see the four dogs get off the boat.

"Where do we go now?" Denver asked.

"We go left, because that is the fastest way to reach the caves and for you to be on your way to China," Buck said.

"So, we are going to the left," Denver said.

The dogs started walking and they couldn't help but realize that Russia's landscape had been similar to Canada's.

"This doesn't seem that bad," said Caramel. "I don't think that it will be hard to find a house here."

"Yes, that is what I'm telling you," Buck said. "This is the perfect place to settle down and have a family."

"Yes, this is a perfect place. I will love a home here," Shorty said.

Buck murmured to himself.

"You won't be able to find a house, because in about a mile my pack will eat you into little pieces."

"What's that?" asked Denver.

"Oh I just like talking to myself. It's a bad habit." Buck said

"Oh, okay so lets get on our way then." Caramel said.

So they started walking in the direction that Buck confirmed as the right way to go. They got about four and a half miles in the direction, and Buck started getting ready. Then they turned a corner to get around a mountain. Then all of a sudden four wolves appeared out of nowhere. The wolves got closer and closer.

"Hey guys, there is no need for there to be a fight because we are all part of the same family." Caramel said as he tried to negotiate with them.

Then out of nowhere, they jumped onto Denver, Shorty and Caramel.

"Buck, can you help us out here? I mean we are in trouble," Denver said, in a frantic voice

"I'm sorry, Denver, I can't do that." Buck said.

"Why not?" Denver said back.

"Because I tricked you. I am really a wolf and I have fooled you this whole time." Buck said in an evil way.

"So helping us with all that stuff was just a trick to get us here so you could kill us," Shorty said in a whimpering voice.

"Yes. And now you are going to die and be food for me and my pack." Buck said.

With this said, Caramel became enraged with anger.

"You are not going to kill my beautiful Shorty," Caramel said to Buck.

All of sudden Caramel got his arm free to put a couple of scratches on the wolf that held him. He got up and scratched furiously at the wolf until the wolf showed no signs of movement. Then he went after the one that had

Denver by the throat. He tackled the wolf and bit his neck so hard that the wolf died instantly.

"Denver, you go get Buck and I'll get the other wolf that is holding Shorty." Caramel said in a demanding voice to Denver.

So Denver rushed over to where Buck stood and became angry with him. He stopped right in front of Buck and got ready to attack him.

"Buck, you betrayed us and you wanted us dead. You almost made Caramel and Shorty not to be together, and you almost made me not be able to see my family. But it ends here! You are going down." Denver said in a determined voice."

"Then, let's get this done with." Buck said.

Buck rushed at Denver and took him to the ground. He clawed at him several times, but using his quickness, Denver dodged them. One of Buck's claws clipped Denver. That got Denver mad. His eyes lit up and he instantly picked Buck off him and flipped him over. Then he got on top of him and started furiously clawing at him. Denver kept clawing over and over again, and he didn't notice until about fifteen seconds later that Buck lay there dead.

Denver got off of Buck and started to calm down. He got up and rushed over to Caramel and Shorty. He noticed right away that they were free and were looking good except for some of the scratches on Caramel. Then, Denver's eyes left them and focused on a cave that loomed right behind them.

"Hey guys, do you see that? That looks like a good spot to live, I mean, you guys are secluded from everyone so you will have privacy. Also it looks like it is protected from wind and snow so the inside will be warm and dry." Denver said.

The two other dogs went to go check it out.

"This is perfect for us. We are safe and protected from

any danger because of these mountains and we are away from others." Shorty said.

They looked around and instantly loved the place.

"Well I guess this is where we say our good-byes," Shorty said, looking at Denver.

"I guess so," Denver said, a bit sadly.

So, Denver said good-bye to his friends that he had gotten to know and started on his solo trip again. He traveled about thirty miles and saw a train that appeared to be boarding passengers. There were a lot of people boarding, so he thought that he might just get on board and no one would notice. So he got onto the train and he looked at the chart. The chart listed Shanghai as the fourth stop. The stops were North Korea, South Korea, Beijing, and then Shanghai. The overnight train ride gave Denver the time he needed to rest and get his strength back. Denver dozed off as they pulled into the first stop in North Korea. He went to bed that night feeling confident about everything. He fell asleep dreaming of the day he would be reunited with his family. The next morning, he woke up to the sound of the train leaving the South Korea train station.

"Well, I guess, I still have a while on this train." Denver thought to himself.

He fell back to sleep again with a smile on his face.

"If I'm going to see my family, I better get some more rest," he said to himself.

For a while Denver slept, until he heard on the intercom that they would be arriving in Shanghai in a few minutes. He felt so happy that he got up from his laying position and started to wag his tail.

As he arrived at the Shanghai station, he happily waited for the doors to open. He was one of the first people that got off the train. As he looked up he realized, he arrived in a place in Shanghai called "Puxi". However, the family letter he carried from Chicago read "Pudong". He thought he had to take another train. He looked for the train that would take him close and he found one. The schedule told him he had to go to the Science and Technology Museum.

Realizing, that he currently stood at the "People's Square Station" and the museum was far away. He boarded the train and sat down. The train appeared to be different from the previous one. More crowded and less comfortable, Denver realized he had boarded a Shanghai subway car.

After four stops, a person came on the intercom saying that the museum would be the next stop. He got off his chair and waited for the door to open. As the train arrived at the station, it really shook Denver. He stumbled a bit, not being used to the bumpy ride. He got off the train and went to the nearest exit. As he started walking out, people were trying to get him to go to their stores and buy something. He thought the sight had been the weirdest thing he had ever seen. He got outside and tried to find the nearest taxi. Lucky for him, he found a taxi driver that knew English writing and could interpret the writing on the letter Denver had. To Denver, it seemed like a lifetime, but took only ten minutes. Denver couldn't remember the last time his tail wagged so fast. It could knock a person out with one wag.

The driver pulled up to a building that read "15." He didn't have any money, so the driver said he would cover him. Denver had been so lucky to meet such nice people in his adventure. Denver ran up to the building, but the building had a security code. No one could get in without a card. So Denver had to wait. A few minutes later a guy came up and opened the door. Denver quickly got in and got to the elevator. He looked at the letter and it said, "Room number 802." Denver got into the elevator. He got on his hind legs, and pushed the button to the 8th floor. He got up to the floor and got out. There were two doors. One said "802" the other said "801". Denver went to the door that read "802" and scratched at the door. The kid with the blond dfchair answered the door. He looked at Denver in a weird way. Denver started wagging his tail.

"Mom, there is a dog here and I don't know why he is here?" The little boy said.

"Check his collar, that will tell you who he is." His mom replied.

The little boy checked the collar. He looked at Denver in amazement.

"Mom, this reads that his name is "Denver" from the Brewer household." The little boy said as he looked at Denver. "Denver, you are really here!"

The little boy hugged Denver and let him inside.

"Mom, Dad, Denver is here for us" he said.

"Is that really, "Denver?" the parents said as they rush to hug Denver.

Finally together again, the family decided never to take Denver for granted again.

The Land of the Enchanted Pearl Tree

By Hannah Brown

"Ready or not, here I come," shouted Molly's mother. "Molly, I give up, where are you?"

Molly and her mother frequently amused themselves with a game of hide and seek in the back garden. They usually played hide and seek while they waited for Molly's father to get home from work. Molly had been crouching in the same place for an entire twenty minutes. For one hiding spot, twenty minutes was a personal record. Sometimes she just didn't have a good enough hiding spot. Other times, she never kept her mouth shut.

Molly knew her mother would never find her there, so she had to come out. It was time for dinner, and her mother had been calling for her to come out for quite some time now. Molly never disobeyed her mother, so she dragged herself back towards the house where her mother stood on the front veranda, in front of the little red front door. As Molly became visible from between the trees, she ran and ran until she finally reached her mother. Her mother's arms reached out and grabbed her under the arms, only to pick her up and start spinning her around and around until she made Molly dizzy.

"Where have you been, Miss Molly? I could not find you anywhere!" said her mother as she held open the door to let Molly in the house.

With no hurry, Molly told her mother all about the magnificent new hiding place she had found down by the pond. She told her each and every distinct detail about it.

"It's a big hollow tree that I found just down next to the pond. But it is an enormous, towering oak tree." Molly loved the hiding place so much that she even asked her mother if she would let her go back there after dinner. Her mother seemed a little unsure of the idea at first, but then agreed, and told Molly to sit down and eat her dinner.

Nothing but a particularly awkward silence hung over the dinner table. Molly scoffed down her food so fast that she eventually got hiccups from eating too quickly. Her mother asked her several times why she acted so strange and why she was being so rude at the dining table. But Molly was so busy stuffing food down her throat that she didn't have any time to reply with out her mouth full. The plate that sat in front of Molly got completely cleared after about two minutes. After that, she swiftly got out of her chair, ran out the back door, and back to the big old tree down by the lake.

Running as fast as possible, she felt her brown frizzy hair that was tied back in two braids, flying behind her head. An icy cold wind blew across her rosy cheeks, and pulled back her white dress. Arriving at the sight of the old, beautiful, and magical tree made her smile with joy and great delight. She saw something there that she had never seen before. On the right side of the tree, sat a short and slanted wooden sign that said, "Welcome to the Land of the Enchanted Pearl Tree."

Trees are very similar, but Molly remembered this exact tree. It stood straight and tall on the right side of the pond in a strange, but interesting way, and it almost looked like the trunk of the tree twisted around several times. Its leaves were a beautiful orange and red color, and they would turn a vibrant green in the summer.

She peered into the Pearl Tree, straight through the entrance. It became pitch black inside; consequently she could not see anything. Leaning in a little closer, her feet neared at an edge; she felt them slip from beneath her. She kicked and screamed until she landed on her bottom with a loud thud at the foot of the tree. She set down her hands on the ground to see where she was. She remembered that the last time she was here was just before dinner when she was hiding from her mother. She was sitting down inside that same tree, but she didn't fall last time. This time she did.

After a moment of time, she heard sounds of something rummaging around. At first, molly had thought a rat ran around at the bottom of the tree. But she soon realized it wasn't. The figure's silhouette appeared from the shadowy darkness. Molly did not say anything. Instead, she crawled to where she saw a rock big enough for her to hide behind. She tried as hard as she could to stay quiet as a mouse so that no one would hear her. Whoever, or whatever this thing creeping towards her could have been, she didn't do anything about it. It would not stop coming towards her and she had nowhere to go. Suddenly, she felt a hand over her mouth, one around her waste pulling her in, and another two holding each of her arms. They pulled her in through a massive black door.

*   *   *

When Molly woke up, she had no idea what had been going on. These people had brought her into a room where she had a bed to sleep on, and that was it. There was not one sound she could hear until out of nowhere, she heard a bird call that sounded so beautiful. A bird, out of the corner of her eye appeared a vibrant orange colored bird sitting on the windowsill. It flew towards her.

"Greetings my friend! My name is Pippa, Pippa Lee to be exact. But you can just call me Pippa."

Molly was so confused. First she had fallen down into a great big tree.

Then she was "captured," and now a little orange bird is talking to her! She had never heard of a talking bird before... She must have been imagining things.

"Why will you not speak to me? Are you afraid? Scared?" Pippa looked back at her wondering.

Molly had no idea what to say. Was this bird called Pippa really as sweet as he looked? Or was he just another part of what seemed like an evil plan to plot against her? Pippa seemed sweet, but there really was no way of telling wether or not he was going to do any harm.

"I'm sorry, uh...I am just...shocked, that's all. I have never met a talking bird before." Even though Pippa had confused Molly, she decided to just be polite.

Her and Pippa had a great time together talking, and talking, and she eventually had no suspicions about Pippa like she did before. It wasn't until about four days later when Molly asked if they would ever be getting out of there.

"How about you come with me? I would like to show you around my home! It is a great place."

Molly simply nodded her head and followed him. Pippa flew over to the cabinet by the door. He lifted up his right wing and pulled out a key. Molly wondered and hesitated to ask Pippa what it could be for, but she just decided to keep her mouth shut. Molly could see Pippa heading for the door. The key seemed heavy for him, so Molly swiftly ran to the door, where Pippa had trouble getting the key into the door. After Molly had seen the key, she realised why Pippa had trouble holding it up. The key obviously hadn't been made for tiny little birds like Pippa. Molly took the key from Pippa and placed it in the keyhole. With a quick flick of the wrist, she turned the key and opened the door. The sound of the turning key made a snapping sound when it popped the door open.

"Finally! We're out of there!" Molly exclaimed. "If everyone is so nice here, then why did you capture me?"

Judging by the look on Pippa's face, it looked like he didn't want to answer that question very much. "Just my orders from the boss. That's all."

When Pippa said that, it made her wonder why he was so vague. Who is the boss? And why did Pippa have to take orders from him?

Molly and Pippa were dying to get out of there, it had been four whole days, and Molly's stomach wouldn't stop growling! She wondered where Pippa would be taking her because he covered her eyes with a black blindfold so that she couldn't see where they were going. She thought of so many places that Pippa might be taking her. Places like the carnival, or the beach, or even somewhere out in the wilderness. But she assumed that none of the places she guessed would be anything like where they actually are going. At first, they walked down a tiny, long, and narrow corridor that was dark and scary. But, after a while, the corridors became wide and light shone through the windows. Soon before they reached their destination, Pippa covered Molly's eyes with his wings and tied a blindfold over them.

"What are you doing? Why are you blindfolding me?" Molly shouted

Pippa said in a calming voice, "It is okay Molly, you are going to be okay. I just want what I am showing you to be a surprise. I think you are going to like it."

Pippa was really starting to worry Molly. First he's a talking bird, then he sat with her in her room for four days and talked to her. And then he unlocked the door with a massive key that was hiding under his wing. And now he is blindfolding her and taking her somewhere. She so badly wished that Pippa would tell her where they were headed because this place was already strange enough. If Pippa would tell her then she could be prepared for whatever strange thing will happen next. As they took slow steps up the spiral staircase Pippa counted for Molly.

"Left foot...right foot...left foot...right foot."

Molly slowly and cautiously walked up the stairs. On the second last step she made, she went to place her foot down and only her toes made it to the step. She slipped, and fell straight on her face with a loud yelp that made the whole corridor echo.

"Oh no! Molly! Are you okay?"

"Yes Pippa, I am fine, thank you for all of your concern though."

"Thank goodness Molly! You scared me so much."

Molly smiled at Pippa's caring comment even though she couldn't see where she was smiling. But it reminded her of how kind her mother was to her. Still blindfolded, Molly thought about what her Mom would be thinking of her right now. It had been four days since she last went home and her mother had no idea at all of where she was. She had not given her mother a thought until now. But the sad emotion quickly passed through her head, and Pippa continued to help her up the last two steps.

"Stand still for a second Molly, I have to open the door so we can get out."

"Get out? Get out to where?"

Soon after no one gave a reply to Molly's concerning question, a warm gush of air blew against her rosy cheeks. Pippa seemed to have opened a door to somewhere that was outside. She heard Pippa's voice come pop out next to her.

"Welcome to the Land of the Enchanted Pearl Tree."

She couldn't stand not being able to see. She opened her mouth and just started to complain about how her left knee hurt from when she fell down the stairs about five minutes ago. But then she realised where she was.

Standing just outside the door, the shock of the beautiful view was from where ever she was, was amazing. Words were trying to come out of her mouth to ask Pippa where they were. But nothing came out. The view was so breath taking as she stood there gazing at it. From the looks of it, Molly thought they were in a wooden tree house of some sort. Walking over to the part of the tree house that over looked the Land of the Enchanted Pearl Tree, Molly noticed where she was. She leaned over the edge of the railing and saw that they were miles off the ground.

"Oh! Pippa! How far off the ground are we?"

"Only around forty meters. Why do you ask?"

"It just seems so high! I feel like I am a bird flying high in the sky."

The river flowing through the middle of the Land of the Enchanted Pearl Tree, reflected the light of the sun back into the sky. Trees bordered it until there were mushroom and flower houses. Pippa told Molly that the mushroom houses were for all of the creatures that worked for the Master Aza. The creatures that worked for Aza all lived in mushroom houses because those houses included electronics and facilities that were useful to them. Pippa also told Molly that the other flower houses were simply for the citizens that lived in the Land of the Enchanted Pearl Tree.

"Look! Pippa! I can see my house from up here! It seems so far away, but I bet you if my Mom went and stood out on the front veranda I would be able to see her. She would probably look like a tiny ant though. Do you think she would be able to see me from here Pippa?"

Pippa tried not to give a curt reply, but it was hard not to. "I don't know..." he said.

Molly began to think about her Mom and Dad who hadn't seen her for almost five days now. They must be worried about her. But, what could Molly do? She was off having a fun adventure with some of the best friends she has ever met in her life. Presides, whenever she missed her family, she could always come up here to the tree house and look back at her house.

*   *   *

It was an extremely long time before Molly finally began to get bored of the amazing scenery, but when she did, Pippa dragged her back down the tree house. They walked through Feather Lane and took a left at Swan Road. Molly was beginning to get sick of not knowing where she was going all the time. It was slightly annoying having Pippa dragging her around to these random places that no human being even knew about. Deciding to keep her mouth shut, she soon realized where they were going. Swan road consisted of mushroom houses on each side of the road.

"Well, here we are, number forty-two Swan Road."

Pippa seemed a little bit nervous to show her through his house. In general the mushroom houses were very nice. Molly did not see one single fault in them.

"Pippa, these houses are extremely nice. But, I can't help but wonder why I am here. Surely I would be going back home sometime soon tonight?"

The look on Pippa's face concerned Molly. It seemed like there was a feeling burning up inside of him that he wanted to tell her, but he couldn't.

"Sorry Molly, I am sure that you miss your family a lot. You have to stay in the Land of the Enchanted Pearl Tree for a little bit longer though. Master Aza told me so."

Who is this Master Aza guy? Why has Pippa obeying him like he is the king of the world? It all seemed very strange to Molly. Maybe it all seemed strange because he was so vague about everything. If he wasn't then it would be easier for Molly to know what was going on and she wouldn't have to be wondering all the time. She got a strong vibe that there was some sort of a secret that Pippa really couldn't tell her because of this so called Master Aza.

Pippa took her hand and lead her into the kitchen, and then to the living room. Molly was sick of wondering where they were going all the time. Pippa never told her anything.

"Pippa, can you please tell me where we are going? It's getting slightly annoying not knowing."

"Molly, It's okay, I just wanted to show you where I will be staying, and then where you will stay tonight. You should really stop stressing out about things like this Molly." Pippa smiled.

Molly felt so ashamed of herself for accusing Pippa. After they had walked down the hallway, Molly and Pippa entered Pippa's room. It turns out that his room is inside a hollow tree, which was connected to the mushroom house, by the "S" shape hallway. His room was very simple, and very small. Which made sense to Molly after a little bit of thinking time. He's a small bird! No wonder his room was so small, however it was a reasonable size for Pippa. After this they went up a fairly large spiral staircase that lead up to Molly's bedroom for her stay here in the Land of the Enchanted Pearl Tree. Molly's room was a little bigger than Pippa's. It was still small, but big enough for her to survive. It was a circular room with a pointed roof and a big window that wrapped around the whole room and looked over the whole of the Land of the Enchanted Pearl Tree.

*   *   *

The next morning, Molly had woken up and gotten ready for whatever her and Pippa were doing today. Pippa was in the laundry folding up the washing when there was a ring on the doorbell.

"Molly, would you mind getting that for me?"

"Who is it? Are you sure it is someone that you know?"

"It is one of my friends, she knows that you're here, just answer the door."

Molly walked over the door and anxiously opened it to let their visitor in. The guest seemed nice, but Molly really didn't have any way of telling.

"Hi! My name is Shadow. You must be Molly?"

"Yes, I am Molly. It's nice to meet you Shadow."

Shadow had come over for breakfast and then they were going up to the tree house to update the Land of the Enchanted Pearl Tree map. Molly, Pippa and Shadow all had such a great time at breakfast together. They had Molly's favourite; pancakes and waffles with maple syrup. After they had finished breakfast, she was so full, but she had to finish it all. Her mother always taught her to never leave anything on the table because there are starving people out there and we can't let the food go to waste. Pippa had made more than enough food. If Shadow hadn't have helped Pippa make them, then maybe there wouldn't have been left overs.

As they were walking towards the tree house where Molly was with Pipa yesterday, Molly noticed something different about it. The tree house seemed much more alive than it was before. When se was walking up the staircase, a vibration coming through the floor and up into Molly's body was making her heart beat faster and faster.

"Pi..." Molly was interrupted at the sight of Pippa and Shadow both gone.

A sudden sound, the flapping of wings came into her ears. She turned quickly to see what was flapping behind her. Nothing appeared. Continuing to walk up the stairs, she heard another flapping frenzy, but this time she didn't bother to turn around. She assumed that it would just be Pippa and Shadow flying around, trying to scare her. Step by step she walked up the wooden spiral staircase. Every step she took made a creek and the creeks got louder and louder as she got further up the stairs. She eventually got up to the top step. The whole time she walked up the stairs she looked down at her feet. When she reached the top, she felt two tiny feet on her right shoulder and two bigger feet on her left. She turned her head suddenly.

"Pippa! Where were you? I thought you left me on my own."

Instead of answering her question, Pippa and Shadow nodded slightly to indicate to her to look ahead.

"Surprise!" All of the creatures from the Land of the Enchanted Pearl Tree were in the tree house with party hats and streamers everywhere. There were cakes and party food everywhere. Not only was there party food, there were all of Molly's favorites; fairy bread and chock chip cookies!

"Welcome to the Land of the Enchanted Pearl Tree, Molly!"

"But, Pippa, I thought we were coming up here to update the map of the town."

"No, Molly, I just told you that so I could get you up here without you suspecting anything."

Pippa introduced Molly to so many creatures. There were much to many names for her to remember. Molly could only remember a few. There was Snow, Raven, Star, Rowan, Amber, and Crystal...That could have been Willow, though. Molly wasn't sure. All that she knew was that she had a great time. She wished that the party could have gone on for so much longer than it did. But it was time to go home, and go to bed. It was getting late. They had practically spent the whole day up in the tree house at the party.

Molly almost had as much fun at the party as she

did when she was playing hide and seek with her mother when she was waiting for her father to come home from work. That was the day that Molly found the tree that had the sign in front of it saying "the Land of the Enchanted Pearl Tree." She loved it here in the Land of the Enchanted Pearl Tree. But there was something that deeply saddened her. She didn't know what though. What could it be? She just had one of the best days of her life and one of the best parties of her life yet she was upset about something.

Sadness hung over Pippa and Molly as they were walking home. The whole way home, down Feather lane and left at Swan road neither Molly or Pippa said a word to each other. As soon as Pippa unlocked the door to his house, Molly suddenly ran inside, straight to her room.

"Molly? Are you okay?"

Although Molly heard Pippa, she decided not to reply. She knew that she really should have thanked him for the amazing party that he organized for her, and she didn't want to be rude. She just needed some time to herself.

Finally, she figured out what was wrong. All this time she had been having so much fun, for almost over a week now, and she had barely even given one thought to her Mom or Dad. She couldn't help but think about how selfish she was for not thinking about the two people in the world who were closest to her. Molly cried for hours and hours. She wasn't crying now because she felt selfish and careless for her parents. It was mainly because she missed her mother and her father so much now.

Days and days passed. Pippa tried to get Molly out of her room. Nothing would work. The only time she ever left her room was when it was breakfast, lunch, or dinnertime. Even then she grabbed the plate or bowl and took it straight up to her room. She didn't want to talk to anyone or do anything with anyone at all.

It had been almost a week since Molly had come out

of her room. She still wasn't on planning on going out until the hour after lunch when she heard a knock on the door of her room.

"Molly...Can I please come in? I think it would help if I talked to you."

Molly lifted her head and thought about her decision for a moment. She didn't know whether she should let him in or just ignore him one more time. She slowly got out of bed, deciding to answer the door. After she tiredly lifted herself out of the bed, she creped to the door and unlocked the door. As she turned the door handle, it clicked, and popped open the door. Molly peered her head out into the hall way from the inside of her room. She saw Pippa hovering outside her door.

"Yes?"

"Molly...Are you okay?" Pippa hesitated, "You haven't come out of your room in a while."

Eventually Molly did come out of her room but it took a lot of persuading from Pippa. Molly knew that Pippa was worried about her, but she didn't want to tell him what was going on, she thought it would just worry him more. Pippa had told her that it would make him feel so much better if she told him though. After a long moment of Pippa and Molly sitting on the bed together, while Molly was thinking, she finally told him.

"At first I was upset because I hadn't given my mother or father one thought since I have been here and I felt so selfish and unkind. Now I guess I am just upset because I miss them so much. It has been almost two weeks since I have been home and I am wishing that I could go back."

Molly burst into tears; she couldn't help but think about how worried her parents would be right now. She also worried about were going to do to her when she got back. Would they be mad? Would they be happy to see her back?

* * *

"Let's go Molly! Big day, today, I am pretty sure this will cheer you up!" said Pippa.

Soon after they left the house, Molly found herself on a shore somewhere near Pippa's house, sitting on rocks talking and playing with the mermaids that lived there. Charlotte was by far the most beautiful. She had long, luscious red hair that stretched down to her lower back. But the most beautiful part of her was her beautifully long tail. Greenish scales covered it the whole day down. Until the end of her tail where it fanned out into two where it turned a light turquoise.

"Molly, why don't you come with me? I want to show you something very special. Not very many people get to see this." Charlotte's beautiful voice calmed Molly. She nodded her head and began to follow the mermaid. Charlotte grabbed hold of Molly's wrists and flung her over her back.

"Hold on tight, Molly. I am a pretty fast swimmer."

Without hesitating, Charlotte dove into the water and began to kick her mermaid tail. It was a very beautiful lake from underwater. It was filled with colorful coral, sea stars, and so many other beautiful sea creatures. After a couple of seconds down under the beautiful blue water, they went inside a cave that must have gotten closer to the surface as you went in because there was air at the top where they stopped.

"So what is it that you are showing me, Charlotte?"

"I'm sorry I have to do this to you, Molly. You seem like you are a really nice girl."

"What?" Molly was so shocked at the strange statement Charlotte made, "What is going on?"

The last thing Molly heard from Charlotte was, "I'm sorry" and then she was pushed down into somewhere cold, dark and wet. So now, Molly was back where she started... In a black, dark, gloomy, scary who knows what! How was she supposed to get out of here?

"I have waited for so long to see you, Molly. What took you so long?" A creepy voice said out of nowhere.

Still not being able to see anything was a total disadvantage for Molly. Who the heck was this guy?

"Who are you?" Molly said in a forceful tone.

"I am Master Aza... Like I said, I have been waiting for you, Molly."

Where were Pippa and Shadow when you needed them? Molly couldn't save herself, she was stuck in a big hole in the ground that was much too tall for her to get out of and she couldn't see one single thing.

The next thing she knew it, just like last time, Molly was being dragged by her wrists to somewhere and there was a hand over her mouth so she couldn't scream. Except Molly didn't bother to scream. It seemed like she had been though this ritual one too many times.

"Four questions... who are you? How do you know my name? Why are you here? And what are you going to do to me?" This creature hadn't been answering any of her questions and it was really starting to get on her nerves.

"My name is Master Aza, you may have heard of me. I know your name because Pippa has been with you. He reports everything back to me. There are also cameras all around his house so I can monitor his, and your every move. As for the last two questions, you will find out the answers to those later on."

Molly interrupted, "So what is the story with this place. It seems like there is a big secret going around and I am the only one who doesn't know about it.

"Yes, there is a secret, and you are going to get to find out what it is right now," he paused.

"Well? Are you going to tell me?"

"I am here to capture you Molly. Everyone in the Land of the Enchanted Pearl Tree is evil. They are all in on my evil plan to capture you."

Shocked, Molly exclaimed, "Even Pi..."

Aza interrupted, "Yes, even Pippa. Everyone was against you. Pippa, Shadow, Charlotte, and of course, me!" Aza let out an evil laugh that just made Molly so much madder than she was before.

Molly felt a firm grip once again, wrap around her wrists.

"Let go of me right now!"

"I can't do that now Molly, it's too late"

All of a sudden the grips that held her somewhere off the ground let go. Nothing. Nothing to see, nothing to hear, nothing to feel. She was nowhere.

*   *   *

"Molly? Molly, are you awake? Molly?" She heard the voice of her father speaking beside her.

"Molly! Please wake up." She heard her father's voice again.

A hand on the top of her right hand too. Molly gained the strength to move her index finger to warn her father that she was all right. As she awoke, she gained more and more strength. Eventually she opened her eyes. When she first opened her eyes everything around her was a blur. It took a while for her eyes to adjust, but once she got used to it, it was okay.

"Dad?"

"Yes, sweetie?"

"Where am I?"

The look on her father's face made him look like he was sad and worried, but relieved at the same time.

"You're in hospital. When you went out to play after dinner you went to the big tree down by the lake didn't you?"

"Uh... Yes, I did. I think I did, I can't exactly remember."

"Well, when you didn't come back for a while, we figured there must have been something wrong. So we went out looking for you. It didn't take that long to find

33

you because you were still down by the old tree. You were pretty excited to get there weren't you?"

"Um... yes, I was. Why do you ask?"

"Well, we saw that one of your shoes had come off and it was sitting right next to a huge root of the tree. So we're pretty sure that you tripped over the root, then fell and hit your head on something."

Molly didn't remember any of this! She knew she was in the Land of the Enchanted Pearl Tree, but how did she get from there to the dumbwaiter shaft in the basement? The only time she remembered falling was when Master Aza pushed her down the tree.

A doctor walked into her room. "I heard you woke up. How are you feeling? Are you dizzy, or, feeling ill at all?"

"No, I'm just a little bit tired that's all. May I have a glass of water though?"

"Sure no problem, I'll be back in a moment."

As the doctor walked out of the room, Molly's father began talking again.

"When we found you, you were holding a crunched up bit of paper in your hand. It was a note from someone, but I'm not exactly sure whom. I think you might know who it is. Would you like to read it?"

"Yes please"

The note stated this:

Dear Molly,

When you were upset about missing your family, I wanted to help you, but there was nothing that I could really do about it. I know that Master Aza told you that everyone here was jus an evil plan to plot against you, but I was truly your friend, I really did want to help you get out of this place. A couple of years ago Aza captured me and told me I had to live in the Land of the Enchanted Pearl Tree or I would kill me.

Once he captures you, there is pretty much no going back. He makes you work for him for the rest of your life. One thing I never told you was that I have some magical powers, everyone in the Land of the Enchanted Pearl Tree does. Except, the only bad thing about them is that once you have them you can't get out of this place. That's why there's no going back. I don't use my powers that often; I try to use it only when someone is in danger. Just after Charlotte took you into the cave, I knew she was taking you to Master Aza so that he could give you your magical powers. Aza pushed you into the hole in the cave, yes? Well, that is how you get those powers.

When I heard you scream, I used this magic that I got when Aza captured me and pushed me into the hole. I made the bottom of the hole just outside the Land of the Enchanted Pearl Tree so that your parents could find you. I know that you are in hospital now and you have some serious injuries. But I didn't want you to be captured forever by Master Aza like I am. Living here isn't all fun and games like you experienced when you were here.

You were one of the greatest friends I have had in a long time. Everyone here is so focused on work. I am going to miss all of the fun times we had together. Even though we may not be able to see each other, I can still see you from the tree house I took you to. Go out there every day at four o'clock so that I can see you. Feel free to write to me Molly! I had a great time while you were here.

Thank you for all of the great memories,

Pippa
P.S. I will be watching over you.

*   *   *

Pippa was a great friend to Molly. He had two choices; one was not to save her so that they could be best friends forever, or he could have saved her and let Molly be happy with her parents at home. But he decided to do the write thing and save her to send her back to her home with her parents. They could still write to each other. And every day at four o'clock in the afternoon Molly would go down to her front veranda and Pippa would go up to the tree house to watch over her.

Less is More

By Victoria Chen

Take that! Tears obscured Amanda's vision as she jabbed a piece of greasy meatloaf. A twinge of pain rose in the back of her throat as she tried to subdue her anger. Bits of grease oozed out from the meatloaf, a result from the fork's impact, and slightly soaked her shoulder-length, dingy auburn hair. A grandfather clock clanged seven times; it was seven o'clock at Crystal Orphanage, in the northern town of Tiny Seawington. A single light bulb illuminated the capacious dining hall. Fifty-some girls sat side by side with Amanda at long oak tables. Amanda silently shoved the foul-smelling, almost spoiled meatloaf into her mouth, satisfying her ravenous hunger. Not even a crumb of her stale white bread remained on her porcelain plate.

I couldn't believe it! My mom was coming back for me. This was all a joke. Fourteen years ago, Amanda's birth mother, Cecilia Gold, dropped her off at Crystal Orphanage, right after she was born. Amanda faithfully believed in her mother so much, and waited for her for endless years, only to be let down again and again. Two days ago, Ms. Tobol the head mama (a helper)–and founder of the orphanage–received an email from Amanda's mother telling her how sorry she felt and how she wanted to meet Amanda as soon as possible. Yeah right, as if she cares. Amanda seriously doubted her mother would even recognize her among the fifty girls who live with her. Furious with her mother, because she had never experienced the feeling of abandonment and being unwanted, she sighed heavily. Drowsy with a satisfied stomach, Amanda knew she needed to decide whether or not to trust her own judgement.

"Hey Gwen, will you pass the tissues?" Amanda's voice quivered faintly, betraying her attempts to hide her anger.

"Sure Amanda. What's wrong?" asked Gwen nervously, Amanda's best friend since she was seven. Tears trickled down the front of Amanda's unnaturally pale white face. Amanda's hazel green eyes glistened in the faint glow of the light bulb.

"Oh. Nothing. I'm fine," stammered Amanda, trying to choke back more tears as they welled in her eyes.

Gwen's voice was filled with disbelief. "Really?"

"Yeah. I'm fine." Amanda tried hard to sound annoyed.

But she was not fine. Amanda knew that Gwen could always tell when something went wrong, tears or no tears. Amanda tilted her head sideways to glance at the ancient grandfather clock that stood at the end of the room, careful to conceal her face from the worrisome mamas. She perceived that the moment the mamas saw her face, the realization that something terribly wrong happened to her would hit them.

The steady-burning light flickered once or twice, and then died down. A power failure extinguished the light in the dining hall. Groans and mutters sounded throughout the room as person by person realized what just happened. Each and every face appeared dead and ghostly in moonlight that shone gleamingly through the large windows. Amanda watched as the younger kids, encouraged by their own fear, sprinted around the room. They screamed their heads off, waking all the infants in the orphanage.

"Calm down now girls! Don't worry! It's just another power failure," came Ms. Tobol's benevolent voice over the now loud whispers and cries. "Ms. Katie just contacted the power company, and they told her that the all of the workers just went home. This means we will all be sleeping in the Hearth today." The younger kids' chaotic actions stopped abruptly, and they all sat quietly, listening intently to what Ms. Tobol said. "The older children can go grab their blankets and make themselves comfortable first. The younger ones should go in groups of five back up to their rooms to get their sleeping blankets and back down as well. Be careful and don't trip over anyone! Mamas, you can take your infants and sleep with them in the Hearth tonight as well. I am expecting the house girls and boys to be on a watch for anything wrong. Come on now, out of your chairs or you won't get enough sleep tonight with all this fussing!"

Tugging on Gwen's sleeve, Amanda pulled her off her wobbly chair, and dragged them both into a sea of confusion. Moonlight spilled through the evenly spaced windows, providing light so that the moving crowd wouldn't topple on top of each other. Amanda emerged from the crowd to face the staircase that led up to their dorm room.

"Come on! Or we won't be able to get a good spot near the fireplace!" Gwen shouted over the clamor.

Amanda scurried up the flight of stairs and dashed swiftly into their room. She walked these halls so many times that she didn't even need light to navigate anymore. Amanda could barely make out three bunk beds and three desks that were evenly spaced out in the crowed room. Although she never received much of anything, Amanda loved the orphanage. Home, to Amanda, meant the orphanage. The only place she really ever loved or remembered. The rainstorm that just left town yesterday also left the room and blankets damp with moisture. Amanda and Gwen occupied the bunk bed and desk nearest the curtain-less, dusty window. The sill was covered with peeling, white paint and smooth, old wooden cracks. On a normal morning, ample light shone through it, brightening the whole room. But now, without the light to give the room a warm glow, it looked spooky, eerie, and strangely unfamiliar.

Amanda scurried over to her bed and pulled off the thin, cotton blanket that usually kept her warm even during the coldest of nights. She also grabbed her red cylinder shaped pillow hastily off the foot of the mattress.

She received this as a birthday gift when she turned eight. Gwen constantly insulted her pillow, calling it the "stinky pillow" because it reminded her of Indian food. The story behind is she had once absentmindedly spilt curry on it while eating dinner a while back. Since that day, Amanda never dared to take her stinky pillow down for dinner again in fear that it would just get even dirtier.

As they hastened back down to the Hearth, they passed by the orphanage's nursery. Almost all of the mamas occupied themselves, trying to comfort the crying, helpless babies who knew of nothing. Babies here were either born in the orphanage, or brought there months after their birth. A mama there told Amanda's first story when she was six months old. Tired and sleepy with the weight of her blanket in her arms, Amanda sluggishly dragged her feet to the doorway to the Hearth. She managed to spot a clearing in a corner near the fire and dragged Gwen towards it, careful not to step on anyone asleep. As they settled themselves down, she could hear the first snores appearing from underneath the mounds of blanket and kid, from those who had already fallen asleep.

That night, Amanda slept restlessly. New worries added themselves on top of the ones she already had about her long lost mother. The fireplace by the Hearth provided the only source of light and heat. Outside, the wind blew mercilessly, bringing down the piercing cold, instantly frosting the windows. The December winters in Tiny Seawington always came as a shock to Amanda. The sun may shine brightly and warm one day, and it would be hiding behind frosty clouds the next. Shivering for the first time under her blanket, troubling dreams invaded her sleep.

How little she knew about her mother, not even a picture to remind Amanda of her. Ms. Tobol, the orphanage manager, was the only person who remembered how her mother looked like. According to Ms. Tobol, Amanda's mother's beautiful auburn hair looked just like hers. However, unlike Amanda, her mother also had lustrous hazel eyes that glistened in the light. Amanda decided one thing that night. Never would anyone be able to break her heart like her mother had, leaving her behind, and wanting her again after so many years. Never.

* * *

The Destiny Bell rung at seven sharp ever single day—except for the weekends when it rung at eight. The loud clangs echoed through the halls and up the dorm rooms. Amanda woke up to face the grey and gloomy sky, framed by the window. Water droplets clinging to the misty window pane reminded her of last night's heavy rainstorm. Thunder and lightning blasted at each other in the distance, the war of the skies. Amanda experienced a sleepless night. She stretched her legs and sat up. crack. Ouch. Amanda loved the feeling of cracking her back.

Surveying around, Amanda noticed that Gwen rolled

about a foot away from where she slept last night. Her best friend lay sprawled on the floor, her shiny, long black hair spread out like a fan.

"Hey Gwen! Wake up! Come on! Gwen Anna Kitpal, we won't be getting pancakes for our Sunday breakfast!" Amanda urgently whispered while shoving her, trying to get Gwen to wake up. Sunday pancakes weren't the best incentive as they were usually overcooked with too little butter, but she had to give it a try.

"Uh... Coming. Just wait a second. Like two hours..." Gwen's voice was muffled by her flowery blue blanket.

One by one, the orphans aroused and got up to put their blankets away. Amanda tugged at Gwen's arm, dragging her across the floor.

"Okay, gosh! I'm getting up! With you dragging me like that, people will think I'm a rucksack!" Gwen grumbled, irritated.

The electricians came early in the morning to fix the electricity. Because the sunlight wasn't bright enough yet, luminescent lights lit up the whole Hearth. The Hearth remained as the only room in the whole entire orphanage that contained newly installed lights as a result of the charity sponsorship activity last year.

Just as Amanda and Gwen headed towards the staircase, chiming stopped them in their tracks. With a ring of the Welcome Bell that sounded each time the door opened, a tall, intimidating man with ginger brown hair and hazel green eyes stepped inside. His demeanor alone brought Amanda the creeps. She couldn't even look at him for more than a second straight. Beside him, a scruffy, worn out boy around the age of fourteen shivered in his cut-off jeans and t-shirt. The mighty, bone-chilling wind blew forcefully into the orphanage, and everyone around shivered fragilely.

"Come along now, girls!" Mrs. Tobol, rush the orphans into the hearth. "Oh, look who is here! Everyone, this is Ian White, and he will be joining us at the orphanage from now on," Mrs. Tobol announced, and to the man she assured, "Thanks for bringing him here. We will take very good care of Ian here, and he will be very safe with us. Do you have any of his belongings?"

"Yes, yes, of course," replied the man. His scratchy voice strained to maintain a polite tone. He reached behind his back and handed over a small brown duffle bag to Mrs. Tobol.

"I wonder if that is all he's got!" Amanda whispered to Gwen carefully, eyes still on the boy. Gwen made a face and stuck out her tongue. Amanda knew that Gwen didn't have many possessions, as a matter of fact no one here did.

"Bye, son," the father said absentmindedly, as if he could care less where his son was and how happy he is.

"Bye dad," murmured Ian, his eyes fixed determinedly on the couch in front of him.

"It must suck to be left here after so many years with your father" Amanda whispered into Gwen's ear. "I hope he finds this place more like home." I sure do.

"Yeah, me too. But come on now, or we will never get to eat breakfast. I'm starving!" Gwen whined.

But Amanda just couldn't keep her eyes off of Ian. Something about his gorgeous dirty blonde hair and piercing blue eyes seemed to attract her attention. Reluctantly, she followed Gwen up the stairs towards her now-heated dorm.

* * *

Amanda loved the breakfast that the orphanage served every Friday. As a tradition, the whole orphanage celebrated Ian's arrival with a welcome meal. The curtains were all tabbed, and the sun shone dazzlingly over the town. Amanda glanced around. As she caught people's eyes, she saw that happiness in their familiar faces.

Everything was perfect, well, as perfect as a group of orphans can be.

Ian soon became the topic of everyone's conversation. Gwen even told Amanda about a rumor spreading around about Ian's father. Apparently, Ian's father beat him several times before he finally dropped Ian off at the orphanage. Amanda knew better than to believe in rumors, but she was still very curious about him. She planned on approaching him sometime soon before things got out of hand.

Amanda huddled by the window of the Hearth, reading her favorite book To Kill A Mockingbird. The sun shone radiantly on the Saturday morning and the orphanage was about to have their weekly field trip. This week, they headed toward the town library, which was a fifteen-minute walk away. Amanda loved reading. It was her only comfort to escape to when there was no one else there for her. She could practically live in a novel and be content with it. She dreamed about being an author and illustrator for young adults books. She wanted to share her emotions and experiences with every child who read her books. Amanda planed on talking to Ian today when they were at the library.

"Come on now ladies and gents! We are leaving for the library in five minutes! If you don't want to go, you can stay here with Ms. Katie. If you do, be lined up by the door here ready to go with you coat and boots on. I think it is going to snow today, so be sure to find your mittens! Come, come!" Ms. Tobol hurried across the Hearth into her room.

Amanda stretched out her legs and put her book away. Excitedly, Amanda rushed over to her wooden cubby.

Five minutes later, Amanda, alongside Gwen, was zipped up and ready to go. The welcome bell rang harmoniously as the children pilled out of the orphanage and into fresh morning. Flakes of snow flew down from the sky, melting slowly on Amanda's purple coat. The snow crunched with every step she took, under the weight of Amanda's body, imprinting a permanent mark on the clean white snow. The clouds hid the sun, making the sky a tint gray. The wind caught Amanda's hair in its invisible fingers, tickling her blushed face. Soon Amanda could make out the red brick building that was like her second home. The group climbed up the concrete steps leading to the entrance and up into the library. The war air conditioning welcomed Amanda as she took off her hat and mittens.

She saw Ian walk off into the science-fiction section and carefully followed him, trying not to appear suspicious. As she walked along behind him, Amanda pretended to browse the aisle, titles like Monsters of the future and Into the Future: 3014 filled up all of the shelves. Finally, Ian took his pick and plopped down on a light green beanbag. Without looking, Amanda pulled a book off the shelf and advanced towards the beanbags.

"You like the A Timeless Travel series too? I love them! Especially Gnool." Ian looked up from his comic book at Amanda, his face spread out in a wide grin.

"Yeah... of course!" Stammered Amanda. In all honesty, Amanda had never heard of A Timeless Travel. "Do you mind if I sit down?"

Ian nodded his head once and went back to reading his sci-fi comic. Amanda scanned her surroundings. This section of the library looked very unfamiliar to her. Amanda liked to stick with her fantasy and realistic fiction. However, Gwen did tell her once or twice that there were beanbags in the library, but Amanda never came to see.

"So... Are the rumors about your dad true?" Amanda questioned curiously, trying not to sound too intimidating.

Ian didn't respond, but Amanda could tell he heard what she said by the frown that eased into his face. After what seems like several minutes, or hours, Ian finally looked up. His eyes didn't carry that smile anymore and he looked as if he just puked. Amanda inspected Ian's face, trying to register this unpredicted expression.

Ian's eyes dropped and his head lowered. He suddenly developed a keen interest in his pants. "Yeah."

"I'm sorry. I didn't mean to make you feel bad or anything. I promise I won't tell." Amanda felt bad, really bad.

"Yeah, it's alright. It's just that everyone keeps asking me, and you're the first person I've ever told."

Amanda nodded warily. Not sure if she should be saying anything. She felt so bad for him. She couldn't even imagine how she would feel if her father had beaten her until she was fourteen like Ian. But Amanda wouldn't know, she would never know.

Amanda felt someone shadowing her from behind. The feeling one gets when they can just sense that someone was behind them. Slowly, Amanda turned around and came to face an older version of herself staring warmly back at her. Well almost. She had the same auburn hair, but had light caramel eyes. A smile froze on her face, plastic and perfect looking. Was she like some older clone-gone-wrong of me?

"Hi, I'm Cecilia Gold. Your mother," her face looked so loving and warm. Amanda couldn't believe it. It must have been a joke. She had no mother, and no one would ever be.

"Ha, ha. And I'm Dumbo the flying elephant. Happy April Fools much?" Amanda taunted.

Just then, a warm hand found its way to Amanda's shoulders. "I see you have met your daughter here." Ms. Tobol's voice directed to Cecilia.

"Wait...who?" Amanda raised an eyebrow. "Her? How come?"

Ms. Tobol nodded solemnly.

"Yeah right. For a second I let myself hope." Amanda could feel a twinge of guilt rise for not recognizing her own mother, but at the same time, how could she be? This was so stupid. I don't even have a mother. That little piece of information just ruined her day. It just wasn't possible. Amanda couldn't have had a mother. Even if this psychopath freak was her mother, why did she come back after so long?

"I'm sure this is just like those stupid happy-ending movies." Amanda gasped dramatically, "Oh look! My daughter!" She held out her hands, acting like she just found a long lost child.

"Amanda Madelyn Dawson, I am your mother who gave birth to you on January twenty-eighth fourteen years ago. Is that not true?"

"Well, yes," she replied hesitantly, "But you could have gotten that information from anyone!" Amanda desperately hoped to be right. She was always right.

Amanda saw Ms. Tobol shift her weight uncomfortably. "I'm going to leave you two to catch up with each other."

Amanda took a deep calm breath. I'm going to be fine. Breathe in, breath out.

"Let's start this over. Shall we?" Ms. Gold asked, smiling sweetly.

"Jeez. Who are you, my mother?" Amanda jeered defensively. She wasn't letting this women lift her spirits an inch.

"Hi. I'm Ms. Gold, and I was the one who gave birth to you. Fourteen years ago I left you on Crystal Orphanage's front door steps because I couldn't take care of you anymore. I am deeply sorry. It's just, I was young and irresponsible."

"Who hasn't heard of that before? What did you like pop out of One Tree Hill?" Amanda jeered.

"No actually. Let me finish." Ms. Gold started to get frustrated, "So a few weeks ago, my therapist thought I was ready to take you back. So I contacted the orphanage and they informed me that you are still here. So I flew over here from New York City to convince you to leave here with me. I want to take you back Amanda."

"Wow. Nice speech. I'd give you a three out of a thousand. So how long did you spend practicing in front of the mirror trying to get down that straight face? Maybe I'll even consider taking acting lessons from you."

Amanda saw Ms. Gold's face flush a bright pink. She watched as the women breathed deeply. "I am your mother. And I have the authority to take you back as soon as I can. And I will take you back. Don't fight it because I will be the best mother you've ever had. Better than here at least." Her voice filled with distaste.

"Wow. I'm hurt." Ian finally spoke since Amanda's mother's arrival.

"I wasn't talking to you sir," Ms. Gold snapped.

Amanda saw a flash of her fierce personality in that instant. Ian looked truly hurt, and he took his books and walked away. Slightly slouching with his head dropped.

"You can't make me. You won't." Amanda pouted and folded her arms at her chest. She didn't want anything to do with this stupid woman.

"Amanda, dear. Cecilia Gold is your mother. She even has your birth certificate," Ms. Tobol interrupted their soon-to-be-mad conversation. "She is taking you away after she signs some legal papers."

Shocked at the reality of all of this, Amanda felt outraged and sad.

"I can't leave the orphanage. It's my home."

"I'm taking you home soon, honey!" Amanda's mother used a fake motherly and warm voice. Amanda hated it when people acted nice around others.

"Does that mean I have to leave soon?" Amanda's voice broke as she tried to suppress her tears and rage. She didn't want to run off with this psychopath of a mother; let alone live with her. Amanda wanted nothing with this stupid mother of hers.

"Well, as I've told you, your mother needs to do some

straightening with the court. Then you will be free to go with her," Ms. Tobol soothed, as if she thought Amanda wanted all of this.

"But I don't have to go with her, right? I mean America is about human rights. Can't I be emancipated?" Amanda protested.

"How did you learn about emancipation? Must have been all the reading you've been doing in the library. Never mind that. You are going with your mother in about four months or so," Ms. Tobol directed to Amanda. Ms. Tobol beckoned for Amanda's mother, and Amanda watched the two of them depart.

Amanda was left speechless. She did not want to go with the mother who abandoned her. She did not like the only person she thought as her mother, Ms. Tobol. However, Amanda sensed that the only way to be safe was to stay at the orphanage. She needed to think of a way to stay here as long as she could.

Ian walked back over and broke her train of thought. "So what do you think all that straightening is about?"

"I dunno. But whatever it is, I hope it takes her a hundred years!" Amanda stuck out her tongue at where the two adults had just disappeared behind a bookshelf. "I hate that mother of mine."

*   *   *

Amanda scurried out of one of the bathrooms on the second floor when she heard the Welcome Bell ring. It was a splendid February afternoon, and sleet pelted gently on the orphanage's brick roof. Gwen came huffing up the creaky old staircase. Oval portraits of happy, used-to-be-orphans and their families hung along the side of the wall.

"You have a mother?" Gwen was astonished and hurt. Tears started to swell in her cute large eyes.

Ian was the only one who was aware of Amanda's mother. Amanda wouldn't have told him if he hadn't been there in the first place. The thing was, she didn't tell Gwen. She knew it was wrong and that when Gwen did find out, she would be disappointed. Now one look at her best friend Gwen's face, and all the guilt came rushing back again.

"I'm sorry Gwen. It's just so complicated. It's not like I wanted her as my mother. . ." Amanda's apology was cut short.

"You knew? You knew all along, and you never thought to tell me–your best friend in the world? You didn't think about me?" Gwen screamed with rage and anger. People around them all stopped to watch the commotion.

"Wait. Who told you?"

"I don't know!" Gwen's voice dripped with sarcasm. "Uh, maybe your dream come true mother!" Gwen stomped into our room and slammed the door behind her. Amanda could hear her sniffles and chocked sobs from behind the door. She knew it would take a long time before Gwen forgave her.

My mother? My mother told Gwen? But how?

"Amanda!" Ms. Katie called from somewhere below her on the first floor.

"I'm coming!" Amanda's cracked voice echoed off the walls.

Amanda shuffled down the staircase, careful not to step in the hole on the third to last step. A few months ago, Gwen accidentally slammed a baseball bat into the stairs while she swung it after a game of baseball. As Amanda neared the end of the staircase, her eyes started to adjust to the new vividly bright lights. There was a huge red banner hung from the damp ceiling. On it, had the words "Happy Birthday Amanda!" finger painted in neon paint. The Hearth was abnormally empty. Slowly, Amanda approached the opening. On the couch sat a woman in her late thirties. As Amanda got closer, she realized that it was her mother. Cecilia wore a wide grin on her face, but that was all she remembered seeing when the bright lights suddenly turned off.

"Surprise!" Happy fifteenth Birthday Amanda!" The lights turned back on and suddenly there were hands and faces everywhere. The air filled with the smell of cake and everyone tired to hug Amanda. Scanning through the sea of people, she caught sight of her mother lingering by the edge of the room, talking to Ms. Tobol. Slowly and cautiously, not to step on anyone, she winded her way in the general direction of her mother. As she neared her, Amanda made out a few words that her mother muttered to Ms. Tobol.

"You can't take her away today. You still have to talk to the court about your previous addiction issues. They aren't sure you are ready to take care of a child yet."

Intrigued by what Ms. Tobol said to her mother, she leaned in closer. But just as she neared the crowd and broke free, Ms. Tobol caught sight of her and stopped talking.

"Oh hi, Amanda. I was just discussing about your future here with your mother," Ms. Tobols's eyes twinkled.

"Oh really?" Amanda pretended to be naive. "And what were you guys talking about?" Her voice came out sweet and charming. But inside, she really wanted to hear about her mother's "addiction," not that she would ever admit she wanted to know more about her mother.

"Nothing much. Just about how excited I am about taking you home real shortly!" Amanda's mother beamed with an uplifting grin.

"Yea! Happy day! Not." Amanda still hadn't changed her mind after three months of Ian trying to make her optimistic. Ian would always reason with her, saying: "It's a change for once; don't you want to get away from the place you've been forever?"

"Actually, I'm taking you from this place today!" Ms. Gold announced as if she hadn't heard a word Amanda just voiced.

"We aren't sure yet." Ms. Tobol's voice came stern and steady.

"Oh no. Too bad. Another day wasted when I could be spending time with my mother." Amanda smiled angelically. Her voice full of sardonicism.

"I just have sort out some legal issues. Nothing much." Ms. Gold shifted her weight, her head slightly tilted down. "You can go find your friends. Yeah, that would be nice. Show me around?"

"Whatever. You don't belong here. I don't want you in my life." Amanda stomped towards the middle of the room where one of the tables from the dining hall was placed. There, Gwen was lighting Amanda's chocolate birthday cake. Gwen struggled to recover from her breakdown, but Amanda cheerfully realized that she was halfway forgiven.

Once Amanda neared, Gwen set down the matches and walked over hesitantly.

"Happy birthday Amanda Panda," Gwen hugged her and whispered softly into her ear. "You are not forgiven yet, but you can explain later."

Amanda knew that Gwen was always like that. She would not forget this incident soon. Her best friend was the type of person who forgave but never forgets. She let go of her best friend in the world. Amanda could not believe herself for not telling Gwen about her own mother.

Amanda saw Gwen dig through the panda bag that she always carried around. She gave her that panda bag for her tenth birthday. Gwen took out a parcel wrapped in a blue piece of wrapping paper.

"Aw. Thanks Gwen! You didn't have to."

"Don't worry about it! It's a gift from the orphanage."

Everyone got at least one present from the orphanage every birthday. The present was bought with Ms. Tobol's own money. This was so every orphan, no matter how abandoned, will always get a birthday gift.

"Open it!" Gwen squealed with excitement.

Amanda delicately peeled the tape off, careful not to rip the paper while doing so. She had this idiosyncrasy of not ripping wrapping paper so she could save every part of the love given to her by the orphanage.

"You are such a perfectionist!" Gwen's voice carried a joking hint of annoyance.

As she removed the last piece of tape, the package unfolded and a sky-blue knit scarf, Amanda's favorite color, fell into her lap.

"Thank you, thank you, thank you!" Amanda hugged Gwen hard, crushing all sixty-two pounds of her.

"How did you know I wanted a scarf?" Amanda asked jokingly.

"Well, I don't know! Maybe because you've been talking about how much you wanted a scarf since last Christmas? Maybe huh?" Gwen smiled proudly, as if she just beat the Guinness world record for mind reading.

"You know me too well. You know me way too well."

Amanda watched Gwen as she left to find some more paper napkins so that she could serve the cake. Amanda felt someone behind her chair and she looked up, trying to see who it was. She came face to face with Ian.

"Oh my gosh! Don't scare me like that!" Amanda gasped.

Ian grinned down at her. "Sorry, I didn't mean to scare you," he apologized, looking truly sorry.

"It's okay. Just don't tower over me like that anymore."

"Okay. But I didn't mean to scare you."

"Oh, I have a question for you. I over heard Ms. Tobol talking about how my mom can't take me because of some addiction she had. Not that I really want her to take me." Ever since that meeting with her mom in the library, she and Ian constantly tried to figure out what the legal "issues." Ian had mostly been trying to convince her that it's not that bad to have a permanent parent. However, his attempts were not failed ones. Amanda began to soften up on that matter.

"Really? Did you ask your mom about it?" Ian looked instantly interested and pulled up a chair beside her. That's what Amanda loved about him. He always listened. Sometimes it seemed like he listened to her more that Gwen could.

"Actually no. But I know my mom is hiding something from me." Amanda knew there was something fishy about this situation, but she just couldn't figure out what.

"Well I think you should go ask," Ian's voice sounded firm and hopeful. "I honestly think it could help your relationship with her."

Amanda spotted Gwen coming back with a stack of blue napkins in her hands. She hummed to a new song they had learned from listening to the radio station FM103.5.

"Hey!" Gwen took Amanda's hands and leaned towards her. She wore the zebra-print sweatshirt that a charity clothing drive gave her.

"Hey! What are you? The leaning tower of zebras?" Amanda knew her humor was terrible, but she still tried to make Gwen laugh to make up to her.

"No!" Gwen frowned sarcastically, her bottom lip sticking out, pouting. Amanda knew she struggled against the urge to smile.

"Ha . . . Ha! That's funny!" Ian chuckled lightly.

Amanda blushed. Determined to find out about the addiction, she stood up slowly. Amanda stretched her legs and felt her knees and back crack. Ouch. Slowly, she stumbled over to where her mother stood. Amanda was determined to get it out of her mother. She needed to know. She wanted to know if she had a reason to hate her mother. As she neared her, Ian came up from behind.

"I want to be there for you." Ian smiled and stood a few meters away from my mother, acting preoccupied with his shoes.

Amanda nodded. She took a deep breath and walked on.

"Hey, Mom!" Amanda smiled cheerfully.

"Hey, Amanda. How are you enjoying being fifteen?"

"Ishy ishy. . . It's been good. I feel so old though." Amanda's eyes sparkled in the bright light, playing along. A fake smile plastered onto her face. "I have a question though . . ." Her voice turned serious.

"Yeah? Ask away." Her mom looked so cheerful. However, Amanda knew her mother tried to put up an act.

"What are all the legal papers you have to straighten up? Is there something wrong?" Amanda's voice filled with feigned concern.

"Well, no of course," her mother bit her lip, "nothing to worry about."

"Really? Because I overheard you and Ms. Tobol talking about an addiction."

Surprised and shocked, Amanda's mother made a quick recovery. "Oh, it's nothing. Truthfully speaking here, I used to drink a lot. Before I became pregnant, I would drink tons everyday. Your father wasn't he nicest fellow in the world and I often felt sad and depressed. Well I couldn't forgive myself for being so horrible of a mother, if I can even call myself one anymore. And I just, well I looked for a way to relieve that anger and guilt. I found beer. Mind you that was a long time ago. I've been perfectly sober now for almost two years."

Amanda bit her lips. If her mother really was an alcohol addict, would she continue her bad habits? Now she was a bit afraid of her mother, besides that fact that she was an insane freak. Amanda shifted her gaze to the damp, moldy ceiling. The paint now peeled from all of the spring raining. Music from the radio drifted toward Amanda. She tried to focus on not tearing up in front of everyone. She had to be tough.

"Why didn't you tell me that earlier? Why did you lie

to me and say it was legal papers you had to sign? Well, I guess it's just another thing to add to my 'Reasons Why I Hate My Mother' list!" Amanda's temper rose. She hated being lied to. It's one of those things she cannot stand in a person.

"Well honey, it's because I love you. I wanted what was best for you." Amanda's mother pulled on a caring face.

"If you really love me, you would have told me from the start. How could you keep that away from me? Oh right, sorry. I forgot. You don't even know me!"

By now everyone around had stopped what he or she was doing. The music stopped abruptly. Everyone stared at Amanda. The lights suddenly brightened too much for Amanda's liking. She felt faint after all of that yelling. Amanda shook her head, trying to keep her mind clear. She needed to lie down and get some rest.

Turning back, she took one last glance at her lying mother, turned around, and stumbled out of the room. Racing past all the people, she took the stairs two at a time until she reached the top. Tears streamed down her face. Huffing and puffing, she came to a stop. Ian stood there at the top, waiting for her. She tried to walk past him, hoping more than ever that she would turn invisible. Amanda pushed past Ian, determined to get to her dorm room before he caught up with her. To Amanda's dismay, Ian soon caught up with her and was by her side, stride for stride.

"What's wrong?"

Amanda didn't utter a single sound. She wasn't going to confide anyone in this. She was the one who was always there for others. She was made to help others, not to receive help.

Briskly, Amanda strode towards the door, trying to get to it faster. Just as Amanda was about to turn the brass knob on her white washed wooden door, Ian's foot blocked her.

"Listen to me. You need me to help you. Just let me listen. What happened?" Ian's voice rung in her ears.

"I ... Don't ... Need ... Anyone," sniffled Amanda.

Amanda saw Ian's foot step and side and she pushed the door open. The moment she stepped in, she was greeted by her familiar surroundings. The window was stained with dirt from the rain last night. Without thinking, she sprinted over to her bed and climbed up the ladder, onto her bed. Amanda let her body fall back onto her bed, her head landed precisely thin pillow. Sounds of footsteps slowly approached her and she knew it was Ian. As much as she wanted to make him go, her words were stuck in her throat.

"I know how you feel. My mother didn't win the 'Best Mother of the Year Award' either. Well, My mother died when I was seven..." Ian voice trailed off.

Amanda closed her eyes. She tried to think of all those dreams she had of her mother. How her mother was smiley and happy and nice. Never in the world did she imagine her as an alcoholic or an insane freak.

"It's gonna be fine," Ian cooed.

"I don't want to live with my mom. No matter what, I will get emancipated and come back." Amanda's voice trembled.

"Don't worry about it. Everything is just alright."

"You promise?" Amanda whimpered hopefully.

"I promise." Ian smiled genuinely.

Amanda knew that Ian was being serious. She just needed to learn to live with her decisions. She had to be tough. With Ian and Gwen by her side, she knew she could go through anything. For now, she would have to live with what she had. If there was one thing she learned while being fifteen so far, it's that sometimes having little was more than having lots.

Kangaroo Justice

By Teddy Huang

"Crack, Crack," the twigs under Greg Koala's feet snapped under his weight. Koala kicked himself mentally for being so loud. The animal he was stalking, a kangaroo, had very good hearing, but it seemed oblivious to his movements right now.

"Maybe I should go around and jump it from behind," thought Greg. Greg had developed an incurable disease that comes and goes. He had a sudden need for blood whenever the disease struck. This was one of those times, and the kangaroo grazing on the fringes of a meadow seemed like easy pickings. This was because it was close to the woods and, therefore, easy to drag prey into the safety and confinement of the woods.

Greg would have surely been caught for murder by now had it not been for the fact that he was the judge for the animal council's court. Greg had diverted attention from the recent murders in the region by stating that the predatory barbaric animals that lived beyond the border that separated the safe from dangerous areas were sneaking in and killing animals. So far his plan had worked; he had even gotten the money that the council gave to repair the fence.

Whoosh. Greg jumped from the tree and landed on the kangaroo's back. He promptly sunk his filed claws into her neck, searching for the line of life that, once severed, would gush out the water of life. He clawed three times, and on the fourth he found it. He lifted his crimson claw and licked it greedily. He would feast tonight on raw kangaroo.

*   *   *

"What? No, no way. You have to be kidding me, my mom just went out to pick some vegetable for dinner today; she didn't even go beyond the safe zone," a very bewildered kangaroo Joey exclaimed. She had just received news that her mother's body had been found in the woods, with several severe lacerations to her throat area.

"I am sorry to say that this is true. After looking through the personal items in her pouch, we determined her to be one Margaret Willow. Who is your mom," replied old detective Tortoise. " I offer my condolences to you. I promise that the Council will take this murder very seriously since this has been the third murder this year."

"Do I also have your word that you will punish the criminal to the full extent of the law," asked Irene Willow, the Joey.

"Yes you do, and if there is one thing that old age brings, it is the reluctance to get young people mad at me," answered Tortoise.

"Then please leave my house. I want some time alone," commanded Irene.

Tortoise offered, "Do you want me to send anyone over to help you around the house?"

"NO, I can take care of my house. NOW GET OUT," yelled Irene.

"Alright, alright. I'm going, jeez..." mumbled Tortoise as he left the thatched hut.

* * *

"*Boom, boom, boom,*" went the judge's gavel. Greg looked pristine tonight; his body showed no trace of blood. A long and silky dress robe that he only used for such occasions

"Today's meeting is to determine the cause of Margaret Willow's murder. If we do find and identify the culprit, we will also determine the appropriate punishment," said Greg in his most authoritative voice. "We will start by asking anyone if they witnessed the murder firsthand."

At this point, a mole rat nervously raised his hand. "I did not see the murder as it happened; however, I did hear the screams. I got a glimpse of the murderer as he dragged the body into the forest; however, the murderer had a small stature. It was not a predatory animal this time," said the mole rat, named Stella. "Many of you probably wonder how I can see. Well, I will tell you this, I have recently invented an eye helper. To make this-"

"Enough, we do not need to hear the rest. Are there any questions for this witness at this time," asked a slightly shaken Greg.

Irene raised her hand. Irene was clothed in typical jungle mourning attire. She wore white frock with a white, circular hat. Irene questioned, "About how tall was the figure you saw?"

To this Stella said, "It was about three feet tallish, maybe Jude Greg's height. It actually looked very similar."

Detective Tort then butted in, "This is good, since there are not that many Koalas that live around this area, identifying the killer will be relatively easy."

"Yes, yes, a short killer was identified, but it does not mean it's a koala. Who would actually believe what a mole rat saw, anyways," concluded Greg the Judge.

"Are there anymore questions? No? Then this meeting is adjourned. The next meeting's time will be posted on the board in the Tree Square."

Irene couldn't help speculate that Judge Greg could be the killer. He just seemed so uncomfortable when Stella said that the killer looked like Judge Greg. Oh well, it was just speculation. "Better get some sleep, I am willing to bet that tomorrow will be a long, long day," thought Irene.

"Hey, I'm going to a party. Would you like to come," asked Irene's friend, Calvin. Calvin was a kangaroo like Irene. He and Irene had been friends ever since she could remember.

"Eh, you have obviously not heard of recent events..." responded Irene.

"Actually, I have. I wanted to invite you so you could regain a sense of normalcy," explained Calvin.

"You are so insensitive, you know. Why would I want celebrate after my mother died?" questioned Irene. And with that she slammed the door in Calvin's face.

"People these days..." Irene thought just as Calvin rang the doorbell again.

"WHAT DO YOU WANT," she yelled.

"Sorry, sorry. I just ran into the Judge. He's starting the session an hour early. So...yeah. He told me to tell you," answered Calvin.

"Oh, OK thanks," muttered Irene.

*　*　*

"This meeting to determine the killer of a kangaroo is now in session," yelled Greg. "Anyone with any new information may raise his or her hand now." No hands went up. "Well in that case we are wasting our time. This meeting is adjourned until further news has been dug up," Greg hastily finished. The koala did not want to risk a chance that some animal might have seen him killing the kangaroo.

During his walk back to his eucalyptus tree, Greg could not help feeling that someone was watching, following him. He took the stairs up to his apartment two at a time and slammed the door close.

"Did you catch anyone following me," he asked?

"No, do not worry. Remember you are a ninja koala," replied his master, a crow by the name of Ivan Murry Bad, or I.M. Bad. I.M. Bad was large for his species, a two-foot-high crow with pitch-black feathers. He had taught Koala the art of being a ninja.

"Besides, she's a young girl, about as naïve as kids get, and she probably believes that there are wild animals out in the woods that hunt so close to our territory," continued I.M Bad.

"I know, but there is something about that daughter of hers... She will kill to get revenge," said Greg.

"But she does not have the ninja skills that you have, does she," crowed I.M Bad. "There is only one thing to fear. If she finds Iain Terry Bad, then things get trickier."

"Iain Terry Bad... you mean THE Iain T. Bad? Your brother," asked Greg.

"The one and only," replied his master.

* * *

Irene ran home sobbing, "I knew it was him," thought Irene. It was so obvious now. The way Greg had been acting during both hearings, how he had rushed the last hearing and how he so quickly changed the subject when the mole rat said the killer looked like him.

"I must find somebody to train me," Irene wondered out loud.

"I have been following you for sometime now kid, and I'd like to train you," said a bird flying above her. "I am Iain T. Bad, brother of I.M. Bad, the person who trained Koala in the ways of a ninja."

"Yea, OK, got it. You can go now strange talking bird," answered Irene.

"Listen to me girl. I know what you want. Which is exactly what I want, which is to kill Greg Koala. Actually, I don't want to kill him, but the process of killing him will embarrass my brother, which is what I want," explained the pure white bird.

"You have a point," said Irene, "how about a trial lesson?"

"You got it. When," asked Iain.

"Now. I'm going to try to beat you up, if you can stop me then we'll see," said Irene.

The fight didn't last one minute. Before Irene knew what hit her, she was on the ground with a bloody nose.

"Good enough for you," asked the bird.

"Yep, when are you free," asked Irene.

"Well, I really don't do anything but sit around my house all day and smoke and drink plum beer, so anytime is fine with me," answered Iain.

"OK, I'll get back to you on that. Where can I find you," asked Irene.

"I'll find you, just call out my name," said the white bird.

"OK, Mr. Stalker, geez..." Irene mumbled as Iain T. Bad flew away.

* * *

"I do not want to rush into this ninja business because I might get killed, and if I'm killed I don't do anyone any good. Maybe if I can make Greg look so shaken up that the council suspects him, I won't have to go ninja and possibly kill someone," Irene thought on her way home. "I know, I'll ask Calvin to help me. I'll tell him to say that he went to the judge's home to sell some wild strawberries to him, but before he could knock on the door, he heard the judge talking to someone."

* * *

"Hey, Calvin there you are. I've been looking for you everywhere," yelled Irene.

"Oh, hey. You changed your mind about the party or something," asked Calvin.

"Only if you help me out with a problem," answered Irene.

"Eh, OK. I'll see what I can do," Calvin agreed.

"Right, I can't tell you this in public. Lets go back to my place," concluded Irene.

* * *

"I have recently become aware that Greg is my mother's killer, and I need you to testify in court for me," explained Irene, "I need you to say that you were going to Judge Greg's house to sell him the wild strawberries that everyone knows he likes. Before you could knock on his door, you heard him talking to someone. You overheard him talking about the murder case and me. You then heard the 'someone' say, 'Besides, she's a young girl, about as naïve as kids get, she probably believes that there are wild animals out in the woods that hunt so close to our territory,' those exact words. Can you do that for me," implored Irene.

"Of course I can do that, but you have to come to the party, OK?"

"Fine, but postpone it. I want to get the sad stuff over first, then I celebrate," answered Irene.

* * *

"*Bang, Bang, Bang,*" went the judge's gavel. "Right, lets get this over with. Calvin Mullark, please speak now," said a rather bored Judge Greg.

"Yesterday, about ten minutes after the previous meeting, I decided to go to Judge Greg's house to sell him some strawberries. However, before I knocked on the door, I heard him and another person talking. Judge Greg repeatedly confessed his anxiety to this person, while the stranger calmed him saying that he was a 'ninja'. The stranger then went on to say this and I quote, 'Besides, she's a young girl, about as naïve as kids get, she probably believes that there are wild animals out in the woods that hunt so close to our territory',″ said Calvin, "That is all I have to say."

The court was so silent that you could hear a pin drop.

"Are you accusing me of murder," asked Judge Greg menacingly, "Do you have any evidence to back this accusation? A witness?"

"N-n-no," stuttered Calvin.

"Then this piece of evidence can now be judged null and void," concluded the Judge. "If there are no other pieces of information, then this court will be adjourned."

"Well, now I've hit a dead end. Anybody accused of murdering someone would respond in the same way," Irene thought as she left the courtroom. "I guess there is no other alternative than to learn the ways of the ninja."

There are wild animals out in the woods that hunt so close to our territory,' those exact words. Can you do that for me," implored Irene.

"Of course I can do that, but you have to come to the party, OK?"

"Fine, but postpone it. I want to get the sad stuff over first, then I celebrate," answered Irene.

"Now how am I going to find that bird," wondered Irene.

"Are you ready to learn now?" asked a mysterious voice behind her.

"Oh, jeez. You scared me," said Irene as she exhaled. "Yes I am ready. I see no other alternative to solve this problem, the only way is to cause pain."

"Good, then we begin now," concluded Iain T. Bad. "The first thing you need to learn is how to throw a decent punch-"

"Were wasting time..." Irene cut in.

"No were not. I doubt you know how to punch correctly," replied Iain.

"Fine, I'll punch you, and then you judge," retorted Irene.

"Go ahead," he responded. And with that, Irene started to pummel his body; the flurry of blows did not produce a squeak out of the bird.

"See, I can punch," panted Irene.

"No, naïve young one, you cannot," said Iain. "If you had punched correctly, I would be on the ground writhing in pain."

"Fine, but I'm a girl, so we can kick too," Irene retorted.

"Go ahead, do your best." Irene then proceeded to try to kick Iain T. Bad in the groin area, however, each time she got close, the bird would just hop up in the air and dodge the attack.

"Hey, no fair, you are a bird, birds can fly. Greg is a Koala, Koalas can't fly," yelled Irene.

"Yes, but he does not need to fly to be able to dodge your attacks. He has something called anticipation. He can guess what you are going to do and when you are going to do it," said a very calm Iain. "I think you are too frustrated to learn right now, how about the same time tomorrow?"

To that Irene said, "No I need a break, I haven't slept well for a few days. How about the day after tomorrow?"

"Yea, that would be fine with me," said Iain.

The two departed and went their separate ways, Irene went back to her tree apartment and Iain flew back to wherever he lived, no one knew. Irene thought long and hard on her bouncy way back to her house. She needed something to calm herself down. "I know," she euphorically thought. "I'll bake some cookies. It always helped when mom was still alive." So, Irene went back to her apartment and baked, and baked, and baked. The anger was not driven away, but she was so tired that she eventually fell into a deep sleep.

* * *

Irene ate cookies for breakfast the next morning, needless to say. She then ventured outside for a walk in the sun.

"Hello, hun," said Iain T. Bad.

"I though I told you that I needed some time to myself," yelled Irene.

"Are you still dreaming sweetie, you've been asleep for more than a day. Don't ask me how I know, I'm just that good at stalking," answered Iain.

"OK, first of all, stop calling me all these names. I barley know you, and you already sound like a close relative. Second, can you quit being such a stalker? I get no privacy now a day," yelled Irene.

"Jeez, girl calm down. You should go to yoga class and learn some techniques to calm yourself down when you are angry," said Iain. "And also, you will start to show me respect. I know you case is different than most, but the fundamental respect still needs to be there. You will now call me Sensei."

"Fine, but you have to stop stalking me. Sensei," said Irene.

"Deal," concluded Iain. "Alright, lets get started. The power from a punch is not from the fist itself. The fist is only the part of your body that transfers the energy from you to the person. You get the energy from the ground. I need to know something first, are you left or right handed?"

"I am right handed," she replied.

"Okay, then the first step is to step forward with your left foot while bringing back your arm. Then you twist your back while bringing your arm forward. The last part is to snap your arm straight. Like this," said Iain, while demonstrating. "Here try hitting this piece of bark," he said as he ripped a piece of bark off a neighboring tree.

"*Thunk*, OW," yelled Irene. And the training started.

Many days of training had passed. Sensei Iain had put Irene on a strict muscle building diet consisting of raw quail eggs, carrots, and frog meat. Each day started at 5:00 A.M. Irene would first go for a three mile run which usually took her twenty-five minutes. Then she lifted large tree branches. After that she practiced her tai chi and yoga. Only then did Iain show up to teach her martial arts form.

Irene's friends played a big role in helping her get into shape. Liz the friendly platypus got to her tree bright and early to wake her up and make her breakfast shake. Calvin was there to keep her company while she ran; he also spotted her when she lifted branches. Over the course of a few months, Irene transformed from a spontaneous teenager into a cool-minded young adult.

"I think you are ready know," stated Iain T. Bad one day after a vigorous round of sparring. "You must remember one thing though; Koala will be fighting for his life, he will not hesitate to use a low blow, you must also pick the right place to kill him."

"Yes, I will keep that in mind. Thank you for your training Sensei," said Irene.

"My advice would be to ambush him while he is on his way from his house to the council building where he works. No one ever goes that way because he is the only person to own a house there," said Iain.

"Yes, Sensei," said Irene.

*   *   *

Irene crouched on a tree branch observing Greg as he walked to work in the morning. For the past month, Greg had only diverted from this route on the weekends and when he needed to take a dump on the side of the road.

From what Irene discerned, Greg never left did anything differently.

Irene sat alone at her house later that day wondering how she would kill Greg. "Should I do it clean, or make him suffer?" she thought. "Well, if you consider the Golden Rule, Do unto others as you would have them do unto you, then I would have to slit his throat. Yea, that sounds good."

Irene then proceeded to write a letter to her friends in case the plan failed and she was killed in the process of assassinating Greg Koala. It went like this:

"Dear Friends,

I, Irene Willow, am about to embark on a risky expedition. Earlier this year, I came to the realization that our council judge, Greg Koala, killed my mother. Hoping to resolve this matter peacefully, I employed our friend Calvin to testify that he overheard Greg openly admitting that he killed Margaret to some mysterious person. Needless to say, this plan failed and I took matters into my own hands. I learned various forms of martial arts from a very talented teacher. I have observed the murderer go to work everyday since the start of the month. I now believe that I am ready to attack. The time to wait has passed. If I do not return alive, know that I have had a great life with all of you guys

Your Friend,
Irene Willow"

*   *   *

It was the day of the attack. Irene woke up early in the morning to prepare herself. She drank her special shake as usual and ran three miles. She then went to her pre-planned spot and waited.

*   *   *

The morning started out same old same old for

Greg Koala. He got up, brushed his teeth, ate a bowl of Eucalyptus leaves, dressed up, and headed for work. He had a feeling about today, but he couldn't classify it, it was both good and bad.

Greg started out the door. He took his usual route to work, a walk down his private road, a stop at Old Man Frazier's bakery, and finally the council building. Halfway down his private road, his stomach started hurting. "Ooo, I forgot to take my morning dump," he remembered. He abruptly stopped and turned to go to the side of the road.

That's when he heard a thump behind him

*   *   *

"Oof," Irene landed most ungracefully where Greg Koala had been just moments before. "Could he have possible known that she was going to ambush him here and today?" she wondered.

"What the-," Greg exclaimed as he turned around.

"Go no further murderer," said Irene as she staggered to her feet.

"Oh, I see where this is going," said Greg. "I knew someone had overheard my me and my mentor's conversation, but that doesn't matter. I highly doubt that you can kill me judging by your less-than-graceful fall from that tree."

"I've learned," said Irene with a smile.

"Lets see it then," answered Greg who followed this remark with a quick jab at Irene's face. Irene easily sidestepped this blow and responded with a right hook. This caught Koala by surprise. "Mmm, good stuff," he said while rubbing an increasingly big bruise. Koala then threw a jabbed at Irene's face that was followed by a quick kick to her leg. This landed and Irene squealed in pain.

"Enough with the small stuff, I'm going to kill you," yelled Irene. The anger consumed her and she lashed out with all her might. Greg remained calm through the storm of blows, easily deflecting them with a flick of his wrist. "You are good, but I've seen better," said Koala, faking a yawn. Koala then dropped the defense and went on the offense. Both animals fought ferociously, their bodies intertwined as if they were part of a violent ballet, at one moment they were close together, then the next they were repelled away from each other.

Then Greg landed a blow at the base of Irene's skull that sent her reeling backwards. He advanced menacingly, filing one of his claws against a tree. Irene was still dazed by the time that Greg reached one of his talons under her throat.

"I am going to kill you just like I killed you mother. One clean swipe of this claw and you will die within ten minutes," Greg menacingly said.

"Not, if I do this," said Irene. She kicked Greg in his groin area, sending him reeling. He tripped over a log and fell flat on his back,

"No...fair," he gasped. It was now Irene's turn to advance menacingly. She ruthlessly broke one of Greg's arms and positioned his claw on top of his jugular.

Irene paused, "Should I really kill this disgusting animal?" She then concluded out loud, "You don't deserve the quickness of death, therefore, I will torture you on Earth." Irene then proceeded to break every single major bone in Koala's body. She then half carried half dragged an unconscious Koala to the council building and put a sign across his body that read, "Please take me to jail. I confess guilty on all charges for killing Margaret Willow, mother of Irene Willow."

* * *

Epilogue

It had been a week since Irene had completely incapacitated Greg Koala. The following day, he had shown up in court with a full body cast on. Irene had talked to him the day before the trail and threatened death if he did not truthfully answer the questions. Greg Koala was sentence for 125 years in prison without chance of early parole.

"Hey Irene," yelled Calvin after the trial. "Were having a party tonight. I'm counting on you to come."

"Yea, I guess I owe you guys after all you did for me. Is there anything you want me to bring?" replied Irene

"How about some of those cookies that you baked a while back. I could help sneak a few while I prepared your breakfast. They were so good," answered Calvin

"Okay then, I'll bring some baked cookies, but you have to have some drinks, the cookies start to make your mouth itch after a while," said Irene.

"Right, see you later Irene," finished Calvin.

"Bye."

As Irene walked away, she couldn't help marveling at how great life was and how great her friends were.

What's the Human?

By Janie Jang

"Class! Your assignment is to finish reading 'Romeo and Juliet' by the next class. Please don't forget; excuses are strictly not acceptable. You're now dismissed."

When our English teacher, Ms. Brown, finished her last sentence, I ran to my locker, collected my books, and packed them up. When Stephanie arrived at her locker and unlocked it, I was all ready to leave.

"Elizabeth," called Stephanie, "wait for me!"

"I'm waiting for you, madam. Come on, we're going to be late." I shouted at her.

"Gee, stop bugging me! By the way, did you tell your parents that I'm gonna stay with you today?" she asked me loud enough to be heard in the crowded corridor.

"Yes, so please hurry up. Come on."

"I'm nearly done. Give me a minute."

*   *   *

"Hey! Don't you dare upload them!" I cried. Stephanie

had shown me the photos that she had taken during her birthday party. Honestly, those photos were so embarrassing; I closed my eyes in almost every photo! I seriously considered running away with her green laptop. Stephanie stared at my blushing face and began laughing hysterically.

"Elizabeth, look into the mirror." she giggled. "I can hardly breathe!"

"Steph, it's not that funny!" I shouted. But when I ran to the bathroom and saw myself, I couldn't stop laughing. Just as Stephanie said, my face was bright red as if I were facing my crush.

"Oh, my gosh." Suddenly, my mom came into my room. "You Freshmen!"

"Hi, Mrs. Owen," Stephanie said, smiling. I ran back to my room and hugged my mom.

"Welcome, Stephanie," answered my mom. "I don't know what happened a minute ago that made you two laugh so loudly, but please remember that we're not the only family who live in this town. Okay?"

"I'm sorry, Mrs. Owen. I'll control my volume."

"Thank you, sweetheart. Would you like something to eat?"

"No, thank you." I had a strong feeling that Stephanie and mom would talk forever, so I politely asked my mom to leave us. Fortunately, my mom accepted my "request" and went back to her room.

"Anyway," Stephanie shouted when my mom left my room, "let's go back to our photos. It's going to be hilarious! Everyone will love them! You look so cute in those photos! Come on, Liz!"

"Shush. My mom will yell at me if we're still loud, not at you." I warned her.

"Fine. I'll be quiet, but those photos are so hilarious and cute, you know!"

I stared at Stephanie's laptop screen. I could see myself with "Gucci" bag and sunglasses. We didn't buy them, but the clerks in the department store where we had gone kindly allowed us to hold them and take the photos. I strongly suspected that those clerks allowed us to take the photos only because the President of the United States was Stephanie's dad.

"Um, Steph?" I asked. "How's your dad?"

"Busy, as usual," she replied. "Ronald called me last night and told me that Dad is focusing on Israel and Palestine's complicated conflict. To be honest, I'm not interested in politics."

"But you should know that you're special. Everyone would like to be the President's daughter and you are!"

"No, everyone wants to have the privilege of the President's daughter, not a child of the President. And everyone is special and equal."

"Well, everyone is special, but you have two, smart, big brothers or a dad who can help you with your homework. Besides, you have many privileges because your dad is the President of the United States! You could have gone to some exclusive boarding school! You could have lived in the White House with its exclusive qualities! You have your own driver, chef, and bodyguards who are probably waiting for you outside! You should admit that you're special, Steph!

"That's true, but they don't know how stressful it is to live as a President's daughter."

"Who are they?"

"Crowds, including you. By the way, why the heck are we talking about my dad and how lucky I am?"

I couldn't say anything, not because I don't know the answer to her last question, but also I felt myself belittled whenever I talk to Stephanie. Although our GPAs were similar and we went to the same school with the same teachers, I felt as if I were a child who didn't understand anything about society. Stephanie knew a lot about the world. She knew a lot about current events. And she knew a lot about people.

I stared out of the window. It was dark now, dark in where I lived, Wildwood Ave, Ocean City County, New Jersey.

I stopped daydreaming and came back to the present, when she loudly asked for my final permission to upload the photos. I simply nodded. Soon, she updated the gossips and rumors that were about the freshmen in our school. Of course, when she abruptly announced that she planned to go to Washington D.C. to visit her parents, I gasped! She chuckled for a while and said her mom begged her to visit them because of her birthday.

"So when are you leaving?" I asked.

"Next Monday. It's like five days after my birthday, but I will be back on Thursday night, so I will go to school on Friday. I will tell you what happened in Washington D.C. when I'm back."

Our chatter didn't stop until it was time for Stephanie to go back to her house. Stephanie promised to text me later. We shared a goodbye hug, and Stephanie left.

* * *

Friday finally approached. It was a day that Stephanie promised me to come back. When I saw her, I couldn't help myself but gasp. Stephanie didn't look well. Her pale face had vivid dark rings underneath her eyes, and she didn't participate in our literature class discussion. Something must have happened to her while she was with her parents.

"Did you read a newspaper this morning?" That was the first thing she said to me.

I replied that I didn't. She groaned and then sighed.

Stephanie wasn't the only one who had changed. It seemed like everybody in the entire school had changed. Whenever Stephanie and I walked through the corridor to go to the class, students suddenly stopped their chatter and stared at us. That was unusual. Everyone knew that

Stephanie was the President's daughter. Stephanie hated it when people treated her special because of her dad. But all the sudden, every eye was upon us; Stephanie, more specifically. Silence filled the corridor whenever Stephanie and I walked.

"Hey, what's happening to this school?" I complained loudly. But Stephanie kept up her abnormal silence. Then, I found today's newspaper on the floor. One of the seniors must have dropped it while heading to his class. When I read the headline, I couldn't believe my eyes. Stephanie's picture covered the whole front page. It said,

"A Secret Revealed-our President has the President of Gucci"

"What's this?" I yelled. "Why the heck you are covering the front page?"

"I have something to tell you," Stephanie suddenly whispered. "Can I go to your house after school?"

"Sure."

* * *

"So, tell me Steph," I demanded. "What's wrong? What's happening?"

When the bell rang, I packed my stuff as fast as I could, grabbed Stephanie's hand, and went to my house. Even though I asked her several times, she never gave me a hint at school. Stephanie complained on the way home, saying that she forgot her geometry book. But to me, that didn't really matter. I wanted to know why her picture covered the front page of the newspaper and what happened when she was with her parents. We ran to my room and when we arrived, I interrogated her as if I were a police officer from the CIA.

Stephanie sighed and said, "Please don't be shocked."

"I won't. So just tell me."

Stephanie sighed for a second.

"Politicians," she finally spoke.

"I'm sorry?"

"A group of politicians who were in the Republican Party saw the photos we uploaded."

"So? What about them?"

"They used, or are using the photos to criticize my dad."

It seemed like the light bulb in my brain turned its light on. Stephanie's dad was in the Democratic party. He was against the politicians who were in the Republican Party. Of course, the politicians would happily "attack" poor Stephanie's dad.

"No way!" I shouted. "It's just the photos that any high schoolers would take! Even some of middle schoolers take those kinds of photos and upload them on the Internet! I think they did the same thing when they were our age! They must be mad! Are they crazy or something?"

"Calm down, Liz," she said. "And I don't think the media will give up easily. It's a good chance for them to "attack" my dad. That's not even funny. I have absolutely no idea what am I going to do."

She sighed for the third time in my room.

"What are you going to do then?"

"Hand me the newspaper." she suddenly asked. "I want to see whether the media just made the news up or not."

I faithfully handed the newspaper to her. She read through it, sighed, and gave it back.

"I knew it," she cried. "They're writing an interesting story, Elizabeth."

I read through. The article said that Stephanie had a mental problem, and she took the photos and uploaded them to be the center of attention instead of her dad. It mentioned that Stephanie indulges herself in extravagant tastes and habits. The journalist ended the article by saying that the President should take care of his children as well as taking care of the United States.

"They're mad. This can't be done in this world," I told her. "What are you doing to do?"

"I told you. I don't know."

Stephanie began to cry; it was first time that I saw her crying. I held her hands and hugged her. "It's going to be fine, Steph," I tried to calm her down.

* * *

There were many significant changes since the article about Stephanie and photos has been printed. I believed that the media made up the story, as I totally trusted Stephanie. Besides, Stephanie's dad would have an official announcement about this matter. However, the entire school seemed to believe what it said on the newspaper. Just like what happened in the corridor on last Friday, there was an unpleasant silence whenever Stephanie and I passed the other students on the way to class.

Stephanie and I usually ate lunch with Sandra, Jessica, Patricia and Michelle. When I joined the lunch table, the girls welcomed me and didn't stop chatting, but when Stephanie joined the lunch table with us, they immediately stopped laughing and talking and stared at her. Even though it was very rude, they didn't stop staring at her. Eventually, on Thursday, Stephanie and I sat alone at a small table.

"I'm so sorry, Elizabeth," she apologized. "I know it's all my fault. I should have listened to you."

"It's okay. I don't trust the media anyway."

The publicity changed Stephanie and my school life, although it didn't affect our friendship at all. Stephanie's dad must have thought that I influenced Stephanie in somewhat of a bad way, which led to taking photos and uploading them on the Internet. He modified Stephanie's schedule immediately, so I didn't have any classes with her anymore. Because Stephanie's parents didn't allow her to go out and hang out with me, she had to go back to her aunt's house right after school. Her aunt picked her up, so she couldn't run away. I didn't mind not having a class with her, but I thought that Stephanie's dad overreacted.

Stephanie didn't come back to school that entire week. Stephanie didn't tell me anything, but I was pretty sure that she went back to Washington D.C. Our homeroom teacher informed us that she wouldn't come back until the new school year starts.

On the first day of May, I enjoyed a relaxing weekend; watching the television and a DVD. I have just finished final exams and was waiting for the summer to come. I went outside, collected the newspaper, and swiftly scanned the front page. When I finished, I felt my heart pumping and my hands shaking. The headlines read,

"The President of United States vs. The President of Gucci in Court"

"Oh my gosh." I murmured. "What the heck is going on?"

* * *

After I read the article, I immediately called Stephanie. Fortunately, Stephanie answered.

"What the heck, Steph?" I yelled. "Are you serious?"

"Yes, Liz. What the heck?" she asked back. "What are you talking about?"

"Are you crazy or something?" I shouted.

"Okay. I seriously don't know what you're talking about."

"Dude. You accused your Dad! You and your Dad's pictures are covering the front page of newspaper!"

"Oh. I'm going to go back to New Jersey next week," she said calmly. "I'm going to answer you when I'm there."

"Okay. Look. You made some stuff up, and you're just making things bigger and bigger. And all of a sudden, you accused your dad and now what. Telling me to wait until you come back? Besides, I thought you were not coming back to school until the next school year."

"I'm not. I'm just going back to New Jersey and that's it."

"Honestly, I have no idea why you're not living in the White House with your parents."

"I think I answered that questions for like a zillion times. It's my dad's secret plan."

"Fine. See you next week then."

*　*　*

Stephanie came to my house next Friday. Fortunately, it was Teacher's Work Day, so I didn't have school, and I was the only one at home. She told me that she arrived in New Jersey on Wednesday and stayed in the local inn for two days so that she could avoid the media. She looked pale and there were two dark rings under her eyes, which reminded me of pandas living in China.

"So, Stephanie," I called, handing her a cup of orange juice. "You have to tell me what happened, what is happening, and what will happen."

"Wow, Liz," she said in an unusual quiet voice. "Ms. Brown must be so proud of you. You're finally able to use tenses."

"Shut up and just tell me," I yelled.

"Fine. So stop yelling at me," she complained. "Please don't be shocked."

When Stephanie told me what happened to her in Washington D. C., it terrified me. She told me that her dad didn't allow her to go outside, and forced her to stay only in the White House. Her dad told her to be accompanied with at least five bodyguards and three housekeepers wherever she went. She also said that she saw a file named "Stephanie and Her Friends" on her dad's desk. I was stunned when I heard about a file from Stephanie's lips.

"The bodyguards and housekeepers followed me so I

couldn't read it but I guarantee to you that there will be something about you." she warned me.

The news about a file named "Stephanie and Her Friends" was enough of a shock to me. I desperately hoped that her bad news would end. However, despite my hope, she told me that she planned to accuse her dad.

"Are you serious?" I shouted. "I thought the media was writing another interesting story!"

"The media might exaggerate some facts," she calmly answered. "But I wasn't lying when I said that I'm going to accuse my dad. And although it's rare, media sometimes tells the real facts to people."

"Look, Stephanie," I called. "You should remember your family's position in this world. Your dad is the President of the United States. Since the US is being a police officer of this world, he's busy enough handling the global conflicts. If you accuse him, your family wouldn't be the only ones who will be shocked. It's the world that will be shocked. Besides, if you accuse your dad, the world won't like America. This isn't just you and your privacy. It's the world and their reaction that we're talking about."

"Don't you think I haven't thought your points before? I know my dad is the President of the United States. I have been trying to understand my dad and help him. But this time, he stepped over the line. I can't believe that he had a file called 'Stephanie and Her Friends.'"

"You don't even know what's in that file."

"If I saw your name and your photos in that on my dad's desk along with that file, I wouldn't say that I have absolutely no idea what's that file about."

"What the heck are you talking about now? Didn't you tell me that you haven't seen the profile?"

"Listen, Liz! I didn't see the profile yet. I just told you what's on my dad's desk!"

The silence filled in our room immediately; it seemed like an invisible tension drew a line between. Stephanie sighed and glared at me. I thought the most reasonable reason why would the President of the United States would want to know about me. Imagining the President, who had a dark brown hair and green eyes, reading a profile about me didn't help me to feel better.

"Why would he want to know about me?" I questioned, breaking the silence. "Why me?"

"That's probably because my dad wants to know who 'influenced' his daughter."

"What do you mean?"

"I've been a good girl of the President of the United States, you know." she explained. "But since I came here, I've been doing something that my dad doesn't want me to. Taking photos and uploading them on the Internet is one of them."

"Then, why don't you go back to the White House and go to the private school in Washington D.C. instead of going to the public school in New Jersey?" I asked her sharply.

"Well, considering that there was an election last year, and my mom prepared for the transition from the middle school to high school, that's probably because my dad probably wouldn't want any unnecessary criticism because of me going to a private boarding high school."

"So your dad used you." I concluded. "Your dad just sent you to New Jersey to make sure that the public would know that the President is somewhat smart, well-mannered, and one of the people right?"

"Yes," she answered calmly, which surprised me. "That's why I didn't have any privileges because of my dad. I didn't come here because I wanted to. It was included in my dad's awesome plan to be elected."

I stared at her. I couldn't believe what I just heard. The President used his own daughter to be elected?

"So, what are you gonna do?" I asked. "You hired a lawyer? You have enough money to hire one? What?"

"I have already got a lawyer," she replied. "And of course, I have..."

"What do you want me to do? Did you hope that I would help you in this nonsense idea? No. Honestly, I think you're just making that profile stuff up."

"Liz. Listen to me. I saw it through my own eyes! I really..."

I didn't want to hear anymore. It was just nonsense. Stephanie wasn't thinking what would happen if she accused her dad. And obviously, she wanted me to help her. Although we've been friends since the first day of school, she went across the line this time. I guaranteed that she made the whole entire story up. I believed that she was smart enough to distinguish between right and wrong. It was my bad judgment that I trusted her and helped her. Leaving her in my room, I ran outside to calm myself down. I saw a shiny and luxurious black BMW and around six bodyguards wearing a sunglasses and a black suit. I walked over to those bodyguards to ask them to leave my house with Stephanie.

"...yes, sir. She's with her friend, Elizabeth Jessica Owen. The information in profile is accurate. I checked that she has a brown eyes and a dark brown hair."

I immediately stopped. My heart pounded and I could feel butterflies flying in my stomach. One of the bodyguards talked through a brand new "Samsung" phone and he said, "sir" at the end of every sentence. I pretended that I had come outside to collect a newspaper. Of course, the bodyguard stopped talking immediately as soon as he recognized me.

"Good morning." I smiled.

"Good morning, Ms. Owen," he said back without smiling.

I came back to my house with the newspaper. Stephanie was still at my room, staring at the outside. Her eyes were somewhat watery. I felt sorry for her. I regretted my actions; I was at fault. There were an intense silence left in my room between Stephanie and I. I coughed several times before I talked to her.

"I overheard the phone call between one of your bodyguards and your dad." I confessed. Stephanie didn't either move or respond.

"I didn't do that on purpose." I continued. "I honestly thought that you were lying. Forgive me if you feel you have been insulted."

"Are you going to help me then?" she asked. "I need help desperately. All you need to do is to listen to me, and give me your opinion of my decisions that I will be making in the near future."

I didn't agree immediately. I couldn't leave my parents without telling them.

"My plan will work during the summer, you know," she said as if she were reading my mind. "You still can finish school and help me during the summer. It won't take a lot of time though; it will take like two weeks or so."

"I gotta ask my mom what's her summer plan though." I added. "I don't know whether I will go to one of the summer camps or not. Also, I may have to study for SAT before it gets too late to study."

"Right," she said. "So, does that mean yes or no?"

"I told you. I don't know yet."

"Fine. How about you call me when you make your final decision. You have to call me before June. Otherwise, I will just think that you won't help me, and I will do my plan."

I nodded. She picked up her phone, iPod, and jacket and said it was time for her to go back to the hotel. She gave me her new phone number, and asked me to call if I needed any help.

"Hope to see you soon." I waved her as she went into the car.

"Same here, Liz," she said, smiling.

I went back to my room after the car turned the corner and out of my sight.

"What do I have to choose, friendship or my future?" I murmured.

* * *

"So you're going to help me?" I heard her questions through her phone. I nodded.

"Hey, answer me. Are you seriously gonna help me?" she asked again.

"One more time, and then I'm going to hang the call up." I warned her.

"Fine. But how did you persuade your mom?"

"I just told her that I wanted to help you, and they said okay. I still have to study for SAT, though. Besides, my parents know who you are and the truth."

"Right. That's fantastic!"

"I know. Dude, so how can I help you if you are in the Washington D.C.? I'm in New Jersey."

"It's going to be awesome if you come to here because there is absolutely no way for me to go to New Jersey. When do your summer holiday start?"

"The second day of June, so we have like two more weeks to go."

"Wicked. Can you come here on like June 5th? You don't have to worry about the ticket. I can buy you one."

"If you're going to buy a ticket for me, that's no problem for me."

"Excellent. And your camp starts on June 20th?"

"Yah."

"Ah-ha. That's just fantastic, Liz. You don't know how I felt when you said you're going to help me. I love you, Liz."

"That sounds wrong. Anyway, I gotta go. My mom's yelling at me to eat dinner. Talk to you later."

"See you on June 5th."

"See you then."

*   *   *

On the fifth day of June, I found myself holding a passport in one hand, and my luggage in the other. I headed to Washington D.C. to help Stephanie. Although it wasn't an easy decision, I didn't regret it. It was not only because Stephanie was my best friend, but it was also because I desperately didn't want my name and personal profile to be spread out or read to people. I shared a goodbye kiss with my parents, and went to a gate to go to where Stephanie would be waiting for me.

A few hours later, Stephanie's driver headed to the White House with Stephanie and me. For once, I saw her smile on her face. She attempted to chat, but I was too exhausted to talk to her. Fortunately, Stephanie let me sleep for about an hour when we arrived to the White House. She had kindly offered to share a room with me. It was better for both of us because we obviously didn't want to be interrupted when we were talking about the "plan"

*   *   *

"So you mean you just hired this dude?" I asked. Stephanie nodded. After dinner, I stayed with Stephanie in her room. Her room was, of course, bigger than mine, but didn't have anything except a few books and her bed. The view of the city from her room was absolutely beautiful. However, I didn't have any chance to enjoy the view because Stephanie began to talk about her plan. She handed me a profile about her lawyer that she hired for this court.

"Benjamin Peter Gibson. Graduated from the Harvard Law School. Fairly smart dude, isn't he? Hm... Works for B&M Law Company? Dude? Where did you find him?" I questioned again.

"Don't you realize who I am?" she asked back. "My

dad used me. And I'm using him. I know it's mean and I shouldn't do that, but it's my dad who crossed the line in the first place."

"Hold on. What's the point of doing this? Because of your privacy and your friends, including my privacy, right?"

"Pretty much. Why?"

"Then we might need some evidence to prove that. The problem is, where the heck are we going to find any strong evidence?"

"That's what Benjamin, you and I have to do; find the evidence."

"What do I have to do then?"

"Help me find the evidence?"

"Evidence that your dad broke into your privacy, right?"

"Yup."

"When will I get to see Benjamin? What do I call him? Benjamin? Mr. Gibson?"

"I call him Benjamin just because he told me to. I guess you can call him Benjamin, too. He said he will come and see me tomorrow at noon, so you can see him tomorrow. Just wait until noon."

"Okay."

*   *   *

"So you're Elizabeth, right?" asked Mr. Gibson. "Elizabeth Owen?"

I nodded. He was approximately six feet and one inch tall and had brown hair, blue eyes, and wide shoulders and was wearing a black suit with blue necktie.

"Yes. Can I call you Ben instead of Mr. Gibson?" I asked.

"Sure, Liz. So, you two will help me to find the evidences, right?" questioned Ben.

"Yeah. Last night, we concluded that our main point is that we need evidence that my dad broke into my and my friends' privacy. I think that profile is the best one," replied Stephanie.

"Look, both of you," he called, leaning forward to us. "The situation is, that we can't just go to the court and say, 'my dad broke into my privacy! I don't like this!' You're correct; our main point should be that your dad broke into your privacy. But it should be something impactive so that everyone would agree that your dad was overreacting. The profile is one. But that's it? We probably need at least two or more pieces of evidence, including those profiles. Your job is to find at least one. Remember, that we're having a court case against the President of United States. While you guys are finding the evidence, I will write the speech up for you. Please send me the evidence before next week Friday."

"Okay, Ben," I replied loudly with a giggle.

* * *

The day to stand in front of judge finally arrived. I sat between Stephanie and Benjamin, wearing a black suit for this court. I was attending this court as a witness. I signed the oath that I would tell the whole truth, and nothing but the truth.

"Is it true that President Simon Rupert Lloyd Watson has a profile of yourself, Ms. Elizabeth Jessica Owen?" asked the judge.

I gazed at the President for a moment. He was about six feet three inches tall, and had dark brown hair and green eyes. For some reason, he whispered with his lawyer. Apparently, he looked very irritated and annoyed. When Stephanie officially announced in front of the media that she was accusing her dad of violating her privacy, it was too late for him to cancel the court. Immediately, he hired a lawyer and prepared for the court, which surprised me because I heard the President could not be brought to court until he was no longer serving as President.

"Yes," I replied.

"Is it true that President Simon Rupert Lloyd Watson used her daughter, Stephanie Rosemary Watson, to reinforce his reputation by sending her to a public school in New Jersey?" questioned the judge again. The President turned to me immediately and gave me a half-puzzled and half-irritated look. Stephanie and I shared a look. Stephanie slightly nodded at me, smiling.

"Yes," I answered. "Yes, he did. According to Stephanie Rosemary Watson, the President's daughter and my best friend, she confessed to me that her dad forced her to transfer to the public high school in New Jersey for her dad's fame and reputation during the election."

I saw our President standing up. I could see his mixed emotions through his eyes; irritated, frustrated, and betrayed.

∗   ∗   ∗

"Elizabeth, wake up!" I opened my eyes when I heard my mom calling me. I checked my phone to see what time it was; it was six o'clock, April 20, 2010. I wasn't in the court anymore; I was lying on my bed, wearing a plain grey shirt and basketball shorts.

"Weird dream." I talked to myself. "I really thought I was in the court."

It was an ordinary day today. I had my classes with Stephanie and ate a lunch with her, as well as Sandra, Jessica, Patricia, and Michelle. It seemed like I was the only one who was sitting on the court with the President of the United States.

"Class! Your assignment is to finish reading 'Romeo and Juliet' due next class. Please don't forget! Excuses are strictly not acceptable. You're now dismissed."

When I heard Ms. Brown's last sentence, I packed my stuff and waited patiently for Stephanie. Soon, I found myself heading back to my house with her. She showed the photos she took on her birthday party. Amazingly, it was exactly the same photos that I saw in my dream.

"It's going to be hilarious! Everyone will love them! You look so cute in those photos! Come on, Liz!" I heard Stephanie shouting in front of her laptop screen. "Please?"

"No." I answered, trying to look serious. "Not again."

My Neighbor

By Alex Kim

"Sir...Please.... Let me go home."

I fixed my eyes on the sharp metal pointed straight at my neck. As he twisted slowly, the knife shined by the reflection of the dim bulb light. I looked back at his plain solid black eyes.

"Home?" Not a muscle of his plain face flinched.

"I really want to go home..." The fear freed my tears from my eyes. I panicked following the rapid pacing of my heart. I felt my blood slowly diffusing to the bottom of my body, leaving my head completely bloodless. I started to shake, the pizza slowly greased down my hands.

I inhaled deeply and added, "You said I could go home once I finish my pizza...Let me go home please..."

"Go," added the man without moving a muscle. He suddenly twisted his head and grimaced. "Who said you couldn't, Lauren? Go."

I slowly moved my focus to the door, I carefully examined the basement. As I did, I spotted a huge trunk case with a pickaxe lying on top of it. My muscles started to tense and I couldn't focus on anything anymore. His smile grew bigger and he spit out a sneer. "TRY to go home..."

The whole background slowly blurred, I began to feel nauseous. 'Oh why out of all the time.' I thought. I choked out a little laugh, a laugh mocking my stupidity. How could anyone be so dumb to follow a man who you know nothing more about than that he is your neighbor? Helen...! Helen must be having a fit by now. I never expected my death would end in such a way. If I did, I would have gone back home and told Helen how much I loved her and how thankful for her being my stepmother.

All the people whom I've walked past today flicked through my head like a fast-forwarding film: John Tomlin, Sydney Langly, Mrs. Langly, Helen Wilson, Ryan Brown, Rudolf Johnson, Mr. Tong and finally, Mr. Walker–the murderer beside me.

*   *   *

Mrs. Wilson

As always, a thin breeze squeezed through the window and awoke her up. Mrs. Wilson stared at the clock blankly for a moment "7.05 P.M", 'How long have I been asleep?' she looked out the window, the black clouds has already dominated the white ones slowly by slowly like a black ink spreading across a thin piece of paper. 'I suppose it's going to be another heavy shower.' "By the way, has Stanley taken his umbrellas with him today? I don't remember..." She got up to her knees, carefully arranging her hair. She walked towards the kitchen heavily. As she tried to stomp ahead, she stared at the front door blankly. "Today...? No, can't be." She shook her head with a force and took out several dishes to prepare for dinner.

'Tock... tock...tock...tock...[chopping carrots]'

'Pi... Pi... Pi... Pi... [dialing front door lock]'

While Mrs. Wilson continued chopping a carrot, someone attempted to dial her front door lock. She looked up in shock but tried to ignore the noise. The inevitable noise.

'Pi...Pi...Pi... [unlock]'

"Mom...I'm back home."

She lowered her face to the ground, putting all of her focus to the carrot. She couldn't stop herself from thinking whether she should look back, but she knew she wouldn't be able to bear the pain that will follow up.

"Mom..."

Mrs. Wilson exhaled deeply and continued chopping the carrot, however this time with much force and rapidity.

She soon exhaled deeply, too and walked passed me toward the room. She stared at me blankly from her door and her face pleaded me to give her at least a glance. She shook slightly and poured back her whole attention with much effort to the carrot. When she realized she has slipped the knife on the edge of her index finger. She slowly turned her head to the door. The door was closed firmly as it had been a week before.

Her daughter has been constantly coming to the house for a week since her death...

*   *   *

Rudolf Johnson

"Why, hello, sir! Thank you for coming again!"

Five foot nine, always a black shirt over a white shirt. Large wrinkles deeply placed under his eyes. Plain, solid black eyes that are far too dark than any other customers Rudolf has seen. It seemed though that he likes 'PIZZA PALATE', as he often brings a cup of coke and a burger with a logo plastered on it to Rudolf's store. He guessed it was Mr. Walker again.

He strangely looked at him as though he didn't understand what he has been talking about.

"He-he-he, don't you remember? You came by last time, quite a lot of time actually..." Rudolf added.

Not a smile drawn on his face.

"Come on... You did come often..." he said, forcing a cheerful smile.

"Really..." stared the customer. He slowly placed the cup on his desk and pulled an annoying look.

"Ha, ha, I must have mistaken then! So how can I help you?" he added, feeling awkward of the silence.

He slowly lifted his burger and grabbed a huge bite of it without taking his eyes off me. He felt a light shiver his back, feeling uneasy with the awkward silent moment. As he munched on his burger he added, "A traveling trunk case."

"Oh! Which size do you need?" Rudolf said politely.

He slowly examined Rudolf's store and suddenly his focus fixed on the corner. Rudolf turned to see, which has drawn his attention; the black trunk case that has been plastered in dust in the corner of my store.

"This one?" Rudolf asked.

"Yes," he added.

"Ha, ha, good choice, sir!" Rudolf brought his handkerchief and lifted the bag on the desk to whip the dust off it. "You've got great sense taste for bags! To travel, large ones like this is always useful. It's strong and tight, so you wouldn't have to worry about the quality of it. Ha ha. You must travel a lot?"

"No. I need it, because I'm moving soon." Mr. Walker said.

"Oh well, you can't get these bags anywhere but my store actually. My store has large collections of great quality and cheap bags! This is the biggest I have in store! It's sure big enough to even fit a human insi—" As he blabbered on about the bag, he met Mr. Walker's stare so he quickly stopped. He continued whipping the bag.

he slowly lifted his eyes to examine the man. He froze like a statue, not taking his eyes off me.

"Is there something...wrong, sir?" Rudolf carefully asked.

"Just hand me the bag," he responded.

Rudolf lifted and examined the bag and finally handed the bag slowly to the man and added:

"Its...fifty dollars. It's the best I can offer for this!"

He dropped his food down on the counter, saying no word at all. He went through his wallet, always with a furious face.

"You...can use credit card if you like. Then I'd offer forty dollars."

"It doesn't matter, I don't use cards anyway," Mr. Walker handed Rudolf the money, took the bag with him and left his store. The door opened, the light gushed out. As he walked out, Rudolf glanced at the money he gave him, at the back of the money something was written.

'John Tomlin' and the bottom it had his telephone. John Tomlin, *but isn't he Adam Walker? Strange.* Then who else would this be? Why would he write this on the back of the money. All these questions flew into his mind like water into an empty bowl. While he struggled with the questions, he saw the counter and found out that Mr. Walker left his food there.

"hmm...I haven't eaten dinner yet..." Found out that he kept ignoring the whole time what his stomach was up to. Rudolf stuck a little note saying, 'I'm gone in a while so contact me if you need. 138-1872-3488'

He went outside, freshened his mind and washed away his questions, all that he wanted to think of is where should he eat. Then unexpectedly, a raindrop fell on to the tip of his head slowly after one by one, then it started have a heavy rain. He had to go somewhere, and then he found a little pizza store. "PIZZA PALATA".

* * *

"Yes, there's various choice in our store, we sell pizza, burger and spaghetti. We also can deliver," the man in a uniform announced.

"Oh, that's great. Then can I have a cheese burger with coke please?" Rudolf offered.

"Yes, sir."

"I'll make the food, and you deliver this pizza to Green court villa, building number 14 and room number 1A," the cook said, handing the worker the large sized pizza.

"Alright."

Then Rudolf spotted the worker's name tag– 'John Tomlin.' Then he swiftly searched for the money that Mr. Walker had gave him. It was the exactly the same name, 'John Tomlin'. *What's going on?* he thought.

* * *

It felt a wind had blown inside his store like a cat trying to sneak in to the rat's habitat. He turned on the television.

"Important news for the day. A seventeen-year-old girl wearing a school uniform was found decomposed in a buried trunk case in the middle of Manhattan Forest. Once the police investigated the identity of this girl, it turned out to be that she was one of the reported missing person *ten days ago.* As a result, three out of eight missing people have been found dead. The police have confirmed it to be a serial murder case. The young girl's body..."

The traveling bag... Then he startled, his eyes went wide. The traveling bag that the girl got buried, it was the exact same bag that the man who came to his store, about ten days ago bought, the last and exactly the same one.

* * *

Sydney Langly

Raindrops fell endlessly crashing against the ground, forming overlapping ripples. Rain always looks beautiful to her but today, it strangely looked gloomy. Maybe it's an excuse of a dark clouds forming a terrifying wind penetrating through her thin shirt.

"I'm back home!" Sydney shouted across the room as she admitted to her house.

"Oh, Sydney!" responded Mrs. Langly.

"You were all stressed out organizing the conference meeting, weren't you?" she said, giving her a smile. "Organizing a conference is great but you should take care of your little daughter bit more, mom. I got all wet."

"Why did you come so early?" asked her dad.

"Oh my, you are all wet! Why didn't you call me then?"

Sydney laughed, "I had a test today so we got dismissed early," she said. "Well, I was trying to call you but it said it was busy all the time."

"Oh...I'm sorry, I was busy calling people reminding them for the conference. Next time I will pick you up," said Mrs. Langly.

"You really have to pick me up next time." She laughed, raindrops slightly dripping off from her silky brown hair.

* * *

John Tomlin

"I'll make the food, and you deliver this pizza to Green court villa, building number 14 and room number 1A," the cook commanded.

"Alright," John said. 'Hmm...Mr. Walker again? Strange, he came and bought burger in the afternoon, and now he's ordering pizza?' he thought.

It rained like buckets, pouring on his hard helmet and he felt his pants slowly sticking on to his skin, getting wet. "Oh, darn, I really don't like delivering in rainy days..."

He rode a motorbike making his way to the house and he forced himself against the rain fighting him in the opposite direction.

As he reached to the house, he took off from the motorbike and got the pizza out. He knocked on the door several times, waiting for a rapid answer but evidently he was wrong, it hadn't answer for a while. He stood there stupidly, staring at the plain door. As he took a deep breath, John yelled, "Pizza is here!"

It quieted for a while, then he heard a tiny footsteps approaching. Someone started to unlock the locks on the door. He's never seen any more locks than this one before, the man took a while unlocking them.

He finally opened the door, except for one lock he missed, or maybe purposely didn't unlock it.

He stared at John coldly through a little space, his eyes were burning as if John had interrupted him for doing something important.

"You ordered pizza, haven't you?" John asked. "Can you open the door, please?"

"Just shove the pizza in," Mr. Walker said rudely.

"Um...Sir, as I have told you several times, If I shove the pizza in this small space the toppings of the pizza would fall off." John tried smiled in a gracious possible way.

"Fine then, wait," said Mr. Walker rather irritably. He closed the door firmly and started unlock the lock. He opened the door and John went inside his house. His house seemed to get darker at the end of the corridor. One little light bulb dangled from the front corridor.

"Here's the pizza and a bottle of a coke. It would cost you fifteen dollars." As John laid the pizza on the floor, he felt little empty and cold. He glanced down, there was a basement downstairs. And then there were little sounds that tickled his ears, as if someone wildly banged their heads against a wall. It got louder and closer, I thought strange, why would the man just stand there when there's such a sound downstairs?

"Uh...there's a strange sound down—" I looked up. I saw his face, his eyes. "—Stairs." John paused for a moment, the man's wrinkles were folded twice as he looked down, his eyes were terrifying as it has been before.

His face got darker and he finally said something, "Hand me the pizza and go."

"Ha...ha...Yes, of course." John said. His heart felt clenched toward each other, he felt his blood running upside down, never been terrified like this before. *Was I not suppose to say that?*

He handed me the money. "Thank you, and you have the coupon card right? I'll have to stamp on it," John said.

He didn't say a word, and he took out the coupon card from his drawer.

"It's already eight stamps, one more stamp then you would get one free pizza." John smiled gracefully.

"Ten stamps would be better."

"Huh? Oh, nine stamps is enough..." John said carefully. He stamped it firmly, and wrote the date. Then John realized that Mr. Walker has been ordering pizza every ten days. John stared at it blankly. *Hmm... Why is it always something fishy going on here.* He handed back the coupon card to Mr. Walker, and he practically forced John to get out.

"Then, I'd better get going." John said at last.

He slowly closed the door, his pupils were as small as a marble, reflecting John on his eyes he seemed to be very enraged. As soon as the door got closed, he started to lock all of his locks speedily.

The way he speaks, the way he looks at John...What's wrong with him? Such a strange man, John thought.

* * *

He slowly went down the dark basement stairs, making sounds as he went down, holding a pizza on his left hand. Then the dark door, locked firmly appeared, and he opened the door, then a girl came into view. Her hands and her legs were bound in rope, her mouth were covered in electric tape. She looked fearful, as of course she should. A tiny light bulb was shining in her eyes brightly, reflecting the man approaching closer her. There were fresh blood deadly dried on the walls, and spider webs clinging everywhere. It was a cold basement room, which had frozen her feet rapidly.

"Hey," the man said.

"I told you to keep quiet," the murderer said.

"Let's eat."

* * *

It rained endlessly. *That's still very strange, I really heard something down the basement.* "Ah, it's non of my business." John said to himself, comforting that nothing unconventional would happen that he needs to care about. He tried not to be too suspicious with a man who naturally has bad-manners.

He hopped on to my motorbike, making his way back to the store.

Rains on the ground were splashing as John rode over them, it jumped up and down like a fish dying for water.

Then a girl came running without looking up and he literally rid right across the area. John kept riding as he didn't notice her since of the bad weather, as they were about to collide, John immediately stopped the motorbike. Water flew all on her, then she screamed, "Ahhhh! Oh my gosh."

"Oh, I'm really sorry." John said. "Oh...I'm sorry, your clothes are all wet, It's all my fault."

"Ha, ha, it's okay. I'm fine." She smiled warmly. "It doesn't really matter because it was wet anyway." She laughed. She looked a senior, and she had a nice smile, which made his blood warm that made him forget that he had been suffering in coldness of the rain.

I said nothing, only staring at her. "Uh, uh– next time, I'll give you tons of free services when I deliver to building 14-1B!" I said. I knew I faltered but I decided to blame it on the coldness.

She looked at him in huge confusion.

"Huh? I don't live in 1B," she said.

"You don't?" John said. "I guess I was confused with someone else then."

"Well, I got to go, when you come delivering building 15, room number 3C, you'll have to give us tons of service then." She ran off as she waved at him. She has been sweet to him but then he realized he's been wasting his time so he went on with his own business.

*   *   *

Ten days had passed surprisingly there has been no customers.

"No orders, no delivery..." John said hopelessly. He got dulled, nothing to do so he turned on the computer. *Huh? What is this?* John said to himself, looking at the latest news.

"Serial murder...?" he said out loud. "They still haven't caught him, yet?" he typed in 'serial murder' in a search box. Then he found news that had happened in Manhattan, very close to where he lived.

"Ten days apart? Moron." It said, he's been killing senior girls every ten days. But then that dinged his head. *Ten days apart...Ten days apart....*John suddenly searched for the coupon card, as soon as he saw the dates. It was intimidating, *Wait... What is this? April 2nd,*

April 11th, April 22nd, May 3rd, May 12th, May 22nd, and June 2nd, June 12th... The dates...match...!

* * *

Ryan Brown

"What the?"

"Argh...Darn it. Why did this person parked his car over here?"

"No phone number, huh?"

"Blocking my car not to go through then you should at least put a note." Ryan, a tough man who has been dealing with money and beating any old men who is not able to pay back money. He spit on the car.

He noticed a tiny little paper saying, "14- 1A"

"Hmm... building 14, room 1A?" I said to myself then Ryan swiftly made his way to the house.

'Ding dong' He pressed the bell several times but there were still no answers from the house.

"Open the door! Now!" Ryan bellowed.

"Anyone there?"

He started to bang the door loudly. He yelled at the house. Ryan did everything to get its attention. Then suddenly its neighbor's door slowly started to open. He guessed, about forty years old woman, who had her hair dyed brown and tied it back, peeked out from the door. She only stared him without a word.

"Not you," I shouted. "Wait, do you know who lives here?"

She shook her head and slowly closed the door, still keeping her focus on me.

"What's up with her? Getting all rotten." He said to himself. As he saw the house that the woman lives, he started to wonder, *was it that house whose daughter got kidnapped and got murdered?* Suddenly, someone started to unlock the locks. Then the man finally showed himself. Except for leaving one lock locked.

103

"You were inside the whole time?" Ryan asked irritably. "Is your car black? If it is, it's blocking the way."

"Black car...I guess it's mine," he boldly closed the door and quickly unlocked his lock.

"I'll move the way out then," he said as he opened door. He moved his way to the parking lot silently.

"What the heck is wrong with him? Didn't even apologize?" Ryan mocked him, purposely right behind him as he followed him. Then he turned his back and glared at me. Ryan really didn't care.

"What you looking at? Move your car." Ryan said.

His eyes were glowing dark, his glare wasn't normal like anyone else but it could never frighten Ryan as he's been dealing much more furious men in his whole life.

He got on to his car and started the engine.

"This is my spot so don't you dare park it here again." Ryan warned.

He spotted the spit trace that Ryan spitted earlier. Then he looked back on him, "Hey, you," he said, "did you spit on my car?"

"No duh."

He said nothing, only staring at me aggressively.

"Why you lookin' at me like that?" I said, giving him a little sneer. Then I spotted large cuts across his left arm.

"Oh. So you have some cuts on your arm, don't you?" I said. "And the last one seems to be a recent as the blood still hasn't dried, yeah? Just move the car."

He never said a word 'I bet he's scared as he spotted large tattoo on my right arm.' Ryan smiled.

"Let's stop staring at each other, you know. Let's get back to business, boy." Ryan said. "I'm not that easy-going and I don't have much to time hang around here, so move."

He started to move his car, *finally*, Ryan thought.

When everything settled, Ryan went in to his car.

Ryan glanced at him. He stood there and then gave him a huge grimace and left.

*   *   *

Ryan came back from his own business. He parked on the spot that he usually park and came out of the car. He stretched his legs but then he felt like he was stepping on something. He looked down to his toe. It was ads of his job. 'Ah...nothing is working out these days.' Then he spotted someone's foot stepping on the ads as well, Ryan looked up.

"Who the—"

"Hey." It was the police, the police that they knew each other too much by Ryan going to police station unusually a lot. "How's your job?"

"Kevin J?" Ryan said. "Move your feet."

"Oh, ha, ha, ha, I'm very sorry," he said sarcastically.

"Why are you following me everywhere I go?"

"I was wondering what you've been up to," he added. "Ryan Brown. 38 years old. Divorced two times. Fraud. Physical assault. Blackmail. It's not even a year yet you came out of the jail, and now you're trying to kill a senior girl."

"Shut your mouth." Ryan said.

"Let me ask you a question, what have you been doing on June 12th?" he asked.

"What are you talking about."

"Well... if you can't answer, I guess you'll have to come with us then." It has been hectic after then, Ryan found out that he had the highest possibility to be the in suspect of murderer. The murderer of the girl who died in this compound. They told him that he lived in a same compound with her. Also, they said if he don't know exactly what he did on June 12th, everything would go upside. Ryan would be suspected then. As he got in to the police car, everyone in the compound was staring at him and whispering to each other.

Ryan looked back at them, as soon as he got in he spotted a man. The man who lived in 14-1A. He continuously looked at Ryan through his tiny window. And he slowly smiled.

Ryan came back from the police station, feeling all disgusted and angry. He reminded himself what Kevin told him...

* * *

Mrs. Wilson

Meanwhile, Mrs. Wilson never knew who lived in her neighbor.

"Do you know who lives here?" A man that she couldn't recognize glared at her.

She could only shook her head and slowly closed her door, as her eyes were blurring the scene. She came in silently.

Day one, 8:00 P.M-10:00 P.M

Mrs. Wilson was under the table, shivering and waiting for her husband to arrive. She had no comment for her own behavior, but she just knew that she's terrified, and no one would know how she felt.

She looked up, staring at the room where her stepdaughter used to use. The door was closed as it has been ten days before. Then, her memory started to tickle her mind. It made her flew to the past...

"Um... Have you seen my hair band while you were cleaning the house?" asked Lauren. She stood there so still like a manikin, as always.

"A hair band?" I asked in wonder.

"The hair band that I always used to wear. The purple one," she said cautiously again. "I left it on my room but now I can't find it."

"Hmm...I haven't cleaned it up, dear. Who would take it anyway?"

"...I really liked it ..." she seemed suddenly depressed of my respond. She avoided my eyes, searching the hair band with her eyes motioning around the house. 'I'll buy you one. I'll buy you a new one'. I kept repeating to myself the same sentence but the sentence that would never roll out of my mouth.

"I'll—" I was about to say as I felt comfortable with my mouth mouthing it several of times, but then she went inside her room right before I started to talk. I had no courage to go inside her room and tell her. 'Ugh, lost the chance again by hesitating.'

"I can buy you a new one." It's not that hard at all. I can just say it out loud, it's nothing embarrassing nor mean, it's just offering ... as a mom.

She came back from the past, she felt more dejected than before. Then unexpectedly, the front door opened.

"You..." It was her husband, his dark circle has been down to earth than anybody else. He seemed tired, he seemed to be gloomy as he has been last ten days ago. "...are still like this?"

"I have to go in a minute," he said as he undid his necktie. "Give me some clothes to change with."

"Stanley...!" She shouted as she climbed out of the dinning table. And she asked cautiously, "Do you need to go again?"

"I told you, I'm not doing this for my own good. There's too many things to do," he replied.

"Honey... I...don't want to be home alone this late." She said bravely.

"...She came...again yesterday," she said. "Our dead daughter....came home last night again..."

"You are saying that again?"

"Lauren...She definitely died, she came home all wet again," she said. "She walked pass me and she went inside her room." She shivered, reminded herself of Lauren's hideous appearance that day.

"Really...? Did Lauren come here again and went inside her room?" he asked as he was getting sick of hearing the same news every time. "Come here." Then he started to walk to Lauren's room and opened the door widely.

"See! There's no one in here! NO ONE! This room is completely empty, Lauren died! She died!"

She only stared at the empty room vacantly.

"It's exactly the same since she left," he said forlornly.

"But...I saw her, I really saw her!" Mrs. Wilson started to argue the fact that her husband had denied long time ago. "Please, don't go. She's going to come again today."

"Just stop..."

"She always come at the time when her school finishes, she's definitely going to come. I'm so scared."

"Stop...I told you, we are going move house..."

"Honey, don't go. Don't leave me a lone. Please."

"Stop..."

"I think she's coming to revenge or something. I don't know, so that's why she comes when I'm alone in the house..."

"Please stop...!" his voice started to raise up. "Stop making nonsense stuff up!"

"If...I've had pick her up that night...then–"

"JUST STOP IT!" he yelled. "You! When are you going to stop saying that! I'm tired of this....when I'm home, I think about Lauren and it drives me crazy...!" then he added. "Do...do you even know how it feels?"

"Stanley..."

"For you, she's nothing because she's not your *real* daughter," he yelled. "But for me, she's the only daughter!"

"Honey...!"

One year ago, he had a daughter, Lauren Wilson. She

lost her mom when she was young she's been growing up alone with Stanley.

That time, Mrs. Wilson was forty-five years old. She hasn't given birth to any child. That time, Lauren was sixteen years old, and only thing similarity was that they were both girls. Therefore, it has been awkward between them. Mrs. Wilson tried to hold her hand like any other mom would do, but she'd been never brave enough. It wasn't easy for her. That time, she should've held her hand, tight.

"Honey..." she said. "How can you say that to me? I...I...I've thinking of Lauren–"

"Lauren...was my daughter...What was she for you?" he cried.

"How...can a mom be scared of her own daughter...?" he asked. "It's because you couldn't accept Lauren as your daughter...that's why it's so scary for you." Then he added more. "I...want to see Lauren, the girl you always see at night, I just want to see her."

His tears splashed upon their ground. Then he dashed out the house as he wiped his tears.

'I was alone again...'

* * *

Mrs. Wilson

Day one, ten P.M

That night, she didn't know what happened to Lauren.

The telephone rang, she got up and stretched her legs to reach the phone.

"Hello?" she answered.

"Oh, this is Lauren..." said Lauren with a quiet voice like a mouse.

"Oh, you still at school?" I asked.

"Uh...is dad there?"

"Hmm...He's not here yet. It's only six."

Their phone line got silent. She took a deep breathe and asked, "Why? Is there something going on?"

"No..." Lauren said. "Uh... What are doing now?"

"I'm just watching T.V." Mrs. Wilson started to wonder why is asking her those random questions.

"Oh, okay..."

"I'm just tired so I'm going to take a nap soon."

"Okay...I'll hang up now."

"Hello? Lauren?" she hung up already. 'That was unexpected...She never used to call me.' She said to herself and continued watching television.

$*$ $*$ $*$

Lauren Wilson

Lauren basically got soaked by the rain pouring on top of her. There were several of mothers waiting for their children to arrive from their school bus. Except for her. It was awkward, hoping her mom to be here too. But it was just hard to call her and tell her to pick her up. Because she wasn't used to her, she's just her foster daughter. The bus arrived, it slashed rainwater on her skirt as it stopped, and all the students started to shift out of the bus and they were all in hurry to hug their own mother. And there it was only her left in the bus stop, she waited even though she knew it was pointless. She peeked at those daughters and their mom. She could never be jealous than anything else. They were holding the light umbrella together, linking their arms, talking and laughing and smiling. 'I wish that I could be one of the daughters there, at least for a minute.'

As she knew this would not make her feel any better, she started to walk her way to home by her own. Rain poured on her head and flicked out and it flew to the ground.

"Hey, there!" Someone bellowed. She looked back.

"Who—" She couldn't determine who it was, as the man covered his face by the umbrella.

"Ha, ha, don't you live in 14-1B? I've seen you several times." He was Lauren's neighbor, well, that's all she knew about him.

"Uh... yes. You live in 1A."

"Yeah, and it's pouring," he added. "Do you want to share my umbrella?"

She hesitated, giving him a shy shook.

"We live in a same apartment anyway."

"It's fine. Thank you."

"You would catch a cold then. It doesn't really matter because I'm only your neighbor." *Polite*, I thought . Maybe only in that situation.

"Then...okay..." She couldn't say no, it was too rude and she thought it would totally be fine because he lives right next door.

He smiled for a reply. They walked together, they talked together, he smiled and he laughed. Things that she could never imagine doing it with her mom.

When they arrived at the back door, he phoned the security guard.

"Hello? I live in 14-1A which is right behind the back door, my drainage system is not working, you should come and fix it now. Thank you."

Their apartment wasn't behind the back door. "Um... front door is over there," she said carefully.

"Oh, right. I was confused," he said. "Come on, if you don't want to get wet."

Lauren had nothing else to say.

"The security guard would be all confused," she said.

"Well, yeah."

They arrived at the front door, and then to their apartment.

"Thank you for the umbrella," she said and made her way to her house.

"Hey, wait!" he shouted. "Can you hold the umbrella for a second? I need to do the code."

She suddenly felt nervous for some reason, she didn't want to hold it for him but then she had to.

"Sure..." She held his umbrella, she watched him as he was about to do the code.

"Um...Can you look somewhere else?"

"What?" She said. She got scared but then she realized that she has been stupid.

"Oh, right."

'Pi...Pi...Pi." [unlock]

He opened the door.

"Here is yo—" Lauren looked up, his face, his eyes and even his wrinkles were clenched together and she just realized how stupid she was, again.

He grabbed her mouth so that she couldn't speak his left hand grabbed her stomach to stop her from moving.

"Mo...Mo..." She faltered, she got terrified. She wanted someone to save her, she wanted her mom in that moment. She felt her heart was clenched together, her blood stopped from moving, her breath got slower, and the scene got blurry. She knew she had to be awake, she had to be strong but...she couldn't.

"MO...Mo...!"

"Shhh..." he softly whispered into her ears. "Don't go 'Mo, Mo'. Just be quiet and you will be spared."

He took her with him to his house, the door slowly got closed, she stretched her arms attempt to reach for her house, even though she knew it wouldn't work but she had to try. She had to live. But it was too late. The door got closed firmly.

$*$ $*$ $*$

"MO...MO...!"

"Don't go 'Mo, Mo'. Just be quiet then you'll be spared."

'Mo...Mo...' Lauren pictured herself with her mom, in a umbrella together, linking arms, talking and laughing in the rain. It was beautiful. It looked real and she would never get jealous of anyone else, they would probably get jealous of her. She and her mom in one umbrella is the only wish she could've done before all of these.

"Mo..!"

"MOM...!"

*   *   *

Sydney Langly

"Mom! Mom!"

"Huh?" Mom said startled.

"Ha ha, what were you thinking? Conference thing again?" Sydney asked in a worry. "You always organize the conference. It can't be that hard?"

"Yeah, but the woman who lives in 14-1B concerns me. I don't know how to put in words to talk to her. She's depressed about what happened earlier."

"Actually, the daughter of the woman, she goes to our school...And she lives in same villa with us but I couldn't talk to her." She said. "She's always alone...Quiet..."

"Oh..."

"What about her mother? How is she?"

"Well...I guess they are alike, she doesn't talk at all," said mom. "She hasn't come out of the house for awhile."

"Well..." Then she spotted the conference sheet. "Is this the conference sheet? I don't think you should give this to the woman...She would be all sad then."

"I was thinking if I should meet her up and talk about it...I don't know," she looked down, feeling forlorn as well. They stood there quiet as Sydney studied the sheet. Then she realized that the conference starts at ten o'clock in the evening.

"Why is the conference starts so late?" she asked.

"Oh, it's because every parents are all busy in the afternoon. And I thought this conference was important and I want everyone to come."

"Wait, but ten o'clock is when I come from school then you can't pick me up this day. You know that we have after school lesson until ten. It's for our exams," she said.

"Really? Oh...Don't worry, I'll pick you up anyways." Mom smiled.

"Seriously?" Sydney got excited, these days it's dangerous for senior girls to walk home alone.

"You're really going to pick me up? You've changed a lot mom!" She said in excitement. "You used to don't care about it but you know that world is getting harsh and stuff."

"Don't you worry, mom will always be there for you, okay?"

*　*　*

Mrs. Wilson

'That was unexpected...She never used to call me.' Mrs. Wilson said it to herself and continued watching television... But if she had been aware of the pouring heavy shower outside...she would have called Lauren back...Everything would have been changed, it would be different and such tragedy wouldn't have happened. Only if she did that one call...

"Lauren, where are you now?"

"It's pouring heavily outside, do you have an umbrella with you?" she might have asked.

"Wait there, I'll pick you up."

*　*　*

Mr. Tong, the security guard.

"Hello?" said Mr Walker. "Are you the security guard?"

"Yes, sir." he said.

"Oh, I live in 14-1A and the water is flooding here and I think you should come and fix the drainage system now. Thank you." It was raining cats and dogs that night. right after he hung up Mr. Tong went to Mr Walker's house and checked. There there were no problem with the drainage system.

"Haven't you called me to fix the drainage system?"

"No, no at all! I don't have any problems with my drainage system."

He went outside to the slathering raindrops dripping. Then he saw the back door. It was strange, 'he did call me to fix the drainage system which is in front of the back door.' 'What's going on?' I thought to myself. 'Who would...' He paused. 'Maybe...'

"Um..Can you look somewhere else?"

"What...?" She said. She was scared but then she realized that she was being stupid.

"Oh, right."

'Pi...Pi...Pi." [unlock]

He opened the door. He was about to grab her mouth with his hand, if Mr Tong was there.

"Were you the person who called me?" he might ask. "Haven't you called me to fix your drainage system?"

"Yes, he did." Lauren would respond.

And the killer wouldn't say anything.

"It wasn't the back door, it was the front door." Mr. Tong might say. "I was going to move on but then it's my job." If he had done that... Nothing tragic would happen like this.

* * *

Rudolf Johnson

It felt a wind had blown inside my store like a cat trying to sneak in to the rat's habitat. I turned on the television.

"Important news for the day. The decomposed body of a seventeen-year-old girl wearing a school uniform was found in a buried trunk in the middle of Manhattan Forest. Once the police investigated the identity of this girl, it turned out to be that she was one of the reported missing persons ten days ago. As a result, three out of eight missing people have been found dead. The police have confirmed it to be a serial murder case. The young girl's body..."

'Nah...Maybe it's just a coincidence...' He thought. 'I shouldn't be suspicious with my costumer, and if I'm wrong then my store's reputation would go down and no one would want to buy anything from me. I should just forget about it... But...! this is about someone losing their life or not. I have no other choice but to call the police.'

"Is this police? Well...ha, ha, I'm not pretty sure but I was just watching the news about the serial murder, right?" He might say. "The girl who died in a trunk case... so... I'm the bag store owner and...I remember selling that same bag to this man..." If he had done such thing, nothing tragic like this would happen.

* * *

John Tomlin

"Ten days apart? Moron." It said, he's been killing senior girls every 10 ten days. But then that dinged my head. Ten days apart...Ten days apart...I found the coupon card lying down on the counter. As soon as I saw the date, It was intimidating, I was shocked. Wait... April 2nd, april 11th, april 22nd, May 3rd, May 12th, May 22nd, and June 2nd, June 12th... The dates....match...!

It's a coincidence... It's impossible... 'Because what kind of murderer would order pizza every ten days? the chance of that the possibility would be like 1%.' John thought. 'And if I tell people about this, then they would probably laugh at me.' But...! if that 1% is...possible...Then I might save that 1% of a person's life...!' If he thought of it in a different way, if people laugh at me, he wouldn't care if he hated that. He would drive his motorbike and go to the police station.

"Um...I'm the pizza delivery person." John might say.

"Huh? We haven't ordered any pizza..." the police would answer.

"No...it's not that." He might say. "I might be exaggerating but I couldn't just move on...so...Have a look at this coupon card." He might have handed the coupon card to them, John would ignore their stares, glares and laughs at him but if this is the way to save one's life then he wouldn't mind.

"The coupon dates are all matching..." If John had done this...Then nothing tragic would happen like this.

Ryan Brown

"Listen, Ryan, this murder happened in this vila. A senior girl got killed. After that we've been investigating profiles and everything and the quality of the murderer was very similar to you. The murderer is about twenty to thirty years old. He might not have any specific job, and he lives alone. And all of these quality, there's you who can be suspected."

"I'm going to murder that guy if I find out who it is." I said to myself.

And if he had thought, 'wait....the murderer lives around the same compound, he's about twenty-thirty years old, and he lives alone...'

"What the heck, there's one guy who has the same quality as me." Ryan might say. And as he remember,

Kevin J told him that there were eight people who's been missing and...he had eight deep cuts. 'Argh. I shouldn't be suspicious with him, I'm just going to go up to him and beat the kid up.'

Ryan would be banging on the 14-1A's door again and would yell him to come out. Then lets assume what's going to happen next.

∗   ∗   ∗

Sydney Langly

"Oh darn...It's raining again..." Sydney tried to call her mom but she wasn't getting a phone, she told her that she was going to pick her up yesterday but an hour had passed. No one was there in the bus stop. "Maybe she forgot" Sydney felt shameful, she knew that these days it's dangerous to walk home alone but there was no choice. She walked home, it was ten o'clock in the evening, she got feared but there were no one in the street, she already caught a cold and she shivered as it rained that day.

"Hey."

She looked back, there was no one. She started to feel more petrified.

"Did anyone call me?" Sydney carefully asked. There was no respond, she continued walking.

"Do you want to share umbrella with me?" Sydney looked back again. One man stood against the wall with his umbrella covering his face.

"Who are you?" she asked.

"You know Lauren, right?" He was coming towards her, his face was blurry and then he finally lift his umbrella up and his face came into view. "You can be my next victim."

Her film got cut then, she couldn't remember after then but when she woke up she was in a basement room and a pizza right in front of her. She got tied up tightly as almost risky to breathe.

"I'll let you go home when you finish your pizza." He smiled. Sydney looked at the door to see any chance to escape. Chance? It was a chance for her to die. A huge trunk case and a pickaxe laid on top, just like what Lauren saw right before she died. "My life is over now."

Suddenly there was a huge knocking on the door, Mr. Walker growled and he went up. She had no hope, who would it be? 'I wish my mom was here.' Suddenly huge sounds got dominated upstairs, she couldn't predict anything but breaking and hitting noise were going on. She started to feel dizzy, her eyes started to blur and her energy couldn't handle anything anymore.

When she woke up, she got surprised, her mom was next to her smiling. It was a dream come true.

"Mom?" Sydney said. "How...what happened?"

"Shh... Let's keep it quiet, okay?" she said. "I told you, mommy is always there for you no matter what." She kissed on her cheek. She couldn't feel any warmer than this. Later Sydney found out that Mr. Tong shadowed her the whole time. When he saw her fainting and got forced into Mr. Walker's house, he called the police right away and tragedy got prevented.

So, what happened to Mr. Walker? Well, that's another story.

The Forest

By Jacob Kim

"Halt! Stop right there!" yelled Mr. Stucker, with all seriousness, from the other side of the cafeteria. "You boys will follow me."

In the cafeteria of Concordia International School of Shanghai, Jack and Kyle got caught playing Call of Duty 4: Modern Warfare, a popular first person shooter video game. In the meantime, Janice and Christine got caught for breaking the school's uniform policy for the fifth time. Normally the students would get a detention. Unfortunately these guys made a bad decision at the wrong time. The eighth grade community busily planned for the upcoming eighth grade trip to Beijing. The eighth grade teachers and faculty members of the school were all busy because of the trip.

"Hmm..." said Mr. Smith, the middle school principal, while looking at the calendar. "You students know about the upcoming trip to Beijing, right? You won't be going to the trip and that will be the punishment. Since all the teachers are busy planning for the trip, there isn't anyone to give you a detention."

"You're funny Mr. Smith," giggled Kyle, who had no idea how serious Mr. Smith was.

"What! No, you can't do that! Everyone's going! And didn't our parents already pay for the plane tickets and everything?" exclaimed Jack.

"I'm serious. Unless you come up with another punishment, you students will be staying home next week," insisted Mr. Smith.

Janice and Christine's faces lid up as if they came up with an idea, and they looked at each other.

"How about we make a handbook about the trip for students?" asked Janice.

Jack, a computer master, easily made a handbook about the trip. After two hours, Kyle, Jack, Janice, and Christine passed out handbooks in the eight-grade hallway.

"Hey man, take this. It's a handbook for the upcoming trip to Beijing," explained Kyle to a random guy he never met, assuming that he's an eighth grader.

"I don't even want to go on the trip! I could just stay home for a week and play basketball or games," complained Kyle.

"Oh, stop complaining Kyle. If you don't go on the trip, you'll be so outdated and you won't get any of the jokes," explained Christine. "You'd be a loner. Would you like that Kyle?"

Kyle stared at the handbook for a while and started handing out handbooks again, this time with more energy.

At the end of the day, Kyle didn't realize but he knew almost everything about the trip to Beijing. Maybe it wasn't that unfortunate to skip the detention and get another punishment. Maybe Kyle was destined to be on the trip.

That night Kyle fell asleep unaware of the people in

the forests of the Great Wall of China and the danger that waited for him. Thunder rumbled and lightning flickered in a village in the forests of Great Wall of China. People gathered around a fire pit, dancing and singing to an unknown language. These people were dangerous. To Kyle and his oblivious friends.

The day of the trip arrived and it excited Kyle but also made him anxious. He was excited that he would be having fun at Beijing and he worried that he might cause trouble during the trip. Kyle looked for Jack, Janice, and Christine in the crowded hallway. Once they found each other they got on the bus and headed towards the airport.

"What's up?" asked Kyle.

"Nothing much. Just a bit tired because I couldn't sleep last night," answered Jack, looking out the bus window.

"Same here! I couldn't sleep at all last night. I guess we're all excited and nervous," said Janice.

"Oh, by the way," cut in Kyle, "the teachers are gonna be keeping an eye on us so we have to be careful of what we do."

"Oh yeah. They're giving us three chances or something. I'm so nervous. I just hope we don't get in trouble or anything," said Christine, quietly.

The bus stopped at the airport and everyone got off. There were a lot of different people at the airport. After walking by a lot of people and having shoulders touch each other's shoulders, Kyle got on the plane.

Kyle and his friends chatted for a while. He looked outside the window of the airplane and saw the Great Wall of China. He anticipated the Great Wall hike the most in the trip. Kyle slowly fell asleep while his friends chatted.

Kyle felt someone shaking him. "Wake up," Jack said. "We're almost there."

Kyle blinked a few times and stretched his arms out

while yawning. He stared at the information screen in front of him. It said that in ten minutes the plane would arrive in the Beijing International Airport. Ten minutes flied by very fast and everyone started gathering their luggage together. When everyone got off the plane and went through the security check, it became evident that the girls' luggage was a lot bigger than the guys'. Kyle wondered why; he packed everything listed in the packing list, but maybe girls' sizes were different.

"Jack, did you notice that girls' bags are so much bigger than guys' bags?" asked Kyle while waiting in line for the security check.

"Hmm... Probably because brought everything on the list," replied Jack, scratching his head.

"You didn't bring everything on the packing list? Dude don't tell any of the teachers that!" whispered Kyle.

"Yeah! Jack, you were suppose to bring everything on the packing list," laughed Kevin, standing behind Kyle.

Jack looked away as if he didn't hear anything. It became Kyle's turn to go through the security check. Kyle put his belongings on the security check desk and walked by the scanner. The gray LED lights above the scanner turned red and made a beep noise. The security guard walked up to Kyle with a security scanner bar. She swiped through Kyle's body with the bar, from head to toe. When it reached his waist, the bar started to beep. Everyone's eyes were on Kyle and the security woman. Kyle reached into his pocket and felt a wooden handle. He wrapped his fingers around it and took it out of his pocket. It was a knife. Everyone's attention changed to the knife. The knife had an ancient look with brown handles and reflective metal. Kyle found four craved letters on the knife: LOST. Everything confused Kyle. The security guard took the knife and opened Kyle's luggage to check if anything else had to be taken away. They didn't find anything in Kyle's luggage and anxiously let him pass the scanner. Kyle thought back and realized that he never owned a knife and never put it in his pocket.

"Dude," said Jack, as he walked up, "what's with the knife?"

"I don't know," replied Kyle, as he tried to listen to the murmurs around him.

"Why did you have that knife in your pocket? Did you put it in?" asked Jack, curiously but also frightened.

"I've never seen that knife and I don't ever remember myself putting that knife in my pocket," replied Kyle.

"Then how'd it get there?" added Jack.

"I have no idea," remarked Kyle.

Kyle and Jack walked with their luggage to where the chaperones were. After a brief talk with the chaperones the school headed to the hotel. As soon as Kyle got off the bus, there were gigantic letters on the wall saying: Butterfly Season Hotel. Sounded like a typical four-star hotel. Jack and Kyle were roommates and so were Janice and Christine. The chaperones handed out the keys and when Jack and Kyle turned to head off to their rooms, the one chaperone made a quick announcement.

"Where do you think you're going?" barked Mrs. Stucker. "Okay so, it has been a busy day today. Once students get their keys, they may quietly go to their rooms. Lights must be out by ten o'clock and there will be punishments if that's not done. Do any of the teachers have announcements?"

The teachers shook their heads and the Mrs. Stucker gave the crowd a hand signal meaning that we can go. Jack and Kyle continued their way to their room. They were the first to get their keys so they got on the elevator alone. After pressing the fifth floor, Kyle quickly pressed the close button so that no one else gets on the elevator. With an alarm sound, the door opened. Kyle stepped from the lighted elevator into the dark, quiet hallway. They went up to the closest door and it read 502 and their room was 510. Kyle went left and Jack went right to see which way was to 510.

After about ten seconds Jack claimed," Kyle, it's this way"

Kyle started to walk towards the other way. He slowed down when he felt like something followed him; he felt a dark aura. He didn't dare to turn back and started to walk faster. Somebody watched him, somebody who Kyle doesn't know but knows Kyle. As Kyle started to run he yelled, "Go! Go open the door!"

Jack started to run and as soon as he reached the door he plugged the key in. To Kyle, room 510 felt very far away when it only took about four seconds. By the time Jack opened the door, Kyle stood right there. As soon as the door opened Kyle pushed Jack in and slammed the door. Kyle nervously double locked the door with his shaking hands.

"Ow..." murmured Jack, "Why'd do that for?"

"There was something... I don't know" hesitated Kyle.

"You're acting very weird today..." added Jack.

Kyle didn't respond and just sat on his bed. They started unpacking their luggage and after few conversations they were normal again. The clock read nine o'clock, which meant one hour away from lights being out. Despite the fact that it wasn't allowed, Jack and Kyle decided to call Janice and Christine through the hotel phone.

"Hello?" answered Janice, with her bright voice.

"Hello this is Butterfly Season Hotel's administration office. We just got a complaint from 404. Please be quiet a little."

"Oh... Ummmm," hesitated Janice, thinking of the fact that Janice and Christine were never loud, "Okay..."

"Ha, ha! It's Kyle, Janice," laughed Kyle, "How's it going?"

"What!" yelled Janice. "Christine and I are just, you know, talking about stuff. So how are you?"

"Wait let me turn the speaker on," said Kyle. "Hey can you hear me? Okay. Jack and I are just chilling."

Jack, Kyle, Christine, and Janice chatted for a long time. In fact they're call never ended with an ending. After about thirty minutes of chatting, there were frequent white noises in the call. A few minutes later the white noise got louder and louder and covered up the whole conversation.

"Yeah. But—" murmured Janice.

Kyle couldn't hear anything so he hung up and the white noise stopped.

"I think someone tried to listen or interrupt our call," said Jack.

"Yeah," agreed Kyle, "But Who?"

"I guess the teachers did it."

Kyle nodded and started to write his trip journal, which was a grade for Language Arts. It became about ten o'clock when Kyle felt tired and sleepy. They turned the lights off and went under their blankets. Kyle couldn't sleep for a while. When he wrote his journal, he realized that a lot of mysterious things happened to him today. The airport security, the hallway, and the phone call brought great confusion to Kyle. Kyle started to have a bad feeling of the trip again. He slowly fell asleep, confused by the day's events.

Kyle and Jack's morning alarm was the door knock of Mr. Stucker, their Algebra teacher. As soon as they greeted the teacher and checked that they were awake, they closed the door and hopped back in to their beds. It was nine o'clock and they had to be down at the hotel restaurant by nine thirty. Kyle thought of just sleeping for ten minutes, of course the same with Jack. Them two slowly fell asleep.

"KYLEEEE!" yelled Jack, as soon as he woke up. "Wake up! It's already ten!"

Kyle burst right up and rubbed his squinted eyes. They quickly put on their clothes and ran out the door still trying to comb their hair. When they ran down and arrived to the hotel restaurant, everyone already finished eating. Their Algebra teacher greeted them with an evil look. As he came closer, Kyle and Jack looked down to their shoes.

"No breakfast for you guys," punished Mr. Stucker. "What's with you two and trouble? I'm giving you three chances, one down, and two more to go. Understand?"

"Yes, sir," responded Kyle and Jack.

Few minutes later Kyle and Jack sat next to each other on the bus to The Forbidden City.

"Hmm Forbidden City," repeated Kyle. "A Chinese imperial palace from Ming Dynasty to Qing Dynasty."

"Wow," said Jack, "Impressive but very nerdy."

"I know. I know," laughed Kyle. "I found it stored somewhere in my brain."

The bus ride lasted about forty minutes. Kyle and Jack both fell asleep miserably, even though they slept more than others. Kyle woke up few minutes before the arrival. Everyone got off the bus and was amazed but Jack and Kyle were starving. As the group entered the palace, exclamations and amazements were all over the place. The tour guide guided us around the rooms and the buildings in the palace.

"Whoa," murmured Kyle, while looking around the room.

Jack and Kyle totally forgot about their hunger and became amazed how the palace is so detailed and gigantic. There were high thresholds on doorways, unusually high. Kyle stepped on it and walked pass the door. The local Chinese people squinted their eyes and stared at Kyle as if he did something very rude.

"Uhh," confused Kyle, "why are—"

"You stepped over the threshold," explained the guide. "It's a Chinese traditional thing where they have high thresholds to stop the ghosts from coming in. Don't step on them next time."

"Oh..."

Kyle was sort of confused but also understood since it's a traditional act. It became around eleven o'clock and Jack and Kyle couldn't resist their hunger anymore. Fortunately the chaperone announced their break time. Jack and Kyle walked by a lot of shops while touring in the palace.

"May we go to the bathroom?" asked Jack. "And where is it?"

"Yeah sure, go straight and turn right on the first hall and there should be a sign," explained the chaperone.

Jack and Kyle walked towards the bathroom at a fast pace. When they noticed that the chaperone's eyes weren't on them, they quickly turned right and headed towards the way they toured from. The shop came in to their sight and after few seconds Jack and Kyle were there. A sandwich that normal people would think it's bland, looked really delicious to Jack and Kyle. It caught their eyes as soon as they arrived to the shop. They bought two sandwiches with no hesitance.

"When you're hungry no matter what you eat, it tastes good," faltered Kyle while trying to cover his mouth with his hand after taking a bite of the unpalatable sandwich.

They slowly headed back to their group, thinking there was enough time because another ten more minutes remained. As they walked Kyle felt the aura that he felt in the hallway last night. He pulled Jack and started walking fast again. Kyle turned left and ran with Jack. They ran in the bathroom hall, which the chaperone told about. As they ran through obstacles, Jack looked back.

"Who is that!" yelled Jack looking at the stranger attired all in black.

"I have no idea! JUST RUN!" shouted Kyle.

They ran until the end of the small street and started to lose the stranger. They arrived at a bigger street filled with people so they started to walk and hide in the crowd. They walked about five more minutes and finally lost the stranger.

"Phew," sighed Jack. "This is so crazy. What's going on?"

"I know right? I think that's the person who I ran away from in the hotel hallway," explained Kyle. "This is so—"

"Hey that's Janice and Christine!" exclaimed Jack, cutting Kyle's words.

"Janice! Christine!" yelled Kyle, waving at them.

Fortunately break time came, so they were able to chat. Jack, Kyle, Janice, and Christine talked about how amazing the palace was. Jack and Kyle didn't mention anything weird that happened.

"Ha, ha, yeah this place—"

"Oh no! It's already twelve o'clock!" yelled Jack. "We had to be at the break place by eleven thirty!"

"Oh! Sigh," remembered Kyle. "I think it's too late, let's just tell Janice's chaperone we got lost and we can tour with their group."

Jack and Kyle explained that they got lost trying to find the bathroom to Janice's chaperone. The chaperone looked very unsure but agreed to let them follow Janice and Christine.

Kyle enjoyed touring with Janice and Christine. Time passed by and it was already lunchtime. Fortunately they could have better food, but unfortunately the groups come together when eating. Which meant Jack and Kyle would have to deal with Mr. Stucker. Jack and Kyle saw Mr. Stucker in sight when they got closer to the restaurant.

"My favorite math students!" said Mr. Stucker, to Jack and Kyle while they were trying to ignore him. "I heard you got lost while trying to find the bathroom when the chaperone told exactly where it was. Plus you guys went the opposite way. Two down, only one more to go."

They quietly went to lunch and tried to enjoy it. Kyle

worried because trouble always followed him when he didn't intend to cause it. Kyle felt sorry for Jack because Jack always got it trouble because he was always with Kyle. After lunch there was another hour-long tour in the palace. The palace was enormous; more than eight thousand rooms and ten thousand buildings. Soon everyone got back on the buses and headed back to the hotel.

"Phew," sighed Kyle. "I'm so tired."

After few conversations, Jack and Kyle both fell asleep. By the time they arrived at the hotel it became four o'clock. Everyone went up to their rooms and rested before dinner.

"Forbidden City actually interested me," said Kyle.

"Yeah," agreed Jack. "Oh I almost forgot about it. Who do you think that black attire person is? What does he want from us?"

"Well he surely is following the wrong people I guess. We're just normal students from Shanghai."

"Do you think we should tell the teacher about this?"

"Nah, it'll just be a hassle and plus, even if we tell the teachers, what can they actually do?"

"Ha, ha, nothing I guess. Anyways I feel really dirty, gonna take a shower"

After Jack took a shower, Kyle took one too. Despite the fact that the teachers told students to save water and take short showers, Jack and Kyle took about thirty minutes to shower. After getting dressed, Kyle and Jack went down to the hotel lobby. The school ate dinner at a different restaurant this time. They got on the bus again and headed towards the restaurant.

"Dude, don't you think we use the buses like a lot?" asked Jack.

"Yeah," replied Kyle. "I wonder how much it costs to use these buses."

After few minutes of the conversation, the bus arrived

at the restaurant. By the look of it, it looked like a pretty deluxe restaurant. The food came out and Jack and Kyle's eyes opened widely. The plate contained tacos, their favorite food. As soon as the waiter put the trays down, they grabbed a taco for themselves and took a bite off the taco.

"This is—," hesitated Kyle, while trying to sallow his taco, "the best taco I've ever had!"

Jack and Kyle forgot about all the strange things that happened during the trip and fell in love with the tacos. Kyle had two tacos in his two hands, biting off them one by one. Time passed by like an airplane when Jack and Kyle were eating tacos. They wanted to eat more but they were extremely full. They wished they could somehow save the tacos and eat it when they want to.

"Bye tacos!" cried Jack. "We'll miss you!"

Everyone laughed and got back on the bus. When they got back to the hotel, Mr. Stucker gave an announcement.

"Did everyone love the dinner?" asked Mr. Stucker. "Who said no? Anyways again lights out by ten and don't forget to write your journal. Good night everyone!"

This time, a crowded elevator greeted them. It got a lot more comfortable when the girls got off at the forth floor. Most of the guys, including Kyle and Jack got off at the fifth floor.

"So tired!" sighed Kyle as he threw his bag on his bed and jumped right in to it.

"Ah me too," agreed Jack.

Kyle and Jack really didn't feel like calling their parents today. They hesitantly picked up their phones and dialed their parents.

"Hey mom," said Kyle.

"Oh hey, how's Beijing?" said Kyle's mom.

"Beijing is really cool mom. We went to The Forbidden City today, the place is super big! Also we had taco for dinner!"

"Oh that's nice! What are you guys doing tomorrow?"

"We're going to The Great Wall of China! I'm so excited!"

"Ohhh, have fun! But also be careful! Keep your heads up all the time."

"Oh, you've been there mom?"

"Yeah, once. Anyways hope you have fun!"

"Thanks mom. I gotta go, lights have to be out by ten."

"Oh okay. Bye! Have a good night!"

"Yup you too."

Kyle just had one of the longest calls. Kyle put his phone down and looked at Jack's bed.

"Boo!" yelled Jack, while shaking Kyle.

"WHOAA!" screamed Kyle, jumping to the other side of the bed.

Jack and Kyle laughed for few minutes and relaxed. When they relaxed and got back on their beds, they started writing their journal. Kyle thought today had been a confusing day, the stranger at the hotel hallway and tacos. He couldn't stop frowning when he thought about the stranger, but he couldn't stop smiling when he thought about the tacos.

"Good night," murmured Kyle, while falling asleep.

*   *   *

Kyle opened his eyes because of the sunshine. The sun shined and the sun glared beautifully with no hint of clouds. It was the perfect weather for the Great Wall hike. Kyle didn't squint his eyes; he smiled and burst right up. He woke Jack up and they got dressed. This time they went down early, earlier than anyone else. After having breakfast they were the first to be ready to leave. When everyone finished, everyone got on the bus as usual. When the bus headed towards great wall, Mr. Stucker had another announcement.

"Okay, so I hope everyone brought a hat, water bottle, and proper shoes, right? Today we will be hiking the Great Wall of China. First half would be mandatory and when you're done you can either go back down or go to the other half. The other half is a bit harder and steeper than the first half. Only people with proper shoes will be allowed. Always—"

Kyle chose not to listen because his mom told him everything. Expecting the bus ride to be really long, Kyle fell asleep resting his head on the window. When Kyle woke up, people were laughing at him. He felt like something happened when he fell asleep. He always had that feeling when he took a nap. Jack fell asleep too. A camera caught Kyle's eyes. Then he realized everyone had his or her cameras out. Kyle instantly turned around and looked out the window. He saw plain land, nothing special. The friends weren't taking pictures of outside.

Then he suddenly thought, 'Oh no—'

He caught his friend flipping through his photo album and there were pictures of Kyle sleeping with his mouth wide opened. Kyle quickly burst up and flied for his friends camera. The bus became a disaster. Kyle jumped around all around the bus searching his friend's cameras. When Kyle was done deleting pictures of him on his friends' cameras, the bus arrived at The Great Wall of China. After another quick announcement and safety talks, Kyle was good to go. Kyle decided to hike with Jack, Janice, and Christine.

"Ready?" asked Kyle, excitedly. "Let's go!"

They all started hiking, in a line. They walked at the same pace, step by step. An hour passed by really quickly and they weren't that tired. Kyle's legs were starting to hurt but everything else was okay.

"This isn't that bad!" said Janice, breaking the silence.

"Yeah," said Christine, "but we still have like few more hours."

Kyle's interest and attention was on the scenery, he took pictures while walking. They walked for another hour and took a little break.

"Are we fast or slow?" asked Jack. "Cuz I don't see anyone like around"

"I think we're pretty fast," answered Kyle, "I think we're fast than everyone else except for the guide."

After a short conversation there came another silence. They walked for thirty minutes, and they didn't realize but they were not on concrete anymore.

"Phew," sighed Kyle, "getting a bit tired."

"Yeah," agreed. "You guys?"

"Same," answered Janice, "Wanna—"

"Guys! Have you realized we're not on concrete anymore?" exclaimed Christine.

Everyone looked down to the ground and realized that they were on dirt.

"Where are we?" hesitated Kyle, while looking the way they came from.

Everyone stopped, confused. Trees were surrounding them, and they thought that was the normal Great Wall of China. Kyle heard small footsteps from the bushes. "Guys be quiet!" whispered Kyle.

A rabbit hopped out of the bushes with a frightened look. "Never mind," sighed with a relief.

"What is this place? Is this supposed to be The Great Wall of China? It's a forest?" said Janice, with full of confusion.

"This is the Village of the Creators. Creators are the people who built The Great Wall of China. Who are known as 'dead' in the outside world." said a stranger, who just walked out from the bushes. He wore black traditional Chinese clothes. He didn't smile, nor show sympathy for four foreigners who got lost in the Great Wall of China. "The village knows your parents Kyle. About fifteen years ago they were the first people to find the village. Your mom had you when she stayed here, that's how we know you. We have hatred towards people in the outside world, because they didn't care about us. They didn't respect us. When we are the people who made this beautiful, magnificent wall. Anyways."

The stranger pulled out a knife that looked like the one Kyle had at the airport. The stranger ran towards Kyle with the knife in his hands.

"Guys! Run!" yelled Kyle while running the opposite way.

Kyle kept on running, confusion and thoughts raced through his mind. He heard a yell from Christine but he kept on running. When he ran until he didn't see the stranger and his friends, he stopped. He panted. He suddenly collapsed. He realized that he left all his friends behind and betrayed them. He felt like he killed someone. He felt so miserable. He burst right up and started running back to where his friends were.

When he got to where his friends used to be, he realized they were gone. He panicked; he pulled his hair and worked his brain. He ran in to the bushes the stranger came out from. He ran and ran without having any emotions, or feelings. He saw the sun shine come from far away in the forest. His body was heavy as a stone but his legs were light as fur.

"Oh my—"

A cliff. He ran with all his power and he reached the end. A cliff. The cliff was about a hundred meter high. A river went under the cliff. Kyle closed his eyes and slowly took one step. Pictures of his parents and his friends popped up in his mind. He took another step and *splash.* Kyle was gone.

I Am My Own Enemy

By Joyce Lam

May 21, 2003

"Ow! Ow! My head! It hurts so badly!" Twenty-one-year-old Taylor Colburn awoke in her dark dormitory to a sharp stinging in her skull. Clenching her teeth, she clutched at her temples so firmly that she nearly yanked out a patch of hair. Tears streamed down her pale cheeks.

"Make it go away! Please make it go away!" Taylor wailed desperately and glanced around the room for anything to relieve her pain. She spotted a Tylenol bottle on her desk, which she snatched up frantically, only to find that it was empty.

"Oh, right. I had a similar headache attack yesterday, and I took the last pill," Taylor recalled. By now, she felt as if her skull was about to explode, and, on top of that, she also began to experience nausea. Taylor forcefully squeezed her head and pinched her eyes shut, but nothing would ease the pain. In a desperate last resort, she seized her phone and punched in 9-1-1.

*   *   *

A fiery radiance tinged the horizon as the morning sun peeked above the Pennsylvanian hills. The first rays of sunlight crept stealthily into Saint Mary's hospital and cast a ruddy glow over all that lay in its path. As patients began to stir, nurses bustled through the wards, engrossed once again in their routine hospital duties. In the waiting room, however, where Taylor sat alone with hands folded tightly, absolute silence dominated. The lanky girl stared wide-eyed into blank space and pursed her lips in a thin grim line.

Suddenly, a door leading from the hospital's east wing squeaked open, and a middle-aged man in a long, white lab coat emerged. He held a tan folder containing a thick stack of papers. Taylor turned her head wearily, but at the sight of the doctor, she immediately leapt to her feet.

"Doctor Morrison, what are the results? Is there anything wrong with me? How did you get rid of my headache?"

Richard Morrison, the head doctor of the oncology division at Saint Mary's Hospital, opened his folder and shook his head. "I'm so sorry, Ms. Colburn. According to the MRI brain scans that we did for you earlier, a malignant tumor has formed from the glial tissues in your brain. You have developed a case of glioma, which is a type of brain cancer. As for the headaches that you have been experiencing, they are symptoms of having a brain tumor, and to get rid of them, we simply injected a dose of rizatriptan. I'm very sorry about your condition."

"You have developed...a type of brain cancer" were the only words that Taylor heard. Her heart skipped a beat as the statement sank in slowly. She inhaled and exhaled deeply to try to appear calm, but her shaking voice betrayed her. "So... So what does this mean, Doctor? Should I undergo surgery to remove the tumor? Or... Or will chemotherapy work better? How much longer will I live? Do I have to stay in the hospital?"

Richard paused for a moment and sighed sadly. "Ms. Colburn, I suggest that you neither undergo surgery nor treatment."

"Excuse me? Did I hear you incorrectly?"

"No, Ms. Colburn, you didn't. I'm very sorry, but you are already in the final stage of brain cancer. A tumor the size of a golf ball has firmly lodged itself in your cerebrum, and there is little we can do about it. Performing surgery on the brain would pose to be extremely dangerous, and there is only a thirty percent chance that you would survive the operation."

"What about treatment? Will treatment be able to improve my conditions? Would I be better off if I stayed at the hospital?"

"Ms. Colburn, please do not panic and let me explain. In the brain, there is a biological structure called the blood brain barrier, which monitors the entrance of chemicals into the brain. Because of this barrier, many chemicals in typical cancer-treating drugs are unable to enter the nervous system to destroy malignant cells. Therefore, there is only one type of treatment that is able to successfully treat brain cancer."

"What is it, Doctor? If it works, I would like to undergo this treatment. I don't care how much money it costs. I'll get a few part-time jobs or something. And if I have to stay at the hospital, I don't mind that either. I'll do anything, anything to destroy the tumor in my brain."

"Ma'am, if you had been at a less critical stage, I would gladly give you my consent to undergo treatment. However, the treatment lasts for over a year, and it has been predicted that you only have one more month to live. I'm sorry, but we have already done our best."

A huge lump formed in Taylor's throat; she struggled to speak. "One more month? Only...Only a month until I die?"

"I'm so sorry, but I believe so, Ms. Colburn." Doctor Morrison ran his hand through his graying hair and bowed his head. Finally, after a moment's pause, he spoke again. "Ms. Colburn, I advise you to make good use of your remaining time on earth and spend it with your family. Since you are not required to remain in the hospital, complete all the tasks you wish to complete, and visit all the people you wish to visit. But most importantly, make sure your family members know that you love them."

With moist, glistening eyes, Taylor nodded a grateful thanks to the doctor and hurried to leave. Tears poured down her cheeks, and a cloudy film blurred her vision the entire walk back to her college dormitory. "My life is one big blotch," Taylor thought as she dried her eyes with the back of her hand and brushed a clinging lock of golden-brown hair from her damp face. "How could this happen to me? I'm only twenty-one, and I already have cancer! For goodness' sake, I only have one more month to live!"

"I only have one more month to live," Taylor repeated gravely with a sniffle, murmuring this time. "I guess I'd better decide soon what's important to me and what isn't. After all, I'm slowly dying every second."

Memories flooded through Taylor's mind, and she struggled to organize her thoughts. She remembered herself as a child, helpless and fully dependent on her parents, and as a teenager, rebellious, insolent, and headstrong.

Flap, flap, flap. A fluttering noise suddenly broke into Taylor's thoughts, and she looked down to find that a leaf had landed onto her shoe. She paused briefly to peel it off, and in that moment, a memory from her teenage years floated into her brain.

Like today, it had been spring, Taylor remembered. She had stolen some money from her parents and had been convinced that they would never find out. But when they found out about her scandalous act weeks later, they stopped treating her as their daughter. They constantly gave her the cold shoulder and turned a deaf ear to her.

"Maybe they overdid it just a bit," Taylor thought, "but I guess I deserved it. And I never sincerely apologized, went to visit them, or even called them, so that's probably why we haven't been on good terms since then." As Taylor arose from her crouched position and continued to amble along, she jotted down a mental note to be sure to mend her relationship with her parents before her time was up. After all, family was important to her.

$$* \quad * \quad *$$

"Where am I?" Taylor thought as she groped blindly for a light switch. She tried to sit upright, but her head whacked a smooth wooden surface.

"Okay... This is odd. Why can't my legs move around? Why does my whole body feel so cramped up?" Fingering her surroundings, Taylor drew the conclusion that she was in a wooden box. She raised her arms and tried to push open the top of the box, but to no avail. The lid didn't budge one bit. Where could she possibly be? The air smelled strangely damp, almost like how the earth smelled after a light, spring drizzle. Could she be underground?

Suddenly, Taylor heard someone call her name, Taylor Anne Colburn.

"Who's saying my name? Will somebody help me? I'm in here!" She pounded the walls of her virtual prison, hoping that somebody would hear her cries, but the only reply that floated down to her was the sound of a funeral dirge.

Then, the truth of the situation hit her like a blow in the face. Taylor froze for a second and opened her eyes wide. "No! This can't be!" She shrieked and banged on the wooden panels. "They buried me alive! No! Help! I'm not dead! Get me out of here!"

Taylor awoke to find herself tossing and turning in anguish. Her face dripped with sweat and tears left damp streaks down her cheeks, for which a drenched pillow posed as evidence.

"Phew. It was just a dream," Taylor reassured herself. She clapped a hand over her pounding chest and breathed deeply. "It's okay. I'm still alive. I still have one more month to live. Speaking of which, I had better not waste my time lying in bed."

Taylor kicked her covers to the end of her twin-size bed and flung her legs over the side. She swung her legs idly for a moment, then shuffled her feet into a pair of fuzzy slippers. Outside, the sun glimmered and winked playfully, while birds serenaded one another.

"I wonder if there's enough time for me to take a quick stroll around campus before class starts," Taylor inquired curiously. But one glance at her watch already gave her a straightforward answer. Groaning, Taylor leapt out of bed and hurried to get dressed. Her economics class was scheduled to begin in fifteen minutes.

May 25, 2003

Ring, ring. Ring, ring. Ring, ring. Ring, ring. Taylor leaned casually on the dorm wall and drummed her fingers on the bedpost. "Why isn't anybody picking up?" She kicked her slipper across the room in growing frustration.

Over the past few days, Taylor had recalled and pondered over Doctor Morrison's advice about spending more time with her family, and after much consideration, she had finally decided to put the advice into action. But for the time being, her plan hung precariously on the thread of whether anybody would even pick up the receiver at the other end of the telephone line.

"Hello? Colburn Residence."

Taylor breathed a deep sigh of relief. Her hopes of reuniting with her family weren't in vain after all. "Um. Hey, Mom. It's Taylor."

"Taylor?"

"Yeah. Your daughter, Taylor. Mom, I sort of need your help wi-," Taylor bit her lip as a strident, annoyed voice interrupted her sentence.

"Taylor, I'm really busy. And why are you calling all of a sudden? All these years that you've been at the university, you never came to visit. You never called us. You wouldn't even let us visit you! Now, you suddenly want our help?"

Taylor shivered at the harshness of her mother's caustic remarks but gathered her courage and continued. "Mom, I'm...I'm sorry, and I know we've never been on good terms, but I really just-," Mrs. Colburn's shrill voice cut Taylor off mid-sentence again.

"Don't tell me you want money, because you're not getting any. Five years ago, you already took more than enough."

"Mom, I don't need money," Taylor lied. She had planned to ask for some cash to pay medical fees, but after receiving her mother's surly comments, she spontaneously made a decision to give up on that request. Feeling defeated, Taylor sighed and stated meekly, "I'm sorry about what I did five years ago. Right now, I just want to come visit you and Dad."

"I beg your pardon? You're sorry? You want to visit?" Mrs. Colburn asked incredulously, spitting out the words one by one.

"Yeah."

"What for? Oh, I know. You can't provide for yourself, so you want us to provide you free room and board, even if it's only for a few days. So you're indirectly asking for money after all."

Taylor gritted her teeth. Mustering the last of her

patience, she forced a sweet reply. "No, Mom. I just want to visit. Is there anything wrong with that?"

"No, nothing at all. In fact, tell you what, Taylor. You can come visit us, but you have to pay rent for as long as you stay. You also have to pay the electricity bill, the water bill, and the grocery bill."

"Wait. But didn't you guys buy the house?"

"Yes."

"So, why do I have to pay rent?"

"Taylor, don't argue with me. This house belongs to your father and me, and we can do whatever we want with it. In this case, the house works somewhat like a hotel for you."

"Are you serious? I have to pay rent to visit my own parents? I have to pay for my own food? That's the most ridiculous thing I have ever heard!" Taylor's cheeks burned with indignation.

"Well, it's up to you. If you don't want to pay rent, you don't even have to visit us," Mrs. Colburn responded coldly. "Call back later, after you've made a decision, and make it quick, 'cause I have lots of work to do." With that, the phone line reverted to its monotone beeps.

"Ugh!" With one strong swing, Taylor hurled her phone across the room. It whizzed through the air and struck the opposite wall with a resounding smack. "My life couldn't possibly be worse," Taylor muttered as she plopped down on her bed. "If I don't visit Mom and Dad, I'll feel really bad when I die, but if I do, I'm going to have to pay rent! What should I do? What should I do? I don't exactly want to get a job, but how else am I going to earn enough money to pay both my medical bills and my visiting expenses?"

May 26, 2003

"'Do you need a babysitter? I am a responsible twenty-one-year-old girl who loves young children. I can change diapers, feed toddlers, and entertain children, and I charge $10 an hour. If interested, please call 706-852-9048.'

"'How would you like to have your car scrubbed shiny and clean? I am a hard-working twenty-one-year-old girl who enjoys washing cars, and I charge ten dollars an hour. If interested, please call 706-852-9048.'

"'Need somebody to walk your dog? I am a trustworthy twenty-one-year-old girl who loves all breeds of canines, whether they be golden retrievers, Chihuahuas, bearded collies, or anything else. I charge ten dollars per walk. If interested, please call 706-852-9048.'

"'Are you having difficulty managing your lawn? I am a diligent twenty-one-year-old girl who is skilled with mowing and weeding lawns. I charge ten dollars for regular mowing and fifteen dollars for mowing and weeding. If interested, please call 706-852-9048.'"

Taylor read through all four of her ads one more time before tacking them down to the telephone pole. She didn't think that the cheesy descriptions, high prices, and old-fashioned money-making methods did her much good, but she desperately needed some cash. "Well, at least I don't have any grammatical errors or spelling errors," Taylor assured herself. "These ads will just have to do." In one deft motion, Taylor attached the papers onto the pole. She crossed her fingers in hope that a kind and generous benefactor would shortly come across her flyers and would notice the urgency portrayed by her four ads. After all, the effectiveness of these pamphlets determined the future stability of her family relationships.

* * *

Taylor gathered her history textbooks and shoved them into her backpack. As always, all of her classmates had already hurried to their next classes, minutes before, leaving her alone with the professor. "Note to self," Taylor mentally jotted down. "Don't be so slow in packing up." Taylor slung her backpack over her shoulder and scrambled towards the door.

"Wait, Taylor."

Taylor swiveled her head around to face the professor. "Oh no! I must have done something wrong," Taylor thought in panic as she nervously approached her instructor. She faced a brief temptation to bite her fingernails, but she managed to maintain her poise. "Yes, Professor Goodrich?"

As if reading her mind, the professor emitted a good-natured laugh. "Don't worry. You're not in trouble or anything," he lightly replied.

Relief flooded through Taylor's whole being.

"I saw your ads for babysitting, lawn-mowing, dog-walking, and car washing, though."

Taylor froze in her steps as she felt her face flush the color of a ripe strawberry. "Aw man," she complained to herself. "Of all people, why did my teacher have to see those pamphlets?"

"So, I was wondering if you were available this evening from five o'clock to eight o'clock," Professor Goodrich continued. "My wife and I are going out to dinner, and we need someone to watch the kids. Are you up for the task?"

"Um, sure. Why not? How old are your children?"

"My older daughter is eight years old. My younger daughter is four."

"Oh. Okay. I don't think that will be a problem."

"I'll even pay you $15 an hour, since I know that you have a lot of homework to do."

"That's very kind of you, Professor Goodrich. Thanks."

"Here's my address," the professor added as he handed a business card to Taylor. "Be there by 4:45 if possible."

"Yup. You can count on me," Taylor replied jauntily. She turned and practically skipped out the door. Then, she checked her watch, and her skip suddenly quickened into a sprint. Muttering under her breath, Taylor repeatedly pinched herself for not being quicker. Her biology class had begun five minutes ago.

May 31, 2003

"Dear Diary," Taylor wrote. "It's been ten days since I first found out that I had brain cancer. So far, I haven't been having any more headache attacks because the doctor prescribed that I take a few rizatriptan tablets every day. They help a great deal. I still remember clearly how at the hospital, the doctor advised me to spend more time with my family, since I only have one more month to live. So, I tried. Here's the case. Mom and Dad won't let me visit unless I pay rent and all of the bills. Sad, right? Anyways, if I don't visit, I'll feel terribly guilty when I die, so for the past few days, I've been trying to earn money. That's right. Taylor Colburn is earning her own money for once rather than stealing. So far, I have $280. I think that should be enough to cover all of my expenses for visiting Mom and Dad. As for the medical bills, I'll figure something out, although I haven't decided what I'll do yet. Well, I'm going to call Mom today to confirm about my visit next weekend, so wish me luck!"

Taylor gently closed her journal and wedged it under her mattress. Inhaling deeply, she reached into her jeans pocket and withdrew her now cracked phone. "Please let this go well," Taylor prayed to an unknown source. "I just want to let Mom and Dad know that I'm sorry about what I did back then and that I'm a different person now. I hope that I'll be able to reconcile my relationship with them before I die. That's my only request." Holding her breath, Taylor punched in her parents' home telephone number and apprehensively waited.

April 5, 2003

Sparrows flitted playfully in the cloudless, cerulean sky. Flowers held their heads high above the dirt, proudly displaying their delicate beauty. A gentle zephyr swept through neatly trimmed lawns. Peace frolicked contentedly, manifesting itself in all aspects of the Pennsylvanian suburbs.

To Taylor, who rang the doorbell of house 108 on Elmwood Drive, however, the picturesque landscape went unnoticed. A single thought pervaded the girl's mind, and that thought was how she would interact with her parents over the next two days.

Taylor propped up one arm on her suitcase's retractable handle and used the other hand to smooth out the nonexistent wrinkles on her blouse. She pasted a feigned smile across her face and silently rehearsed a few greetings.

Suddenly, the door creaked open and a dainty figure emerged. Small, beady eyes quickly inspected Taylor from head to toe, and a disapproving demeanor immediately came across the woman's face.

"Um. Hey, Mom," Taylor said unsteadily.

"Hello, Taylor," a cold voice replied.

"Long time no see. How are you guys?" Taylor cringed to hear her own awkward attempts at making small talk.

"Well, we were perfectly fine until you came along."

Ouch. That hurt. Taylor clenched her teeth and balled up her fists at the harshness of her mother's statement. "I'm just going to pretend you never said that. Now, where were we? Oh, right. Are you going to let me in?"

"Actually, your father and I have decided that you'll be staying in the gardening shed. You'll be sleeping on a cardboard box, and you can have as much privacy as you want."

Taylor's jaw dropped open. "You have got to be kidding me. That's as crazy as making me pay rent!"

Mrs. Colburn shook her head in disdain. "You should be grateful that we're even giving you a place to stay. But luckily for you, that was just a joke." The woman turned abruptly on her heels and disappeared into the house's vast foyer, leaving Taylor to glance around unsurely.

"That was definitely a great start," Taylor thought sarcastically. "I wonder what Mom's gone to fetch." Not knowing how to kill time, the girl smoothed down her hair and twisted at her golden-brown locks.

Just then, an irritated face reappeared at the door. "Ahem. It looks like somebody's over-obsessed with her looks. Are you coming, or not?"

"Oh. Sorry," Taylor muttered. She fumbled for her belongings and staggered into the house, unable to imitate her mother's brisk pace.

"You had better keep up, or you're going to get lost," Mrs. Colburn snapped.

Taylor knew better than to protest, so she merely stared at her mother's ankles and plodded on. But to tell the truth, she itched badly to glance upwards. The decorative floor tiles suggested that the rest of the house's features held a much greater beauty, and Taylor was certain that compliments would soften her mom's temper.

Seconds ticked away slowly; minutes dragged on for what seemed like forever. "How big is this house?" Taylor wondered. She felt as if she had been walking for hours, and her weary legs could barely support her body weight. Then, just when Taylor's energy supply began to run dry, Mrs. Colburn halted abruptly in front of an elaborately carved wooden door.

"Oof," Taylor mumbled as she collided with her mother's back.

"Watch where you're going!" Mrs. Colburn barked gruffly and, with disdain, brushed off nonexistent pieces of debris from her back. "You'll be staying here, in the guest room. And don't forget that you have to pay for everything." After shoving open the room door with one strong push, Mrs. Colburn immediately turned on her heel and marched out of sight.

Taylor took a step into the room. Her jaw dropped.

"Wow. Mom and Dad must have gotten the house renovated since the last time I was here. This...this is beyond amazing." She unconsciously dropped her bags on the ground and spun around slowly to admire her Victorian-style bedroom. A four-poster, canopy bed took up a quarter of the room, while a full size wardrobe lined one wall. On the right, a door led to a private bathroom, complete with a tub, shower, sink, and toilet. Glaring sunlight streamed in from two windows on either side of the bed, and a Victorian desk stood proudly in the corner. Rendered speechless by the magnificence of the furniture, Taylor could only gape at what would be her accommodations for the next two days.

Suddenly, a knock at the door interrupted Taylor's thoughts, and she leapt up in surprise. Catching her breath, Taylor tugged the heavy door open wide and poked her head out. Her eyes immediately widened.

Taylor blinked and stared blankly, for a moment resembling a deer caught in headlights. "Dad?"

"Hello, Taylor," a gravelly voice greeted. "It's been quite a few years since we've last seen each other, and it looks to me like you're very well off. Do you have a job, or are you 'borrowing' money from people as you used to?"

Taylor tilted her head and inspected her father's features, which she had last seen three years ago. To her, his brown hair seemed to have grayed a bit, and his eyes sunk deep into his cheeks. Without thinking, she suddenly blurted out, "Wow, Dad. I think you're beginning to look more and more like Grandpa."

Mr. Colburn's eyes popped open in rage, and his reply struck Taylor like a sharp blow on her face. "Insolent child! How dare you insult your elders? You know, maybe I have gray hair and wrinkles because I'm old! And maybe it seems like a big difference to you because you never came to visit all these years!"

Taylor bit her lip. "I'm sorry."

Mr. Colburn ignored the apology and continued to

rant. "Maybe I look older because I get stressed out at work! But at least I earn my own money, unlike somebody who takes advantage of her parents' hard work! You know, Taylor, you had better learn to keep that mouth shut and be more grateful. If it weren't for my money, you would probably be living on the streets right now!" Her father's face had turned a bright scarlet, and he looked as if he would blow up any second.

"Dad, I'm sorry. I hadn't meant my comments to come out like that. And just so you know, I don't steal money. Why are you and Mom still holding that grudge against me? That happened five years ago."

"I don't care how long ago it happened! The only thing that matters is whether you did it, and you did. The consequences will carry for the rest of your life."

"I don't under—," Taylor began, but a gruff remark from her father cut into her sentence.

"Taylor, I'm not going to waste my time arguing with you. Just accept the facts and get on with life! You made a wrong decision, and you'll never be able to erase it from your life transcript!"

"But..."

"There is nothing more to say. I came up here only to tell you that dinner is at six o'clock sharp, and you better not be late."

With a brusque twist of his head, Mr. Colburn turned around and headed down the hallway.

"Wait, Dad," Taylor called. "Where's the dining room?"

"That's not my problem. You should be smart enough to find it yourself."

"Wow. Thanks a lot. That really helped," Taylor replied sarcastically. She slammed her room door and leaned against it with her eyes closed. "I can tell this is going to be one tough weekend. And since dinner is in two hours, I had better start searching for the dining room."

• 　　*　　　*

Silverware clinked at the Colburn's mahogany table as Taylor curled up with a book. She had been sitting in the dining room, or dining hall as she had discovered it to be, for the past hour and a half, attempting to kill time by reading. Now, dinner time approached, and Taylor's stomach rumbled with anticipation.

Two dignified figures entered the room and slid into chairs on opposite ends of the long table.

"Oh. Hi," Taylor greeted, glancing up from her book and immediately closing it.

"Good evening," both parents replied in unison.

"Suzie!" Mrs. Colburn tapped her spoon on her plate until the housekeeper emerged from the kitchen. "You may serve dinner now."

"Yes, ma'am," the rotund woman replied and scurried back into the kitchen, returning soon after with three steaming bowls of soup.

"So, um, I guess I should start off by thanking you guys for letting me stay," Taylor began.

"Ahem. Speaking," Mr. Colburn gruffly responded, "is not permitted during dinner time."

"Oh, I'm sorry. I guess you can't expect guests to know all of the rules right away. You'll have to forgive me," Taylor remarked with a simper.

Mr. Colburn ignored his daughter's comment and began to spoon soup into his mouth. Shrugging, Taylor picked up her own spoon and imitated her parents. All through dinner, not one sound emerged from either Mr. or Mrs. Colburn; only Taylor slurped and chomped noisily. Then, when the plates were finally cleared at around 6:30 p.m., Taylor could stand the silence no longer and began to speak.

"Dad, Mom, are you guys still upset about how I took some of your money when I was in high school?"

Mrs. Colburn squinted at Taylor with her hawk-like eyes. "I'm surprised that I hadn't already made the answer obvious."

"Okay, so I guess you guys are mad. But that was five years ago! Why can't we just get along?"

"Taylor Anne Colburn! Don't think that you can sort out this problem so easily! You stole eight hundred dollars from your father! You tell me whether you consider that something to be easily forgiven!"

"Mom, I'm sorry, okay? I already apologized like fifty billion times over the past years."

"You never meant one word of those apologies, and you never made any forms of restitution."

"Can't you just forgive me? I desperately needed that money back then. If I didn't get it to Jesse by the end of the month, she and her gang would literally cut me up into pieces!"

"Why? You borrowed money from them? Don't you have enough common sense to know that you shouldn't get involved with dangerous gangs?"

"I didn't borrow money! I made a bet with them about a basketball score, and I lost the bet! It's as simple as that!"

"You gambled? That's even worse! And it was about a sports score too! That's despicable! How much dumber can you get? You lost eight hundred dollars!"

"Actually, I lost a thousand dollars, but that's beside the point. Look, Mom, I was so sure I would win! The team that I was rooting for was way ahead at half time, but they ended up losing by one point! I thought that I had found an easy way to make money, and I was sure that you would be so proud when I came home with a thousand dollars. I never imagined that I would lose the bet! Since there was no way for me to find a thousand dollars in a month, I gave two hundred from my own account and borrowed some from you. Back then, I didn't think it would be that big of a deal. I thought that I would just pay you back some time, and you would never know that I took money to begin with. Then, Jesse betrayed me and hinted to you that I had mysteriously acquired large sums of money. When you counted your money, you realized that eight hundred dollars was missing, and you immediately suspected me."

Taylor paused and took a deep breath. "So, I admit that I took some money from you, and I know it was wrong."

"Yes, and that's exactly what you said five years ago. You acknowledged the fact that you stole some of our money, but you never explained what you needed it for." Mrs. Colburn stubbornly rejected Taylor's apology and stood firm in her accusations.

"Well, now I told you, and it's the absolute truth. I promise I'll pay you back one day. But please just forgive me," Taylor pleaded, widening her hazel eyes imploringly.

Mrs. Colburn's menacing demeanor softened slightly, and she turned to Mr. Colburn for input on the matter.

Mr. Colburn cleared his throat and stared sternly at his daughter. "Taylor, your actions were extremely irresponsible. You took money from us without permission, you didn't notify us about what the money was for, and you never paid us back. So, let me simply warn you of one thing." Narrowing his eyes, Mr. Colburn leaned toward Taylor until their noses were inches away. "If you continue in your insolence, and you don't return eight hundred dollars to us by the end of this year, I will surely disown you. Understood?"

"Yes, Dad," Taylor gulped. She had never before looked at her father from such a close range.

"Good. Now, you may return to your room."

Taylor scooted backwards in her chair and stood up. "Goodnight, Father. Goodnight, Mother," she said with a nod, mocking her parents' formality.

"Goodnight," Mr. and Mrs. Colburn answered curtly.

Taylor trudged from the room and turned a corner toward the direction of the guest room. Then, she halted abruptly as hushed but fierce whispers began to drift from the dining hall. Retracing her steps, Taylor returned to the hall and pressed her ear against the wall.

"Robert! Do you really want to forgive her? She stole eight hundred dollars from you and possibly even more!" Mrs. Colburn's voice sounded viciously threatening.

"But, Genevieve, I feel that she has repented, at least in part. We should give her a second chance," Mr. Colburn reasoned.

"A second chance to do what? To steal more money from you? Be logical, Robert. If you feed a cat once, it will keep returning to you for more food."

Taylor's cheeks burned at the way her mother compared her to a cat.

"Well, I have to admit that she's quite lacking in manners and politeness, and it's necessary to reprimand her once in a while, but Taylor's just a child! Good morals and ethics will come with increasing age."

"She's not a child anymore! For goodness' sake, she's twenty-one! She can take care of herself, and she should know to behave better. She was only sixteen back then, and she already committed a crime! You can't just let her go! Next thing you know, she'll rob a bank!"

"I'm sure she knows better than to do that."

"She ought to go to jail! In fact, if you hadn't intervened, I wouldn't have even agreed to let her stay here for the weekend!"

Taylor had heard enough. She spun on her heel and tiptoed, or at least walked as quietly as her rage allowed, back in the general direction of her room. As she wandered, the dark halls seemed to glare and snarl at her, and Taylor quickened her pace, praying that her room was near. Finally, Taylor nudged open a door and caught a glimpse of her checkered suitcase. Breathing sighs of relief, she slipped into the room and shut the door.

"If Mom and Dad don't want me here, I won't stay," Taylor convinced herself. "I have no problem with that.

In fact, I don't even like it here. It's way too big. Better yet, if I leave tonight, I won't even have to pack anything. How convenient!"

Taylor laughed dryly and plopped onto the bed. Then, she grabbed her bag and briefly rummaged through it until she found a pen and a sheet of paper.

"Hm. How should I begin?" She tapped her pen on her chin a few times and began to write.

"Dear Dad and Mom,

Thanks for letting me visit, if only for one day. I don't want to be a burden to you guys, so I'm going back to the dorm. The two hundred dollars that you find along with this paper are to pay for rent, food expenses, and whatever else I used during my short stay. I just hope that you guys will forgive me for taking the eight hundred dollars from you five years ago.

Your daughter,
Taylor Anne Colburn."

Taylor reached into her jeans pocket and withdrew her wallet, from which she extracted two hundred dollars. Then, she placed the bills onto her note and set down both articles on the mahogany desk. Sighing, she tugged open the door and began her search for the foyer.

"So much for my hope of reconciliation," Taylor muttered as she groped in the darkness. "But I guess it's mostly my own fault for being a terrible daughter. I wouldn't be surprised if a month from now, Mom and Dad are overjoyed at the news of my death."

April 18, 2003

The sun sank reluctantly beneath the hills as the sky dulled to a tinted purple. Alone in her dorm room, in the exact position she had been in two hours ago, Taylor ecstatically counted and recounted her total earnings from babysitting, car washing, lawn mowing, and dog walking.

"Seven hundred seventy— seven hundred ninety— eight hundred— eight hundred and five! Yes!" Taylor threw her hands up victoriously and punched her fists in the air. "Success! I've finally made eight hundred dollars!"

Taylor couldn't wipe the grin off her face. "Mom and Dad will be so-," Taylor paused. "For the first time in my life, they'll be so proud of me." She beamed with pride and chuckled to herself, at the same time clumsily shuffling all of her profits into an envelope and gently tucking the envelope into her shoe. Taylor stood up and stretched, then glanced at the clock.

"Oh, it's only seven," she read casually. Then, Taylor's eyes suddenly widened in panic. "Oh no! It's seven! My doctor's appointment was at five-thirty, and I forgot about it! No! This is so bad! Now, I don't have any more rizatriptan tablets to take. What should I do? The pharmacy closed at six thirty!"

Taylor scurried around the room in a frenzy, grasping her head one moment, then waving her arms frantically the next.

"Okay. Calm down, Taylor," the girl quieted herself. "Let's think of what will happen if I don't take the pills for a night. I don't think it'll be that bad. I mean, it's just for one night, so I should be fine."

Taylor clasped a hand over her chest and breathed deeply. "Phew. It should be all right, and I had better stop worrying, or a heart attack may kill me sooner than brain cancer does."

* * *

A painful throbbing in her head roused Taylor in the middle of the night. "No! No! Not the headaches again," she cried in anguish. Grabbing her phone, Taylor instantly dialed 9-1-1. Within moments, medical staff rushed into the dorm, and seeing Taylor thrash desperately in her bed, they hoisted her onto a stretcher.

"Wait!" Taylor mustered the last of her strength. "Take my shoes and my phone. Please."

A paramedic swiftly snatched up the items and hustled everyone from the room. "Every second counts! Get her into the ambulance!"

"Thank you," Taylor gasped. Then, she lost consciousness.

April 19, 2003

Beep. Beep. Beep. Beep. Taylor blinked blearily. "Where am I?" She asked herself as she examined her surroundings. Sunlight streamed in through a window to her left, while pulsing, jagged lines covered the screen of a heart monitor to her right. Taylor shifted in the bed and tried to sit up, but her body seemed strangely devoid of strength. Wires attached to all of her limbs restricted movement as well, so Taylor sighed and resorted to a recumbent position.

A few minutes later, a slightly familiar-looking woman strolled into the room. "Good morning, Taylor. You're finally awake."

Taylor nodded politely, trying to figure out where she had seen the woman.

"The shoes and phone that you wanted me to fetch last night are on the bedside table beside you." The woman gestured and smiled pleasantly.

"Thanks," Taylor replied weakly. She now recalled that the lady was one of the paramedics who had rescued her the night before. "By the way, um..."

"Katherine Thompson. But you can just call me Kathy."

"By the way, Kathy, can you call my parents? I don't think I have enough strength to do it myself."

"Actually, we already did. We looked through the

contacts in your cell phone this morning, and your parents should be on the way."

"Thank you," Taylor murmured again.

Suddenly, two sophisticated figures appeared at the door.

"Dad. Mom," Taylor acknowledged with a weak smile.

"Taylor, why didn't you tell us you had brain cancer?" Mrs. Colburn rushed to the bed, with tears in her eyes. Taylor had never before seen her mother so emotional.

"I guess I'll give you some privacy," Kathy remarked and exited the room, closing the door firmly behind her.

"Well, I didn't want to worry you guys. Besides, you already had more than enough reasons to be angry with me."

"Taylor, honestly, eight hundred dollars isn't that big of a difference," Mr. Colburn asserted. "I know I made it seem like money was my most prized possession, but, in truth, your life is way more important. I was so hard on you because I didn't want you to grow up to be a thief."

"Speaking of the eight hundred dollars, I promised I would pay you back." Taylor reached feebly for the shoe on the bedside table. She extracted an envelope from it and handed it to her father. "I worked hard to earn the money. I didn't steal it."

Mr. Colburn's eyes began to water. "Taylor, you knew all along that you would die soon, yet your priority was to set things right with us? You earned all this money in the midst of your sickness and suffering?"

Taylor nodded. "Family's the most important thing to me. I know I messed up in high school, and I made a lot of wrong decisions, but I hope that you'll still be able to forgive me. You were great parents, but I was a wayward daughter. I'm sorry. I was the one in the wrong all along."

A tear trickled down Mrs. Colburn's cheek. "It's all right. I forgive you."

"I forgive you too," Mr. Colburn added. "But you need to hold on. Don't die. You still have such a great future ahead of you."

Taylor shook her head, her own eyes damp. "I can't," she gasped. "I just don't have any more strength. So, I want you guys to know that I'm sorry for everything and that I love you both very much."

Mrs. Colburn began to weep, and she clung onto Mr. Colburn's arm for support. With shaking shoulders, they managed to choke out, "We love you too, Taylor. We always have."

Then, Taylor smiled contentedly and shut her eyes for the last time.

Get Up and Fly Away

By Quincy Larson

"Freedom?" a shrill voice asked. Confused I turned around, and realized what she referred to. She talked about my shirt. "Okay then. If you want freedom, I'll give you freedom. Freedom from that hideous outfit!" The girl screeched as she dumped her soup all over me. I turned around slowly, taking in what had just happened. Soup dripped down my shirt, along with my hair, face, and arms.

"Chick fight! Chick fight!" the crowd chanted, enjoying my little time of torment. I collected my thoughts and inspected the damage done to my newly acquired shirt, ruined. Ugh! That brat! The usually kind, sweet, and quiet manner faded. Ruining my new and expensive shirt was a hard blow.

"You gave me freedom over my hideous outfit, so I'll give you freedom of your greasy hair!" I screamed as I did the finger quotation thing around hideous, and poured my protein shake over her hair. I didn't know why she would call my outfit hideous. I thought that it was kinda

160

cute. It's like most of my outfits, simple. I wore a pair of my dark skinny jeans, a new light grey T-shirt, with a darker grey "freedom" running down the side of it. Topping it off was a leather jacket with the theme of the movie Grease. I am greatly influenced by the T-Birds, and I think John Travolta in that movie is the hottest thing on the planet!

Oh, wait! I'm in the middle of a fight. Now she was the one inspecting the damage done to her own clothes. My protein shake had done the job. Sighing, I thought, this all could have been avoided. It all happened because I bumped into her in the lunchroom. Finding a place to sit, I passed a group of girls that were giggling. All I saw was pink. The sight sickened me and accidentally ran into one of the girls sitting at the table.

Apparently she was the wrong person to bump into, because everyone in the cafeteria went silent. The next thing I knew she screamed and poured her soup all over me. That was how my first day of school started in another new town. I just groaned and walked away so I could clean up the chicken noodle soup that clung to my body.

This had been the most eventful fist-day-of-school I had ever experienced. Obviously, I moved a lot. It was not something I did voluntarily, but instead it was something that my parents inflicted upon me. I hadn't really minded anymore. There were three things I had learned in my extensive moving knowledge.

First of all, my parents didn't care about me. They didn't care what I did or what money I spent. They worked all the time and didn't have time for me. I had accepted the fact and had learned to be alone. Secondly, fist impressions were critical. I was pretty sure I had just bombed mine at this school. Thirdly, I was going to have to deal with this first impression because I was here for three years.

I was a sophomore and apparently my mother had

just landed a "jack pot" job, so we were there until I graduated. This was something I was definitely not used to. It's not like we really needed the money. I stared at myself in the bathroom mirror and saw myself the way everyone else did. I wasn't this quiet girl. I actually loved hanging out with friends, when I had them. I was also freely formed my opinions, but I never got to show those opinions. I walked out of the bathroom; suddenly a body crashed into me. The impact sent me smashing into a brick wall, and I dropped the books I was carrying.

"Whoa! I am so-o sorry!" I opened my eyes and looked up to see a surfer model. Or a fifteen-year-old version of a surfer model, take your pick. The surfer dude helped me up with a long, tan muscular arm and pulled me to my feet. He picked up my books, handed them to me, and then walked off with a wink.

I just stood there and stared, unfortunately with my mouth hanging open as well. I was so surprised that someone had actually been nice to me. The bell rang into my nice, little, happy, rainbow moment. I freaked out and dropped my books again trying to find my schedule. I stared at the piece of paper, and my eyes scrolled down the classes: AP US History, AP Psychology, AP Chemistry, and finally found what I was looking for.

Free Period, Sweet! I walked leisurely toward my locker. I saw at the other unlucky sophomores that were sitting in normal sophomore classes. My "genius status," as the principle called it, gave me some liberties, such as free period. I walked to my locker and after about a minuet, finally, got it to open. A note fluttered down to the floor when I opened the locker door. I put my books onto the locker shelf and picked up the note.

Hey Annaleigh
I want you to come to the dance room and take in what
you see.
See ya there!

Okay, I was not usually the curious one, but this note made me really curious. Fist of all the person had spelled my name right. If you hadn't know before, A-N-N-A-L-E-I-G-H isn't the normal spelling for my name. I had learned to ignore the wrong spellings and just dealt with it. I knew I shouldn't just go off somewhere for no apparent reason. I should've been sitting in the library, studying for my AP classes, which turned out to be almost all my classes. Studying, really Annaleigh? It's the first day of school, and you're already thinking about studying? That's just sad. I mentally scolded myself. I had a two minute-mind debate, which wasn't unusual for me, and decided to go with my curious side. The only problem was that I had no idea where to find the dance room.

* * *

"Finally!" I nearly yelled as I started to walk toward the door labeled Dance Room. It had taken me nearly the whole period to find this stupid room. Who knew that there could be five dance rooms in a school? Honestly, who needs a dance room for polka? Who even dances polka? I pushed the door open as I saw three other doors open. That was weird. What a coincidence.

The coincidence moment was lost when I realized what I was staring at. One of the other people that entered the room, at the same time I did, screamed. I had the same reaction in my mind. My body trembled, too shocked to do anything but stare and cry. There was a woman hanging from a noose that was, in turn, hanging from the ceiling lamp fixture. I should correct myself and say a dead woman was hanging.

The three other people in the room came closer and looked at the pathetic scene that portrayed in front of us. The head drooped down as if someone had snapped the neck and left it to just hang there. The head's skin was pale, maybe even blue. It reminded me of a sickly bruise color. I would be able to deal with the middle-aged clothes that were stained with blood, and the tangled hair that meant the person struggled, and I would even deal with the puncture wound to the abdomen that still dripped blood. The set of eyes stared me down and pricked me deep in my heart. It seemed as if they could see straight into my very being. They were sad, yet had a sort of madness that a person would get if they were fighting for their life. It reminded me of something that I couldn't put my finger on. Then I remembered, lifelessness. I sat down and started to weep and was soon joined by another girl that came over to sit by me. I didn't know who cried, but it didn't matter. The shock overwhelmed me too much to care. I just embraced the girl and wept. I didn't know the poor woman's identity, but it didn't matter, even the most cold hearted person couldn't keep dry eyed when faced with this image.

"It's Ms. Stegglar from the library," someone's voice finally broke the heavy silence after an excruciating five minuets. I looked up from my crumpled position on the floor to the speaker. The speaker turned out to be a boy my age—and abnormally attractive. I didn't know why or how, but his eyes were talking to me and I was getting a weird feeling. I shivered and held up my hand so he could help me up. Instead, another boy walked up and bumped him out of the way so he could help me up. He also helped up the other crumpled girl that was beside me.

The fist boy seemed a little annoyed at this action but ignored it and repeated what he'd said. "It's Ms. Stegglar from the library. She helps you if you have a question or if you need to find something."

"Helped, she won't be doing it anymore," the other girl corrected. Her voice chocked up, and she started to cry again.

I remembered the once happy, boisterous lady that had help me earlier today get my AP books. The bell wrung a loud shrill ring and we realized we needed to get to class or someone might suspect something and come find this horrific sight.

"We have to get to class, or someone might find this place and . . . her." I knew I couldn't miss one of my first AP classes so I just blurted out the first thing that came to my mind. "Come to my house today after school. We have to talk about this later, after we've breathed for a while." I told them my new address and then we all scrammed to get to class. To get to my new AP Art class, I needed to go by the office again. I left a unanimous sticky note on the secretary's desk, who was out at that moment.

I slipped into class at the last moment and realized what I'd seen. I'd seen a murder and only three other people knew about it. As I was getting over the shock I realized something else, one of the people I shared this burden with was the same girl that dumped her soup on me this morning! Great.

*   *   *

I was walking to my house through the woods, when a movement caught my eye. I started to go into super-freaked-out mode. I turned slowly in a 180° circle and started to stroll in the opposite direction. I noticed a figure going behind me as if it was trying to follow me. As quick as you can say that really cool word from Marry Poppins that's really long, I spun around and squared a kick right on my stalker's chest. The figure, who turned out to be a boy my age, toppled over with an "oomph."

"Who are you and what are you doing following me?" I put my hands on my hips and tapped my foot as I waited for the answer. The boy turned over, exposing his face.

"I'm following you because I forgot your address." He grunted as he tried to get up off the ground. "I'm one of those kids who found that . . . woman." His voiced choked at this and I knew he'd really seen the sight I had. I apologized profusely as I helped him up off the ground.

"Annaleigh!" A voice carried through the woods and startled the boy next to me, but being used to my housekeeper's exceptionally loud voice, I just smiled. While I started to walk toward the general direction of my house, the boy behind me tripped which led to me having my face in mud. We were a bundle of two humans, mud, sticks, and anything else you'd find on a forest floor.

"If I'm not disrupting anything, Annaleigh, you have guests." Both of us jumped up at the presence of another person. There stood my housekeeper, Victoria, with a spoon in her hand. She had a skeptical look on her face.

I tried to explain the awkward situation she'd found us in, but was interrupted by Victoria saying, "Yeah, yeah. I don't want to know. You and You," she said gesturing with her spoon, "go get cleaned up then see to the guests who just arrived at the door." With that she turned and walked away. I took this as an exit and started to walk, carefully, toward my house. This time making sure I didn't fall.

"My name's Alex." The boy, who evidently was Alex, said.

Without turning back I said, "Annaleigh Grace."

"Yeah I kinda figured that out on my own. Nice lady that housekeeper is, she's very mellow." I turned to face him and glared. He just smirked.

I started up my front porch steps, when I heard a whistle coming from behind me. I smiled knowingly and asked, "what? Never seen a 12,000 square foot house before?" I already knew the answer. Most people hadn't, it was quite abnormal. But as I've already said, my parents were super rich. If I really wanted, I could've had one bedroom for every day of the month. Even though my parents are millionaires, I like to keep the rich thing on a down low. Exploitation isn't one of the characteristics I look for in a friend.

The doors slid open from the inside by my two butlers, or two of the many I have.

"Afternoon Joseph, hey Bob. Where're the kids that Victoria was yelling about?" We were all accustomed to Victoria, so when I mentioned her, the butlers smiled.

"Afternoon Ms. Annaleigh. Your guests are in the second sitting room." Bob answered with cheer in his voice. I was pulled aside by Joseph, who said,

"I like the boyfriend. He's very cute, a little quiet though. By the way, what have you been up to?" He asked with a skeptical look.

"He's not my boyfriend! " He looked more skeptically at me when I explained further. "We tripped and that's why we're so dirty." Then I grinned at one of my closest friends and walked toward the second sitting room. Alex was right behind me, marveling at everything that most kids hadn't even seen in movies. Walking into my second sitting room, I saw the other boy and girl that had seen the murdered woman. The mood in the room changed as we all remembered the horror we'd seen.

The tall surfer guy that bumped into me this morning, who turned out to be the other boy in the room, broke the tension by saying, "Man. What on earth have you guys been up to? Is there something we should know?" There was only one laugh in the room, which led to two, which ended up with all four of us laughing loudly.

"She looks like when I poured soup all over her face! Sorry about that by the way. I get moody when I'm around those horrible people at school. " She looked at me and silently pleaded for me to forgive her. Man, that girl knows how to give you Bambi eyes, I thought.

"Of course I will!" She leaned in for a hug then noticed my clothes and stopped. I chuckled and held out my hand. "Annaleigh," I said.

"Alexandra, but don't you dare call me that. It's Lexi." She said with slight annoyance in her voice. Shaking my hand she smiled and winked.

"Hey! I'm Christopher, but most people, well, everyone calls me Chris." Chris then squeezed my hand.

"Alex." A voice said behind me. I turned and noticed Alex was still covered in mud and sticks, then I noticed I was too.

"Alex and I are going to go clean up. You guys can go toward the kitchen, I think Victoria's making cookies." Grabbing Alex's hand, I walked out of the sitting room.

"Uh. Annaleigh? Where exactly is your kitchen?" Lexi asked from behind. I laughed and asked the maid stationed at the door to show them the way. Thanking her, I left with Alex. I took him up the stairs to one of my bedrooms. Giving him clean clothes and pushing him toward the bathroom, I left to go to my main bedroom.

I shut the door and striped. I threwed the dirty clothes I had worn into a basket and headed toward my bathroom. I had this obsession with hot showers so I turned the water up and waited. Climbing into the shower, I sighed a content sigh.

"Wow." That was the only thing that came out of my mouth that could've described how I felt. I'd never had so many friends at one time. Well, actually, I'd never had so many real friends at one time. I had a feeling that maybe this school wouldn't be so horrible. Maybe, just maybe, I'd be okay at my new school.

I turned off the water and wrapped a towel around myself. I faced the mirror and saw something. It was the same thing that hindered me from having a real family. The same thing that made all my friends abandon me. There was something I hadn't said about myself. I had wings.

I had been born with wings. That was why my parents isolated themselves as much as possible. They didn't know how to deal with a freaky child. The only mother figure I had ended u being Victoria. She hadn't cared that I was different. She raised me and loved me.

I stretched out my wings and looked at them. I couldn't

have ever hated them. I hated what they did to my life, but I couldn't ever hate the part of me that's most beautiful. They were slender, but strong at the same time. They were pure white with black tips. They were beautiful.

The part that I hated was what came with them. I was an angel, or supposedly I was. The angel of freedom, that's what they called me. I didn't know why I was an angel of freedom. I didn't feel free of anything. I didn't help other people become free. There was no connection with freedom in my life.

"Why do you cause me so much trouble?" I asked. Of course I expected no answer, but I wished for one. Sighing, I started to get dressed. I was almost done dressing, I had everything on except my shirt. I stretched my wings out all the way before I'd have to put them away until, who knows when.

"Oh my goodness, Annaleigh. Victoria makes the best cookies on the . . ." That's where Lexi stopped. The door was open, and in the doorway were my friends. They just gaped. I stood there, my back facing them. I had no shirt on, but that wasn't the issue. My wings were spread out in front of them, thirteen feet wide.

I pulled my wings in and stuffed my shirt over my head. While I turned around, dreading what I'd see, Lexi screamed. Oh man, here it comes. Instead of being looked at like I had leprosy, I was given a huge hug.

"Oh my goodness! I can't believe you have wings too!" Wait, what?

"Lexi, do you have wings?" I asked. I already knew the answer, or at least I thought I did. How could anyone else have wings? Even if there were other people with wings, what are the odds that they'd live in the same small town?

"Yep. See?" She spread out her wings from two slits in her shirt that I hadn't noticed before. Her wings were beautiful. They were a little smaller than mine. They were a chocolate brown with pink feathers dotted here and there. No wonder she likes pink so much.

I'm positive I was glowing. The happiness grew inside of me, making the moment the happiest I've ever experienced. The commonness between us would keep us together forever. The one thing that no one could take from us, we all had in common.

As we did a little girly, happy dance, strong arms engulfed both of us. We turned to see Chris crying. He dropped us and wiped his eyes. Spreading out his wings, he said, "I'm so glad that there's someone else who has a secret like I do." His eyes searched ours to see if we approved. I just smiled.

"Chris, your wings are gorgeous. " They really were. They were just like him, totally eco. They were light brown with green feathers spotted around. He pulled them in as I spoke. "I can't wait to be your friend forever." He gave me a rib-crushing hug. Then he gave Lexi a rib-crushing hug.

I squealed as strong arms wrapped around my waist. I turned my head to see Alex. A single tear rolled down his cheek as he whispered in my ear. "My whole life I've been alone. No friends, family, anyone. I've had this burden with no one to share it with. Now I have you."

I turned when he said this and gave him a peck on the lips. I don't know what made me do it, but it felt right somehow. I noticed his wings outstretched behind him. His wings were the exact opposite of mine. They were strong, black with white tips. We turned when we heard two people clapping. Chris and Lexi were standing there clapping and whooping.

"Chris, you look like a jumping gorilla!" I said laughing. Chris pouted in the corner until I went over and hugged him. Hugging him I said, "Goodness Chris, you're almost as bad as Lexi!" This made Chris laugh and hug me back.

"I don't receive that." She said from behind me. Just

as she was about to rant, the light flickered and then shut off completely. That made our happiness vanish and Lexi's comments forgotten.

I whipped my head around when I heard Alex scream. "No, no! This can't be happening." I rushed to his side.

"Alex, Alex. What's going on?" He looked like he'd just seen a ghost. It even looked like he'd seen something worse than a ghost.

"Are you guys angels?" He squeaked out. He looked up at us with hope. I wondered if that was a hope we were or weren't angels. I looked at the other two and wondered. Could it really be that we were all angels? I doubted it, but I was going to tell them anyway.

"Yes. I'm the angel of freedom." I looked around the room, at the mirror, the shower, the toilet, at anything but his face.

"Me too. Except I'm the angel of humanity," Chris said. I was going to start tearing up again.

"I'm the angel of passion, that's why I change emotions so often." I stared at her. No wonder she changed emotions in the lunchroom so quickly. "Honest." She looked at me with a worried expression. I could feel a little giggle coming out. I tried and failed to keep it in. I burst out laughing at the same time Chris did. We stopped laughing when we heard,

"Oh man, oh man, oh man. You guys have got to leave." Alex started pushing me toward the window. I struggled and turned. What on earth is going on with him? Does he know something? "You've got to go too." He told Chris and Lexi. He looked like he wouldn't give up so they went to the window and opened it. I just shrugged when they looked at me confused. I had no idea what was going on either.

At that moment, there were shouts outside. I couldn't make out what they were saying, but I could tell they weren't supposed to be there. Footsteps started to run down this hallway. I could hear them echo off the walls, chilling my bones and sending goose bumps up my arms and legs. I knew at that moment where Alex was getting his sense of urgency.

I whispered at Chris and Lexi, "You've really got to go. Slip out slowly so the people down there won't see you." Chris nodded, while Lexi just stood there stiff with fear. "Man, we're only fifteen. What is wrong with us?" That managed a smile on both of them.

They jumped out of my window effortlessly and spread out their beautiful wings. Lexi flew up to the about the roof level where she waited for Chris. Chris hovered at the window. "Where do you want to meet?" He asked.

I answered, "The dance room." He nodded knowingly and flew up to Lexi. He turned around and winked before he headed toward the school. Lexi just did a girly wave, which I returned, and flew after Chris. They looked like some supernatural being. Well, they looked like angels. I turned around, ready to argue with Alex. I wasn't going to leave without him. He either leaves with me, or I stay with him here.

As I prepared to state my argument, he blurted out, "Please. Just do it for me. Please." He pleaded with his eyes and I knew I had to do it. I reached up and kissed him, the turned toward the window. I was on the window sill when someone spoke behind me.

"Well done Alex." The voice was cold. I could feel the hatred and evil coming off his words. I turned slowly, dreading what I was going to see. I saw a man, all in black. He wore a mask so I didn't know what type of person he was. He was shorter than Alex, but with his eyes glaring, you couldn't pay attention to anything but them. They were a deep blue. It were the kind of eyes that made you think that if you only looked hard enough you could see their inner being.

I knew I had to get out of there, so I did. I locked eyes with Alex then flipped out the window. I fell a couple feet and then surged upward. As I passed the window that seconds before I had been sitting on, I blew a kiss to Alex.

I beat my wings with as much power as I could give them. I did a little spin then slowed. Out of their reach, there was no way they could get me up here. I hovered a little while and marveled at my gift. Everyone wants to fly, there's a reason for that. Flying is like the ultimate roller coaster ride. It takes all the self-control in the world not to put your hands out like superman, trust me I know. Wind flips through your hair, your wings beat fluidly and gracefully, but it does get a little cold.

The night air was making me shiver. Note to self: next time creepy dudes are trying to get you, bring a jacket. I looked out at the black sky and marveled at the sky. Nothing can get me up here. Just as that thought was going through my head a small prick came shooting up my leg. I screamed. I turned and saw a small dart sticking out from my lower calf. *Dear God*, I thought. With that I closed my eyes and fell. I couldn't do anything except fall. Soon the dart would take over my mind and I'd go completely unconscious.

Before my mind switched off I heard Alex yell, "No! Annaleigh!" And with that I blacked out.

*　　*　　*

In the dance room:

Chris and Lexi were sitting in the cold emptiness. The thick air reminded them of the body that hung there hours before. An hour since they left Annaleigh's house, and the other two still weren't back. They were both frightened and didn't know what to do. Finally Chris broke the silence.

"Let's go get 'em." He said. Lexi looked at him with a tear stained face, confused. He explained with newfound confidence, "Let's go get our angels back."

*　　*　　*

"Annaleigh? Are you awake." My eyes felt heavy in my head. I couldn't open my eyelids yet. I couldn't speak, so I just groaned. I had no idea where I was or what had happened. All I remembered was falling.

My eyes fluttered open to find Alex hovering above me with a worried expression. He flopped down beside me and sighed when my eyes opened. We just laid there. My drugs were waring off, but I still felt like every limb was a brick.

"What do I see here?" Alex tensed beside me. Where do I know that voice from? I wondered. I knew when I looked at the glass covered observation area. It was the man from my bathroom. That's what I'm going to call him from now on, the Man. I giggled and Alex looked at me like I had suddenly turned into a psychopath, which probably had happened. I'd made a pet name for the person who drugged and imprisoned me. Maybe the drugs haven't worn off as much as I thought.

"I'm glad you find this enjoyable. This will be fun," I heard the smile in his voice. "It will be fun for me, but I honestly doubt it will be fun for you." He did a little evil laugh that sorta reminded me of a movie.

"You've got me a long time ago, do you really need her?" Alex asked as he stood up. His eyes pleaded with the Man. What does he mean by 'you've got me a long time ago'? I managed to lean up on my elbows.

"Alex, what do you mean?" I asked him. I hoped it was what I thought. Alex couldn't know the Man. Could he? His eyes looked down on me with shame. Uh oh.

"I'm so sorry Annaleigh. I didn't know. . ." His voice got clogged in his throat. The Man took over.

"Oh dear, you haven't told her? Well dearest Annaleigh, Alex's an angel too. Except your friend here, or boyfriend, isn't all goody, goody like the other three of you. He's the angel of death." I gasped and looked at Alex. He looked away. I could see his shoulders shake, he was crying. I scolded myself then. What's so bad about the angel of death? Nothing. "Exactly. He's a horrible person, hated by everyone. I took him in when he had no one else. It was quite sad really." I got up slowly and sent the Man death glares. He looked as if he was going to go on.

"He's not hated by everyone. Chris and Lexi love him and I love him!" I screamed at the Man. I came the realization as the words came out of my mouth. Alex turned around with surprise on his tear-streaked face.

It was obvious the Man didn't like what I'd said very much. "Well then you wouldn't mind then if you died with him." He growled at me. He pulled a lever positioned near the right of the microphone he spoke into. I heard a creak and a groan as a piece of the wall slid up.

I was surprised by how much water shot out. Gallons after gallons shot out. It was like a mini tsunami coming straight for us. Alex stood in front of me and shielded me, just as the water crashed into us. The impact was unbearable. The weight of a million tons of water shooting at your body was more than I could handle.

I opened my eyes under the water and noticed where the light was coming from. I swam with all my might toward the surface of the ever-growing pool. I reached the surface just in time. I gasped and flapped my arms until I was level. I breathed heavy and tread water until I got my mind around what had happened.

Alex! Alex had jumped in front of me so the water must have been worse for him. I have to find him, was all I could think. I saw a head of black hair rise to the surface. I swam as fast as I could toward Alex in a growing pool of water.

"Alex! How are you?" I asked when I reached him. He was barely conscious, so I had to lift him up as best as I could.

He managed to squeak out, "I can't feel my body. I'm sorry Annaleigh. I didn't mean to kill them, I never do. Wherever I go, someone dies without me even touching them. It's because I'm the angel of death."

"No. There's nothing wrong with being the angel of death." I managed to swim over to the air conditioning vent so I had some support while holding Alex. "Death's not a bad thing. As long as you have God and hope you'll be fine. You bring people the peace and freedom they deserve. Alex, you're a good angel as long as you believe it yourself. Do you believe it?" His eyes changed. He contemplated it for a minuet, thinking about the lie that had been fed to him his whole life. He then looked like he was going to answer me, but the next thing I knew he was gone.

The water reached my chin, and a strong current pushed against me––getting stronger every second. I saw a body a couple feet below me flying through the water with the current. "No!" I screamed. This couldn't be the end. Think Annaleigh. What can you do? I asked myself. I knew I couldn't go into the current or I'd be swept away. The door! I could kick down the door, and the water would flow out.

Before I could dive down into the water, the Man said, "I told you he killed her, or at least he thinks he killed her. Of course he doesn't know that I killed all of those people before, just like I killed Ms. Stegglar. I then blamed it on him so he's forever the bad angel of death in his mind. You can't win you know. It's been ingrained in his mind that he's evil for so long. There's no way you could make him free." I smiled and thought, what an evil man. Too bad he doesn't know I'm the angel of freedom.

I took a deep breath and dived down. My eyes stung as I searched for the door. I found it below me and started to kick at it. It didn't budge. That door wasn't going anywhere. I gotta breath! I pushed my legs against the door up toward the surface. My body soared upward then jerked back. My pants were caught.

I struggled at the pant leg. Come on, come on. Every second my air was running out. I couldn't afford to stay underwater, but my leg was caught. I started to get light headed. It felt as if my lungs were going to burst. I'm so sorry Alex.

I knew I was going to die here. I cried a single tear and was about to breath in the killing gulp when a light surrounded me. It was coming from me! It happened so soon that all I know is one second I was going to breath in water and die, the next I was surrounded in light coming from me.

I sucked in the air, good clean air, overjoyed by the life giving air. I didn't move for a couple seconds before I remembered Alex. "Alex!" I managed to croak out. I wanted to rush over and find him, save him somehow. Unfortunately, no matter how hard I asked my body to do it, it didn't budge.

"Annaleigh. I'm right here." Alex stood over me with concern, but a slight smile was spread across his face. I was astonished so much that I started to weep.

"How?" was all I could manage to say.

"I don't know, but you set me free. You did it Annaleigh." He gave me a peck. "Look, you blew the door down and the observational glass was blown in. The Man is dead." He helped me up, but supported me as we walked toward the door.

I didn't expect Lexi and Chris to run though the door, but they did. They were panting and looking proud. They hugged us even though we were both soaked.

"I was so worried about you. You have no idea what sort of scenarios that go on in a person's mind." Lexi said as she squeezed me. I laughed. We walked through the door to see two of the guards hanging upside down by vines.

"Smooth." I turned to Chris and giggled. We then passed the other two thugs who were now sitting there with dead expressions.

"Oh my goodness! They were coming at us and I screamed. And not like a normal scream or anything, like a really, really big scream. Oh my gosh, it was awesome!" Lexi said at about ninety miles per hour. We just stared for a minuet and then started to laugh. I laughed hysterically as Lexi gave me a sly smile and winked. Lexi and Chris jumped into the air first and waited for us to join him. I was about to when Alex interrupted me,

"I believe Annaleigh." With that he jumped up into the air and joined Lexi and Chris. I smiled and I knew. I just knew I was going to be okay.

What Faith Can Do

By Seth Lee

"Watch out!" cried Jeremy. A silver Audi sedan with a broken bumper swerved past the double yellow line and right into the way of Jeremy's van. Panicked, Mr. Chui, his driver quickly maneuvered the silver van into the lane on the right. "That was close!" Jeremy exclaimed as his driver made a U-turn.

However, Mr. Chui remained calm and relaxed. "Don't worry boy," Mr. Chui said, "nothing bad will happen to this Buick. A holy man blessed it."

As they continued on their way to Jeremy's new school, Jeremy looked at his surroundings. Trees lined both sides of the street. Cars crammed the streets and caused traffic. It was so unlike Tianjin, but Jeremy would have to get used to it.

Mr. Chui parked the van outside the school and smiled at Jeremy. "Wow, what a big school. Well, have a good orientation." Mr. Chui said as Jeremy stepped out of the Buick and through the school gates.

Jeremy stood in awe as he admired the tall silver

179

building that was the high school. A bridge connected the high school building to the middle school building, which was also silver. Blue windows aligned every floor, and it was a magnificent sight for Jeremy. He recalled that his previous school in Tianjin only had one tiny building that all the students were crammed into.

As Jeremy walked towards the high school building, he noticed an electronic bulletin board that read, "Welcome new students to Shanghai International School. We hope that you will have a great time during this orientation."

The wind billowed at Jeremy's black shirt, and his long blue jeans touched the floor as he walked. He stopped to push his green and silver glasses tightly against his nose and then continued to walk.

Posted on the door to the high school building, was a sign that read, "All new students are to report to room H21." Jeremy pushed open the door and admired the interior of the building. The white marble floor shined brightly, and the entire place was extremely clean. Jeremy found the directory and made his way to room H21.

As all the students found a place to sit, a tall man with blonde hair and hazel eyes walked towards the wooden podium. His red tie flapped against his white shirt as he walked. His long black trousers touched the ground, covering his shoes. The man adjusted the microphone and then announced, "Hello everyone, my name is Dr. Finimore, and I am your head of school. Welcome to Shanghai International School, or as some people call it, SIS. I want all of you to know that we don't want SIS just to be a school to you, but to also be your home. We want you to enjoy your studies here and have a great time. And just to let you know, our school theme this year is "joy," so I want you all to have a joyful year. Now today you are all going to be meeting with some people who work in the office to check to see if your profiles are accurate and to introduce you to our school's website. Afterwards, you will be divided into groups and be lead by two ambassadors. They will take you around the school and show you everything that you need to see. So, I hope that you all will have a great school year, and I look forward to getting to know you all."

After Dr. Finimore delivered his speech, the students were instructed to line up outside different rooms and were to wait for their turns to enter. After waiting patiently in line for what felt like an eternity to him, it was finally Jeremy's turn. A tall man with black hair and brown eyes sat on a wood chair behind a metal desk that supported a silver Macintosh desktop computer.

"Hello. I'm Mr. Wang. Come in and sit down. Now what's your name?" the man asked.

"Jeremy Tai," Jeremy answered, as he sat down on a wooden chair.

"And how do you spell your last name?" Mr. Wang asked.

"T-A-I," Jeremy replied.

"Okay," Mr. Wang said, as he typed on his keyboard, "I think I've found your profile. Are you Singaporean?"

"Yes," Jeremy answered.

"Are you thirteen right now?" Mr. Wang inquired.

"Yes sir," Jeremy replied.

"You've lived in Tianjin your entire life, and you attended the school Tianjin American School. Is that correct?" Mr. Wang questioned.

"That is correct." Jeremy responded.

"Good. Now your student ID is 2014112, so remember that. At this school, we have a website called Student's SIS where students turn in their work and receive their assignments. Come here now." Mr. Wang instructed, as he got out of his chair. Jeremy obediently walked to the desk and sat down. Pointing to the screen, Mr. Wang said, "This is the website. Your schedule and class information are all on here." Jeremy looked at the site. Written in blue was "Student's SIS", and there were links to Jeremy's classes and his schedule underneath. "Your username is jeremy2014112, and you get to choose your password, so type it here." Mr. Wang instructed as he pointed to a rectangular box next to the word password. After thinking for a moment Jeremy typed in "Tianjin". To Jeremy, it is a reminder of where he used to live.

As Jeremy prepared to leave, Mr. Wang handed him a sheet of paper along with a blue card. "It's your schedule and student ID card. The ID card is used for buying lunch or snacks from the cafe and for checking out books from the library." he explained, "Now, you're in Michelle Lee and Fred Huang's ambassador group. Just go to the high school gym and look for the sign with their names."

After leaving the room Jeremy made his way towards the gym. As he passed by the entrance of the high school building, he gasped. A silver Audi sedan was parking outside the school. The bumper was damaged badly from a crash. Jeremy stared in shock as he recognized the car that had nearly taken his life.

"Are you admiring my car?" a voice asked behind him. Jeremy whirled around to find a tall Eurasian boy standing behind him. He wore a mischievous smile, his hazel eyes carried a playful gleam, and he wore a white shirt with the word "ambassador" written in yellow on it. The school mascot, a red falcon, was below it. On his chest was a sticker that read, "Fred Huang."

"That's your car?" Jeremy asked with surprise.

"Sure is," Fred replied casually, "it's a bit scratched up from when my driver crashed it, but anyway, you don't happen to be Jeremy Tai do you?"

"I sure am," Jeremy answered.

"Good, cause we're waiting for you," Fred said, and he led Jeremy to the gym. On the way, Fred pushed an Asian boy with spiky black hair and rectangular glasses against the wall.

"Why did you do that?" Jeremy asked him.

"He's a loser, and that's what happens to them in this school." Fred replied.

"But isn't this a Christian school?" Jeremy pressed on.

"I'm already a Christian, so don't preach to me," Fred answered annoyingly.

"But if you're a Christian, then why did you push him?" Jeremy questioned. Fred turned around, his face filled with annoyance.

"Look," he said roughly, "he deserved to be pushed, and right now you're getting on my last nerve. So zip it, or I will zip it for you!" Then he turned the other way again, and they continued to walk. Jeremy remained silent for the remainder of the way to the gym.

They arrived at the gym, and Jeremy stared in amazement. It was the largest gym Jeremy had ever seen. A huge bleacher was on one side, and smaller ones were on the other. Fred led him to a corner where five students stood. An Asian girl, about Jeremy's height, who wore rounded pink glasses, came up to Jeremy. Her hair was tied in a ponytail. Like Fred, she wore a white ambassador shirt. She shook his hand. "Hi, you must be Jeremy." she said. "I'm Michelle Lee. Welcome to SIS. Now that you're here, we can begin."

She nudged Fred, who was listening to his iPod Touch, and he casually removed his earphones. "Okay, so this is the high school gym." Fred began "This is where the whole school chapels will be held. That's all you need to know about it."

Michelle gave Fred a look of annoyance and cleared her throat. "What?" Fred demanded.

"You're supposed to talk about the pep rallies, you moron." Michelle scolded.

"Oh! Right! When a new sports season in the high school starts, we have a pep rally. So we'll all come to this gym and watch cheerleaders perform and some demonstrations by the sports team. Is that good enough, Miss Lee?" Fred sneered.

Michelle murmured something about boys being

immature, and then led the group out of the gym and into the middle school building. "Okay people, the eight grade classrooms are on the second floor. All of your classes are generally on that floor, but if you're in band, strings, choir, sculpture, or painting, those classes are in the fine arts building. We're on the first floor right now, and as you can see, the nurse's office, cafe, and library are all here. Right now we are standing in the cafeteria, and we also call this area the commons." Michelle explained. She then showed them the different stands in the cafeteria, what to do when he forget his ID card, and explained how books were checked out at the library. Jeremy followed the rest of the group into the cafe.

"Fred, it's your turn to talk," Michelle said.

Fred, who was still listening to his iPod Touch, looked at Michelle with annoyance, "Look, I only signed up for this to get into NJHS. Do you think that I care about introducing them to everything in this school? Well forget it!" Fred exclaimed. He then walked away from the group and out of the building.

"What a jerk," Jeremy commented.

"I know! Oh, my gosh! Why did I get partnered with him!" Michelle cried. She looked as if she were going to burst with anger, but she quickly regained control of herself. She turned to the group and explained, "Right now we're standing in the cafe. Most students hang out here during break. We can buy smoothies, croissants, sandwiches, hot chocolate, sushi, Jello, and plenty of other foods."

Michelle then led the group back to the commons. "Okay people, you're all going to take a math test and a Mandarin test. This is to see how much you know in these subjects so that the school knows what level to put you in. So everyone, find a separate table to sit at. The Mandarin and math teachers will be here shortly to hand out the tests," Michelle instructed.

Jeremy walked to the far end of the commons and sat

down at a round table. A large woman with white hair and round glasses came up to Jeremy and handed him a packet, a pencil and an eraser. "Hi! I'm Mrs. Gerrard; I'm a math teacher at this school. This is the pre algebra test, and when you're done with it, just raise your hand and I will come and collect it." The lady explained.

Jeremy found the test very easy as he took pre algebra in his old school. Everything on this test was so simple to him. He finished the test within ten minutes.

Jeremy raised his hand and Mrs. Gerrard came over to him to take the test from him. "Jessica, he's finished, can you come and give him the Mandarin test?" She called out to a short Asian woman wearing rectangular glasses. Then she left to help another student with his test.

The woman called Jessica came over to Jeremy and introduced herself as Ms. Zhou. "How long have you been speaking Mandarin?" Ms. Zhou asked.

"Mandarin is the first language that I've learned." Jeremy answered.

"Okay then. This is the hardest test that we have. Let's see how you do on it." Ms. Zhou said as she handed the test out to Jeremy.

He took one look at the test and immediately knew that this would be harder than the math test he had taken. He wrote definitions for Chinese phrases, analyzed poems, made phrases with characters, answered questions based on stories, completed sentences, and wrote an essay. Jeremy finished the test after forty-five minutes. When he looked up, he saw that everyone else was already done with their tests and waiting for him.

Jeremy raised his hands and Ms. Zhou came over. She took the test from him and headed out of the commons.

Michelle called out to the group, "Okay people, we've had a long day, so now we're going to have lunch. You all should have your lunch cards, each with one hundred RMB on it. We're also sitting in our ambassador groups to get to know one another better." As soon as Michelle finished her explanation, students from other ambassador groups flooded into the commons for lunch. Jeremy chose to go to the Italian stand and was given a plate of spaghetti. He found the table where his group was eating and joined them.

"Move," a voice demanded from behind where Jeremy sat. He was so startled that he jumped up from his seat. Jeremy turned around and found Fred standing behind him with a bowl of fried rice. "Don't make me repeat myself. Move!" Fred demanded. Obediently, Jeremy moved to his right and sat next to Michelle. Fred sat down where Jeremy had just sat and started to eat.

"Okay people, let's all introduce ourselves. Fred and I will start. Fred, would you like to begin?" Michelle asked politely.

"My name's Fred," Fred began, "but you can call me Freddy. Oh wait," he casted a glance at Jeremy, "I take that back, only cool people can call me that." A few people snickered, but were quieted down by Michelle. "I'm from Michigan," Fred continued, "and this is my seventh year at SIS. I'm good at practically any sport, and that's about it."

Michelle cleared her throat, and then introduced herself, "Hi everyone, my name is Michelle Lee. I'm from San Francisco, and this is my second year at SIS. I enjoy reading, listening to music, and playing soccer." She looked to an Asian boy with long hair that reached his shoulders. "Why don't you introduce yourself to everyone?" She asked.

"My name is Jake," the boy began, "I'm from Michigan."

"Yeah!" Fred exclaimed, and he gave Jake a high five.

"I like to play soccer and I play guitar. That's about it." Jake concluded.

Next was a beautiful girl with golden brown hair. She

had brilliant hazel eyes that sparkled with excitement. "Hi everyone!" She said enthusiastically, my name is Elizabeth Strayer. I'm from Michigan and I love to dance."

Next two twin brothers introduced themselves as Tom and Jerry. They were from Korea. Jeremy couldn't tell them apart. They combed their hair the same way and wore matching clothes.

"What about you Jeremy? Tell us about yourself," Michelle inquired.

"Hi. My name is Jeremy" Jeremy began, "I'm Singaporean, but I grew up in Tianjin. I'm a Christian, and I've never lived anywhere but China. I like to read, listen to music, play my clarinet, play Go, and play badminton."

"What a loser!" Fred exclaimed. "Dude! You have no life! Reading, music, clarinet, Go, and badminton! Badminton isn't even a sport. It's lame!"

Jeremy didn't know what to say, he was so taken aback by Fred's comment.

"Fred!" Michelle scolded, no longer calm. "You have no right whatsoever to criticize him! Apologize right now!"

"I don't take orders from you!" Fred exclaimed and he walked off leaving his unfinished rice on the table.

"I'm so sorry Jeremy. Fred just gets out of control sometimes," Michelle apologized.

Jeremy didn't respond, he was staring at where Fred had gone. *Am I really a loser? What if the other students don't like me either? How will I ever fit in?* Jeremy thought to himself.

Elizabeth reached over and touched his hand. "Are you okay?" She asked.

Jeremy looked over to her and nodded.

"Anyway, put your food away, you'll all get the chance to meet your teachers now. The only teachers that you don't need to visit are P.E, math, and Mandarin teachers. The P.E teachers are organizing your team building games, and the math and Mandarin teachers are giving other groups their tests right now. I suggest that you compare schedules with each other and go with those who share the same classes with you. Be back here in thirty minutes, then we will dismiss all of you." Michelle instructed.

Jeremy found that he shared the most classes with Elizabeth. She was in his homeroom class, band class, Math class, Science class, P.E class, and Religion class.

"So you play clarinet?" Elizabeth asked while they were on their way to their band room.

"Yeah, how about you?" Jeremy asked.

"Alto saxophone," Elizabeth answered, "but I also play electric guitar."

"Nice!" Jeremy commented.

"So what's it like in Tianjin?" Elizabeth asked.

"It's a lot colder there and the buildings aren't as large as they are here. Shanghai is kind of better than Tianjin. It's a big city with large shopping malls and cars everywhere. It's very modern here. This is also the first time I've been in a big school like this. My old school only had four hundred students." Jeremy answered.

"Oh, cool. What's Singapore like then?" Elizabeth inquired.

"Well, I only go back twice a year. It is really hot and humid there. Large trees line the roads, and it is very clean there. I love Singapore." Jeremy said wistfully.

"Is it true that you can't chew gum in Singapore?" Elizabeth pressed on.

"Well, it isn't illegal to chew gum in Singapore. You just can't buy gum there. You can bring gum from other countries to Singapore. Just don't litter," Jeremy explained.

After thirty-five minutes Elizabeth and Jeremy had visited all their teachers. They walked back to the commons where the rest of the group was waiting. Fred had rejoined the group and was standing against a pillar with a look of annoyance. "What took you two so long?" Michelle demanded.

"Our teachers talked too much." Elizabeth explained.

Michelle sighed, "Okay. Well, we're looking forward to this new school year with all you guys. You can go home now.

As Jeremy turned to leave, he heard his name called out. Elizabeth ran up to him and asked, "Jeremy, where do you live?"

"Green Apartments," Jeremy answered.

"Awesome! I live there too! How are you getting home?" Elizabeth inquired.

"My driver is picking me up." Jeremy answered.

"Great! I know that it is only five minutes away, but I'm too lazy to walk. Can I hitch a ride?" Elizabeth pleaded.

"Of course," Jeremy smiled.

On the ride back, Jeremy asked, "So what block do you live in?

"Block fourteen," Elizabeth answered.

"Really. I live in block fourteen. What floor do live on?" Jeremy asked.

"Fourteenth floor," Elizabeth answered.

Jeremy stared at her, "That means that you're my next door neighbor."

"Wow! That is so cool!" Elizabeth announced.

They arrived at the block and entered the building. In the elevator Jeremy asked her, "Is this your first year in Shanghai?"

"Nope. I went to Shanghai Western Academy last year, but my parents wanted me to go to SIS." She answered. As the stepped out of the elevator, Elizabeth went to the left and Jeremy went to the right.

"See you tomorrow!" Elizabeth said.

"Yeah. See you!" Jeremy called back.

"So how was your day?" His Jeremy's mom asked him.

He filled her up with the day's events. "I really don't like that Fred boy, but this Elizabeth girl seems very nice. Maybe you two can be friends." His mom commented.

"Yeah. I guess." Jeremy answered.

That night, before he went to sleep, his father came and gave Jeremy a blessing. "Oh Lord," he prayed while putting his hand on Jeremy's head, "I pray that you will be with Jeremy and guide him in what he does. May you grant him peace and success in whatever he does and I pray that you will grant him protection and friends in his new school. May you be with him and may he be an example to others, as you are to us. Forgive him of his sins, and deliver him from evil. Amen."

Jeremy quickly drifted to sleep.

"Beep! Beep! Beep!" Jeremy's alarm sounded.

He reached over and slammed his hand on his clock. Kicking off his covers, Jeremy stumbled into the bathroom and took a quick shower. He then got changed and headed downstairs for breakfast.

"Morning Jeremy," his mom greeted as he walked down the stairs.

"Morning Mom. Did Dad leave for work already?" Jeremy asked.

"Yeah, you just missed him. Now hurry and eat your pancakes, or do you want to be late for your first day of school?" his mom instructed.

Jeremy gulped down his breakfast and picked up his backpack, clarinet, and helmet. He then headed out the door to get his black bicycle. Elizabeth was already outside with her pink bicycle and waiting for the elevator to come.

"Morning!" she called out.

"Morning!" Jeremy greeted.

They got into the same elevator and rode to school together.

Jeremy was excited. It was his first day at school. He sat next to Elizabeth and a large Asian boy with circular glasses. Fred, Jake, Michelle, Tom, and Jerry were all in his class. A tall woman with orange hair entered the room.

"Hi everyone," the women greeted, "My name is Ms. Zane. I am your homeroom teacher. We're each going to come up here and introduce ourselves. Why don't you start," she pointed at the boy sitting next to Jeremy.

He walked up to the front of the room and said, "Hi, my name is Steve Hong. I'm a Korean born American, and I'm from Michigan. This is my third year at SIS."

Jeremy, Elizabeth, Fred, Michelle, Tom, Jerry, and everyone else in the class followed afterwards. Jeremy recognized the last boy to introduced himself. He was the same boy that Fred had pushed aside at the Orientation. He spoke with a strong Malaysian accent.

"Hi. My name is Oliver Choo, and I'm from Malaysia. I've lived my whole life in Shanghai." For the rest of the period, the class got to know each other better.

Humanities turned out to be Jeremy's favorite class of the day. Mr. Umpetuna, his teacher, told them stories of when he was in the military, and showed the class a bullet wound he had taken to the knee. Everyone had to simper at his jokes, but in the end, he made everyone laugh. "You may think that my jokes are unfunny," he began, "but in the future you're going to be in a meeting. And the director of the board will tell a joke that is really unfunny. And you guys can sit back and laugh, because you've heard worse."

At lunch, Jeremy decided to sit with Steve and Oliver. Jeremy soon learned that they shared similar interests, and had a great time talking with them. Recess wasn't so pleasant for him though.

Steve, Oliver, and Jeremy were playing basketball, when Fred, Jake, and a tall blonde Caucasian boy called Lance came and stole their ball. Jeremy tried to get it back, while Steve and Oliver walked away defeated.

"Ha! Your friends have deserted you! What are you gonna do? Fight me for the ball?" Fred taunted.

Jeremy was furious, but he couldn't do anything about the situation, and followed Steve and Oliver. "Why didn't you guys fight for the ball, it was ours?" Jeremy demanded as he sat down with Steve and Oliver.

"Oliver and I don't get into fights or arguments Jeremy. Nothing good comes out of it." was Steve's answer. The same incident happened everyday after that until they eventually stopped playing basketball.

Life in school turned out to be a living nightmare for Jeremy. The teachers were nice, and the work wasn't difficult, but the people in school were really mean towards him. Fred had a big influence over the students in school, and whomever he hated, they hated too. They rejected Jeremy and scorned at him whenever they could. Steve and Oliver were too afraid to defend him, and Jeremy himself didn't know how to get out of his situation. He thought that spending time with his friends might help. Every Sunday, you would play badminton with Steve and Oliver, and he would hang out with Elizabeth every Friday after school. However, this did not change the way the other students treated him in school.

The first quarter passed quickly, and Jeremy had his first three-way conference. Jeremy announced, "I think that my strength is that I am a good public speaker. My goal is to be able to get into NJHS, as I want to be able to help my community. I think that my weakness is that I don't double check my work."

It was his mom's turn now, "Jeremy, you're strength is that you have a really kind heart and that you are nice to all those around you. I think that your weakness is that you lack confidence. Everyday, you'll come home from school, all sad and gloomy. You'll tell me about your day at school, and what those other students say about you is just horrible. You need to have more confidence in yourself Jeremy."

"I agree," Ms. Zane put in, "You seem very sad in school. I've heard what the other students say about you. Those comments aren't very nice. I think what you need is to have more faith in yourself. So let's set a goal for you. How about you build up your self confidence by the next conference."

The next day, Jeremy's mom talked with Jeremy. "Jeremy, there is a youth group in Puxi called SOAR. It is a very nice place, and I think you might want to go there." Jeremy agreed and went the next day.

A tall Asian boy with rectangular glasses came up to Jeremy and greeted him, "What's up man?" the boy asked.

"Uh, nothing really." Jeremy replied.

"Is this your first time?" the boy asked.

"Yes," Jeremy replied.

"So what's your name?" the boy asked.

"Jeremy Tai," Jeremy answered.

"Whoa! We have the same last name. I'm Shaun Tai." the boy introduced himself, "Where are you from?"

"Singapore," Jeremy answered.

"Awesome! So am I!" Shaun exclaimed.

"Alright," a Caucasian man in his early twenties called out to the group, "come take a seat on the floor."

"So, any new comers today?" he asked.

Jeremy raised his hand.

"Alright!" the man called out. "My name is Kenny and I'm the Youth Leader. Stand up, tell us your name, where you're from, what grade you're in, and what school you go to."

Jeremy introduced himself and half the people there cheered when he announced he came from Singaporean. "Alright!" Kenny exclaimed. "Now my question for you is what do you put your faith in?"

"I don't know," Jeremy replied.

"That's alright. Now, let's begin." Kenny announced.

They began by singing praises, and Jeremy found that

he enjoyed singing with them. After that, Kenny gave a talk.

"You are here for a reason. You are all here to learn. Our lesson today is what we put our faith in. Some put their faith into experience, some put their faith into facts, and others put their faith into assumptions. But let me tell you, the only place where your faith should be is in God. He can do anything. Just now we were singing, *into marvelous light I'm running. Out of darkness, out of shame. By the cross You are the truth, You are the life, You are the way. Sin has lost its power. Death has lost its sting. By the cross You've risen, victoriously!* That is just beautiful. God has conquered the grave. Because of his sacrifice, sin has lost its power and death has lost its sting. Now you tell me, that God can't help you with your problems. Now you tell me that God won't be able to save you. Cause no matter how much you argue, you're wrong. Nothing is stronger than God. Nothing. I want you to go home with that in your mind."

As Jeremy turned to leave, Kenny called for him to come over. "Look at that wall," he instructed.

Jeremy read, "Even youths grow tired and weary, and young men stumble and fall; but those who hope in the LORD will renew their strength. They will soar on wings like eagles; they will run and not grow weary, they will walk and not be faint. Isaiah 40:30-31"

"You see Jeremy," Kenny said, "put you're faith into the Lord, and he will help you with whatever problems you may face."

That day, Jeremy returned home full of excitement. "Mom, I love SOAR! The people are so nice and welcoming. The youth leader is great too, and he is very understanding!" he declared.

His mother couldn't be any happier for him, and Jeremy went to SOAR every week from then on. His self-confidence was built up, and his faith grew as well. The people in school didn't treat him any differently than they did before, but they noticed something was different about Jeremy. He was a lot more confident.

During one SOAR meeting, Kenny made an important announcement. "Okay guys! Our October retreat is coming up! We're gonna call it Thirst, because we should be thirsty for the Lord's Word. If you want to get baptized at the retreat, just tell me at the next meeting. I've checked with all your schools. You will all have holiday that Thursday and Friday."

Jeremy discussed the retreat with his mother and father, and they greed that Jeremy should go. "I think that I'm ready to be baptized." Jeremy declared.

"You sure Son?" his father asked.

"Yes. I'm sure," Jeremy replied.

The next Thursday, Jeremy arrived at the SOAR house with all the belongings he was bringing for the trip. "Be safe Jeremy," his mother instructed.

"Mom, it's a retreat. I think I will be very safe there," Jeremy assured her.

After Jeremy had checked in and paid the money for the retreat and his mother had left, he sat down with Shaun on the couch. "So are you excited about the retreat?" Shaun asked.

"Hell yeah!" was Jeremy's answer.

"So the problems that you have with people in school, have you overcome them?" Shaun asked.

Jeremy never hid anything from Shaun as he was his trusted friend. "Their comments don't bother me anymore, but the way they treat me still hurts. I'm like an outcast. I get left out in games. I'm scorned at when I get within shouting distance. It's not really their comments that hurt. It's their hostility and their hatred towards me that hurts. I can ignore it, but I can still hear their comments. If only they would show me some respect, I would be having a great time at school," Jeremy explained.

"Wow, school is a pretty complicated place. Good thing I'm home schooled." Shaun commented.

"Okay youths! Let's go get on the buses and head to the retreat!" Kenny announced. Everyone cheered and they ran for the buses.

The ride to Silver Pool Garden, where the retreat was, was two hours away. Jeremy talked with Shaun for the entire journey.

"So, you seem to be great friends with Elizabeth? Do you like her?" Shaun teased. Jeremy elbowed Shaun in the gut playfully.

"We're just friends." Jeremy announced flatly.

"I'm sure you are." Shaun said sarcastically. "Hey we're here." Jeremy turned around and saw a huge complex filled with white and brown cabins.

"Okay youths! We're getting off shortly!" Kenny announced. A massive applause and cheers followed his speech. Each person was then arranged into groups. "Group F is Jeremy Tai, Shaun Tai, Mark Wang, and Paul Crandall. Your leader will be John Choi." Kenny announced.

When the bus had stopped and every stepped out, Jeremy and Shaun found their group. A tall Asian man with hair that reached his shoulders was holding up a sign that read, "Group F". Standing beside him was Paul, whom Jeremy knew from SOAR, a tall boy with curly brunet hair who wore a name-tag that read, "Paul Crandall." Next to him was a short Asian boy with a name-tag that read, "Mark Wang" Jeremy and Shaun quickly joined their group and were given name tags and booklets.

"Hi. My name is John Choi, but you guys can just call me John. Let's head to our cabin, then we can formally introduce ourselves." the man introduced himself. He led them to cabin 46, and they headed to the fourth floor. They all shared one big room. Jeremy and Mark were to sleep on the beds, while Shaun and Paul were to sleep on mattresses. John would sleep on the couch. The whole group gathered together and they introduced themselves. "So, my name is John Choi. I'm a Korean born American. I'm thirty-two years old right now. I'm an architect in New York. I came to Shanghai cause Pastor David Choi asked me to be part of his team for this retreat." John introduced himself. He then indicated for Mark to introduce himself.

"Hi, my name is Mark Wang. I'm Cantonese and I go to Shanghai Western Academy. I'm thirteen years old, and I'm in eighth grade. I'm here because I would like to know more about God." Mark introduced himself. Next came Paul's turn.

"My name is Paul Crandall. I'm from Minnesota. I'm home schooled. I'm in eighth grade and I'm fourteen. I'm here to renew my relationship with God." Paul introduced himself.

Both Jeremy and Shaun introduced themselves, and John then told them what they were going to do. "You're going to choose a workshop, then listen to a sermon today. Tomorrow is the baptism. Is anyone getting baptized in here?" John asked.

"I am," Jeremy answered.

"Excellent. Well, you won't regret this. Now look in your booklets and choose what workshop you want to do," John instructed.

Jeremy chose to go to the workshop "Dealing With Bullies", while Shaun chose to go to "Why Does God Allow Suffering?"

John was leading Jeremy's workshop, so he remained in the cabin and waited for other people to arrive. After twenty people had arrived, John began his workshop.

"Now. There is one thing that we absolutely hate in school, bullies. They scorn at us, reject us, outcast us, and push us around. You all are probably pretty mad at those bullies right? Well let me tell you something, don't seek vengeance. In the Bible, Jesus said that if an opponent hits you on one cheek, turn around and let him hit the other cheek. Let the bullies push you around, but let me tell you this, 'God always brings justice.' In the end, the righteous will be rewarded and the wicked will be punished." He then went on to talk about how to stand up to bullies and how to befriend them. After an hour, it was time to go to the sermon.

Jeremy headed to the clubhouse and sat in the theater with all the other kids. Pastor John Choi began his speech. "You are here for a reason. Don't say that you only came because your parents made you. You know that isn't true. You are here to learn about God. You are here to renew your relationship with him. You are here to build up your faith in him and in yourself. Let me tell you, you will get what you have come for.

"I know a lot of you are facing problems from peers. Well, let me tell you, do not fear them. Our God is mighty to save. He is with you when you face your problems. He is always there to protect you and guide you. Trust in him, and he will work through you. Do not take on your enemies with force, for it is not by force, nor by strength, but by the spirit of the Lord Almighty."

After another hour of the sermon, Pastor David Choi called for an alter call. "If you want to repent your sins to God, then come up here and do that. If you want to trust in the Lord and put your faith in Him, do that. Come. I will pray for you!" Jeremy got out of his seat along with many other people, and he went up the front of the theater.

"Oh, Lord," he prayed, "Help me stand up to Fred and the others in school. You are the one who gives me strength. I put my faith in You from now on."

Pastor David Choi came and said a prayer for Jeremy, and as soon as he finished, Jeremy felt a presence of something Holy surging through him. He cried. He cried out with all his heart. He cried with joy.

That night, each member of the cabin shared their experience during the sermon, and they were all awed by each other's testimonies.

"Jeremy Tai!" Pastor David Choi called out. Jeremy stepped from the group of people and stepped into the lake with the pastor. It was early the next morning, and Jeremy was going to be the first to be baptized. "Because of Jeremy's confession of faith, we're going to baptize him in the name of the Father, the Son, and the Holy Spirit. Jeremy, do you accept the Lord as your savior?" Pastor John Choi asked.

"Yes," Jeremy replied.

Then he was dunked into the water. "Fill me with your presence oh Lord. I am ready to face my enemies," Jeremy prayed. Then he submerged. "I'm ready," he declared, "It's time I stood up and faced them."

"Do you feel any different?" asked Pastor John Choi. Jeremy smiled and looked into the pastor's eyes. The pastor immediately knew that Jeremy had changed.

"Definitely, "Jeremy answered.

Snakehead Kid

By Eric Li

"Make a decision Phil. It's either you leave this place a man with honor and pride, or you leave this place a coward."

Grandpa Carey held tightly onto the rail while changing his line of sight from the colorful Los Angeles Carnival to his trembling grandson, Phil. Grandpa Carey's gray hair hovered in the light breeze as he watched the moment of truth. The instructor tightened the harness on Phil. In Phil's mind this was impossible. Even though he thought this, he made a decision.

"Grandpa Carey, I'm not gonna let you down." Still trembling, Phil stepped onto the wooden plank overlooking the ocean of people bellow him.

"One, two, three, jump!" shouted, Grandpa Carey. After those long three-seconds, Phil jumped up and into the depths of the crowd. Maybe bungee jumping wasn't so bad Phil thought, but the worst part wasn't here yet, once the falling person reached the lowest point, the person would shoot right back up and down again.

"Don't worry Phil, it'll be over soon," yelled the instructor at the dangling Phil whose face looked like he was about to cry.

"I am never doing that again," Phil whispered to himself as the instructor slowly reeled back up.

*   *   *

Back at school, Phil was no genius but he was good at sports. He was just a normal student trying to make it to college to create a good life. He had many good friends. Phil was in ninth grade now. There were only a few students in Phil's school that weren't his friends, they were the bullies, Ryan, Jeff, and Lester. They were fat, dumb, and didn't care about others. They would often take others' lunch money or just beat them up for self entertainment.

Phil walked down the hallway, carrying his books for the next class when Ryan and Jeff came up to him. Lester was at detention because he argued with a teacher.

"Hey, heard you were scared of going bungee jumping," shouted Ryan loudly, so that even Lester two floors above in detention, could hear him. Ryan and Jeff started laughing after the insult.

Phil angered by the insult replied, "Well at least I didn't fail first grade three times because I couldn't spell my own name." Ryan left with his head down as Phil continued to get to his classes.

Though Phil didn't get straight A's, the teachers still liked him and gave him much support and encouragement. Phil participated in many after school activities such as the karate team and the track team. He was the captain of both teams.

Phil entered his boring classroom, with his classmates already seated.

"You're late Mr. Carey," said Miss Cole in a monotone voice.

"I'm sorry I got caught up..."

"Sit down."

Thirty minutes of class passed slowly, it was reading time in class. Phil read a magazine on tigers. The speaker suddenly spoke, breaking the silence.

"Phil Carey, please report to the principle's office." Miss Cole slowly raised her head from what looked like a pillow and dismissed Phil to go to the principal. Phil thought, was this meeting because of the encounter with Ryan, and Jeff? Approaching the secretary, Phil was directed to a different room, other than the principal's room. There in the room sat a man. His face showed neither emotion nor feelings. He was Chotte Beasley, commander of The Special Operations. Phil sat down, not knowing what was about to happen.

"You must be Phil," said Chotte in a low voice, adjusting his glasses.

"Yes, I'm Phil, and you are?"

"I am Chotte, Chotte Beasley that was. I am the commander of Special Operations, and I am here to recruit you."

Phil replied, "Me? You want me? Out of all the secret agents of the world you want to pick a teenager that has no skill at all?"

"No skill? Let me see, you're the captain of the karate team. I would take that as skill. Also you won many awards on the track team."

"Fine. But why exactly do you need a teenager? Aren't all secret agents supposed to be at least twenty or more?"

"Phil, Phil, always a curious little boy. Our mission was for a family of two, father and son, to be illegally smuggled from Asia to America. The mission starts in a week. Out of all the teenagers on the list we have, you seem to be the most skilled and suitable for the job.

"What about my education? What about my disappearance?" Phil was eager to find out everything he could possibly know. "What about my Grandparents, do they know?"

The secretary popped in suddenly, answering Phil's question, "Your Grandparents are being dealt with. We told them that you're going on a school trip and that you'll be back in two weeks time."

Phil puzzled asked, "And who are you?"

The secretary, still standing at the doorway replied, "I am Mr. Beasley's assistant, Carina Walker. I should get back to my cover now."

Chotte coming out of his silence said, "So Phil, you in?"

"Yea, I'm in."

*   *   *

"We're going in deep, and were going in hard."

Five men and one teenager rappelled down a ten story building in record time. Once hitting the ground, each pulled out a submachine gun and started shooting the targets trying, to reach the checkpoint. Phil, having done this a million times now, was no rookie at this.

Phil had already been at training camp for six days. He did not need advanced training. If he got into any kind of trouble, his five other companions were to protect him at all costs.

"Faster, faster, faster!" shouted Chotte, who was the trainer of the men. These men were trained to go with Phil on a mission code-named: Snakehead. Snakehead was a deadly organization, they dealt with illegal immigrant smuggling, drugs, and much more. Their mission was to take down Snakehead.

After a week's training, Phil was ready for action, and got to his new companions. Fox, Hunter, Hawk, Sparrow, and Falcon were nicknames for the five men that were going with Phil. Phil did not know their real names but didn't really care. Hunter, Hawk, Sparrow, and Falcon were to play the role of civilians.

Fox, (the leader) would be playing the role of Phil's father. Their mission was for Phil and Fox to immigrate illegally with the Snakehead. Fox would be playing the role of a unemployed man with a teenage as a son, who wants to go to America for a low wage. Together Fox and Phil would immigrate illegally with the help of Snakehead. When arriving in America, Fox and Phil would follow the Snakehead members, hoping that the members would take them to the Snakehead Headquarters.

"Okay ladies get back to your rooms, we have a big day tomorrow!" shouted Chotte at the six well trained soldiers that stood before him in a straight line, their backs straight, and their minds focused on the tough man before them.

"Sir, when exactly do we leave for the mission?" asked Phil, not knowing if it was the right time to ask.

"We leave tomorrow!" yelled Chotte.

Those were probably the last words that Phil was ever going to hear before he was going to be put into a mist of danger.

* * *

The rain fell from the sky, as the small jet took off into the misty gray sky. Inside the plane sat seven men, one of them holding a glass of champagne, and the other six drifting asleep.

The seat belt sign lit up as the pilot announced, "Flight attendants, please prepare for landing."

Phil, still dazzled from his nap looked out the window. Indonesia looked like a wreck from above. The polluted river was already turning a shade of turquoise, the buildings all looked run down and unstable, and the worst part about it was that there were clouds of pollution surrounding the plane.

The jet landed in the Indonesia International Airport. Phil and Fox walked down the stairs of the plane, breathing the hot summer air.

"Hey Phil, you think your ready?" Fox asked Phil as he carried their multiple carry on bags onto a bus.

"I'm just scared that something bad was gonna happen. What if we get captured or something? What if we got lost?" Phil was as nervous as he was on his first day of school.

"Don't worry, that's what Hunter, Hawk, Sparrow, and Falcon are for."

Hunter's main job was to take out anyone that would interfere with the mission. That's where his name came from. Hawk's main job was to keep an eye on Phil and Fox, to see if they get into any trouble. If they do, Hawk would be there to help. Sparrow's main job was to organize the team. Sparrow would stay in a hotel, controlling the team, telling the team where to go, what someone should do when in need of help, and that kind of stuff. Sparrow also specializes in gadgets used for missions. And finally Falcon, Falcon specializes in disguise. If anyone needs to blend in, Falcon was the person.

Fox and Phil walked out of the airport searching for the car that would be picking them up. After fifteen minutes of standing in the humid heat, an old Honda parked in front of them. For a fugitive, this wasn't a bad car Phil thought. Fox and Phil got in the back, as the driver wearing a tux put their luggage into the trunk. Once the car had started, the driver took off his hat, revealing the Hawk's impassive face.

"Hawk? I thought you were still on the plane," asked Phil, confused from the fast transition.

"I went to the car rentals after you guys got off the plane," replied Hawk.

"I thought Snakehead was picking us up here," asked, Phil.

"We're supposed to be Indonesian remember? Do we look anything like Indonesians?" replied Fox.

"How are we gonna do that? I don' think we packed

any thing that would help us in that matter," said Phil, getting even more confused about what was going on.

"Your about to find out."

The Honda parked in front of the Indonesia Holiday Inn hotel. There at the entrance of the hotel stood a tall man that looked very familiar, but Phil couldn't tell who it was because the man was wearing sunglasses as well as a hat. As Hawk and Fox carries the suitcases up the stairs, the mysterious man took off his glasses and revealed his face as, Falcon.

"So I'm guessing Sparrow was upstairs waiting for us in a room," asked Phil

"That's right," said Falcon, leading the two into the hotel as Hawk went and parked the car around in the parking lot.

*   *   *

It was the month September, where it was hot and humid in Indonesia. Fox, Phil, and Falcon entered room 112 where they saw Sparrow sitting there sipping on a cup of hot coffee.

"Ahhh...welcome, welcome. How do you do Phil?" said Sparrow admiring his hot cup of black coffee.

"I'm okay I guess, a little nervous at times," replied Phil.

"Well, let us get this kid to look like an Indonesian," stated Falcon, breaking the silence.

Getting Phil to look Asian wasn't easy, Phil would have to dye his brown hair black and bathe in a tanning liquid. The hard part about this mission was that Phil had to act like an Indonesian kid, he would be more attracted to Indonesian characters than English, and he would need to speak with an accent if he was forced to speak, otherwise Fox would do all the talking. Everything had to be done carefully so that Phil's look wouldn't give himself away. As for Fox, Fox's hair was already pure black, his skin was quite dark, from all the training, but only his eyes gave himself away.

Later that day at seven o'clock in the evening, Phil and Fox would meet up with members of the Snakehead to discuss their illegal immigration. If anything went wrong, Phil and Fox may be killed.

"Phil, you need some gadgets," said Sparrow pressing a button on his desk.

Immediately the hotel's wall slid open revealing a cabinet lit up with small lights on the side.

"Welcome, to the cabinet of newest gadgets of the Special Operations."

Sparrow clapped his hand twice, and immediately 3 of the cabinet drawers opened. In the first drawer was a retainer, in the second drawer was a packet of gum and Mentos, and in the third drawer was a pencil.

"This here my friend, is the ultimate retainer communicator, go on put it on," said Sparrow, enjoying his inventions going to work at last.

Phil reached out at the retainer and put it in to his mouth, surprised that it was a perfect fit.

"Now this was how it works. Slide your tongue on the left side of the retainer three times to send a signal to this computer, (Sparrow pointed at the computer next to him). The signal means that you are in trouble and that you need our help. Now, rub your tongue on the right side of the retainer twice, to send a signal to the same computer, telling us that you have found the location of Snakehead head quarters and that you need extraction," said Sparrow, almost losing his breath.

"Now, to continue on with the gadgets. The gum and Mentos are very dangerous items, so don't use them foolishly. In this gum packet, there are six gum sticks, the wrapper of each gum stick holds a tiny metal blade, which was able to cut through almost anything. The Mentos, was a highly explosive device, licking the edge of the Mentos for three-seconds will cause the Mentos to launch the timer of the little explosive inside it. The explosion was powerful enough to blow a metal rod in half. Finally the pencil, my favorite invention of mine. If you press the eraser, the tip of the pencil will extend, causing it to become a small needle, if you press the eraser again, a type of poison will be shot out of the needle."

"Wow, that a lot of gadgets!" said Phil trying to remember everything that Sparrow just said.

"Well, I must wish you luck! Fox and Hunter are waiting for you down stairs.

As Phil made his descend down the elevator, Fox and Hunter were getting ready for Fox and Phil's departure to the Snakehead check point where they would be picked up and brought to a waiting point.

*   *   *

The car drove slowly as it reached Chinatown, this would be where Fox and Phil were to meet the members of the Snakehead. Phil had already put on his retainer, because you never know when there was going to be trouble. The gum and Mentos were located in his left pocket, as his special pencil was located in his backpack.

The car stopped in front of a rundown shanghai style dumpling hotel, this was the checkpoint. Hunter got out of the car scanning the place for any danger. Fox and Phil got out of the car, if no one stared at them awkwardly, then that meant that they were camouflaged well with their new, and uncomfortable appearance. Hunter carried out their luggage slowly one by one.

After unloading the luggage, Fox and Phil walked into the rundown hotel nervous, as there was no walking back now.

Inside the hotel stood two men by the door, each looking Chinese and dangerous. In the middle of the room, sat a man wearing sunglasses. His name was Wu

Hong. Wu Hong was one of the powerful members of the Snakehead. He was the head of the immigration section, his father was the head of all Snakehead sections. Wu Hong's father, Wu Xiao, was on the top five wanted list of the world, but the Snakehead was a big organization, finding just one man, in the billions of Chinese people was like finding a specific needle in the Pacific Ocean.

"Ahhh...you must be Mr. Huang, (that was Fox's cover name). And this must be your son, Jackie, (that was Phil's cover name). Welcome, you and I shall discuss the matters in another room, your son can wait here.

Wu Hong led Fox into a private at the end of the hall, leaving Phil alone in the filthy room. An hour passed as finally Wu Hong and Fox came out of the room.

"It's a deal, our next shipment was tomorrow, you will leave then." said, Wu Hong.

"Thank you so much, it has always been a dream of mine to go to America, but it's just that we don't have enough money for a plane, thank you sir, thank you." said, Fox trying his best not to sound American.

Fox walked over to Phil taking a nap on the floor, tapping his head trying to wake his up.

"C'mon, we have a big day tomorrow, you need all the rest you can get."

*   *   *

The black sedan parked in front of the large ship Fox and Phil would be taking to get to America. Fox took the suitcases, as Phil followed the Snakehead member leading the way to board the boat.

"Where are we going to be?" asked, Phil

"From me and Wu Hong's conversation, we're going to be in a container at first, then moved to a small room, then before we get to the docks of America, be sent back to the container, just for low profile."

Fox and Phil got onto the boat, and were leaded separate ways.

"We're not in the same container?" asked, Phil.

"Looks like not, but don't worry, we're still going to be going to the small room where we'll be spending most of our time." replied, Fox.

Phil was led to a blue container marked, "Indonesian Toy Industries." There was a hatch under the container which Phil would be entering.

Fox's container was red. It would be impossible for Phil and Fox to find each other. On the other side of ship, Wu Hong on his bed, watching T.V., enjoying the life. Phil was in a small container which contained six other people. There was an old man, a couple with one child, and a brother and sister going to America for a better life. Each person was given a two slices of bread, and three bottles of water, this would be their journeys food supply.

Twenty hours had passed since the boat kick off. Phil could stand it no longer, he had to get out. Using the Mentos pack in his pocket, he took out a single Mentos, licked it, and stuck it onto the lock that was holding the hatch door shut. In less than three seconds, the hatch lock burst into pieces opening the hatch. Everyone in the container was surprised, was it true? A teenager stepping up against the Snakehead?

Phil climbed out of the container, realizing that it was dark out, he smiled as he knew the darkness would help him have a low profile. Phil ran past many containers, trying to look for a red one, which may contain Fox. Phil didn't see any red ones, but there was another way to find Fox, maybe Fox was already in the small room which they were going to be in. Phil had to take all chances. Running along the deck of the ship, Phil spotted two men holding mini Uzi's walking down the deck. This was a chance to prove that Phil was worthy of this mission. Phil hid behind a small barrel located near the edges of the ship. Once the two men walked past him, he would make a stealth attack, lashing at the first guard's stomach and disarming him.

Once the two men walked past Phil, Phil lashed his fist toward the man's stomach. Once the man crashed to the ground, the other man stood back, and aimed at Phil.

"Stay back or I'll shoot!" shouted, the guard sounding very threatening.

Phil raised his hands looking at the man he had just attacked, it was Fox.

*   *   *

"So, trying to make an escape Jack, which may not even be your name!" cried, Wu Hong looking furious.

"Take them into custody, tie them up and watch them twenty-four seven!" hollered, Wu Hong. This kind of matter couldn't happen again.

"Just to show these two idiot from I don't know where what will happen to them if they do this again, we will kill the old man in the blue container!" shouted, Wu Hong.

Someone was going to die because of Phil's foolish actions, Phil thought he was hero, but his heroic actions caused the death of one, and the injury of another Fox. Fox was in much pain, when Phil lashed out at him, Phil's hand had hit a nerve on the side of Fox, causing him to have inner bleeding. Luckily it wasn't too severe.

Phil and Fox had been led to a small room located under the deck. They were both tied to chairs, with one man inside the room watching, and another outside guarding.

*   *   *

The ship reached the dock of California. It was very nice outside, the sun shining, the wind blowing, and everyone happy except for two people. Fox and Phil. Their capture led to their bodies breaking down bit by bit,

211

they had not eaten in two days, their muscles were sore, and their tied up hands were losing their feeling. After orders, the man inside the room untied both of them. Fox and Phil didn't have the energy to stand up, and so the Snakehead member hit both of their faces with the bottom of his gun. Inside Phil's mouth, the retainer broke in half. The retainer! Phil thought, why haven't I thought of the retainer.

Help could have already been on the way. Phil was now highly displeased with himself, he had cause the death of one, caused Fox to have inner bleeding, and he just missed the chance of being saved and going back to his normal life.

*   *   *

Fox and Phil got out of the Snakehead car standing directly in front of a large building in a desert, this was the Snakehead headquarters. Around the building were eight guard towers, each containing five armed guards, as well as snipers, and dogs. Getting out of here would be close to impossible.

Fox and Phil were led into the building, inside the building looked like a perfectly normal office in America, but the people sitting in their cubicles were all Snakehead agents, tracking people around the world that Snakehead was going to assassinate, the people in the office were also in charge of all the drug dealing, and much more Snakehead business.

Fox and Phil were brought into room, where there was a man sitting behind a desk.

The man was Wu Xiao.

Wu Xiao was no ordinary man, he was the one that brought the Snakehead to its power, he was the one that started all the drug dealing in the world, he was the one that was going to decide what to do with Fox and Phil.

"Ahh...we finally meet, my son has said some bad stuff about you."

Wu stood up walking to the back of the room behind Fox and Phil.

"Here's what I am going to do with you, I am going to kill you obviously, but in a proper fashion, bring the tiger!"

Phil remembered about the retainer still in his mouth, would it still work? Phil needed backup from Special Operations meaning that he would have to rub his tongue of the left side three times, but Phil had also found the Snakehead headquarters, meaning that he should lick the right side of the retainer twice. Phil made a decision, he would lick both sides.

The fierce looking tiger was brought into the room, as Phil was pushed into the cage.

"Now, don't take too long." said, Wu sitting down drinking tea, enjoying the boy about to die.

Phil didn't know what to do, all he could think of was the pencil. The pencil! That's it! The pencil would be able to kill the tiger, if Phil stuck the needle into the tiger. Phil took out the pencil from his pocket, pushed the eraser and unleashing the sharp needle, immediately the tiger stepped back, scared of the shiny looking weapon, that may hurt it. All Phil had to do was make a distraction, Phil took off his shoe and threw it out of the cage, the tiger still focused on Phil. Phil remembered what he learned in class one day, that tigers are attracted to blood, then Phil had an idea, he peeled off the scab on his leg, revealing a drop of blood, what Phil didn't think of was that the tiger would see the blood, and attack Phil no matter what. The tiger leaped forward at Phil, Phil with no other choice, raised the needle and pressed the eraser once more. The tiger stopped in its tracks as it fell to the ground. It was dead, the poison had already reached the blood system and killed it.

"Bravo, bravo. Now let me think...how do you get out of the cage?" said, Wu feeling that the killing of the tiger was no big thing."

Phil remembered the gum and the Mentos, which would be better? The Mentos would be faster than the gum. Phil pulled out the pack of Mentos.

"Mentos? You think Mentos was going to help you get out of there?" shouted Wu, bursting into laughter with the other Snakehead members.

Phil licked the side of the Mentos candy, causing the Mentos to start ticking off, until its explosion. Phil put the Mentos candy next to one of the cage bars, as Phil got to the other side of the cage, the Mentos exploded leaving the bars around it broken. Wu couldn't believe this, he ordered his accomplices around him to go attack Phil, before the accomplices could even get to Phil, Fox came from behind, and pulled the two men back twisting their necks to their death. Wu acted quickly and ran for the training base in the headquarters building, that place was definitely safe.

Before Wu could even step outside the door, a man's arm grabbed him, holding him onto the ground, it was Hunter.

"I'm knew I'd hunt you down sometime," said Hunter, smiling at the man he was holding by the neck.

Outside, the Snakehead, and the Special Operations broke into war. Special Operations men and the Snakehead gangs were fighting to the death of the other.

Hunter still holding Wu by the neck led the three of them out of the building, into the extraction vehicle. All was calm now for Phil.

* * *

Three days later Phil came out of the hospital, he had suffered from lack of food causing his body to not function normally, he would often vomit, and his body often had pain, due to the soreness.

Fox was still in the hospital, he was still recovering from the inner bleeding which Phil had caused on the mission.

As for Wu Xiao, he was arrested along with the other Snakehead members including Wu Hong his own son.

After Phil, Fox, and Hunter had escaped from the war between the Snakehead and Special Operations, the building had blown up. When Phil was running for the exit, he had dropped his pack of Mentos. During the fight between the two organizations, there had been a gas leak. Because the Mentos only works with some sort of liquid, the water leak led to the explosion of the whole pack of Mentos, creating an explosion, setting the whole building on fire.

Phil would have two more weeks of rest before going back to school, he needed much time to recover, and calm down from all the madness that had just happened.

*   *   *

"Spies, the government's elite. Devoid of emotion. We have no perspective of our own. We are machines, prodigious killers designed to instigate and quash to our advantage. To be skittish is not an option, we must be willful, we must incapacitate all who oppose us. To do so was to increase the longevity of our lives. Only then can we prosper. After these few weeks, we have found someone who can stand up to such expectations, may I welcome Phil Carey to the stage please!" shouted Chotte Beasley into the microphone.

One week had passed since the mission had ended, everyone that had helped made this mission a success was being awarded, especially Phil.

"Everyone, this was Phil, the star of the mission, he was a hero in this mission, even though he did some things that weren't the best choices, he still did a great job, for someone so young, I award him the Youth Honors Badge!" shouted Chotte into the microphone.

Carina Walker walked up to the stage holding the badge in a crystal case. On the badge was written, "Youth Honors Badge, dedicated to Phil Carey."

This awards ceremony was a secret, no one outside of the room except for Fox knew about it. If the world knew about Phil, his life would never be the same.

*   *   *

Phil walked into his grandparent's house as he pulled his suitcase with him behind him.

"Phil! How was your school trip! I heard it was wonderful." said Grandpa Carey surprised to see Phil get back so early.

"It was wonderful grandpa, I made new friends, went to Indonesia, went to California, I even got a badge for helping out the poor in Indonesia.

"Wow, that sounds wonderful, do you think you will go on this trip again? asked Grandma Carey.

"I have to say, it was a once in a life time experience, but I think I'm to tired for all that again." replied Phil yawning, acting as if he was half a sleep.

Phil walked up the stairs reaching into his pocket and pulling out the packet of gum, and the broken retainer, he threw them into the trashcan to recover the best he could.

Not Without a Fight

By Sarah Lynch

Thick, dark clouds raced by the windshield as her aircraft began violently plummeting toward the ocean. Audrey glanced over her shoulder at the increasing size of the blazing fire, which had started because of a mechanical glitch in the engine. Flames furiously made their way from the engine into the cockpit. Trying not to panic, she reached for the radio to contact authorities, but in the few seconds between her looking over her shoulder and turning back around, the fire reached the cockpit. Audrey's hand brushed the radio controls just as they burst into flames. She let out a scream when the fire burned her left hand; she quickly used her unscathed hand to pull the eject switch, and catapulted into the air high above the rough ocean waters.

Audrey scrambled to free herself from the parachute as it pulled her down deeper into the cold depths of the salty ocean water. She finally broke free and swam to the surface, gasping for air. After flipping her black hair out of her face, she inflated her lifejacket. Looking around, the flames from the crashed aircraft illuminated what appeared to be an island not too far in the distance. To prevent further injury from the cold water, Audrey hurriedly swam to land.

Pain burned up her arm from her injured hand and exhaustion made the short swim seem like an eternal ordeal. Audrey wanted to kick off her boots, but she figured that she would need them, so she struggled against the waves and current. As she stumbled in the squishy sand after the long swim, she remembered that back at the Air Force Base in Anchorage, she had less time than usual to inspect her plane. Even the flight mechanics seemed a little dazed while checking the aircraft. Those few minutes would have made a big difference in her flight. Had they been more alert, they probably would have noticed that something was wrong.

* * *

Audrey's burned hand throbbed, and she finally found time to clean it with antibiotics from her first aid kit. The burn would eventually leave a huge pink scar that would stand out on her tan skin, but Audrey only cared that it would heal without further damage.

Although weak from the ordeal, she still managed to scavenge for sticks to build a shelter. Using some limbs from the nearby forest, some leaves off of trees, and a few large vines, Audrey managed to build a small lean-to shelter. The shelter, while small and not very sturdy, shielded any wind or rain and kept her warm inside.

Soon after finishing her shelter, the sun slowly sank behind the horizon and hunger set in. Audrey figured her twenty protein bars to be enough to keep her fed for at least a week; rescuers were sure to find her before then. As for water, she always had a purifier at hand. She was all set. Besides, she thought, humans can go awhile without food. Audrey thanked God for being able to find this island; had she stayed in that frigid water for just a few more minutes, she wouldn't have survived.

Slowly drifting to sleep, Audrey wondered how long it would take for people to find her. She knew she landed somewhere between Russia and Alaska, but on which island, she had no clue. Her handheld GPS, along with her radio, had been lost during the crash. She didn't put them in a secure pouch. Instead, she held them loosely in her pockets; a mistake she made while frantically trying to escape the blazing plane. Looking back now, she realized what a huge loss that had been. She thought that the Emergency Location Transmitter on her plane would help people find her, but the tide was too strong.

"With this tide, who knows where the plane could be now?" she said to herself. A new, but disturbing, thought came to her: Audrey flew a brand new plane. She was one of the first pilots to use it; it had no tracker or satellite to follow it. "Ugh," she grumbled as she dragged her hands down her face in frustration.

Audrey worried mostly about the fact that her mission to gather intelligence about the Russian military would not be completed and she wouldn't be able to notify her superiors. She smacked her face, wondering why she hadn't taken the time to inspect her plane.

Audrey sighed, "Only my third mission. Could I be any more of a failure?" A sudden burst of thunder startled her and interrupted her thoughts, but she let the sound of rain outside help her fall asleep, grateful she had taken the time to build shelter.

As the sun rose the next day, Audrey explored the island, mainly on the coastline. She knew that if there were anyone else here, the beach would be a good place to look for tracks. Also, the forest seemed too thick for anyone to want to settle there. Returning from her exploration, Audrey concluded that she did, indeed, reside all alone on this island.

The days went by very slowly on the windy and rainy

island, and after three days passed, Audrey knew that her chances for rescue grew slimmer each day. "The Air Force has so much technology!" she yelled toward the sky. "How could they not have rescued me by now? Over the days, she never spotted a plane in the sky searching for her.

"This island can't be that remote," she lamented. "It has to be charted. I mean, how could an island like this not be the first place they looked for me? The Pacific Ocean isn't that big!" She snickered sadly at the realization that the Pacific Ocean was, indeed, very big; she had started to lose her mind. Still, Audrey wondered why she had not been rescued; she had followed her flight plan. In the mean time, she decided to make herself comfortable on the island.

With her stash of protein bars slowly, but surely depleting, and her other stash of small game that she had hunted almost gone, Audrey decided to go for a good hunting trip. She desperately wanted something more filling. Fingering her pistol with the idea of a good meal, she headed into the thick, green forest.

A few squirrels and many wasted bullets later, Audrey tried making her way out of the forest. She thought she became lost, but then happened upon some footprints. She knew how to identify different footprints, and these were definitely human footprints. "But I explored this island," she said to herself. "I'm the only one." She nervously laughed at her gullibility and realized she must have been going in circles. It was probably her own footprint. Audrey turned around and bent down to examine hers and compared them to the new one. They didn't match up. A smile suddenly spread over her face at the thought that these people could help her; she dropped her catch at her shelter on the beach and then came back and followed the prints.

On her way, her mind was racing with thoughts of who these people could be. The fact that they hadn't already found her and she hadn't already found them made her feel a little bit uneasy; nonetheless, she wouldn't dismiss the idea that they could help her. She remained near the edge of the forest and near the coast because that was where rescuers would normally start looking for her. "If they haven't found me yet, then they probably weren't looking for me," she muttered, thinking out loud.

Despite those facts, knowing that there was someone else on the island relieved her. But she felt something in her gut, something telling her to be careful. After all, this was a very remote island in the northern part of the Pacific Ocean. If someone considered this island to be vacation-worthy, they must be crazy. At that, Audrey stopped following the tracks and decided to wait a little bit before checking them out; finding her way back home took her longer than expected and tired her out. She would come back the next day.

Having pondered her earlier experience, Audrey came to a conclusion over a small dinner of squirrel, which she had roasted over a tiny fire. "The print didn't look too different from my own. It's pretty muddy here, so the bottom of my boots must be filled with dirt, and that's what made them different," she reasoned while running her fingers over the tiny ridges that lined the bottom of her boots. Content with her idea, Audrey made her way to bed and had a good rest.

Another day passed on the dreary island, and Audrey became even more paranoid. She had spotted more footprints and some differences in the make up of the forest that were obviously a sign of human interaction. She had no clue who they could be, yet she felt that she should exercise some caution. However, curiosity and the thought of being rescued took over and she ran into the forest. At this moment, she only thought positively; the pain in her hand from the burn subsided and the thought never crossed her mind that these people could be mean.

Thirty minutes later, Audrey found herself in the cover of bushes observing a small group of men in a clearing. Upon reaching the end of the trail of footprints, she peeked into the clearing. To her dismay, these were not friendly campers; not by any means. These were tall, muscular, angry-looking men with machine guns. The sight of this had her heart racing. A myriad of thoughts ran through her mind, and she didn't know whether to be scared or excited. Just as she wondered who these men were, another man walked out of a tent. She immediately recognized him, and her heart stopped. He was the terrorist America had been trying to track down for over three years. It was Htrad Redav, the maniac who hated America with all his heart. He was the biggest, scariest Russian with piercing blue eyes anyone has ever met.

"Holy cow," she whispered as she sat back carefully, trying to remain unseen and unheard, but still keeping an eye on the men. Audrey crawled her way out of the thick forest, and ran until she emerged onto the beach where she had her camp. She couldn't organize her thoughts because she was so shocked. All she could say over and over again was, "Wow." More frustrated than anything at this moment, Audrey knew she had all this information, but there was no one to report it to.

Known to always see the good in situations, Audrey did some thinking. "Okay, so I don't have a GPS...and I don't have a radio...but I can handle things. I know where they are hiding, and I can watch them, and I know how to defend myself if things get rough," she said matter-of-factly, trying to remain the poised person she had been before the crash.

The rest of the day went by smoothly, with Audrey carefully outlining her plan for the next day. She figured to observe them for a little while and find out what she's up against. She also thought to use that time in the morning to find what they were doing here and why. Later on, she would take action. Things were about to get exciting, a good change of pace, she thought. "They don't know what's coming," she sneered.

The next morning, Audrey finished getting ready. She found some sheets of paper in her survival kit along with a pen. She figured she could put these to good use by taking notes on the men.

Making the trek back into the forest where she first saw them was tough, but she had no problem finding them. These were rather loud men. Spotting the place she had previously used to watch them, she settled there. The view wasn't perfect, but those imperfections provided a shield so that no one could see her. It was an advantage to be able to slip in and out as she pleased.

The sun rose low in the Eastern sky, and the terrorist group wasn't doing anything interesting. Audrey observed them cleaning weapons and discussing things that were not important. Regardless, they were interesting to watch. She learned a lot about them from just half a day. In total, the group consisted of five men, two of which seemed completely dimwitted. The other three, however, always had a scowl on their face, always talked gruffly, and stomped around their camp as if extremely angry. They were all obviously Russian, but primarily spoke English. All of them were above six feet, the tallest being around six foot five. Their pale skin was covered with numerous scars, and their arms were bulging with muscle. Their hair ranged from blonde to a dark brown, but all of them had a crew cut. They seemed like an organized group, which Audrey knew had to be dangerous. "They are *definitely* not campers," she jokingly whispered.

They intrigued Audrey, but more so, they disgusted her. They had no manners, spat upon the ground, and it seemed like they were always cursing or making a hateful remark. She wondered how someone became so angry. It didn't deter her from her intelligence gathering, but after eating some berries that she had found for lunch, she headed off. Audrey was satisfied with her morning's work, but after spending some time analyzing some of the information, she became bored. She wanted more.

Audrey made her way back into the forest, eager to find out more about this group. Although the information she had gotten earlier did not have much relevance to it, she was sure that if she waited long enough, good information would come.

She couldn't have been more right. The first few hours of the afternoon were uneventful, and Audrey slowly drifted to sleep. But just as she was about to doze off, something caught her attention. She heard the words "flight plan," "missile," and "Air Force One" in the same sentence. She flinched and tuned in to hear the rest.

After hearing what they were going to do, Audrey was enraged; she was furious that these men thought they could take some missile and shoot down the president's plane. "It doesn't work like that," she growled under her breath. She worked hard to control herself from bursting out in anger. After taking some deep breaths and trying to relax, she listened to more of their conversation. She heard the whole plan.

The men wanted to show the U.S. how vulnerable it really was. They managed to get a ton of information on the president and his whereabouts. The president would be at a gala in two weeks, celebrating Independence Day. He would be travelling from a visit to Thailand and stopping in Alaska to refuel and get some rest. The men had found the flight plan, and according to that plan, the plane would fly right over this island in just two days.

The onslaught that these men were going to pull off seemed so simple. The hardest part was timing the missile right, but even that would be fairly easy; they had precise time charts and a tracker on the missile to make sure it went the right way. These men had extremely high-tech gear; some of their items were still on the drawing board in the U.S.

The scariest part was the missile itself; it was shoulder-held, but still quite large. A chill went down Audrey's spine as she realized that what they were planning on doing was possible. She had two days to do something, and right now she needed a little time to relax. She made her way back to her camp and thought about what she had just heard. She tried to convince herself that it could never happen. Something like that wouldn't work. Plus, she thought, as long as she was on this island, there was no way they were going to get away with this.

Within an hour, she had a plan. She was the only one who knew about this, and because she was the only one who knew about it, she was the only one in the position to prevent it from happening. It came down to all or nothing for her now; she could either act now or forever live with the fact that she did nothing. She chose to act.

That evening she planned to sneak into the camp and do the only thing she thought of to stop this disaster: kill Redav. Knowing that she was about to take someone's life put a nauseous feeling in her stomach, but she was doing it for the greater good. "Desperate times call for desperate measures," she said to justify herself.

She knew she didn't have the most well thought out plan, but it had to do. She had a small pistol and a fairly good aim. She also had plenty of bullets left; the only problem would be Redav's sidekicks. If she shot and missed the first time, they would be after her, in a flash, with machine guns. Then she would be dead for sure. She was going to have to be extremely precise with her plan, or it would be off with her head.

Finally, Audrey decided just to go with it. She was confident with her shooting skills. If she could manage to even just scare the men, it might get them to focus on her and distract them from their plan, and that was the main objective.

Audrey felt nervous and antsy throughout the rest of the evening; she kept running through her plan even though she knew it was better if she just relaxed a bit.

She was convinced she played out every single scenario in her head, and she was prepared for anything, especially her own demise.

The next morning came like it did everyday, but Audrey knew it could be her last day. That thought made her queasy and she tried to focus on the good things. "I've had a pretty good life," she sighed. "I'm doing what I said I was prepared to do, what I said I would be proud to do, when I joined the military: giving up my life for my country...Who knew the day would come this quickly?"

Audrey slapped herself for thinking like that. There was a possibility she could live, but deep inside she knew that possibility was slim. "I'm going to go in there, do my thing, and if I die, I die. I'm not going down without a fight," she exclaimed to pep herself up.

Audrey prepared to invade terrorists' camp. She had her pistol, her knife, her water purifier, and some food. She said a quick prayer before she went, thanking God for her life and her family, also adding in a small plead for things to go well.

"Ha. I sure hope God is listening," she grumbled, half joking and half completely serious. "I really, really, really need His help tonight."

After that, she set off. As Audrey trudged through the forest, her mood kept changing. First, she was nervous. Then, as she thought some more about it, she became angry. She was angry that these men were going to try to do something so atrocious. Then she became somewhat excited, excited that she had the opportunity to help out and make a difference. Her adrenaline pumped by the time she got to their camp, but when her eyes set on the clearing, she became sad and nervous again. There was no choice; she had to do this.

Audrey waited for the men to make their daily trip to the shore on the other side of the island. Redav never went with them; he was so paranoid about his plan that he stayed in the camp going over details almost every second of every day. She thought she saw everyone leave, but she waited a few minutes anyway just to be safe. Redav stood at the other end of the camp, behind some tents. She had to get around to the other side to get a better aim at him, but she had to do this without being seen.

It was like one of those shows on TV where a spy would peek around the corner, make sure no one was watching, and then sneak to the next point. Audrey went a few yards, always keeping one eye on Redav and the other on the nearest hiding spot. Then she stopped to observe. In order for this to work, it was necessary for her to know what Redav was doing and where he was at any given time.

Finally, Audrey's break came as she hid behind a bush; Redav stood in the middle of the clearing to look at a map in the sunlight. With his back turned, she could more than easily shoot him. If she were really lucky, she would be able to shoot, kill, and then grab some other supplies from their camp.

Audrey slowly held up her pistol into a shooting position, her hand slightly shaking with nerves. She took a deep breath to steady herself, put her finger on the trigger, and slowly pulled. After the shot, she raised her head up quickly, searching for Redav. She was sure she had gotten a direct hit. As she stood up, Audrey saw him lying on the ground, a pool of blood next to his chest slowly getting larger. Her stomach felt queasy at the sight, but it appeared that he was dead.

Audrey laughed in disbelief – she killed him– but a sudden movement from Redav quickly halted her laughter. Her jaw dropped in disbelief and terror as he slowly turned over and faced her, a menacing grimace on his face. He started to reach for his gun, but the grueling pain he was in stopped him halfway. In a panic, Audrey shot again and again, hitting him twice in the arm. Audrey knew that his men probably heard the sound of gunshots and were already on their way. She prepared to dart into the forest to avoid getting caught by them, but it was too late. They came running into the clearing, dumbfounded at the sight of Redav on the ground. He gathered enough energy to scream at them for standing there and he fiercely told them to find her. At this, Audrey fled.

Followed by the sounds of the shouting Russians, Audrey used her adrenaline to speed herself away from them. They ran for a good ten minutes before Audrey heard the shouts fade away. The chase was done for now, but she knew they would continue to search for her later. Nevertheless, her plan worked for the most part. She didn't know how much of what just happened would affect their plan, though. They might still be able to shoot the missile.

As Audrey looked around at the boundless trees surrounding her, she realized she no longer knew the best way to evade her pursuers. With no sense of direction as to where her camp was, she knew sleeping in the middle of the forest was her only choice. She spent the rest of the day trying to build a makeshift shelter with branches and grass. She even managed to find a small stream to get water from.

In the late evening, Audrey went to bed. She had trouble falling asleep with the constant threat of being found. After hours of listening for the sounds of the men, she finally was convinced it was safe to sleep and got her much deserved rest.

The next morning, Audrey wandered back to their camp, following her own footprints from the day before. She was surprised the men hadn't followed her tracks, but it may have been too dark to see them. Or, she thought, maybe they were too dumb to think to use them. She eventually found the camp, but hesitated before going to an area where she could see the men. Her experience from yesterday had her jumpy. Audrey nervously paced back and forth, but soon enough found a few ounces of courage and stepped forward. She was not sure if just injuring Redav was enough to stop their plan.

She peered slowly into the clearing, and to her dismay, her efforts the day before had no affect on them. She didn't see Redav, but the missile was out in the open and the other men were around it.

"Aiya," she mumbled. Her plan failed.

Audrey sat back to think. She had tried to kill Redav, and was not able to do that. She didn't want to risk getting killed herself by trying to kill another one of his men.

"Now they are looking out for me. There's no way I will be able to sneak in. It's too early for them to think I'm dead, but I barely have a day until they shoot the missile," she whispered to herself. "Hmm..." She lost all hope until she heard the men start to talk she and leaned over to see.

"Boss told me the plan is still on," said one of the men who came out of the tent. The others groaned slightly.

"How long until he gets better?" another one asked in a strong Russian accent.

"It'll be a long while. He's wounded pretty badly. That girl shot him three times; he's lucky she didn't hit any of them important organs. He's been sleeping for the most part, 'cept for when he feels like yelling at us," he answered. At that, the others looked at each other wearily.

"Well, if he's sleeping most of the time, then that makes us basically in charge, right?" a third one asked.

"Yeah, I guess so. Why?" the main one asked.

The third man looked around and snickered as he suggested, "Then who's to stop us from having a little celebratory event on the beach? Our plan is going to work. I mean, I think we scared that girl enough for her not to come back. There's nothing wrong with leaving Redav here sleeping while we go to the beach, right?"

Everyone excitedly nodded in agreement.

The main man said, "Yeah, that could work. We've worked our butts off for Redav's heist. We deserve a little something." He clapped his hands together in amusement, "Okay, guys. Tonight, six P.M., on the beach. Be there." The others cheered until he hushed them as to not wake Redav.

Audrey gasped in absolute disbelief, "Oh my gosh! Wow..." Joy completely overcame her. "I can steal one of their radios while they're gone," she said to herself as she clasped her hands together, thinking of all the things she could do while they're gone. "Who'd have thought this would work out?"

The placement of the sun suggested that it was about noon. Audrey figured she had time to take a quick nap and get rejuvenated before six, "I can come back at around five thirty. It will give me some time to make sure they are still going through with this. I guess the missile is supposed to be shot late at night, or maybe in the morning. I've lost track of the days..."

She made her way back to the shelter she built the night before and sat down. "There are five tents on the edges of the clearing. Redav is in the one towards the eastern edge," she used a stick to draw a map of the clearing in the dirt. "His tent door is facing inward, so if I can come behind it, I can go to the one next to his. That tent is slightly at an angle, so he won't be able to see me. Hopefully there will be some radios in that tent," she said as she drew a circle around the drawing of that tent. Audrey knew she had about two hours until she went back to the camp. "Time for a quick nap," she said contentedly.

An hour and a half later, she awoke from her nap to the sound of rain pattering on the ground. She groaned as she realized what this probably meant for the party.

"They're going to call it off. There's no way they'd

continue it in this weather." Nevertheless, she decided to still go back to the camp.

"You never know," she said. "They just might be crazy enough to still party."

She started off into the depths of the forests, knowing this was her last chance to stop these lunatics from killing the president. She walked slowly but confidently. "I've made it this far," she said. "There's no stopping me this time." Smiling, she arrived at the clearing, rain still pouring down. She sat down to observe the men, her fingers crossed and hoping they were just crazy enough to go on with the party.

As she looked in, she noticed some good signs. Redav was still in the tent, and the rest of the men seemed to be in good spirits, even though they were walking around in the pouring rain. "Hey guys, it's five fifty. Let's head to the beach now. I just gave Redav some more medicine; he'll be asleep in minutes." The rest of them cheered quietly and started to gather food and cigarettes for the party. They all put on raincoats, too. "They are quite the stubborn bunch," Audrey said under her breath.

Ten minutes later, they were gone. The camp was eerily quiet. To be extra cautious, Audrey waited a few more minutes after they left. She did not want to risk ruining her last chance to make things right.

She finally decided it was time to go in. Audrey let a sigh of relief flow from her as she stepped into the open. She grinned and shook her head as she followed her planned path around Redav's tent. Slowly, she pulled back the door that led into the second tent. Looking around, she noticed there were no radios. "You're kidding me," she muttered.

Stepping out of that tent, she went into the next one. This one had radios, plenty of them. "Now this is what I'm talkin' about," she said as she nodded her head. She went around the tent and looked at the radios, deciding which one to take. Suddenly, a noise interrupted her thoughts. Following that noise were the words in a thick Russian accent, "Hey! Redav, are you awake? You have to rest, man."

It was one of the terrorists. Audrey let out an annoyed groan as she pondered her amazingly bad luck. Foot tapping the ground, she quickly thought of what to do. She had her pistol, but she was trapped in a tent. She hoped he was unarmed and alone. Then out of the corner of her eye, she saw a shadow. The man was making his way into the tent, snarling as he did with the realization that Redav was still asleep and that an intruder was in their camp. With her hands quivering, she grabbed her gun. She closed her eyes for a brief second to prepare herself for what was to come.

As the tent door opened and he stepped in, they both froze for a moment, staring blankly at each other. He glared at her with his scary eyes and sneered evilly as he said in his Russian accent, "You still alive, I see. You are a tough one. I must ask, what do you think you are doing in my camp? Eh?" Audrey pointed her gun and shot at him. She shot continuously until he dropped to the ground and stopped moving. That's when she realized she had used the last of her bullets. She slapped her face, extremely frustrated that she had run out of bullets. She feared that the other men would come back and so she stayed in the tent.

Another voice came, "Hey! Andrei! I heard you shooting, what happened? Was there an animal?" He had no idea Audrey was there. She saw his shadow approach the tent and she grabbed some radios to throw at him. He stepped into the tent, not even seeing Audrey at first because his glance was fixed on Andrei's body.

She suddenly threw the radios at him, hitting him once on his head. Surprised, he screamed in anger and ran towards her, punching hard. She fought back, her anger fueling every swing she took. She ducked and managed to avoid many of his punches, but the ones that he did connect with made her dizzy. Audrey didn't know how much more she could take; she was the one with all the martial arts training, but he was huge. He didn't have to have any training to do some serious damage.

Finally, he knocked her to the ground, and she stared at her terribly bruised arm. She writhed with pain as he stood there laughing. Then she looked up in horror as she saw him reaching for a gun. Without thinking, she grabbed one of the other radios near her with her unhurt hand and got up, running at him. She hit him on the side of his head with all the force she mustered up and he stopped, clearly blacking out as he threw blind punches at the air. He hit the ground with a thud, still alive but definitely not waking up for a while.

Trying to stifle tears from the pain, she grabbed one radio and ran away quickly. The other men were still at the party and had no idea what just happened; they probably wouldn't for a good while. The missile wasn't supposed to be launched for a few hours. She had time to call for help.

She ran far into the forest and once she was satisfied with the distance from their camp, she stopped. She stared in amazement and relief at the radio she held in her hand. She did it. She had the radio and her life; the president was safe, and she could return home to her family and friends. She was going to escape with just a bruised arm and a healing burn on the same hand. Audrey smiled with pride as she dialed the emergency frequency on the radio and explained everything that had happened. The president's flight was quickly cancelled and rescuers would be there in less than an hour.

Abduction of Friend

As blurry trees passed by the window, John caught the glare of the bright sun in his eyes. The wind flowed through his hand as it hung out of the window. The other hand firmly secured the steering wheel, adjusting for every curve in the road. His friend sat in the passenger seat of the rusty truck, turning the dusty knob for the radio. His friend had an odd twitch to him. John contemplated the odd mood. Usually his friend seemed adventurous and daring, but today all he talked about was getting back to his home in Freeport. John, however, wanted to have some fun. He pushed his friend's hand off the radio and turned it to the closest station and turned up the volume. Then he stepped on the gas, and the car sped forward. The squeaky car lurched with its flaky paint falling off. John was surprised the car could even go sixty miles per hour.

John had been friends with Max since he was in second grade. Now they were both ready to go to college. Even thought Max was a great friend, he had a habit of getting John in trouble. When John thought of peer pressure, Max's name came to mind; however, Max got him to step outside of his shell and see the world. Max was a bit taller than John and frequently boasted about it. Even though they had their differences, they seemed to have the same interests. While John was thinking, Max was still sitting tense near the window.

John broke the silence, "You seem a little uptight, everything okay?" John didn't usually ask about Max's feelings because Max got defensive when asked, but something seemed really off.

Max replied, "I'm just tired. Are we there yet? Can we pull over? I'm feeling sick."

Max never felt carsick. It was unusual for him to complain. John saw Max glance at his cell phone, Max looked terrified when he saw the dim screen. John saw Max try to relax his shoulders and lie back. He thought about asking when the trip was over. The trip was to get away from their troubles, and he wanted it to stay that way.

John turned the car to pull over but, Max interrupted, "It's okay. I can wait a few hours. Let's just have fun with the few remaining hours we have left." Max didn't know how true his statement would become.

As John drove his truck past an open field, he saw a black van off in the far corner of his eye. He pulled up to the intersection, the van didn't seem to slow down. Now he could see the van more clearly. Its tinted windows made him uneasy. The van seemed like some car from a nightmare. It seemed out of place in the forested area of New Yamshire. Then the oddest thing happened. John's friend saw the truck and began to freak out.

Max yelled, "Stop!"

Caught off guard, John tried to respond. The brakes had needed to be replaced for weeks, and the brakes didn't have enough power to stop the speeding vehicle. John questioned his friend, "What is going on Max?"

John made an effort to respond, but at that moment the car was thrown across the road, leaving the car on its side. The airbag deployed and he struggled to keep awake. Then his mind drifted into darkness. When he regained consciousness, he discovered that he lay in the car with glass and debris all around him. He noticed his friend wasn't in the car. John saw a man that could not possibly be a rescue pulling Max from the vehicle.

A white man in a black suit dragged Max across the shattered glass to his barely dented van. His black suit added to his pail skin. The scariest thing about his the man was his emotionless expression. His wrinkly face gave no feelings away. John remembered him, but his eyes blurred the man. All John could tell was his friend was being dragged away into a van. The shocking fact hit him. This was no stranger, this was his uncle.

He noticed the faint smell of gasoline and tried to grip the pieces of metal to get out of the car and help his friend. Then his mind went blank. The space around him vanished, and he was left in nothingness. When he woke, three concerned citizens crowded John.

"Call an ambulance!" yelled the first man. The other two followed his lead. When John tried to speak, the man interrupted him. "Don't worry help is on the way."

All John could think about was the man who took Max. John tried to talk, but he figured it was no use. He lay in bed hurt and bruised and soon became unaware of the area around him. His brown hair dropped, and his hands went limp. Soon after that, blinking lights filled the area, and an ambulance transported him to a hospital. When he woke, doctors bombarded John with questions.

He then faked falling asleep to escape them. Many thoughts rushed around in his head. He couldn't figure out why his friend had been taken away. He then just shrugged off the whole story. It must have been a dream, he told himself. When a nurse came in the room, he asked how his friend was doing. She didn't know what he was talking about. Then the realization hit him. His friend had been taken away. He knew the nurse would not know about his abduction, and it would be useless to talk to her, so he hurried her away. He needed to make an escape.

He looked around, assessing his surroundings. It looked like he had only been in the hospital for an hour. He wondered if they had gotten the chance to scribble down his name on a sheet. The doctor had told him in an authoritative tone that he could not leave his bed for a few hours, but that was time he didn't have. He tested his body. Nothing seemed amiss. A blunt pain ached at his arm, but that was expected. On that thought, John lifted himself out of bed. When his right foot made contact with the cold, damp floor, he felt a sharp pain. He must have sprained his ankle. He hobbled into the hall, making his way to the exit. He grabbed the coat and pants next to him and quickly shoved them on. When putting his pants on his ankle became more of a problem. His leg would shoot up in pain each time he hit it.

A man in the distance approached. He had a smile, but he could easily be trying to get him back in the hospital bed. As John hobbled faster, the pain increased, pulsing with every step. Now the man was only about five feet away. The man glanced at him and spoke. Each word frightened John. If he were part of the hospital staff, he would have to wait to help his friend.

"Do you need some help? I noticed you limping down the hall. Can I help you out the door?"

John quickly contemplated his request, "No, thank you. I am fine. I don't need crutches."

The man seemed to understand and hurried down the hall, disappearing into the vast halls of the hospital. John hobbled close to the door and grasped the cold handle. He emerged from the building, and the crisp breeze brushed against his face. Now all John needed to do was get to the crime scene. He awkwardly trudged towards the road, without his car he would need to hitchhike. He pushed his hand into the open air to flag a car. A car pulled up and he got in, heading to the scene.

When he arrived, he saw the debris of the cars that had smashed into each other. He approached; he took in the faint smell of gasoline. Looking around he had no idea what to do. Searching for possible leads, he spotted a quaint little gas station near the intersection. As he came closer, he noticed the rusting door handle and the scraped paint on the building. Stepping into the warm station, he noticed a clerk half asleep at the counter.

When the clerk noticed John, he immediately stood upright and asked, "Is there anything I can do to help you, sir?"

The smiling man seemed a bit plump with a slight bald spot on his forehead. Edging forward John spoke, "Do you know anything about the crash yesterday? Did you see anything out of the ordinary?"

His Uncle stepped back almost afraid. "I saw the crash. A truck and a van collided at that intersection. I went to get some equipment and rushed out there. The only weird thing about the crash was that the van was gone when I got back."

John thought over his uncle's answer. "Are you sure you didn't see anything else?"

"I am not sure what I saw, okay. I might have seen another person in the car, but that is impossible. I only remember one person being taken out of that old car. Are you some sort of detective or what?" said his uncle.

John quickly responded, "I was in that crash and the other person was my best friend." His hands were clenched together. His knuckles turned white under the pressure. All he wanted to do was find his friend. "Is there anyway you can help me?"

After pausing for a second, the pudgy man responded, "I do have a camera near the intersection." He looked worried, and John's erratic behavior wasn't helping. As his uncle led John into the attic, they traveled up a dusty staircase.

The attic had a thick layer of dust covering it. John grasped the railing to the attic and touched the grainy dust. The smell filled his nose. He couldn't help, but sneeze. As his head appeared in the attic, he glanced at the TV centered in a cobweb filled corner.

His Uncle broke the silence, "I haven't been up here in a while. I apologize for the dust." He flicked the switch to the TV brushing off the dusty cobwebs. After a few seconds of messing around with the outdated equipment, he got it to work. His Uncle and John stayed silent through the whole crash. He watched as the van collided with truck, but the most horrific part was watching his friend being dragged from the car.

John didn't know how to react. His mind was racing. Trying to find a reason for all this, John paced back and forth. Then he remembered how out of place his friend was. Max must have known about it all along, but why didn't Max tell him. The oddest part of the whole video was when he saw the van again. He knew he had seen it somewhere.

The storekeeper seemed perplexed by the whole thing. "I just can't believe it. I thought I was hallucinating. I think I can get the license plate number." Squinting he managed to read 1592HS.

John quickly grabbed a piece of paper on the table and quickly jotted down the note. This was a big clue that he needed to use. His dad's friend was a police officer. He hoped he could have the license checked. His newly made friend still sat there with a disturbed face. John needed to leave, time was disappearing and the trail was going cold. He said goodbye to the storekeeper, and started his journey to home. He hitchhiked home.

He traveled in vans, trucks, and some tractor trailers. John never talked about his missing friend in the cars.

The drivers might think he was a crazy. Even though he never talked he thought about it. He couldn't get the van out of his head. It was so odd. He knew he had seen the vehicle before. Through his car rides he thought of all the cars he saw while on the road. A black van never appeared in his memory. The licensee plate was burned into his memory. There was nothing special about the plate 1592HS, but it was the only lead he had.

As he came closer to his home he thought about Max's family. They must be so worried, he thought. Now that he thought about it he realized he should have been home a hours ago. He was already running late getting home and the crash had pushed him back five hours at least.

When he arrived at his street he noticed a few trees had fallen and the mailbox to his house had fallen. When he got to his driveway he stood frozen. He tried to clear his eyes, but it was no illusion. Standing in front of him was a black van with the same license plate from the crash.

Then he realized his mother could be in trouble. He sprinting up the front porch, he burst through the front door. Each step was burned as he ran. The door handle chilled his hand as he grasped it and ran into the house. He couldn't waist any time. The wind brushed past his face urging him to move faster. He ran through the hall looking into every room. He sprinted up the stairs, hoping his mom was not hurt. He burst through the door to his mother's sewing room. His mom was sitting on her favorite chair sewing and talking to his uncle.

Then the realization hit him. He had seen the van before, but it wasn't on the trip. It was his uncle's car. The shock took him by surprise, but he couldn't let his uncle know he was on to him. Then he spoke, "Mom, I need to tell you something." His uncle tensed as he said these words. He inched toward the door. John quickly shut it.

His mom opened her mouth to speak, but she was

interrupted by the uncle saying that he needed to go to the bathroom.

His Uncle edged towards the door and James stopped him. He put his hand out restricting his uncle's passage. His uncle's cold shirt brushed up against his hand. John spoke with a forceful tone, "My friend was kidnapped yesterday. All I know I is that the man who took him drove a ..." Before John could finish his sentence his uncle pushed John into the wall with tremendous force. His Uncle sprinted down the stairs clumsily stumbling at the bottom. John was on his tail, his uncle had a few seconds head start and he was injured. Now his uncle was outside. The smell of pine filled his lungs and forced him to move on.

Now John was only a few feet away from his uncle, with one leap John was able to tackle his uncle. As his uncle tried to catch his breath John punched him in the face leaving his uncle unconscious with a dull expression on his face. His uncle lay motionless, his wrinkly face and black hair covered his eyes.

He was only forty, but he looked as if he was sixty. John was fit and about eighteen years old. No one would have known this man was his uncle. John had brown hair and the man had black hair. John had worn bright colors, while it looked like John's uncle saw in black and white.

While John was moving his uncle his mother would not stop telling him to stop. He had to lock his mother in a closet. He put chair up to make sure she couldn't get out. When his uncle woke John was ready; he had tied the uncle to a chair. He made sure every strap was just tight enough to hurt. The thick rope roughened his hands. John noticed his uncle's eyelids were opening to the fresh light of his basement. John hurled a splash of water toward his face.

His Uncle gasped for air and muttered out a few words. "What do you want from me?"

John spoke abruptly and with force. "Where is my friend! Why are you here and why do you want my friend."

His Uncle opened his mouth and then a grin came upon his face. "I don't know where your friend is. I am just your humble uncle and your friend has been missing for over a month now."

The twisted grin of his uncle scared John. He knew what his uncle had said was partially true. If he checked the police he was sure he would find his friend had been missing. Whatever was going on had been planned for some time.

How else could his friend have been so effortlessly taken? His Uncle who took his friend must have thought about this happening. There were only two questions that remained in John's head. Why had Max been taken and where was he now.

John went outside for a breath of fresh air to think about his uncle. His fresh air was instantly interrupted by his mother. The worried face gave John a scare. He had not seen his mother look this way before. She walked up and slapped him.

John staggered back, he knew he had deserved that.

She quickly retorted, "Why is uncle Charles down there? You have no right to treat him that way. I don't know what someone can do to get that kind of rudeness from you. Go apologize!"

John had no time for his mom's angry tone and her quest for justice. He would need to get out. Without an answer he headed back down the stairs to check up on his uncle locking the door behind him. He went down the stairs to the tune of his mother hitting the door violently and screaming for him to come back up stairs.

John didn't need her though, all he could think about was saving his friend. He did not have anytime for his mother. He needed to focus on his uncle and getting answers from him. The stairs creaked to the sound of his feet and the musty air entered his lungs. When he got down the stairs he noticed something odd. The chair was faced around the opposite direction of him. This odd happening did not bother John though. He quickly spun the chair around.

He was greeted with a solid punch to the face and a kick to his body. The force threw John to the ground. He tried to get back up, but he couldn't seem to get up. His Uncle must have hit him near his ankle, he had wounded in the car crash. John had been ignoring the pain until now. It seemed like it could wait. The pain shot up his leg. The pain pulsed with every second.

Then John noticed his uncle was exiting from the small vent in the basement. He knew his pain needed to be ignored. He staggered to his feet and began to hobble after his uncle. Each step seemed like he would collapse. His Uncle was partially out of the window now. John reached for his uncle's leg, but he leaped out before John could grab it. John hoisted himself on to the window. John grabbed the chair that his uncle escaped from and used it to jump out of the window. The harsh rocks scraped his skin as he managed to squeeze out of the window. His foot was now throbbing, but he ignored it. Now he could see his uncle was getting into his car. John picked up a rock and chucked it at the car, but it did nothing. John broke out sobbing.

His friend would be gone forever and he couldn't do anything. John's mind was racing, but then he noticed something. He saw a piece of clothing on the ground. It was his uncle's sweater. Something about it seemed strange. He looked it over and noticed a fine dust. Not only did he find dust, but the sweater had a piece of paper in it. It was a note. The wrinkly note read,

To Charles Smith,
When you have captured the child bring him to me. You

know were to find me. He will be used for test two. You will be rewarded when I receive the child. Thank you for your service and have a nice day.

P.S if you see the boy again make sure to flee the scene.

The note made John shiver. John feared the worst for his lost friend. Max must be in deep trouble. Now John knew it was a race against time. But how would he follow this man. He had to get help. Then he knew he needed professional help. This was not a job for someone like him. What did he know? He was a high school senior. He knew he had to hire someone. When he entered the door to his home and pulled the rusty handle he was greeted by the second slap of the day, but this time John had an answer to his mother's questions.

John's voice was firm and authoritative as he spoke, "Recently I have gotten into a car crash with my friend Max. You know we were on our road trip. When the car was hit by a van I looked over and I saw my best friend Max being taken away by a strange figure. That strange figure was uncle Charles. When I got out of the hospital I came home as soon as possible. This was so I could tell you what had happened to me. That is why I have been acting so strangely."

Then his mother seemed to take all the information in and asked him if he had injured his head in the crash. A surge of anger entered John. His own mother would not believe him. He knew he had to convince her. He needed her car and money to get help for his friend.

His worried mother said, "I think we should take you back to the hospital and make sure this is nothing serious. I hope no lasting damage was done." His mother let out a concerned sigh.

Then John knew it was no point in arguing. His mother now believed he was a crazy. Then he passed his mother without saying a word, ignoring the pain in his leg. He would just need to grab some of the money in the car. He searched for his mothers keys on the cluttered shelf. He grabbed the keys and headed to the garage.

His mother then stepped in front of him. He could not get involved in her arguments. He needed help and someone who would listen to him. He dodged his mother's attempt to stop him. Then she started to yell. Her deafening roar did not bother John. He was used to the yelling. She never quiet took him seriously.

He grabbed the door handle and yanked open the door to the car. He jumped into the car and sped off. The van he was driving wasn't his dream car, but he had bigger worries than what car he was driving. Luckily his mom was afraid of asking for directions. She left the phone book in the car as well as many maps. He could search for a detective with the address book. Flipping through the tattered pages of the address book he noticed an address for a detective.

The car lurched forward as he sped towards the destination. He knew his mother would not call the police. She was worried about how others would see her son. When he reached a small part of town he noticed the detective store. It was oddly colored with an orange door. The building was colored in a gray. When he entered he noticed small decorations littered the walls. One of the decorations seemed to follow him. It was an owl. Its gaze seemed to chase him. The whole store gave John the creeps. He just wanted help to find his friend.

John aimlessly walked through the store looking for someone to help him. He bumped into a figure. It almost appeared to be a coat hanger, but when it started talking he leaped backwards. The tall man started to talk, "Excuse me, do you need any help? If you have come for detective services I am the right guy."

John was tempted to say wrong store, but he answered politely, "Do you have a moment to look over my case it is urgent." John looked at the man. His face looked cold and in search for a job to feed himself. The man was wrinkly and looked as if he was seven feet tall. John knew he should try to be more friendly, the man could think he was afraid of him.

"Lets sit down his uncle spoke. I do believe you have a case to inform me about." The man sat in a small chair behind his desk. It seemed almost ironic that such a tall man was sitting in a chair designed for children as small as three. As John looked around the store he noticed dust filled it. The air tasted grimy, like it hadn't been vacuumed in months.

John began to explain his ordeal and how he needed to find were his friend was. Throughout this whole case the man seemed very nervous. Almost like the man had seen this same case before. The thought of John not going crazy was the best news he had heard yet. The man's tense facial expressions led John to realize he wasn't the first one this had happened to. When John was finished telling his saddening story the man looked oddly calm. The man had been nervous one second ago and now he was face to face with someone who seemed very sure of himself.

The man smiled at John. "You may have been watching too many movies or not getting enough sleep. This case you are showing me is unbelievable." As the man spoke he almost had fear in his eyes.

John picked up on this. He almost felt like his uncle was trying to hide something from him. His Uncle didn't even seem to think about the idea before declining it. John's anger bled trough when he spoke, "I have been running around getting chased by people, escaping hospitals and chasing suspects and all you have to tell me is that I am going crazy!"

Then his uncle broke. "I may have been misleading you. What you have stumbled on to has not been the first case. The circumstances are usually alike." The detective pulled out maps, charts, papers, and a blank sheet.

"This is what I have from the previous cases. I refused to help them, but enough is enough this has to be stopped." I have been blackmailed by a man for about thirty years now. He is threatening to take my wife. My wife passed away a few months ago, apparently they don't know.

John felt sorry for the tall man. He seemed to love his wife from the tone of his voice. This had to be ignored though. His friend was in danger. "How much time do you think my friend has before something happens to him."

His Uncle replied with a grave tone. "I believe you have about one day. Do you have anything I can use to help me find your friend?" John noticed the man's earnest expression. John looked at the sweater in his hand and the paper in his pocket.

"I have this note I managed to grab off of a man trying to run away from me and his coat." (Don't you think John would tell the detective that his uncle was John's uncle?) John knew these would help quiet a bit in his case. His Uncle's expression proved him right. This evidence was needed to help him find his friend.

His Uncle responded, "Have you noticed the dust on this sweater?"

"Yeah, I noticed when I picked it up it seemed odd to me that someone who lives in the countryside would have so much dust on them."

"This dust is not dust at all it is flour. This stuff was most likely from a flour mill. This is probably the biggest lead I have found on this case in thirty years," said his uncle. His Uncle quickly started to tap away on his computer the screen illuminated his face showing his interest in the case. It seemed like this man's work had been put into finding these people. When he scanned through all the charts and data his uncle had it looked like he had about fifty pages of stuff all on these abductions.

John questioned him as he frantically searched his computer, "How much work have you done on this subject?"

The detective quickly responded, "As long as they have been taking people, thats thirty years of research right there. six cases and sixteen potential cases sit in that packet. Those maps are where I thought they lived, but now I know." His Uncle's face lit up as he clicked a button. "This is it. I found were there hideout is. His Uncle gave John a piece of printed paper with an address on it. This paper shows were there hideout is."

"How can you be sure," asked John. I used that flour mill data you gave me and I found all the mills near the area. Then I noticed a few of them were too close to town to be used as a hideout. That left only one. This area is off the map. It is practically abandoned. When you get there you will want to look for an underground area. From all of my research that is the only safe place they can test at."

John seemed uneasy about all this and was especially worried about having to go alone. He was under the impression he would have the detective as backup. "Won't you be there to back me up? What if it is more than I can handle?"

The detective spoke with force, "You will have to be alone on this. I can not be caught by them and you will have to be smart. If it is too much run and don't turn back. Now I can go there with you if you want, but I can't stay or go inside. I am sure they would kill me and everyone who is close to me."

John saw the man's worry and was outraged. He was supposed to be a detective, but this man was just a coward. When John thought about him being caught, he wondered what would happen if they caught him. He did not want to bother himself with all this information. He needed to take action and on that mindset he replied, "I won't need you to drive me. I don't want someone who won't help me when it is his job"

When John got in the car he put his foot on the gas and zoomed off. Looking through his rearview mirror he noticed the man watching him leave. John knew this place was something to be afraid of, but for some reason he seemed to be focused just on his friend.

When John closed in on the address he began to think about his condition. He was in no shape to fight and he had no chance if he did fight. He would need to be stealthy and smart about every decision he made. If he made the wrong move he could be in for a painful experience. John rolled down a window and let the fresh breeze fill his lungs and blow across his face. This could be it, he thought as he noticed a building up ahead. This was the place he needed to be. He parked a few stops away from the area were the building was just to be safe.

Entering the area John crept close to the flour mill. It seemed abandoned. The windows were broken and the floor was picking up dust. This gave John some suspicion. This flour mill must not be used at all. This conclusion totally falsified what the detective had to say. John began his journey back to the car when he slipped on a can.

The coke can gave John something to take his rage out on. He would never see his friend again and it was all because some lousy detective was wrong. He smashed the can and kicked it at a shed. His friend was practically dead if he couldn't be helped.

Then it hit him. The coke can was fresh. It would have been blown away if no one had been there. This was clue. Then John started to notice other details. Cars had been here, the tracks on the ground looked fresh. This meant he was on the right track. Then he noticed the shed he had kicked the can at a door. The door was slowly opened and John hid. Darting to the crates to the left of him John saw his uncle. His face made John want to charge, but he had to be smart. His uncle went back into the shed. John was quick to follow. He climbed through the door not knowing what to expect.

He found stairs at the back of the shed. The cold

damp shed had turned into a stainless steal lab. John didn't want to make a sound so he stayed at least twenty feet behind the uncle. When he moved from the lab to a separate room John followed closely behind.

When he was close he heard the sound of a faint voice. "Were am I? Who are you?" spoke the barely audible voice. Then two voices responded his uncle and a voice he hadn't heard.

Then uncle said, "All that is important is that you are helping science." The whimper from the faint voice grew louder as John heard the sound of machinery.

Then the voice of his uncle who John hadn't heard spoke, "We are just testing the tools, now go back to sleep."

John had to look at what was going on. He had to see who the voice was and when he peered over the bench he was hiding. He noticed his friend's familiar face and the glow of a knife. It almost looked like his uncle near him had a drill. When he glanced back at his friend he noticed that he was looking pail and ill. No wonder his voice was so faint he was drugged.

He wanted to shout out to his friend and tell him that everything was okay, but it wasn't run-on John still needed a plan to get his friend out of the building. The machinery got louder as time passed. It was only a matter of time. Then John made his move.

He grabbed a wrench from the ground and hurled it at his uncle. The unknown man seemed just as surprised as his uncle, but he was much faster to react. He grabbed a knife and edged closer to John. Each move the doctor became closer. John ran to his friend. The drill was still next to his uncle. He grabbed it and thrust it towards the doctor.

John didn't have time to think about his next move. He grabbed his friend from the table and hoisted him on to his shoulders. He ran to the exit. This was his chance to escape. When he reached the lab he closed the door and jammed a chair behind it. The doctor rammed the exit trying to escape. The door would break any second now. He needed to get out.

Ignoring all pain from his leg he ran up the stairs with his friend on his back. The steps clanked with every step. The air smelled like a doctor's office. The smell of chemicals filled his nose. When he reached the surface he could hear the door being jammed open. He would need to get to the car now. Just ahead stood the car. With all the courage he could muster he ran towards the car. His leg felt like it was going to burst open with every step. Then the doctor came out holding what looked like a gun. John realized he must have grabbed it when he was opening the door.

John was only a few meters from the car when the first shot went off. It rang in his ears. It was just a bit to the left of him. Then two more shots went off. Both missed. He hurled his friend in the back seat and when he go into the van another shot went off. This one clipped his leg. John let out a cry of pain. This was his moment to get out. Each second mattered. His leg was throbbing. It couldn't take that much pressure from holding Max and the shot. He was seriously hurt. He used his opposite leg to drive the car.

The hospital was just down the road. When he got there he was greeted by nurses and later his mother. His friend was safe. They found a few chemicals in his system, but he was mostly fine. When John had time he told the police about his whole story and when they went to the shed everything was there, except for the doctor and his uncle. They were all on the news. Later when Max was back to health he was able to tell John that he had been receiving texts about some weird program. He refused and then Max overheard he was going to be captured. John realized the criminals tried to get Max to come in voluntarily, but it backfired.

Lost in Shanghai

By Lauren Tong

"Mom, are you serious?" questioned Alex.

"Yes honey, I am. I love Jim very much, and he loves me back. I know you're not totally into the new father idea, but we will get through it, together. Jim is a great man, and I'm sure you're going to love him as much as I do! I wouldn't marry a man that I thought would be a horrible father to you. I have a feeling that he's going to be a great father! I want the best for you. I love and care about you very much, Alex! I want you to know that," said Alex's mother.

"Then why did you divorce Dad? He made me so happy, and you knew that. You just had to take him away from me!" retorted Alex.

"Alex, things weren't going so well with your dad and me. You knew that! We grew apart from each other. I still love your father, just in a different way now. I know that you love him very much, but hearing your dad and I argue wasn't good for you. I'm just trying to look out for your needs," answered Alex's mother.

Alex Johnson considered himself to be an average fifteen-year-old teenager. He lived in a little city called Chattanooga, Tennessee, surrounded by beautiful mountains and fresh air. The blue skies made everyday magnificent. Alex attended Chattanooga High School as a ninth grader. His life had been a mess ever since his parents got divorced two years ago. Alex's mom also had fallen in love with another man named Jim. Alex's mom and Jim went to high school together and started dating a year and a half after her divorce. Now, Jim had asked for her hand in marriage, and Alex's mother had said, "Yes," and they planned on getting married in a month.

The divorce totally devastated Alex's life. Everything changed around him, but he didn't want change. Alex wanted to have a normal life, like the other kids in his school. On the outside, it seemed as if Alex didn't have anything going wrong in his life. On the inside, everything went completely wrong in Alex's life. Alex and Jim disliked each other. Although when Jim hung around Theresa with Alex, he acted like a good guy, but when Jim was by himself with Alex, he acted like a total jerk. Alex's mom loved Jim, and Alex made the choice to respect his mom's decision.

Alex hated the fact that Jim took his mom away from him. Even though they were going to be one family, he didn't like that fact that there would to be another man in the house. Ever since Jim and Alex's mom began planning their wedding, Alex's mom never made any time to spend with Alex, and he felt left out. Alex never liked being left out, even when his mom ignored him.

A very strong Christian, Alex attended Oakwood Baptist Church. His Christian faith had turned his life around. Before the divorce, going to God for help made his life great, no matter what else happened.

Ever since the divorce though, he stopped going to God for help. His life became very hectic, and he never found time to talk to God about his problems. Alex just wasn't giving God a chance to help. He had been trying to do things on his own, but nothing he tried worked out right.

Alex's father, Jeff, wanted to take Alex to China with him and his co-workers, so that Alex could spend a little more time with him before the wedding. The only problem was that Jeff didn't have enough money to buy a plane ticket for Alex, if only that problem was to be solved.

Alex's father, a thirty-seven year old man, lived in the capital of Tennessee, Nashville. He moved there after he transferred for his job and got his divorce with Alex's mother. Nashville, Tennessee was about a two-hour drive from Nashville, Tennessee to Chattanooga, Tennessee. Being an advertiser for different companies, he goes around the world advertising for the companies that hire him. Jeff and Alex's mom were married for five years, until they got a divorce.

* * *

"Hey buddy!" exclaimed Alex's father.

"Hey Dad! What are you doing here?" asked Alex.

"I wanted to visit you! Is that all right?"

"Of course that's all right! I love seeing you!"

"I came over here today to tell you something. I have some news to tell you. There's good and bad news. Which do you want to hear first?"

"I guess I want the bad news first,"

"Well you know how I told you that I thought of taking you to China before your mom got married to Jim? Unfortunately, that won't be happening. I can't get enough money in the time that I have. Your Uncle Mark and I have been trying the figure out a way to get the money in two days, but we can't find a way. I really wish I could take you with me though. I'm really sorry."

"Oh Dad, it's okay. I'll be fine here with Mom and Jim. I can toughen it out. I kind of didn't believe that you would be able to get the money in the time."

"I'm glad you understand son, but here's the good news! Do you want to try and guess what it is?" questioned Jeff.

"Not really. I'm a terrible guesser."

"We're going to Atlanta to see your favorite baseball team, the New York Mets, play against the Atlanta Braves tomorrow!"

"Oh my gosh. Are you kidding me? Yes! Thank you so much Dad! I can't wait! Does mom know about this?"

"Of course she knows. I asked her a week ago if I could take you. I felt really bad about not being able to take you to China with me, so I decided to get baseball tickets for you, so we could spend some father-son time."

"I love you so much Dad! It's going to be amazing!"

*   *   *

The baseball game happened to be on the next day. Alex woke up at ten in the morning to get ready. Even though the baseball game started at seven-thirty in the evening. He wanted to make sure everything was set for his day with his dad. He was so excited about this baseball game, especially since he was going to see the New York Mets. He hadn't been to baseball game in almost four years! Alex's dad raised Alex to be a New York Mets fan, since he was a New York Mets fan.

Jeff arrived at Alex's house around twelve in the afternoon, to make sure that Alex was ready. They planned to depart from Chattanooga, Tennessee at around four in the afternoon, so that they could get to Atlanta, Georgia in time for the game. It being a two-hour drive, they wanted to get there earlier than later.

That day, they ate lunch and headed out to their father-son day. Their father-son day turned out to be a hit! There were a myriad of New York Mets fans at the game. The New York Mets won which made the day even better!

After the New York Mets game that Alex and his dad went to, they headed back to Chattanooga.

"Thanks a lot for taking me to the game!" said Alex.

"No problem buddy, anything for you!" said Jeff.

While leaning over to hug Alex, Alex screams, "DAD! WATCH OUT!"

In a split second Jeff's car collided with another car. Alex had a few bruises and Jeff happened to be in a minor coma. An ambulance came right away. Alex's mom and Jim weren't notified about the accident right away. Jeff didn't want them to worry about what happened. The police arrested the drunk driver, and Alex and Jeff were taken to a hospital. When they arrived at the hospital, immediate help was on the way. A doctor examined Alex and told him that he was all right the doctor gave Alex permission to see his dad.

"Hey Dad. How are you feeling?" asked Alex.

"Hey buddy! I'm feeling fine. It wasn't anything too bad. I'm just glad you're all right. God protected us in that accident, and he looked after both of us. I want you to know that God is with you always. I know you've been really confused and stressed lately, but you need to know that He's looking after you. It probably seems as if no one is noticing how you're feeling right now, but God knows everything that is going to happen and what is going on right now. He has so many things in store for you," replied Jeff.

"Thanks Dad, I needed to hear that. I know that God is with me daily, I guess I just needed someone to tell me. You know me so well, Dad. I just hope that Jim will be as great as a dad as you are,"

"Alex, I'm sure Jim is going to be a great father. I've actually given him some advice. Since he's a first time father, he needed some advice. He seems really excited to be apart of your life. You have so many people that care about you. I'm always here for you. If you ever need me, just give me a call,"

"Really? If you say that Jim is going to be a good dad to me, then I guess I'll have to believe you. Thanks again, Dad," said Alex.

Alex's mom didn't answer her phone the first time they tried calling, so Jeff left a voicemail telling her what happened. Since the driver totaled Jeff's 330 Lexus, they had to go rent a car. Since it was two in the morning, Alex's dad decided to get the rental car in the morning when they planned on heading back to Chattanooga. That night, they stayed in a hotel until the next day.

*   *   *

The next day, Alex and Jeff woke up at around ten in the morning to drive back to Chattanooga. Thankfully, nothing happened on the way back to Chattanooga that time. When they got home, Alex's mom came running to the door with a caring and joyful look to her face. She was so glad to see that they had gotten home safe.

"Your mom stayed up all night worrying about you guys," commented Jim.

"Yes I did! I was scared that you guys weren't going to be able to make it back home!" responded Alex's mom.

"We were fine Mom. Dad took care of me! He always does a great job of keeping me safe!" replied Alex.

"Thanks Jeff. I'm glad that you and Alex were able to spend time with each other," said Alex's mom.

"No problem! I love being able to hang out with my old buddy!" said Jeff.

"Thanks again Dad! I had a great time! We should definitely do it again!" said Alex.

"You're so very welcome! I agree! We should do it again! I was thinking though, maybe you and Jim should go though! He likes baseball too, and it would be cool for you guys to hang out together!" exclaimed Jeff.

"Yeah, that's sounds cool," said Jim.

"Uh, yeah. Totally," said Alex.

After that conversation, Alex went up to his room to

go and think about what he just agreed to. Alex didn't even like Jim. He just agreed with Dad so he didn't make Jim feel hated. Alex felt really uncomfortable during that conversation. He had to remember what Jeff said though. God is always with us. Alex got out his Bible and turned to Joshua 1:9. It says, "The Lord your God will be with you wherever you go." Alex pondered on that verse for a while. He realized that God had been working in his life, and he hadn't even had the time to notice. Alex was so grateful to have parents that were God-loving people. Without them, he would have never realized that.

Alex loved being an only child. Of course he sometimes wished that he had a brother or sister, but he had his friends to hang out with. Alex had two best friends, Aaron and Caleb. Aaron, Caleb and Alex were basically brothers. All three of them went to the same high school, church, and they were all the same age. They were a so-called, "trio." They stuck together like white on rice. They had known each other since they were about four years old. Their moms grew up together as well. The three were born to be best friends. Whenever Alex needed some advice about anything, he'd go to Aaron or Caleb. Alex wasn't very fond of going to his parents for answers. Alex and his parents were close, but he needed to be careful about what kind of things he asked his parents for advice on.

Jeff went back to Nashville, Tennessee so that he could catch a flight to Shanghai, China, for a business trip. Right then, Theresa informed Alex that they were going to have dinner over at Jim's house that night. Alex had a bad feeling about going to dinner that night.

"Mom, do I have to go to dinner with you and Jim?" whined Alex.

"Of course you do! You get to see where we are going to be living! It's going to be great! Don't you want to see where you're going to be living?" exclaimed Alex's mom.

"I guess I do, but how long are we going to stay there?"

"No more than three hours. The three hours are gonna fly by! I promise!

"Three hours? Are you kidding me? What are we going to be doing there?"

"We're going to be eating dinner, and then we're going to get a tour of Jim's house! He just bought a house big enough for our family! I haven't gotten to see it yet, so we're going to go tonight! You should be excited! You're going to be able to see where you're gonna live!"

"Yeah, I guess."

That night, Theresa and Alex left their house at around 5:30 in the evening. Jim's new house was about thirty minutes from Alex's house.

When they got to the house, they figured out that the house was gigantic! The house seemed like a mansion! It settled in a perfect area where there happened to be a lot of space, and not much traffic. Alex's mom had an astonished look to her face, and knowing that he would be living in a mansion for the rest of his high school career made him even more satisfied. He liked Jim a little more since he got them a mansion to live in.

Jim came out and saw Theresa and Alex's shocked faces. Alex didn't know that Jim had so much money. He just thought he was a regular guy. Apparently Jim was a wealthy guy who loved Alex's mom.

During the visit, they ate dinner first. For dinner, they had Jim's chef cook for them. They ate pizza that melted in their mouth. After dinner, Alex went up to see what the rest of the house looked like. It looked amazing. The house looked even better on the inside than the outside!

Alex had a suspicion though. Why would Jim buy a mansion? Is it just to look like he's a good guy? Is it just to suck up to his mom? Alex didn't know, but he wanted to find out. Alex decided to go scope out the place to see if anything suspicious was going on. Alex started in the basement of the house. He didn't find anything there. He gradually made his way up to the attic of the house. He found something very abnormal there. He found a travel machine. It wasn't very normal for a person to have a travel machine in their attic. If a person had a travel machine in their possession, they would be killed or they would have loads of money. This travel machine could take you anywhere in the world. You just had to type in where you wanted to go, and in a split second you could be there. Alex began to think that his suspicion might be correct. He wasn't very sure on whether to think that Jim was a terrorist, or whether he was a millionaire.

A few minutes later, he heard Jim stomping up to the attic. Then he heard his mom.

"Alex! Where are you? We're getting ready to leave!" hollered Alex's mom.

Right then, Alex didn't know what would happen if he got caught snooping around Jim's stuff. Especially since Jim disliked Alex, so he decided to hide. Alex didn't know where to hide, so he hid in the travel machine. Right then he knew he had made a stupid mistake. When he heard Jim's voice in the attic, Alex got terrified, not like he wasn't already terrified! When Jim got closer to his hiding spot, Alex began to be frantic with fear of getting caught. He tried not to imagine what would happen to him if he got caught. A few seconds later, he felt the travel machine move and wobble around. He knew something bad was happening.

In a split second, Alex appeared to be in the middle of Shanghai, China. The place where he didn't know the language; or anything! Alex had no idea where he had been taken to when he first got there, but he eventually figured out with all the different Chinese characters around him. Alex had no way of communicating in China, which really stunk for him. He didn't even know where to go! He was a fifteen-year-old boy who was lost in the middle of Shanghai, China.

The next two hours were spent roaming China and trying to figure out how to survive for however long he would be staying there. Alex eventually got to Super Brand Mall, which was located in Lujiazui. Lujiazui is the financial district of Shanghai. It's filled with huge skyscrapers and many Chinese people. When Alex got to Super Brand Mall, he was blown away. The mall was so crowded and noisy! It was way different compared to Chattanooga, Tennessee. Where people had manners. Alex walked around the mall for about an hour and luckily, he had some American money that he had before he left America.

He found a currency exchange machine in the mall. He didn't get a lot of money since he only had fifty dollars which gave him about 340 Yuan, which is China's currency. Now that Alex had money, it was twelve in the afternoon and his stomach was growling. He decided to go eat at McDonald's for lunch. He got a ten-piece chicken nugget, a small coke, and a small pack of fries. It lasted him for about three hours. He went to many different stores and found out that he might need clothes incase he has to stay over night. He went to the store "Quicksilver" and bought a shirt and a pair of jeans. He didn't have much money left after that.

It was around five in the evening when Alex decided to rest and take a break from walking around the mall. Alex decided to leave the mall at around five thirty at night, and decided to walk beside the Huang Pu River, which is also called the Yellow River. That's where something unbelievable happened! It was like a miracle! While walking beside the river, Alex found his dad with a few of his co-workers. When Alex went up to his dad, Jeff had a confused expression to his face when he saw his son in China. Alex happened to be about six thousand miles away from Tennessee.

"Hey Dad!" exclaimed Alex.

"Who's calling me dad?" questioned Jeff.

"It's me! Alex!"

"Alex? It can't be! How'd you get here? Did you take a plane?"

"Nope, I took this travel machine from Jim's attic."

"A travel machine? No one has a travel machine!"

"Well, I definitely didn't come from a plane... It's a really long story, but here it goes. After you left, Mom told me that we were going over to Jim's new house to see where we were going to be living after they got married. We went over, and apparently he is like super rich and has a whole lot of money. He has basically a mansion. It's ridiculous! I was really excited about Jim and Mom getting married. Then I thought something weird was going on. I was really suspicious.

"Oh no, Alex."

"Dad, let me finish. So I was really suspicious, and I decided to scope out the place. I started from the basement making my way up to the attic. There, I found something crazy. Something so abnormal; I discovered a travel machine! WHO HAS A TRAVEL MACHINE IN THEIR ATTIC? Well anyways, I had super bad timing and then I heard Jim's footsteps coming and I panicked, so I hid in the travel machine, which was a stupid idea. I could tell that Jim had been looking for me. In a second, I felt the travel machine shaking and then I ended up in China!

"Alex! Are you kidding me? That's not possible! No one is capable of handling a travel machine. How long have you been here?" asked Jeff.

"I guess for about six hours," said Alex.

"SIX HOURS? You have to be kidding me!" exclaimed Jeff.

"I'm not kidding you. I spent all my time at Super Brand Mall though. At least I'm still alive! The cars here are absurd! They don't let pedestrians pass! I feared for my life!"

"I'm just glad you're safe!"

"Yeah, me too!"

"Wait, before I do anything spontaneous. How do I know that there really is a travel machine, not that I don't believe you, it's just that I need proof."

"Fine, you want proof of the travel machine? Come with me. It's near the huge building. The one that looks like a bottle cap opener."

"The Shanghai World Financial Center?"

"Yeah, sure."

"Well, I don't have much time, but I guess I could spare some time to figure this thing out."

"Okay!"

Jeff's driver took Alex and Jeff to the Shanghai World Financial Center. The travel machine was still there; it hadn't gone anywhere. When Jeff saw it, he stood there in silence, speechless. Alex could tell that he was in shock.

"There you go Dad, there's the travel machine."

"Son, I don't know what to say. I've never seen a thing like this. Sure I've seen it in movies, but I've never seen one in real life."

"Do you believe me now? That's how I got here!"

"Yes, I believe you. Have you tried calling your mom?"

"Nope. How was I supposed to call her?"

"Well, I guess we can call her later. I'm guessing you're pretty hungry. You wanna go get something to eat?"

"Sounds good!"

*　　*　　*

After that scene, they went to the Shangri La, where Jeff had been staying, so that Alex could get freshened up. Alex loved the Shangri La. It was gorgeous. The hotel had everything. Alex got dressed in the clothes he bought

263

at Quicksilver and went out to eat at Element Fresh in Super Brand Mall. At Element Fresh, Jeff's co-workers left and it was just Alex and Jeff. At Element Fresh, they called Theresa and Jim to tell them that Alex was fine. Alex's mom thanked Jim for finding Alex and for keeping him safe. Jim didn't really care, but he tried to sound like he cared. Jeff then told Alex's mom that Alex could stay the rest of the week with him. Alex seemed pretty thrilled that he could stay with his dad for another week. After dinner, they went back to the Shangri La.

"Thanks Dad! It's going to be great spending the whole week with you!"   "You're welcome Alex. Well, actually I'm going to be working this week, but next week we're gonna be able to hang out. I pushed my flight back to Tennessee a week so that we could hang out in China," said Alex's dad. Oh wait, you have your time machine right?"

"Uh, yeah. Why?"

"We could just use your time machine to go back!"

"Oh, okay. Sounds good!" exclaimed Alex.

"Tomorrow I'm gonna be at work, so you can do whatever you want to do, as long as you stay in the hotel. I don't want you to be roaming around Shanghai by yourself. We can do that next week."

"Don't worry Dad. I won't go anywhere tomorrow. I'll stay in the hotel and be a good little boy."

"That's my boy, just exclude the sarcasm part."

"I thought that you always liked my sarcasm! I guess I was mistaken."

"There goes the sarcasm again. I gonna have to give you an attitude adjustment! Anyways, you should get going to bed. It's been a long day for you."

"Yeah, I was just thinking about that. I'm pretty wiped out! Today turned out to be a really interesting day,"

"I'd have to agree."

"Goodnight, Dad."

"Goodnight, Alex."

*   *   *

The next day, Jeff went to work at eight in the morning, and Alex slept in until ten in the morning. After Alex woke up, he decided to go and check out the hotel. Alex loved how they had so many restaurants. Most of the day though, he went to the gym and played around with the equipment. He wanted to look buff so that when he went back to America everyone could see how strong he had become. Especially since he would be in tenth grade next year, he needed to get a girl to notice him. The rest of the week, Alex just went to the gym to work out. He didn't do anything special since his father told him specifically to not go anywhere without him.

After the week was over and Jeff was free from work, Alex and Jeff went sightseeing around Shanghai. The first day, since they were in the financial district of Shanghai, they went to the Pearl Tower. The Pearl Tower was pink and had eleven spheres on the outer part of it. They ate in the revolving restaurant in the Pearl Tower. The second day, they went to the Shanghai Aquarium. It turned out to be pretty cool there. Lots of interesting fish were found in the aquarium, but Alex and Jeff still thought that the Tennessee Aquarium was better than the Shanghai Aquarium; their opinion happened to be biased though. The third day, they went to the Jin Mao Tower. The tower contains eighty-eight stories and had a beautiful view. The fourth day, they went to the Shanghai World Financial Center; its abbreviation is SWFC. The Shanghai World Financial Center is one hundred and one stories high. On the fifth day, they didn't go anywhere. They stayed in the Shangri La and packed and got ready to leave the next day. The Friday they left, they got up early in the morning to go back to Tennessee. Alex and Jeff got to spend a lot of time together, which was good since Alex's mom and getting remarried and he wouldn't see Jeff very often.

Using the time machine, they got to America at

around four in the afternoon. Alex's mom was mainly glad to see the two back in Tennessee. Since Alex never went out of the country, Alex's mom wasn't sure of what would've happened to him. Alex's mom had never even been outside of the country. After Theresa and Jim picked the two up from the airport, they all went to Jim's house. That happened to be the chance for Jim to explain why he had a travel machine in his attic.

"Wow! Jim's house is spectacular!" commented Jeff.

"Didn't I tell you?" asked Alex.

"Yes Alex, Yes you did tell me," replied Jeff.

"It's nothing really. I wanted Theresa and Alex to live in a good house,"

"Well, it's good to know that Theresa and Alex are going to be in good hands, Jim."

"They sure are! You guys can all come in."

"All right!" said Jeff.

Later, Alex talked to his mom by himself. He hadn't gotten to talk to his mom by himself in a while. Alex's mom was usually planning for the wedding, or with Jim. He was pretty happy that he was able to talk to her though. He told his mom the whole story about how he got to China, and about Jim.

"Mom, can you please listen?"

"Honey, I am listening,"

"Well, I know how you told me before that you wouldn't marry a man that you thought would be a horrible father to me? I have something to say about that. I don't think that Jim is the perfect father for me. I'm meaning this from the bottom of my heart. I know that you love Jim, but I know that you can meet a man that is better than Jim."

"Alex James, you cannot talk to me like that. I am your mother, and you are my son. I'm glad that you care about my decisions, but I am old enough to make my own decisions."

"But Mom, Jim doesn't even care about me! You just like him because he has money and lives in a mansion!"

"Alex, I want you to understand that I love Jim for his personality and not his money or possessions."

"Do you know how I got to Shanghai Mom?

"Actually I don't,"

"Jim has a travel machine in his attic! What kind of person has a travel machine in their attic?"

"Oh Alex, that's ridiculous. No one has a travel machine.

"Mom! How do you think I got to China?" Do you remember when you guys were trying to look for me? Well, I was in the attic, and then I heard Jim's footsteps so I panicked. I didn't know what to do, so I hid in the travel machine. While I was hiding, Jim was looking for me in the attic, and he accidentally hit the travel machine when I happened to be in it, and it sent me to China. Don't ask me how this happened though."

"Oh, that's a great story, but I still don't believe this."

"Do you want to come with me so that I can show you proof?"

"Fine,"

Alex took Theresa up to the attic and showed her the attic; it hadn't even moved. After Theresa saw the travel machine, she was really confused and wanted to know why her fiancé had a travel machine in his attic.

"Jim, why is there a travel machine in your attic?" asked Alex's mom.

"Well..."

"Well? What's your reply? I'm really confused, and I'd like to understand what's going on. Now, I'm going to ask again. Why is there a travel machine in your attic?"

"Okay, the truth is, this isn't my house."

"What?"

"Yeah... this isn't my house. It's random person's house that I used."

"Are you kidding me? You tried to impress me by breaking into a random person's house and acting like you lived here?"

"I guess you could put it that way."

"Jim, I'm really ashamed of you. I wouldn't have judged you on what kind of house I would be living in. You know that! I would live in a shack for all I care!"

"Well, I actually haven't gotten a house yet."

"Wait, so you lied to me about that too?"

"Yeah,"

"Jim, this isn't like you. I thought you were someone else. I thought you were a person that I could trust and rely on. Apparently I was wrong. I think Alex and I should get going."

"No, don't go yet!"

"We'll talk about this later Jim."

The one thing that Alex's mom hated when a guy tries to be someone they're not. Alex's mom left the house angry and frustrated at Jim. Alex left with his mom, and Jeff went back to Nashville.

That night turned out to be the end of Jim and Theresa's relationship. Alex's mom cried the whole night; Alex could tell that his mom really loved Jim. Jim ruined everything when he confessed that he was pretending to be someone he wasn't.

"Hey, Mom," said Alex.

"Hey Honey," replied Alex's mom.

"Are you okay?"

"Not really, but I'll be fine."

"Are you sure? I'm really sorry."

"Why are you sorry? There's no need for you to be sorry! You actually helped me. I was about to make a huge mistake and marry a guy that I barely knew. I just thought that if Jim and I could just go back to high school and recreate the fun times we had. Don't ever try that Alex. Live in the present and not the past. Did you get that Alex?"

"Yes Mom, I did. Thank you."

"I love you Alex. Wait for that special person in your life. Okay?"

"I will, I promise."

"Now go get some rest,"

"All right Mom, goodnight."

"Goodnight Alex,"

*　*　*

After Alex had that talk with Theresa, he decided to call his dad. Alex told his dad everything. Jeff decided to call Theresa after he talked with Alex. Jeff drove over to Chattanooga, after he had the chat with Theresa. Alex had already gone to sleep, so he didn't hear about anything until the next day.

The next day, Jeff and Theresa woke up Alex. They told him that everything had been settled, and that they were going to be one family again.

"Alex?" asked Alex's mom.

"What? What's Dad doing here? I thought you were in Nashville!" said Alex.

"I came back, just for a short visit after you had gone to bed. I wanted to see if everything was all right," said Jeff.

"Alex, we have something to tell you. It's good news. I'm sure you're going to be very excited and happy to hear about. You're dad and I have decided to be a family again. It's easier on you, and it's easier on us. I made a terrible mistake, and your father has forgiven me. I realized that it's normal for everyone to fight and argue. Your father and I have decided to become a family again," said Alex's mom.

"Are you serious Mom? This is great! We're going be a family again!"

"I knew you were going to be happy," said Jeff.

"We love you Alex. Now come down and eat breakfast with us," said Alex's mom.

"Okay!"

They were finally going to be a family again. God had been with Alex all along. He just had to have faith and believe it.

That day ended up being the start of a new and normal life... well a semi-normal life.

A few years later, Jim ended up going to jail for breaking and entering and for being responsible for the ownership of the travel machine. After that, the Johnson family never heard of Jim ever again.

Down With the Town

By John Vecellio

The creature let out a thunderous screech that pierced the Professor's ears. The beast grew larger and larger. The restraining straps snapped, and the table that held it collapsed under the weight. Suddenly, the monster stopped growing. It swung its hand to the ceiling, trying to break lose and escape. Some of the goop that formed its arm splashed on the Professor's white lab coat and black boots.

The professor wiped it of and said, "I have finally done it! I, Professor Deen Pexel, have successfully created a monster! Now I can finally lay waste to this trashed town and become the King!" he barked in an evil voice.

The monster seemed perfect in every way, giant and destructive.

"Now Monster, I command you to destroy this town," he barked in a firm voice, pointing his finger to the sky.

The immense creature stopped hitting the ceiling and just stood looking down at the Professor.

"Come on, Go!" Staring blind-eyed at him, the creature

sat down. "No! Bad Monster. You will listen to me and do as I command, now GO!"

The monster let out another thunderous roar that shook the beakers and test tubes. Professor Pexel grunted and sighed. He knew that this was another failure but this was the closest he had ever been in all of his fifty-three years. His failures started way back in 1873, in his current town of Scranton Ville, Britain. At the age of seventeen, he had become fascinated in monsters and had always wanted to create his own. Hoping to become the supreme ruler of the village, so he wouldn't have to take orders from the King any longer. He began his quest to create the ultimate creature that would make him King.

Counting this creation, Professor Pexel had twenty-seven other attempts, but none where successful.

"I guess there is no other choice. If you don't listen to me, then what good are you?" Professor Pexel walked over to a machine along the long, cracked wall. The machine had a number "8" painted in black on it. He punched a long combination of buttons, and the machine started to shake. Then it stopped and went completely quiet.

The Professor grabbed a pin off of machine nine and dashed over to the monster jabbing the pin into the creature's foot. The pin began to flash faster and faster. Finally it stopped. The monster suddenly turned to liquid and oozed through the drain in the cracked, uneven lab floor.

"What is the problem here? Why isn't this working? I try and try but still fail. I wonder what I could do to make this work." The Professor pulled on his gray, coarse hair trying to come up with a solution. "I've got it! My brother Harry is a genius; perhaps he can offer some advice. Better not tell him what it is for though." He might not like what I am doing, and therefore will not offer to help, the professor was thinking to himself. The Professor ran to the phone and punched the numbers.

"Hello, this is the residence of Professor Harry Pexel. How may I be of assistance?" A voice said in a sophisticated manner.

"Harry, this is your brother, Deen. I need your help."

"My help, I thought you always said that you were the better scientist. Why would I help you?" the voice on the other line said smugly.

"Come on Harry, this is no time for games. I have a question for you."

"Okay, speak!"

"For the longest time, I have been experimenting with ectoplasm and trying to create workers with it." Professor Pexel lied to avoid suspicion. "But for some reason the workers will not listen to me. What am I doing wrong?"

"Here's the thing Deen. I have never really experimented with ectoplasm, myself. I am afraid that I wouldn't have an answer for you. However, if I know you, you don't have an assistant. My advice to you would be to find one. Assistants can offer new ideas and give new insight to an obstruction such as this. However, I do warn you, there's been an assistant that goes around helping people. Then when they are close to making a new discovery, he steals their ideas. I am just warning you. Now seeing as it is late at night, I bid you farewell."

Harry didn't even wait for his brother to say goodbye. Now Pexel knew what he needed to do. He had to find an assistant, and together they would try to solve this problem and create their own monster.

The Professor slammed down the phone and raced to his lab. When he arrived, he dashed to the corner of the room to his desk and pulled out a sheet of paper from the drawer. He started to draw. He put in big letters on the top of the page, "Assistant for Hire!" Below that he put some specifications about the job. "Professor Deen Pexel needs your help and is willing to pay top dollar for it. Assistant must have some background in science and be ready to take orders."

The Professor then grabbed the slip of paper and bolted his way to town. As he neared the town, he slowed down to a brisk walk. He passed by the old rickety sign that read "Scranton Ville." As he saw it, he murmured to himself,

Scranton Ville, what a terrible name for a town. If I were in charge, I would name it something with some zing and pep. Pexeltown, yeah, that sounds perfect.

The Professor repeated this name over and over to himself. The Professor then came to an old building that had only a few broken windows, nothing compared to the rest of the buildings in the town. As he opened the door, a bell atop the door rang. Then a clerk came to the counter.

"How may I help you?" said the man that worked the counter.

"I need thirty copies of this." The Professor slammed his "help needed ad" on the table and slid it to the clerk. The clerk picked it up and looked at it with great confusion.

"You need thirty copies of this?"

"Yes, how long should something like that take?"

"This is a big order for this small printing company. We haven't seen an order like this in a while. Should have em' finished by Monday. Come back in five days."

"Thank you." Pexel looked up at the plaque that had prices on it. "Looks like the standard rate of two cents per page."

"As much as we would love that, you get a discount for ordering such a large amount. We will knock off a whopping five cents. That will bring your grand total to, fifty-five cents."

The Professor set the money on the table and walked out the door.

*   *   *

Time passed slowly as the professor waited for Monday.

His heart raced with excitement on Monday morning. He arrived at the printing store as soon as the clerk opened shop.

"Are my posters ready?" Pexel asked anxiously.

"Yes, I will go and get them for you." The clerk walked away from the desk and entered a back room. Then he came back out and set a stack of papers on the desk. "Good Luck!"

Professor Pexel grabbed the papers and scampered out the door.

"I will hang these all over town. This will let people know that I am looking for an assistant and increase the likelihood of someone coming in to interview.

The professor posted his help ads all over town and then returned to his home. He went down to his lab and sat at his desk waiting for a knock at the door or a ring of the doorbell. The Professor sat there anxiously tapping his foot and scratching his head, but no one showed.

As the clock struck ten, the professor gave up and started to walk up to his room, when he heard a knock at the door. He made a mad dash to the foyer and opened the door.

"Hello! Sorry to disturb you at such a late hour, but I saw your poster and had to get here before anyone else got the job. I want to be interviewed to be your assistant."

"Very well, come, come in quickly and grab a chair."

The short hunchbacked man scampered inside.

"Follow me," the professor said. The two walked down into the Professors lab.

As the two trotted down the stairs, Pexel asked, "So what do I call you?"

"I am, Hector G. Zasck!" The short fat man announced proudly. "You must be Professor Deen Pexel."

"Why yes, I am. Before we get started with this, what knowledge do you have in the background of ectoplasm?"

"Well, my previous teacher had success in making

a little gooey ball that would move to the direction you told it to. However, I don't really remember how he did it. I could try though."

"Excellent! Maybe after a few tries, you will remember."

When they reached the lab Hectors jaw dropped.

"Wow! Look at all of this equipment. Never have I witnessed such a work of art. The man ran along the wall with all of the machines, dragging his and along each one of them. These machines are amazing!"

"It seems that you will be the perfect candidate for my assistant. If you want the job, how does fifty cents a day sound?"

"I would be honored to be your apprentice."

"Good show old boy, your work will start in the morning. Be at my doorstep at 6:30 A.M. and not a minute later."

"Thank you so much Professor Pexel! I will not let you down!"

Professor Pexel escorted Hector back up stairs and to the door.

"Wait here I will go get your coat." Professor Pexel said then dashed around the corner. He went to the coat closet and picked up Hectors black lab coat. Then Pexel reached up to the shelf about the coat rack and grabbed a small black journal. He then came back to Hector handing him his coat. Then he handed him the journal and said,

"Here, use this to take notes in. Make sure you bring it tomorrow also."

"Fabulous, I am excited to be able to learn from you. Good night!"

Pexel closed the door and tiptoed up to bed. That night, He couldn't sleep. The excitement overcame him.

He kept talking to himself. "Finally, I will be able to make a monster, a living, breathing, obeying monster that will destroy this village. This Hector person will help me to make this little ectoplasm ball then I will fire him. I know that if he ever found out what I truly have in store, he would call the police. He just doesn't seem like the type of person that would stand by and watch as I take over this town. He seems shy and nervous but brave at the same time. It is really confusing. Oh well, time to call it a night"

The Professor turned over and fell asleep.

* * *

The next morning, The Professor was in his kitchen drinking coffee and reading a book when, just as promised, doorbell rang. He looked up to the clock.

"Six-Fifteen, I like a man who shows early"

The Professor got up out of his chair and answered the door.

"Hello Hector, nice to see you again. I think that it would be best to get right down to business. Follow me to the lab."

Once again, Hector gasped in amazement to the lab and all of its machines. When they got there they walked over to Pexel's planning desk. He already had his formulas to his previous monster laid out.

"Let's make a list." Pexel directed.

"A list for what?" Hector said in total confusion.

"I think it would be best to start from scratch. Every time I tried before I failed. That's because I was using a formula that didn't work. If we start over, then maybe you could catch some mistakes and help out with the thought process. So, lets make a list for supplies that we need. Then we will make the ectoplasm. From there, we will come up with a formula to bind it to DNA. And then finally we will train it to listen to voice commands. So let's get started."

The two rambled on about different ingredients. Each one of them suggested a couple of ideas that sounded completely preposterous, but they saw past their disputes and finally came up with one complete list of seventeen different items.

"I know just the place to purchase these items" Hector exclaimed. "There is a store just outside of town. An old woman named Voodoo Booboo Juju runs it. She has everything on this list. Should we try there?"

"Of course we should go there, what were you thinking?" Pexel shouted in a playful manner.

Pexel marched up the stairs followed by his apprentice. The two gathered their stuff and marched outside. Then Pexel walked into a small shed that sat beside his house. He then yanked out a small wagon through the door.

"Here Hector, you can pull this." The Professor handed him the cart and began to walk down the road. Hector followed without saying a word. The two trotted down the road without speaking until Hector shouted, "There, that is the shop. That has to be it."

The two started to run. Hector parked the wagon and went inside the shop followed by Pexel. No one was there. They rang the bell on the desk and a woman from the back shouted,

"Be with you in a second."

The two stood there waiting. Pexel looked down at Hector's hand and noticed that he didn't have all five fingers. He was missing his ring finger.

"Hector, if you don't mind me asking, what happened to your finger?"

"For your information, I do mind, but I am going to tell you anyway. When I worked with my previous teacher, I did not follow his instructions on how to use one of his fancy machines. On accident I let the machine overheat and caused it to jam. I stuck my hand inside to fix the jam when all of a sudden, the machine started back up again and severed my finger."

"Hmmm... I hope you heed my instructions well because all of my machines are very dangerous. I would hate for something like that to happen again."

As Pexel finished his sentence, an old lady came rushing out of a backroom door.

"Sorry to keep you waiting. Just finishing some personal stuff. Business has been very slow lately. How may I help you?" The woman asked in a frail old voice.

"I will need one of each of these ite—"

Before Pexel could finish, the lady snatched the paper from him.

"One of each, you say? Should cost you about five-fifty. You can sit down over there while I get these." The lady pointed to two dusty old looking chairs. The two men sat there, looking around the shop at all of the creepy, mysterious things that were hanging from the walls and ceiling. There were jarred bats, pickled brains, and whole skulls all sitting on her shelves.

"Is it just me or does this place give you the creeps?" Hector asked.

"You said you have been here before, don't you remember?"

"It was a long time ago. I was in-and-out. I picked up something for a friend."

"Oh okay, but remember how creepy this place is for next time."

"Here you are boys. One of everything."

Pexel counted out five-fifty and put it on the counter.

"Grab some stuff and help carry it to the cart!" Pexel ordered Hector.

"Yes sir."

The two loaded up the cart and began their walk home.

When they arrived back at the Professor's home, Hector and Pexel unloaded the cart and started hauling their ingredients down to the lab. The two set up all of the items on one of the many tables.

"Lets get to it!" the Professor said in an anxious voice. "Hector, grab that beaker over there along with a couple of test tubes." Pexel opened the jar labeled "Eye of a Newt" and dropped it into a beaker. Then he took another can with a skull and crossbones on it, and poured it into the same beaker. The eye disintegrated and all that was left was the juices from it. Pexel then opened another jar and poured a wax-like substance into a test-tube.

"Hector take this over there to that big machine with the large number four on it. Put the test-tube in the slot and twist the dial to number eight. Quickly now, can"t let this solidify. Time is of the essence." Pexel watched as Hector ran over the machine and filled the order. Meanwhile Pexel picked up the beaker and swished it around to keep it in liquid state. Hector raced back and handed the test-tube to Pexel.

"Now open all of the jars that we just bought and poor them into this bowl." Pexel set an enormous bowl down on the floor. Pexel took the beaker and the test-tube and also poured their contents into the bowl.

"Now grab the other end of this bowl and help me carry it to machine nine." Pexel knew that the bowl would be heavy but it surprised him how ponderous the mixture really was. The two wobbled as they neared the machine. They set the bowl on the floor in front of the machine. Then Pexel pulled a device off of the machine. It had a rod on the end of it and he plopped it into the weird bluish mixture. The bar turned red-hot and made the goop turn green. Pexel pulled two masks off of the machine's side and handed one to Hector.

"You will need this. I think it's going to get pretty smelly in here."

"Gee thanks," Hector said.

Both of them slipped a gasmask on and watched as the substance started to shrink.

"Wow, I had no idea that that humungous pot of ectoplasm would shrink to such a little ball." Hector said in surprised voice. Hector then put his had out and tried to pick up the little ball of goop when the Professor slapped it away.

"What are you, crazy? That ball is over one thousand degrees Kelvin. You'll fry your hand off"

"Oh sorry, wasn't thinking."

"It is things like that that make you loose like fingers. You need to start paying attention to your surroundings."

Pexel walked over to a barrel and pulled out a special pair of tongs. Then he pulled a thick pair of gloves out. The tongs had a small cup on each side. He scooped up the ball in the cups and walked it over to the machine with a big number six on it. He opened the tongs and the ball fell into a funnel that connected to the machine.

"This will take a while. We need to let the machine do its work to cool the ectoplasm down to room temperature. What do you say we walk up to the tavern and 'av ourselves some lunch?"

"Sounds like a plan, I am starving!" said Hector.

*   *   *

As the two walked back, something caught Pexel's eye. It was a WANTED sign. On it stood a sketch. Pexel looked at it then looked at Hector. He realized that the person on the sign resembled Hector. Pexel kept on walking and didn't say a word. He thought to himself, *Now is not the time nor place to ask him about this. I will talk to him about it later.* The two came to Pexel's house and, again, made their way down to the lab.

"Looks like it is done," said Hector pointing at a big green light on the top of machine six.

"Yes, now it is done. It is safe to touch. Bring it over to me." Hector ran to the machine and opened a hatch at the bottom of it. He pulled out the ball and rolled it in his hand.

"We made good progress today. Lets conclude by

running some tests and then you can have the rest of the day off."

"What kind of tests?" Hector said in a perplexed voice.

"That's a good question. I really have no idea. See that bookshelf over there?" Pexel pointed to a wall full of books. "On the third shelf from the wall, fifth shelf up there should be a book all about ectoplasm. Go fetch it for me."

Pexel watched as he ran over to the wall, grabbed a ladder, and slid it over to where the book was. He found it funny how he climbed the steps and slid his hand along the bindings of the books.

"Hmmm... Oh! This must be it." Then he pulled a book out and read the title to Pexel. "*101 Ways to Make Ectoplasm* that sounds perfect." Pexel watched as the man did his limp-run and brought the book to him. Pexel opened the book and flipped through the pages to the index. Then turned to page 347.

"Ahhh! Here it is. Test the ectoplasm. First test: consistency. Is the ectoplasm a constant density throughout? The answer is "no" I guess. This side is very squishy but the other side is very stiff. The book says that if this happens, put it in a tumbler."

"Well Professor we are lucky that we have one aren't we?"

"Yes Hector, we are. Do you know how to use it?"

"Who doesn't know how to use a tumbler?"

Pexel handed the ectoplasm to Hector who then ran it over to the tumbler machine two. He set the orb in the machine and closed the hatch. Then pushed the big red button. The machine started slow then gradually got faster. It shook, twisted, and turned. The two watched it for a minute or two. The machine then stopped and Hector lifted the hatch and handed the ball to Pexel.

"Perfect! Now what's next? Hmmm...okay, next test is shape retention. The book says that the ectoplasm should retain its shape if dropped from a high point over ten feet. Okay Hector you run up to the top of the stairs and drop the ectoplasm through the hole that the stairs spiral 'round. Hopefully this will work because it says that the only way to fix this one if broken is to remake the whole substance."

Hector grabbed the ball and hopped up the stairs. He looked down the hole in the center and saw the professor.

"Are you ready, Professor?"

"Ready when you are Hector."

Hector released the ball and it plummeted down to the laboratory floor. Pexel watched as the orb hid the floor, absorbed the impact, the returned to the ball state.

"Perfect!" shouted Pexel. "Good thing we don't need to remake the ectoplasm.

Hector ran down the stairs and joined Pexel.

"Today was a successful day. Lets call it, we both worked hard today. Take the rest of the day off. Come back tomorrow, same time as usual."

"Thank you, sir." Hector marched up the stairs and walked out the door. Pexel heard the door close then he took the ectoplasm and put it in one of the cabinets. He looked up at the clock that read 6:30 P.M. Pexel walked up the stairs and made himself some dinner. Then he sat down and started to read a book. Next thing he knew, the clock struck ten. He packed up his book and when upstairs to bed. That night Pexel couldn't sleep.

I wonder what Hector is wanted for? Maybe since he is a criminal, he would be okay with my plan to take over this town. He might even help. Uhg... What was I thinking? I can't ask him to help me. He would never go for it. Pexel rolled over and fell asleep.

The next morning, a knocking on the door awakened Pexel. He looked a t the clock and it read 6:30 A.M.

"Oh! I must have overslept." Pexel ran down the stairs and opened the door.

"Good morning Hector. I am sorry but I got off to a late start this morning. Come in and help yourself to my kitchen while I get dressed. I will be down momentarily." Pexel ran back upstairs and into his wardrobe. He pulled out his white lab coat and slipped into it. Then he combed his gray, coarse hair and put his long black gloves on and rushed to join Hector.

"All right, let's get to work" The Professor uttered all out of breath. They eagerly walked down the spiral steps to the lab.

"Okay, what's on the agenda for today?" questioned Hector.

"Today we are going to attempt to blend some DNA into the ectoplasm to turn it into a living, breathing creature. The only question is: what kind of DNA should we use? Human? Animal? Bacterial? What do you suggest Hector?"

"I think that my previous teacher used his own DNA from his hair. That worked for him, maybe you should give it a go."

"Of course! I can't believe I never thought of that. A hair follicle should be perfect. I guess we will start with that."

Pexel went over to the cabinet and took out the ectoplasm ball.

"We need to transform it back into a liquid state instead of this jelly state. Then we can mix in the DNA."

"Machine nine?" Hector asked.

"Hey, you're a fast learner. You catch on quick. Yes, machine nine."

Pexel pulled a small bowl out from the cabinet and dropped the ectoplasm in it. Again he took the device with the rod on it and put it on the ectoplasm. It expanded, but not too much. He then pulled three of his gray, coarse hairs from his head. "Ouch" he mumbled under his breath. "So what will we do while it cools down?" asked Hector.

"This isn't like the last time, the ball is much smaller and will cool much faster. We only need to wait probably another thirty seconds."

Soon after he said that, the ectoplasm formed the ball again, and it started to roll around in the bowl. Pexel reached down and picked it up. He opened his hand and it dropped out and hit the floor. Then it rolled around the lab.

"Oh No! It will be very difficult to retrieve it now!" yelled Pexel. Hector started chasing it all around the lab. It swerved all around, weaving under the tables and around the machines. Eventually with sweat dropping from their foreheads, the two of them cornered the thing and Pexel trapped it in a small cage.

"We have to train that thing before we let it out again." Hector exclaimed.

"Lets start by giving it a name to answer to. Hey!" Pexel pointed his finger at the glob. "You *will* answer to the name 2–0–2! Got it? So let's start with something simple.

2–0–2, jump once!" Pexel barked the orders in the blobs face. The little ball took a small leap.

"Oh, it listened!" Hector announced.

"Lets try another one, 2–0–2 run around the cage two times." The little blob rolled around the cage twice then stopped awaiting further orders.

"IT WORKED! IT LISTENS!" Pexel shouted to the whole world. "Now I can crush this town!"

"What? What are you talking about Professor? You are going to do something evil with your new creation, I can just sense it!"

"You are correct my young apprentice. Yes I did use you to help me create a creature out of ectoplasm that would obey me as its Master. Unfortunately you don't know my whole plan. This little ball was just the beginning. I am going to make a full-sized monster that will take this town over and do whatever I say."

"No, there is no way—. I won't let you—!"

"Oh, that is too late. You can't do anything about it."

"Oh, ya? I will make my own monster that will take your monster down."

"How do you plan on doing that? You have no lab, no equipment. I am sorry but there is no chance of anything like that happening."

"I'll figure it out." Hector then ran out of the house.

"I better get to work." The professor took the ball out of the cage and ran over to machine number one. He dropped the ball in and it popped out the other side. It then began to grow. It grew larger and larger until its head touched the ceiling. Still it began to grow, pushing through the ceiling. The monster stood about thirty feet tall. It climbed through the giant hole it had just made and stood there in front of the Professors house.

Pexel ran up the stairs and out the front door. He called out to the monster.

"2-0-2! Can you hear me?" The monster turned to the professor and nodded. "Good. You will obey me is that clear?" Again the creature nodded. The beast kneeled down and extended its arm to the ground. Pexel ran as fast as he could and took a giant leap. He landed on the beasts forearm then climbed up to its shoulder. The beast stood up with Pexel riding on his shoulder.

"March 2-0-2!" Pexel demanded. "Knock down buildings!" the creature extended its arm and slammed it against the buildings on the side of the road. They fell down. The Professor started an evil laugh. It grew louder and louder until the Professor stood there laughing at the top of his lungs. Then the monster stopped walking.

"Here it is, the castle. Once I take that, then I will have the town at my fingertips. 2-0-2! Onward!"

"Not so fast..." said a mysterious voice. Pexel turned around and there stood Hector, beside a monster that looked the same size as 2-0-2. Even made of the same material as 2–0–2. The only difference was instead of being green-see-through ectoplasm it was purple.

"I see. How did you make this?" Pexel barked.

"I went to my old teacher and told him of your doings. He agreed to help destroy you. Together him and I created my monster, Celtic Kiha!"

"Oh you really think that you can build a better monster than me? I have been making monsters my whole life! Ha! 2–0–2Attack!"

2–0–2 made a fist on his right hand and plowed it into Celtic Kiha's chest. The monster stumbled back into a building. He got up and shoved 2–0–2 into the castle wall. Pexel almost lost his balance but he held tight, holding his position. 2–0–2 launched its leg into Kiha's leg and it turned to liquid. Kiha screeched to the sky and its leg grew back. 2–0–2 reached down and picked up a large support beam from one of the broken buildings. Then it thrashed Kiha in the face with the beam. Purple ectoplasm sprayed all over the buildings. Kiha fell to its knees. 2–0–2 hit Kiha again and again until it eventually fell down in the dirt. It didn't get up.

"Ah ha! I told you my monster is better than yours! Now for the grand finale!" Pexel and his monster pushed through the castle gates and made a path up to the highest point. They destroyed anything in their way. The king had ordered his troops to attack. 2–0–2 destroyed them without skipping a beat.

The Professor stood up facing the whole kingdom and announced, "I, Deen Pexel declare this town to be called Pexeltown. I will become the Supreme Ruler. Anyone who resists will face the wrath of my monster." Next, as all of the townspeople lowered their heads and bowed down before him, he looked to the sky and began to laugh.

My fault

By Sydney Wilson

"Where's Dad? He's always home by six-thirty, and it's almost eight," said Hope.

"I have no clue. He's never late, and if he is late, he always calls." I was setting the table for dinner.

My sister Hope and I had grown really close in the past two years. I was fifteen years old and a sophomore. Hope was sixteen years old and a junior at our small-town school, Blue Star High School. We were very different in every way but so close that no one could ever separate us.

Where was dad? He's only been late a couple time and never this late. He always wanted to have dinner with his girls, so where was he? I had a foreboding feeling. I felt it in my stomach. I couldn't quite point it out, but I knew it was there. It was going to happen soon, real soon. Today, maybe tomorrow.

"Hey, was that the door?" asked Hope curiously. Someone rang the doorbell and knocked on the door.

"I'll get it," I said, setting the forks down excitedly on

the table. I was hoping to catch Dad before Hope could hammer him with questions.

"No Angel, I've got it," said our mom, Christina, as she rushed down the stairs and opened the door. "Hey there, John, you want to come in? We just made roast chicken, your favorite."

I stood right next to the bookcase, out of mom's sight, but all the while, I listened and watched the two of them.

My mother wasn't like a typical mom you would find in any normal family; she acted more like a friend. She wasn't strict. She was bubbly and fun to be around. John Pauling was the town sheriff and Dad's best friend.

Mr. Pauling looked strange, as if he were in pain. His voice sounded unnatural. "No thanks, Christina. I came to deliver some bad news."

"What is it John? Come on, it's not like I'm going to get mad," Christina said slowly.

"Christina," Mr. Pauling took Mom's hand in his. "We found Logan. He...um...we found Logan in his car."

"What do you mean? Where's Logan? Is he okay?" Mom pressed on. Logan was my dad. "John answer me. John! John! Where is my husband? Was Logan in an accident? John! Talk to me! Please!" Mom sobbed furiously in Mr. Pauling's tight embrace.

"Mom? Mom! What's going on?" Hope ran in to the living room, a place mat still in one hand.

I followed her closely behind, "Where's dad?" I looked around the room, no one answered. They all stared blankly back at me, except for Mom, who was still silently sobbing. I overheard their conversation, and knew something horrible had happened to Dad. "Mom? Mr. Pauling? Hope? Anyone?"

My long brown wavy hair fell in front my face. I brushed it back. I wanted to know what was going on.

"Hope, Angel, we found your dad," Mr. Pauling turned

slowly to face us, his face looked pinched with pain. "He was in his car. He committed suicide. I am so sorry."

"NO! No, no, no. . ." Mom wailed.

Mr. Pauling held out his arms and wrapped them around Mom, Hope, and me. The moment Mom stopped yelling, the house turned quiet.

After a few long moments, Mr. Pauling broke the silence, "He left you all letters."

"What kind of letters?" Hope asked, wiping tears off her cheek with the back of her palm.

"A letter for each one of you. There was one for me, too," Mr. Pauling said as he handed us the letters.

"Did you read it?" I asked.

"What did it say?" Hope stared at the letter, debating if she should open it or not.

All four us were in shock from what had happened. I couldn't even let myself think about what had happened, that Dad would do something like this. Suddenly a cold chill ran down my spine, and when I realized that Dad was forty-two, the same age as his dad when he committed suicide.

Anger rushed through me, and my hands bunched into fists. Why did he take his own life? Was life so bad that he thought he should punish all of us for it? Why didn't I see this coming? Did Dad love us? Did he love me?

Dad and I had a great relationship. We both loved and breathed soccer. On my fourth birthday Dad gave me my first soccer ball; it was pink with purple flowers. That was the day my dad started to coach me, and the day I fell in love with soccer. He also became the coach for all my soccer teams. He was never a tough coach, but he made sure that we were all motivated and inspired to play. We got so good that we were in the state championships this year, but lost by one point to Niskayuna Central High.

I had to stop thinking about Dad. Tears almost pushed their way out, but I couldn't start crying now. I had to be strong for my family. I had to make sure that my family didn't crumble into pieces. I had to be the person that would bring us up again.

"His letter to me just said not to be sad and that it wasn't our fault," Mr. Pauling was saying. I could tell that Mr. Pauling was trying really hard to fight back tears, but he fail soon afterwards.

"Well, um... Mom should I open mine?" Hope asked.

"Yes, honey, your dad would have wanted you to," Mom said, walking into the kitchen. She looked lost and confused. "John, are you sure that you don't want some dinner. We made enough for four."

Then Mom hid her face in her hair. She sobbed at the idea that Dad should have been the fourth person at the dinner table. She sank to the floor, with her arms around her knees. Mr. Pauling ran over to her and helped her into a chair. Hope and I rushed to our mother and gave her big hug.

Mr. Pauling turned to me. "I'll come tomorrow, if that's okay with everyone?"

I just nodded.

"Yes, please. I think that we'll all need family and friends around in a time of need," Mom said, as she tried to get up.

*   *   *

A week had passed, and Hope and I headed back to school. Our family and friends had traveled from all over the state for the wake and funeral. To me, the week was a blur of sadness, with people sobbing and using up boxes and boxes of tissues. But I hadn't cried. Not even once. I couldn't. Mom and Hope needed me. I had to remain strong.

Mom and Hope had both already read their letters, each three pages long, double sided. They told me Dad had written about moving on, not getting miserable over what had happened and understanding that he had to do this for him. The letters were filled with memories and the good old days; he said we should remember those good days and not this time of sadness.

Hope and I arrived at the school parking lot. I could feel every eye on us. Luke ran up and kissed me on the top of my head. "Welcome back," he said. Taylor was right behind him, as he put his arm around Hope's shoulders.

Luke and I had been dating for about a year and a half. He was a sophomore like me, but he was already sixteen. Taylor was Hope's boyfriend. He wasn't that smart, but he made Hope happy. That is all that mattered then.

Allie started to walk up to us. "Oh my gosh, I'm so sorry about what happened. My mom wanted me to say that our family is here for you two and your mom. Really any time, even in the middle of the night. Just give us a call."

"Thanks Allie," I said. Allie was the kind of girl that had to get into everyone's business and was the first one to know about everything.

We walked to our lockers, and that's when I noticed that every eye was still on me, but not Hope. All I could think of was that there was something on my face, or that I had put my pants on backwards.

"Hey, why is everyone staring at me? And only me?" I asked Luke.

"It's just a stupid rumor. Don't worry about it." Luke grabbed his books and shut his locker. "Come on, we're going to be late for class."

"No," I stood there. My feet were glued to the floor. "Luke, what's going on? And don't tell me its nothing."

"Not now, okay? Later," He started walking towards English again.

"No," I wasn't going to wait. If the rumor had anything to do with my dad, I want to know. "Tell me, and I don't care about class."

"Angel, don't be like this," Luke said, he looked

straight into my eyes. Then he sighed, "Okay fine. But stay calm."

"I'm waiting," I stood with arms crossed, staring defiantly at Luke.

"You know Amy. She loves to spread rumors, like wild fire. Well she started this one. And...well...the rumor is that it was your fault for what had happened to your dad, because you missed that goal in the state championships." He hugged me tightly. I knew he didn't want to see the look in my eyes. "But everyone knows that it's just a rumor. You and I know that it isn't true. Your dad did not kill himself because of you," he whispered in my ear.

"How do you know that? It could be true," doubt filled my trembling voice. "It could be my fault. Well maybe not because of the game, cause that would just be stupid. But we did get into a huge fight a few days ago before everything, about soccer and how he was always trying to push me to go farther. I was just so tired of being yelled at, so I yelled back. Plus I should have seen it coming. I should have stopped him. But I didn't. What does that say about me?"

"Angel, you know it's not your fault. You can't think this way." He placed his hands on my shoulders. "Have you read the letter he gave you?"

"No, I don't see the point. I don't want to know what he wrote to me. He's going to tell me to forget this sad time. Guess what? I'm not going to forget this time. I am not going to forgive him for the pain he has put on our family. I don't want to do anything he wants me to do, including reading the letter." My voice cracked, and my hands shook as I grabbed my book bag.

"Angel read it. Your dad didn't do this to hurt you. Will you just read the letter for me?"

"Yes, fine," I lied. The letter was going to sit on my desk, unread for a very long time.

English class was as boring as ever, but when the class ended Mrs. Brooks told me to go to the counselor's office. I really didn't want to go. I didn't see any reason to. I knew exactly what this was about. I would just go in and say that I was fine. I didn't feel like telling her my feelings. To me, that was just dumb.

I reached the office, took a deep breath and knocked on the door.

"Who is it?" Someone asked from inside the door.

"It's Angel Silver," I answered.

"Oh, come on in honey," said Ms. Alexander. "And close the door, will you?"

I closed the door as she asked and made my way to the sofa centered across from Ms. Alexander. She turned around from her computer and looked at me. "Do you want a piece of chocolate?" she asked.

"No thanks, Ms. Alexander," I tried to be polite.

"Call me Ms. Alex, all the kids do." She got up, tied her blonde wavy hair into a ponytail and sat on the couch next to me. "Is there anything you want to talk to me about?"

"No, not really," I answered quickly. All I wanted to do was leave. I didn't want to talk about my life at all. It was useless to me.

"Angel, I just talked to your sister Hope and she's worried about you. She says that you won't talk about what has happened with your dad. That maybe you are hiding it all in, and that you may need some help to let in all out. She also said that she hasn't seen you cry, is that true?"

"I don't understand why all this matters, plus this isn't any of your business," I snapped.

"Angel, I just want to help, that all I'm here for." She put her hand on my knee, but I shrugged it off.

"So what if I haven't cried yet. Is that supposed to mean something?" I didn't like how I was acting, it wasn't me. But I couldn't tell her what was going on, so I changed the topic fast. "I have to be strong for my family, and I can't fall into pieces like my mom. She is miserable at home. All she does is look at her wedding pictures. I don't know what I can do for her. I try to talk to her, but she's always thinking about something else. I feel like she isn't there anymore, that she's not my mom anymore."

"Well I think the best thing you can do for your mother is to make sure that you tell her that you love her, to let her feel love, and make sure she knows that you will always be there for her. Then you can build your mother up from there."

"Thanks, um...I think I should get to math. Could I have a note?"

"Yes, of course."

Hopefully I didn't say too much.

After school, Luke dropped me off at home. The last thing he said to me was, "Everything is going to be okay." I want to believe him so badly, but I couldn't. I didn't believe in "okay" any more.

"Hey, who dropped you off?" Hope asked, as I walked through the main door.

"Luke," I dropped my gym bag and backpack on the stairs.

"Well that was sweet of him." That's when Hope noticed my gym backpack.

"Oh, I didn't go to soccer practice."

"Why not?" she asked.

"Cause I didn't feel like going."

"Honey!" Hope was worried about me.

"Don't 'Honey' me, okay? I can't go to soccer practice."

It was useless to go to practice without dad as a coach. I didn't love soccer any more without dad, I couldn't. It felt like something was missing without him, something huge. It wasn't worth it for me to play soccer anymore. Soccer was what dad and I shared it brought us together, I just couldn't do it without him.

I stomped up to my room and Hope followed me.

"Hey, so I kinda want to ask you about something," Hope said, as she sat on my bed.

"Sure, go ahead," I said, calming down.

"Well, today I met up with Ms. Alex, and well I was wondering if you did too?"

"Yeah I did."

"I was wondering what you guys talked about." Hope questioned.

"Nothing, really. I was annoyed with Ms. Alex. She has no right to ask me or you about our family." I frowned.

"Did you guys actually talk about anything?" Hope asked.

"I was only in there for about five minutes. We talked about mom and me." I felt the anger rising up. "Why did you tell her that I haven't cried yet? 'Cause you know what Hope? That's none of your business. I don't see how that matters to anything."

Suddenly, I remember my anger at her for talking about me with Ms. Alex. I know she was my sister and all, but I could take care of myself. I didn't need someone looking over my shoulder and wondering if I was okay.

"Of course it's my business. I'm your sister, Angel." Hope stood up. "Look, I'm worried about you. I don't think you've really thought about what has happened. And I've also heard the rumors that Amy spread. Luke and I are both really worried about you..."

"Luke and I! So you two are talking about me now?" I interrupted.

"No, we are just worried. Back to what I was saying if you want to talk about anything, I'm here for you and so is Luke."

"You know what I want? I want to punch Amy because she had no right to spread that stupid rumor."

"I know, I know. But you know that the rumor isn't true right?"

"I don't want to talk about this any more."

"I think you need to."

"No, I don't." Why couldn't she just leave me alone?

"Angel, talk to me, please. Let me in." She reached her hand out to grab my hand, but I pulled away.

We both sat on the floor, staring at the ugly pink and purple carpet.

"Hope, I just don't know any more. I don't know why he did that to himself. He was the same age as his dad when he took his life. Plus dad was really furious when I missed that goal. We could have won the state championship, but we didn't because of me. Also we had a huge fight, I just don't know any more."

"Angel do you really think that dad would take his own life because his daughter missed a soccer goal or because they got into a fight?"

"No."

"Yeah that's what I thought. Look, a lot of people love you in this world. Please let some of us help you and let us in on what you are thinking."

"I am," I lied.

"No, you aren't. For example, right now you aren't, you're not giving me the whole story."

Hope and I sat there in silence for a few minutes, and she looked a round the room and saw Dad's letter on my desk. "Why haven't you opened this?"

"Because I don't want to," I didn't.

"Well, why don't we just open it now?"

"No." I snapped, reached over and grabbed the letter from her and put it back on my desk. "Come on, mom's crying again. I think she has the wedding pictures out again."

Downstairs I could hear her sobbing and saying the words "Why?" to herself over and over again.

The next day didn't get any better. When I opened up my locker I found a note.

Angel, you are right. You know that if you scored that goal, you dad would still be here.

Someone you know

"What kind of sick joke is this?" I slammed the noted in to Amy.

"What are you talking about?" She read the note and shrugged. "This isn't me," she said, flipping her too blonde, too straight hair.

"Then who is it?"

"How should I know? Gosh, who do you think I am? I'm not that mean."

"Look Amy, I'm not going to play games with you, because I don't have the time to and I don't want to. I swear if I find out that you wrote this, trust me you'll regret it."

"Is that a threat?"

I just walked away. I couldn't stand Amy. I need space to think. Whoever put this note in my locker, I was going to find them.

After P.E., Luke was waiting for me by the gym. We made small talk about our day and about classes.

"So um... I heard that you got into a fight with Amy," Luke said when we reached my locker.

"She had it coming. She put a stupid little note in my locker saying that my dad died because of me." I was still really mad about it, but part of me wondered if she was right. I did say some pretty horrible stuff to dad the last time we fought.

"Do you still have the note?" Luke asked.

"Yeah." It was in my pocket. I had forgotten that I put it there but now it felt like it as burning a hole in my jeans. I handed the note to Luke and watched him read it.

"Wow, whoever did this is an idiot. This isn't true." Luke's cheeks turned red with anger.

"It was Amy." Suddenly, I was sure of it.

"You do know its not true, right?"

"I'm not going to have the same conversation with you that we had yesterday."

"Angel..." He couldn't finish because I stopped him by opening my locker. The door slammed into his face.

A piece of paper fell out. Luke picked it up. Suddenly his whole face changed into a mask of pain and shock.

I grabbed the paper from him.

Hey there again. I'm glad you got my first note. Well I'm not Amy, but

you were close, very close actually. I'm impressed. Anyways I have

something to tell you, Your dad wasn't always faithful to your mother.

Look in the yellow pages, search up the name "Cutie pie". You'll know what I mean when you see it.

Someone you know

"I have to go home." I grabbed all my books and ran out the school door.

"Angel, I'm driving you home." Luke ran after me.

We got to my house in about five minutes, only because I yelled at him to go faster every two seconds.

I found the Yellow Pages on the coffee table and flipped it to the letter "C". Finally I found something called Cutie Pie Salon.

"Hope, have you ever been to Cutie Pie Salon?" Hope had just walked through the door.

"Yeah, that's were I go to get my hair cut. Why?" She was looking at Luke and I with a strange face. My stuff was all over the floor and normally Luke wasn't allowed over unless a parent was home with us.

"Where's mom?" she asked.

"At the store. She left a note on the coffee table. Anyway, when did you go there last?" I demanded.

"The last time I went there was with Dad about three months ago, to get my hair cut for yearbook pictures. Why?"

I showed her both notes.

"This is outrageous! Dad did talk to the hairdresser a lot, but Dad loved Mom. He would never do anything like this, never."

"I know I know," I answered. Hope was crying, so I gave her a big sisterly hug. "I'm thinking about going down there and asking the people who worked there a few questions. Do you want to come with?"

Hope wiped off the tears off her face. "Sure, I could help you point out which one cut my hair. I'll leave a note for Mom."

Luke drove us there in about twenty minutes. The saloon was decorated like '80s with bright neon colors, and I could hear "girls just want to fun" playing in the background. "Hi, can I help you?" The receptionist asked us, she had blonde hair with blue highlights.

"No thanks, we're just looking for someone." I looked at Hope to see if she saw the hairdresser.

"There she is. The one with wavy brunette hair that's finishing up with the customer." Hope pointed out for me.

Wow, the hairdresser was beautiful. Her hair fell down to her waist and she had the brightest blue eyes I've ever seen. She wore a dark washed skinny jeans and a Journey t-shirt.

I walked up to her as she finished blow-drying the customer's hair.

The hairdresser immediately recognized my sister. "Hope, hey, are you here to get your haircut again?"

"No, but my sister Angel has some questions for you."

"Oh, hi. I'm Scarlet Daniels."

"Are you dating anyone?" I went straight to the point.

"Excuse me?" Scarlet had confusion written all over her face. "Um...no."

"Did you have an affair with my dad?"

"What? Sorry, what is this about?" Scarlet stammered.

I showed her the second note.

"Oh, wow. I don't know what to say. But the answer is no. I met your dad once about four months ago."

"Three months," Hope corrected her.

"Yeah, never mind three months. I talked to your dad when I was doing Hope's hair, but that doesn't mean I had an affair with your dad. He talked about your mom a lot, and I could tell that he loved her. Your dad came across like the faithful type."

"Do you have a sister?" I asked, she looked really familiar but I couldn't put my finger on who she looked like.

"Yeah, Belle is my sister, Belle Daniels," Scarlet said. "She's a sophomore at Blue Star High."

"That's what I thought." I started to piece things together.

"Angel what are you thinking?"

"You know how the note said that the person isn't Amy but close, well I was thinking Belle Daniels."

"Belle would never do anything like this," Scarlet's face started to turn red with anger.

"Why Belle Daniels? She doesn't have anything against you. I talk to her in class, she's one of the nicest girls in school." Luke was as confused as everyone else.

"I don't think that Belle wrote this, but I think that the person who did wants me to think that it's Belle. I think it's..."

"Stacy, you think it's Stacy don't you?" Scarlet cut me off.

"Whoa, What's going on here?" Hope reached out her hand like a stop sign.

"Yeah, I think it's Stacy, because Scarlet and Belle's dad is the lawyer that helped put Stacy's dad in jail for that robbery." A puzzle was coming together in my head, and only a few pieces were still missing.

"Okay, if Stacy did, then why did she send you these notes?" Luke asked.

"I don't know." I turned to Scarlet. "We have to go. Sorry about the questions."

"No problem, I understand," Scarlet turned around to greet another customer.

On our way home we stopped at our favorite smoothie place. I don't know what it was, but we got lucky cause Stacy was sitting at a table with her gym bag. Luke and Hope went up to the counter to order me a blueberry smoothie.

I walked up to her and sat in the seat across from her.

"Hey, missed you at practice today." Stacy was on the soccer team that my dad use to coach. "Are you coming back?"

"No, I don't think so." I was thinking about Dad.

"Oh, I understand," she looked down at her raspberry smoothie .

"Thanks, have you finished that essay on World War One yet?" I tried to make small talk before I dropped the big bomb on her about the notes.

"No, I haven't even started. Have you?" She asked me.

"No. Anyway, I kinda have something to show you." I took out the notes from my pocket and showed them to her.

"Um...okay. Am I supposed to know what to do with these?" She asked.

"No, but did you write them?"

"You've got to be kidding me."

"Look this is what I think, I think that you wrote these to me to make it look like Belle Daniels."

"Now why would I do anything like that?"

"Because Mr. Daniels help put your dad in jail, and if I got mad at Belle it would kinda be like payback for you. Look I'm not mad at you if you did this. I just don't understand why you did this to me."

Suddenly her face turned white, then red. She buried her head in her hands. "Because I was jealous," she was gasping for breath. "You and your dad had an amazing relationship. He loved you so much, but my dad doesn't even care about me and he's in jail."

"I'm sure your dad loves you, Stacy."

"No, you don't know him. I'm really sorry about the things I said. Your dad loved you so much Angel and he would never kill himself over a goal you missed, even I know that. I heard you and Luke talking yesterday. Amy didn't start the rumor, I did. I just made it sound like Amy. I'm so sorry, I wasn't thinking straight."

"It's okay, and I'm sorry about your dad," I got up and gave her hug to make sure she knew I wasn't mad. "I better get back, my mom is waiting."

"Hey Mom, we're home," I yelled, as we walked through the door.

"Oh honey, I'm in the kitchen making dinner," Mom yelled back.

We walked in to the kitchen and I could smell something really good.

"Hello Luke," my mom gave Luke a hug. "Are you staying for dinner? We have enough."

"Sure, Mrs. Silver," I could see Luke getting excited.

"Mom, Luke and I have homework, so we're going to go upstairs okay? Yell when dinner's ready." I tugged Luke towards the stairs.

"Okay I will." Mom started chopping carrots.

We walked into my room, there was stuff all over the floor. "What do you want to start first math or science?" I asked Luke.

"How about something not related to school," he said as he grabbed my hand.

"Luke what are you talking about?" I stared at him.

He grabbed the letter off my desk and put it in my hands. "I think its time."

"I don't know." It was too soon.

"Come on Angel, now you know the rumors were just rumors and that it wasn't because of you, just read it. Please for me."

"Fine," I sighed, opening the envelope.

Hey there my Sunshine,

I'm so sorry that I'm doing this to you, your sister and mom. I'm going to write you a short letter because you and I both like to have things to the point, but Christina and Hope don't. Anyways honey I know you don't understand why I did this, but I really hope you understand that I had to do this for me. You couldn't have stopped it. Its not your fault. It's my fault. It is something that I needed to do. I can't explain it but there you go. I want you to know that I love you very much, and I want you to kept kicking amazing soccer goals. I'm sorry about getting mad at you at the Championship Game. It wasn't your fault.

I want you to marry a guy that you love very much. If that guy is Luke then so be it. Go to college, and find a great job that you love, and have amazing children (make sure you make them play soccer).

I hope that you live the rest of your life with happiness and love. Most of all, know that I love you Angel. Don't forget that.

I Love You, Dad

"I love you, too," I whispered.

I didn't notice that I was crying until a teardrop hit the letter. I quickly wiped my face, because I didn't want to wreck the letter.

Luke pulled me into his arms and kissed the top of my head. "Your dad still cares about you and loves you,

Don't forget about that. It wasn't your fault, you couldn't have stopped it."

"I know I just wish that he was here, you know."

"Yeah, I know." He kissed the top of my head again. "I think you should join soccer again, your dad wants you to."

"I don't know its too soon, and plus it won't be the same."

"It would kinda be the same. I'll still come to every game and cheer you on, so will your mother and Hope."

I laughed at the thought, because they always make the funniest posters to cheer me on. I've kept every one of them. Some are even on my wall.

"Fine I will, but you promise to keep making the posters?"

"Yes, anything for you Angel. Trust me. Everything will be okay."

I grabbed Luke hand and we headed down stairs. I showed Mom the letter and she, Hope and I hugged, it felt like is lasted for hours. That night, during dinner I heard my mother's laughter for the first time in a long time. That's when I knew everything was going to be okay again.

Justice Kills

By James Zhao

"Viper, catch that boy!" a distant voice shouted.

"Oh God, here we go again!" muttered Chase.

This was the third time in a week that Chase had been caught by 5T 49ers, the dogs of the Triads. He had been sent on a mission to retrieve a roster of 5T spies going undercover within certain organizations throughout Hong Kong.

Chase raced down the streets of Hong Kong, darting in and out of the crowds of people who seemed oblivious to what was going on. Every now and then, Chase looked back, but he could still see the faint outline of two 49ers in hot pursuit after him.

After what seemed like a whole year of running, Chase glanced back. The 49ers were nowhere in sight. *I guess I'm safe for now*, he thought. He slowed down to a fast walk, glancing in every direction for any sign of the 49ers. Cautiously, he pulled a moldy piece of papyrus out of his left pants pocket and unfolded it. On it somebody had scribbled a bunch of Chinese characters, as though they had no meaning. *Great,* Chase thought. *I went through all that trouble to steal some "top-secret information" from the 5T, and all I get is this piece of junk.* He spat at the ground in frustration, and continued walking.

Suddenly, a dark figure appeared out of an alleyway and knocked Chase on the head with a vicious blow. He instantly crumpled to the ground, the stale taste of blood rushing into his mouth. Two strong hands reached out and dragged him into the alleyway. As Chase struggled to regain his senses, he realized that the dark figure had been his 5T pursuers, Viper and somebody whose name he did not know. Without hesitation, the two 49ers ruthlessly kicked him around until he spewed blood all over the place. At this point, Chase could feel his adrenaline pumping at extreme rates. Without warning, he reached out and grabbed Viper's shoe — just as he was about to deliver a kick into Chase's groin — and threw him into the wall. Then, inn one swift motion, he leaped up and delivered a kick into the other 49er's stomach, instantly knocking him out.

Deciding that he was safe now, Chase withdrew the papyrus scroll from his pocket again and peered at it closely. The scroll was a roster of 5T spies working undercover within White Tiger, just as he had been informed. To his dismay, the roster contained some names that Chase had befriended and even formed blood bonds with. Nonetheless, he knew that, if he successfully conveyed the list to Black Shadow, his leader, then the people on the list would be imprisoned, or even executed.

As Chase busily examined the scroll, Viper gradually regained consciousness. Without letting Chase notice, he pulled a little bottle of vinegar out of his breast pocket, and, using every last ounce of his strength, launched the bottle at Chase. This alarmed Chase, and, upon instinct, he reached out and caught the bottle. However, he had such a firm grip on it that it shattered in his palm.

Little splinters of glass punctured his skin; he threw the undercover roster on the ground and grabbed his injured hand. All of a sudden, Chase realized what he had done terribly wrong: he had allowed the papyrus scroll fall into a puddle of vinegar.

"No, no, NO!" Chase shouted, horrified as he watched the scroll slowly disintegrate into ashes.

Chase fell to the ground in disappointment, ashamed that he had let Viper, who was chuckling in the corner, trick him with something as simple as a bottle of vinegar. Nonetheless, the damage was done. Chase had failed his most important mission, and now, because of him, White Tiger would never be able to eradicate the enemy spies that lurked within their system.

Chase Pang was a twenty-three-year-old Cantonese intermediate spy who worked for White Tiger. Being one of White Tiger's most familiar spies to Hong Kong, most of his work took place there and in surrounding areas. As a boy, Chase was trained by his father, a prestigious martial artist, to become a Dragon fighter. Dragon fighters, now defunct, were a league of the most skilled martial artists in Hong Kong, joined together as the Dragon Union. At that time, though Chase had already qualified to become initiated, he never made any attempts to join because his father had been murdered at a Dragon battle.

White Tiger was an underground society that had been working around Hong Kong since 1931. Originally, White Tiger were a triad mainly associated with bootlegging drugs, weapons, etc. Later, after the fall of the Shi Kung Triad in 1961, the weak fledging leaders of the White Tiger became paranoid, thus destroying the entire Triad. Parts of the broken Triad later met in 1963, and came to a consensus on creating an underground police group to corner and wipe out gangs. Soon, it began operation in China, Hong Kong, Vietnam, Malaysia, South Korea, Britain, Italy, and California.

*   *   *

Two big, brawny men dragged the twenty-year-old Chase Pang across the damp floor like a carpet. Their footsteps echoed throughout the endless stone hallway. Miniature windows lined along the walls were the only source of light, casting an eerie glow on the floor. Drips of water rained down rhythmically from leaks in the ceiling and formed puddles in the uneven flooring.

Chase tried to resist the unyielding grips of his seizers, but he was no match for them. "Let go of me! If I can be a gangster, I'm pretty sure I can walk to!" he exclaimed sarcastically.

"You here that, Forest?" The man on Chase's right laughed. "This little whimp thinks he's a gangster!" The man swore. "Shut up, kid. You don't know what the hell you're talking about!"

"Yeah," Forest chimed in, "wait till you meet Smoke, the Incense Master. I'll be surprised if you don't wet your pants! That'll be hilarious! Don't you think so, Wave?"

After their brusque conversation ended, Wave and Forest returned to their originally solemn state. The three continued down the gloomy hallway, their footsteps in synch with the cadence of the water dropping. Chase darted his eyes here and there across the foreboding walls. He had an uneasy premonition of what was going to happen. He was not sure; all he knew was that he had been sent by White Tiger to become initiated into the 5T Triad so he could spy on the organization. He was currently on the way to his initiation ceremony. *Psh, great ceremony. More like a funeral,* he contemplated disappointedly. He never expected the fearsome and prosperous Triad to provide such horrible service for new recruits.

At last, they reached the end of the hallway. It was a dead end, as Chase had dreaded (he knew that when the ceremony ended, he would have to walk all the way back across the hallway). In the middle of the dead end stood a small stone temple. Like the rest of the hallway, the temple dull, simple, and looked like it was built by cavemen. Four round stone slabs were laid on top of each other in decreasing size order to serve as steps. In the middle of the smallest slab, which was large enough for ten people to stand on, four grey pillars stood proudly, supporting big stone roof that looked like it was about to collapse any second. The entire structure had been done extremely crudely; the separate pieces of stone were uneven and failed to dovetail each other, and none of them had been glued together.

Suddenly, numerous candles lit from around the circular walls of the dead end, and a group of young men wearing brightly tinted fuchsia robes walked in and surrounded Chase, Wave, and Forest. A hood covered part of each candle bearer's face, so he failed to see their expressions. However, in the spooky shadow of the candles, their stern and unsmiling mouths proved that they were solemn, even scared.

At the far end of room, two candle bearers diverged from the rest of the circle to reveal a man, who was most likely Smoke, the Incense Master or Ceremonies Officer. He was a short, stout man with tough, deep-set eyes and a pointy nose. His mouth was rigid as though it had been carved straight from stone. He carried a gilded, crowned cane and rings on each finger, as though he were some medieval prince. Like the candle bearers, he wore a big fuchsia robe, except his was embroidered with golden images of dragons, phoenixes, and flowers.

Smoke slowly made his way towards the center of the temple, pacing his steps evenly as though he were afraid of the cracks between the stone tablets. Immediately, every person in the room took a knee, except for Chase. Smoke seemed bewildered by this; Forest jumped up attentively and whacked Chase in the stomach, who let out a yelp of pain and crumpled to his knees.

"Rise," bellowed Smoke in a deep and throaty voice, "What is your name, Blue Lantern?"

It took a while for Chase to recover from the blow and comprehend that a Blue Lantern was an uninitiated member of a Triad. "P-Pang Lau Kung, officer."

"Very good," replied Smoke. He then proceeded to ask Chase more questions, until finally he began the ceremony of the Triad oaths.

"Repeat after me," Smoke explained, "One, after having entered the Han gates, I must treat the parents and relatives of my sworn brothers as my own kin. I shall suffer death by five thunderbolts if I do not keep this oath."

Chase hesitated. He was going to have to lie to these oaths in order to spy on the 5T. And according to Triad superstition, he would be struck dead for this. Slowly, he repeated the sentence.

Smoke nodded in approval and continued. "I shall assist my sworn brothers to bury their parents and brothers by offering financial or physical assistance. I shall suffer death by five thunderbolts if I do not keep this oath."

Chase hesitated again at this oath. All of a sudden, Forest jumped up from behind and produced a whip from his pocket. The whip came down on Chase's back like a crack of lightning. Chase screamed in agony and fell forward at Smoke's feet. Tears sprung from his eyes as his back burned.

"You gonna stall?" Forest cried, "You gonna stall during your initiation ceremony? You call this bull gangster? Well I tell you what, you little twerp, if you hesitate like that again, I'm gonna show you what a real gangster is. I'm gonna whip you till you die!"

Chase tried to swallow back his anger. *You have to do this*, he told himself. *You have to do this. For your parents that this 5T Mountain Master murdered.* After he regained his composure, he repeated the second oath and continued his initiation.

Finally, after what seemed like eternity, Chase finished

repeating all thirty-six oaths, signing the blood pact, and drinking the sacred wine—the three traditional steps in Triad initiation. He was exhausted; he had been beaten and whipped countless times by Forest and Wave, forced to slice open a finger to sign his blood pact, and drink a whole bowl of highly concentrated alcohol. He lay down on the ground and began to contemplate.

Had he made the right choice?

* * *

Black Shadow stormed down the hallway, holding a folded piece of paper in his hand. The end of the hall diverged into two other hallways that went in separate directions. Black Shadow continued towards the wall, as though he didn't notice it. However, he suddenly veered to the right and ran into a small man, knocking him hard onto the linoleum floor. The man cursed as dust that hadn't been cleaned for nearly forty years now flew up all over his seemingly brand-new blue-and-white striped T-shirt and faded jeans.

"Hey, watch it!" he coughed, dust clogging his throat.

"Sorry," Black Shadow muttered as he continued down the hall.

Black Shadow sighed in disgust as he glanced at the faded wooden doors lined along the walls. This was a dormitory that was mainly used by young White Tiger members who couldn't afford their own housing and, apparently, didn't know how to operate a vacuum cleaner. The managers of the White Tiger headquarters had thought that these lower rankers didn't deserve a cleaning staff to do all their dirty work for them. Instead, the board believed that the members had to do everything themselves in order to develop into strong, independent Tigers.

However, this theory failed, as these young Tigers were too lazy to even make their beds. The hallways and rooms were completely covered in a thick layer of gray dust. Years and years of messes and graffiti had reduced the originally snow-white walls to a displeasing tie-dye of faded colors. A sickeningly strong smell of smoke hung in the air; correspondingly, a myriad of cigarette butts littered the floors, giving the average visitor an impression that he was walking through a trash dump.

Black Shadow continued along, disgusted that these youngsters had no idea of what it meant to be 'clean'. As he walked, he glanced at the placards hanging on the doors that lined the walls like big brown soldiers in a military drill. *347, 349, 351...365.* Finally, he had arrived. Inside, he could hear boisterous laughter accompanied by deafening rock 'n' roll music. He heaved a disappointed sigh and opened the door.

Inside, four burly boys hung around the room, each one of them dangling half of a cigarette loosely between their fingers. To Black Shadow's dismay, each of the boys looked as though they hadn't showered for days. They smelled like it, too. As soon as they saw his dark, domineering face, every single one of them shut up.

Black Shadow had no trouble identifying which one of these was Chase Pang. Chase was a fair-skinned, young-looking person set on a muscular frame. On the other hand, his three roommates were fatter and looked a lot older than him. They each shared the same dirty, dusty face and a head of thick, oily hair, and one idea: *Uh oh.*

"Chase Pang!" Black Shadow exclaimed with an earth-shaking roar. The four Tigers cowered and hung their heads to avoid his callous, stone-carved expression.

"Y-yes sir?" Chase managed in a shaky whisper.

Black Shadow unfolded the piece of paper he had brought and shoved it in Chase's face. "What do you make of this?"

Chase took the piece of paper from Black Shadow's hands and peered at it through his squinted, miserably near-sighted eyes; he had forgotten to put on his contacts that day. The paper turned out to be a wanted poster. After months of extensive research, Chase was able to deduce immediately that it was a 5T poster, due to the fancy calligraphy and dragon-embroidered border. What caught his eye was a drawing of a face in the center of the poster. Suddenly, he realized who the face belong to and nearly dropped the paper in terror.

The face, though crudely drawn, was unmistakable.

It was a drawing of him.

"You failed," uttered Black Shadow through clenched teeth, "and now you have half of the city's most powerful gangsters after you. Soon enough, they're going to sniff you out from here in our secret base, and that'll risk the rest of our lives as well as the entire organization. I knew I should never have sent your failing butt to carry out such an important mission."

"I-I'm sorry, master," Chase squeaked. At the moment, he was more afraid of Black Shadow than of getting caught by the 5T. "I-it won't h-happen again."

Black Shadow glared at Chase. He hated it when people promised that "it won't happen again" to him. After so many years of experience with countless fledging spies, every single one of them said they wouldn't mess up again, but they always did.

Since Black Shadow did not say anything, Chase spoke again. "S-so what are the l-leaders going to d-d-do to me? W-will I be terminated?"

Black Shadow laughed his sinister laugh; the one that signaled that he had a mischievously evil plan hidden up his sleeve. "The leaders," he answered, "have decided that they won't do anything to you *yet*. (Chase let out a sigh of relief.) However, (Chase tensed) you have now been exiled and must complete a very special task before you can be reinitiated into the White Tiger.

"It is now your responsibility to discover the hiding place of the 5T Mountain Master, or Lau Pei (a name which he had taken from the famous ruler during the

Three Kingdoms), and terminate him. You will have a year's time to complete this mission. If you fail to meet the deadlines, you will be hunted down by our scouts and terminated. We will supply you with a flick knife and one thousand Cantonese dollars. Simultaneously, we will take from you your ID and all of your current supplies. If you try to come back before you complete your mission, we will have armed scouts guarding all entrances to the headquarters. Upon sighting you, they will gun you down immediately. Now, get out before I have to personally terminate you."

And that was that. One simple bottle of vinegar had caused so much damage. Chase slugged his shoulders, grabbed his jacket, bid farewell to his roommates, and left the dorm in silence. Black Shadow followed closely behind and put an arm around Chase's shoulder.

"Chase," he said in a much friendlier tone, "I'm sorry I spoke like that to you in there. I really don't want to have to do this to you, but I simply can't help it. It was the golden resolution of the leaders."

Chase sighed despondently and looked up at his master weakly. "I understand, master." Suddenly, a burst of confidence and adrenaline surged through him. "Don't worry, master. I shall complete this task in the name of my parents, whom he had murdered. I will find where that lousy scum is hiding and I'll murder him. Then, on this day of next year, I will bring his head back proudly and lay it on our Mountain Master's desk!"

Black Shadow laughed, glad that Chase hadn't suffered too much emotional detriment. "Ah, that's my boy!"

A gang of four dirty and dangerous-looking teenagers hung out in front of a fruit shop, checking out every single woman that walked by, regardless of whether or not they were attractive. Each one of them sported a faded brown jacket that seemed perfectly normal. However, if anyone were to look closely, they would notice that each jacket had a white patch that bore the Chinese character for "five" on the right sleeve and a black patch on the opposite sleeve with the numbers "49" sewn in red. The message was subliminal yet clear: they were 49ers of the 5T Triad. And, like every single other 5T member, they were dirty, bloodthirsty, sexually perverted, and on the lookout for a notorious traitor by the name of Chase Pang, who had recently attempted to convey a 5T undercover roster to the much-hated White Tiger.

The gang had spent the whole morning in front of the shop, yet they failed to spot any good-looking chicks, or anybody whose face matched Chase Pang's. Thus, also to avoid suspicion, they entered the shop and each flashed a card to the old cashier, who nodded and pointed to the back of the store. The gang slowly made their way to where the cashier pointed and disappeared behind a big red curtain. On the other side, they continued down through a narrow corridor that was barely wide enough for them to even walk in single file, turned left at the end, and were greeted by an armed guard who wore the exact same jacket as they did. The man grabbed an AK-47 from a pile of weapons on the desk next to him and jabbed it into the first teenager's ribs, who reacted by pulling out the same card he had shown to the cashier. The guard nodded and pulled his gun back, letting the teenager in. He repeated this routine with the other three teenagers, and closed the door when they had all been checked.

Meanwhile, out on the busy street, Chase Pang put down his cheap pair of binoculars that he had gotten from the fake market and sat up. He had lain prone in the abandoned apartment all morning, spying on the "Wong's Fruit Heaven" that stood dusty and unwelcoming across the street. This was a new entrance to the 5T headquarters that had been opened only a few weeks before. Based on what Chase had been told during his undercover mission within 5T, it was the least conspicuous and thus the least guarded. If what he had heard was accurate, the outer gate—the fruit shop itself—was guarded by Wong, or Fierce Dragon. The inner gate—a large, empty room—led directly into the headquarters and was guarded by Shock, a much more experienced and attentive 49er. All Chase had to do in order to break into the 5T headquarters was to sneak into the fruit shop, pretending to be buying fruits. Then, while Fierce Dragon wasn't looking, he would slip through the gate, continue on to the inner gate, and take Shock out.

However, the more Chase thought about it, the harder it was to believe. It was way too simple. Such a big organization as the 5T wouldn't let their guard down by so much, especially with a traitor on the loose.

That traitor is me, Chase thought.

Suddenly, as though by a miracle, the cashier at the fruit shop got up, walked out into the street, and disappeared into the crowd of people. *Nice security. Better than I expected*, Chase thought sarcastically. He jumped up, stowed his binoculars in his pocket, and carefully made his way down the uneven steps of the abandoned building.

The sun blinded Chase after having been in the dark building for so long. Carefully, he surveyed his surroundings through squinted eyes, trying to detect any suspicious faces. Seeing that there were none, he walked down the street towards the fruit shop, trying to stay as hidden within the crowd as possible.

Chase stood in front of the shop. He cocked his head back and examined the red, faded letters—"Wong's Fruit Heaven". Next to it was an enlarged photo of a man savoring a big, plump peach. *Dang, this place looks more like "5T's Entrance To Hell" to me,* Chase thought. He still could not believe that an entrance to one of the largest and most dangerous crime organizations could be so simple and obvious. What flabbergasted him even more was the fact that Wong had simply got up and left, leaving it unattended to and completely vulnerable.

Surveying his surroundings one last time, Chase silently walked to the back of the shop, pulled back the curtain, and disappeared behind it. What was behind the curtain turned out to be a narrow hallway. Like the hallways of the dormitories in the White Tiger headquarters, the walls were dusty, stained, and graffitied as though they hadn't been cleaned or repainted for centuries. What caught Chase's eye was the numerous black-and-white photos that hung on the walls. He stopped and looked closely at the first photo. It was faded, but he immediately realized that it was a portrait of the first Mountain Master of the 5T Triad, named Lau Pei.

He had created the tradition that each 5T Mountain Master must name himself Lau Pei, after the great Three Kingdoms ruler. Chase moved along to the next photo, which was of the second Lau Pei. He continued down along the generations of Triad leaders that had died of murder, disease, or old age. He stopped dead in his tracks when he reached the last of the photos. Glaring back at him was a face that was all too familiar. It was the current Lau Pei. The exact same Lau Pei that had personally murdered his parents when he was only thirteen years old.

Insupportable anger filled Chase. He smashed the glass picture frame and ripped the photo of Lau Pei up. Before he could act any more reckless, he forcefully regained his composure and continued down the hallway and turned left.

Chase slithered along the wall, surveying the long, dark hallway for any 5T personnel.

"You coward," Lau Pei exclaimed. "Did you think you could simply walk in and destroy my great organization? I'm going to make you die, slowly and painfully, just like your parents did ten years ago." He chuckled, then arched his back, lifted his hands out, and bent his knees, signaling that he was prepared for a kung fu duel.

Chase did the same. Tears rushed to his eyes as an

incapacitating wish for revenge welled up inside him. His adrenaline pumped so fast that his hands were numb. This was it. It was now or never.

Suddenly, Chase jumped up at Lau Pei, trying to catch him off guard. However, Lau Pei was prepared. He leaped to the side, throwing Chase completely off mark. Before he could react, Chase fell in a heap to the ground. Lau Pei reached down and hauled him back to his feet. Though he was fat and stocky, he was extremely strong. The next thing Chase knew, Lau Pei was punching him with his iron-hard fists, slowly but forcefully. Chase was already so exhausted that he considered giving up, but the thought of getting revenge on the 5T Mountain Master reenergized him. He stuck out a fist and thrust out randomly, eventually hitting Lau Pei in the gut. Lau Pei fell back, winded and bewildered.

A sudden crash startled both of them. Two burly 5T 49ers burst through the door, shattering it to pieces. They quickly surveyed the room, and were flabbergasted to see that their master was wounded. The first one shouted something weird to the other, who ran over to the Mountain Master and helped him up. Before Chase could react, all three 5T members surrounded him, each ready to fight.

"Oh, you should have given up when you had the chance," Lau Pei chuckled at him. "You've got no where to go now, Chase. You're as good as dead. Pawn, Warrior, take him out."

Pawn and Warrior charged at Chase, each sticking a fist out and knocking him in the stomach. The blow threw Chase head over heels on the ground. He saw golden stars and could taste blood running into his mouth. The 49ers were too strong for him; nonetheless, he wasn't ready to give up. He launched himself off the ground and at the smaller 49er, whom he guessed was Pawn. He landed on the man's shoulders and squeezed his hard skull between his thighs. As Pawn struggled to get Chase off his shoulders, Chase plunged his index and middle fingers straight into his spine. Pawn threw back his head and let a muffled scream into Chase's groin as he collapsed to the ground, paralyzed. Chase had perfectly executed a Wooshoo Finger on Pawn.

Warrior watched in horror as his partner was defeated, his eyes wide as golf balls. "You scum-wad, what did you do to my brother? I'll make you pay for this!" Subsequently, he hoisted Chase into the air and flung him at the wall, but Chase was prepared. He stuck his arms and legs back like a crab and softly bounced off the wall.

Warrior did not give up. He sprung up on top of Chase and pounded his fists down onto Chase's face. Chase felt his nose crack as hot blood rushed up to his mouth and nostrils. The pain was numbing, and he tried to scream, but no sound came out. He was suffocating; Warrior was crushing his ribs down on his lungs. He wriggled around under the backbreaking of Warrior in an attempt to break free, but to no avail.

Chase was running out of time; he felt himself suffocating to death. His eyes grew heavy and his vision faded. He no longer felt Warrior hammering his face. Fire alarms exploded in his ears. The entire world seemed to slow down to a near stop. Chase no longer had any energy to continue living; he allowed himself to be slowly pulled into the abyss of death.

Suddenly, Chase was overcome by visions of his parents. No, he couldn't just die and let them down. He couldn't fail White Tiger a second time. He couldn't fall in the hands of a filthy gangster. With a new surge of powerful energy, Chase came back to his senses and swung his legs up and into Warrior's scalp. The kick was stronger than Chase expected, and Warrior rolled to the side, cradling his head.

Chase sprung up, feeling fresh as though he had just been born. All the beating had given Chase a black eye. His nose was crooked and bleeding. His heavily, bruised cheeks were covered with fist marks, and his lips were gigantic. He looked around for Lau Pei through his good eye, but he was nowhere in sight. "You sissy," he screamed as he tore furniture from the ground and threw it around, "and you call *me* a coward? Take a look at yourself! Why don't you come out and fight me like your two slaves have?"

Suddenly, Chase felt a hand tap him on the shoulder. He swung around, ready to fight, but instead, to his dismay, was greeted by a bone-shattering punch to his already beaten face. Chase crumpled to the ground, overwhelmed by second assault. Just as Chase was getting up, Lau Pei came down on his stomach with a full-fledged punch. Chase instantly vomited stale, hot blood. All the energy had been drained from him again.

"Get up!" Lau Pei barked. "Get up now! I'm not going to leave without a fun fight!" He delivered two more blows to Chase, this time to his chest. Chase roared in pain as he sensed the sharp pop of a chipped rib. He knew that he could not fight like this, yet he had to defeat Lau Pei and avenge his parents' death. He needed something to do the job...

That was when he thought of it. His knife! White Tiger had given him a flick knife when it exiled him. He glanced at Lau Pei; he had his back on him, still saying meaningless threats to him. He reached with a shaking hand for his pants pocket. He listened dreadfully as his rib began to snap, afraid that if it were to puncture an organ and kill him, he would fail his job.

Finally, Chase had a grip on the base of the knife. He groaned in agony as he pulled his arm back. Despite the pain, he smiled a bloody smile as he flipped open the knife and aimed it in Lau Pei's direction.

"I am going to give you one last chance," Lau Pei thundered, "to get your—" Lau Pei's eyes widened in terror. He slowly cocked his head down, only to see Chase holding a knife in his stomach. With a roar like a stampede of elephants, the Mountain Master drooled blood and collapsed to the ground next to Chase.

Chase rolled over to face the ceiling, clutching his chest. So he had succeeded in defeating the Mountain Master, but he had failed his task. He hadn't told White Tiger where he was, so reinforcements would never make it. 5T would choose a successor and execute him, and it would be as though nothing had happened.

As he was contemplating his failure, he heard shouts coming from outside. *Oh, great. They heard this old bag's scream. I guess I'm dead too,* he thought. To his surprise, the people that charged in weren't wearing the 5T uniforms.

They were White Tiger and the police.

A group of paramedics ran over to Chase and crouched around him. On the other side of the room, the police had arrested and cuffed Warrior and Pawn. *I guess I didn't fail,* he thought, and fainted.

* * *

Chase woke up to find himself completely submerged in a bath of some hard, white substance. He could hardly move; he tried to thrust his head around, and managed to break his face out of the substance. He was in a large, dark, grey room. A man dressed in denim and a black headband sat next to him. It was Black Shadow.

"He's awake," Black Shadow called across the room. "How are you feeling?" he asked Chase.

"Great," Chase replied, "Where am I?"

"You're in one of the White Tiger recovery rooms. This bath that you're in is a special chemical formula that stimulates white blood cells, allowing bruises, cuts, fractures, etc. to heal in a matter of hours, rather than days."

It took Chase a while to comprehend all this information; his head was having trouble thinking correctly. After a moment of silence, three men dressed in suits walked over to him and sat down around him.

"Greetings, Chase," the man closest to him spoke. He was old, with dark, wrinkled skin, sunken eyes, and a withered nose upon which a set of golden spectacles perched. "I am Shi Kang, the Mountain Master of White Tiger. My two friends here are my head officers, Dragonbreath and Star. The three of us are here to commend you and thank you for successfully destroying the 5T. The police have taken care of everything. The sudden death of their Mountain Master has also thrown the 5T organization into turmoil worldwide. It won't be very long before it collapses. Now, let me tell you a little bit about what has happened in the time that you were exiled.

"Immediately after your exile, we dispatched a few spies to sniff out the 5T headquarters. They had discovered it a long time ago, but we decided to wait for you to discover it first, so we could reinforce you when you needed help. When you discovered that the fruit shop was an entrance to the corporation, our spies signaled, and we and a group of police officers entered the shop and positioned ourselves in the hallway behind the red curtain and in the shop itself after you entered. Once we heard Lau Pei howl, we immediately charged in, some of us headed for Lau Pei, others headed elsewhere throughout the facility. Now we are here.

"I also thought you might like to know that the Chinese government was pleased with what we—you—did, and have officially incorporated White Tiger as a governmental organization."

Chase stared at him blankly. He hadn't understood a single word the man had just said. All he knew was that he had done a good job. With that thought, he closed his eyes and allowed himself to be pulled into the world of sleep.

About the Authors

Concordia International School Shanghai is a college preparatory school in Shanghai, China. It offers a high quality American curriculum to 1200 students in grades preschool through high school.